If I Should Die

Donevy Westphal

Cover by Diane Turpin Designs • Diane Turpin—. DianeTurpinDesigns.com This is a work of fiction. Names, characters, places, and incidents are products of the author's imagination or are used fictitiously. Any reference to actual persons, living or dead, is entirely fictional. All scripture references are from the King James Version.

If I Should Die

Copyright © 2020 by Donevy L. Westphal

Published by Westerness Enterprises LTD Box 52 Casey, Iowa 50048

If I Should Die / Donevy L. Westphal

ISBN 978-1-7349256-0-9

ISBN 978-1-7349256-2-3 (eBook)

Printed in the United States of America

Books by Donevy Westphal

Ebenezer: My Stone of Help Series

If I Should Die
As A Lovely Song*
All of My Tomorrows*

* Coming Soon

Then Samuel took a stone, and set it between Mizpeh and Shen, and called the name of it Ebenezer, saying, Hitherto hath the LORD helped us. (1 Samuel 7:12 KJV)

Dedication

When I look at all the people who have helped in this long process it is a difficult decision as to who deserves the dedication award. I would have to single out my dear Grandmother, Margaret (Coe) Magill. It is a long overdue recognition of her quiet behind the scenes care for not just her family, but all of her family, especially her grandchildren. She was the backbone of our family, a family who would not have had a home without her and our Grandfather, Vernon Magill.

Acknowledgements

Many belong here on the acknowledgement page. First is my Adorable Cousin, Beverly Watson, who has poked, prodded, and commiserated with me as we both struggled with our writing. There were the 'reviewers at Writers Edge that encouraged me to not give up, continue rewriting. Then there are those much closer to home: my son Benjamin Westphal, and my other son, Levi Westphal, with his encouragement and his technical work without which this could not have happened. Kudos to my husband, Chris, who suffered silently through untold editors and their crazy edits and my mutterings about such editors and edits. I learned much through ACFW and their courses, especially the one with Patrick Craig and self-publishing. And foremost I praise God who prepared me through life and much more through His wisdom to write this story. May this story be a blessing to all who read it.

~ Prologue ~

What brought me full-circle to the faith of my father was the most bizarre case in my years-long file of missions.

I'd always been formidable. Indeed, I took pride in my Scottish heritage. The almost God-like warrior, in body, mind, and soul, honor-bound to my duty, come what may. But no one is perfect except God, and even though my body was still responding to the challenges thrown at me, I felt like I was losing my mind. PTSD had become the new watchword for some of us from the Viet Nam era, but most of us didn't understand how it worked. All I knew was that I was diagnosed just after my buddy, Mike Germin, had died working on an important assignment. Mike and I met as young recruits in the military and our friendship lasted a lifetime. Mike—codename Snowman—and his team had been tightening the noose around this international crime ring and close to bringing some truly evil characters to justice. Everyone was in place when Snowman hit someone's radar. His murder almost put an end to the mission.

Mike and I were two peppers in the tamale. He had no family, and I had cut loose from mine. My father and I didn't see life exactly the same—not exactly a unique experience for a young person in the sixties. I had been taught better than to dishonor my father . . . but, he was like Santa Claus. He knew when I was sleeping and when I was awake. Worse, he knew when I was in the wrong place at the right time. I had a talent for what my friends called 'Charlie Brown' stunts—and dad al-

ways knew. He had eyes in the back of his head, and everywhere else. If I did something in town, he knew it before I arrived home.

For all of our disagreements, I still loved him, but the volcano of anger and frustration buried it, and, overnight, our once close-knit, loving family turned into a bitter, fractured group. The more my father reached out to me, the more resentful and cynical I became. I wanted out. So at the turn of the decade, I left home to join the Marine Corps. And that's where I met Mike.

I was a young buck of seventeen from North Carolina, ready to confront the world. And just like that, military service relieved me of quite a few of my starry-eyed ideas about myself and my relationships. There is something to the saying that there are no atheists in a fox hole.

With our time done, Mike and I were recruited to become a part of an elite organization that claimed to help "bring peace and democracy to the struggling people of the world." I wasn't for it, but Mike was, and what did I have to lose? I had nowhere else to go. Sure, I was a war survivor with several medals, but to those who mattered most, I was dead. Which was just as well, because after leaving home in a huff the way I did, announcing I would never return, I would never be able to find enough humility to go back and admit I was wrong.

So I put my medals and ribbons in a box and stored them away.

Now this. In just the past year, our special ops force had lost two good agents, including Mike, my wife and child had been forced under protection, some doctor was telling me I had this thing called PTSD, my beloved President Reagan had come under attack, and Oliver North was about to face questioning. And the only response I seemed to be able to muster to it all was this intense desire to go back home and tell my dad how very wrong I had been.

So I turned in my resignation. And then just as my last mission ended, I got one more call.

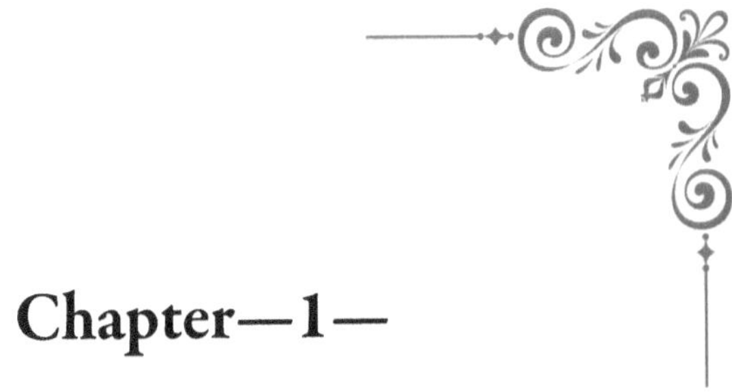

Chapter—1—

Tuesday June 9, 1987

Joshua glanced at his watch before disembarking from the 727 at Narita International in Tokyo. He raced up the flight of stairs two at a time stopping at the gate.

Dropping his suitcase, he slapped his tickets on the counter. "Hold this flight to Chicago."

"Sir, they are latching the door."

"Hold that flight." He flashed his badge at the agent.

The man reached for his phone but kept his eyes on Josh. "Yes, sir, but you'll need to—"

"Send that luggage." He pointed to his suitcases. Then clutching his briefcase like a football, Joshua sailed through the oncoming traffic pulling the black case ever tighter to his chest, as he wove through the throngs, breaking his long run only at the corners. When he reached his gate, he strode purposefully to the desk and presented his tickets before jogging to his plane. He felt the young flight attendant's narrowed eyes as she checked his boarding pass. He quickly surveyed the passengers in first class. Then he took the aisle back to the half- empty economy section.

His seatmate looked up from his book and shifted closer to the window. "That was close, mister."

"Tell me about it."

Joshua frowned, catching his breath. These maneuvers were getting old. How many times had he needed to sprint miles through airports, parachute from planes, dodge bullets, and duck the fists of, capable assassins bent on his destruction?

"Miss." He signaled the flight attendant.

"Yes, Sir?"

"I'd like to stretch out. Mind if I move to those empty seats?"

"Fine," she said. "I could put your briefcase up—"

"No, ma'am, but thank you." He scooted across the aisle and flipped the armrests up, then stretched across the seats, his arms wrapped around his case. Waiting long enough to get a feel for the activity around him, he relaxed. He was used to resting with one closed eye, leaving his mind in neutral.

Wish I hadn't had to use my badge. I don't need the trail.

Regret wasn't a good companion, but since it was already here, he indulged. *Junco, Mai, why is our time always too short? Half an hour in a park. Agent Shields spends more time with you than I.*

When someone jostled his case, he grasped an arm near his cheek.

The attendant gasped, "Sorry, sir. Just wondered if you'd like something to drink?" She rubbed her arm.

Eyes open now, his mind became fully engaged, "Sorry, I startled, ma'am. Get some ice on that, so it doesn't bruise."

"I'll be more careful next time." She frowned.

He looked at her through narrowed eyes. Was there a double meaning to her words? "You'll be back around?"

"Yes, there'll be a meal in an hour."

He tried to relax, not convinced that she was sincere.

"Juice, please?" he said sitting.

This is going to be a really long trip.

WEDNESDAY MORNING, June 10th; On layover in Chicago, Josh found a private one-stall restroom and locked the door. Layer upon layer his reddish-blond hair, blue eyes, and fair complexion disappeared. He worked more skin color into his hands. He brushed his dark brown wig into place, and took a closer look at the brown contacts. *That'll do.* He checked his new credentials. *Yes, Julius C. Armstrong, freelance journalist, you're ready for your next—and last assignment.* And just in time as the bathroom intercom called his flight. One more hour, and he'd be heading for his day's destination: some remote midwestern town called Beetle River.

"I DON'T WANT A WHITE car. Is that all you've got?" Julius glared.

"Today's Wednesday," the rental agent said. "Our fleet has been hit pretty hard this week. Vacuum salesman convention, but bring it back— call first—maybe Friday. We'll have something more along the lines you're looking for," the rental agent said.

"Thanks." Julius grasped the keys off the counter. "I'll call—Have a good day."

Julius found his rental in the lot. Disgruntled he gazed at the white Buick Somerset and shook his head. He'd stand out like an elephant at a flamingo convention. At least the clerk said they'd have another vehicle available—maybe tomorrow or Friday. He slid in and started on the last thirty miles of his trip.

Before hitting the interstate, he found a convenience store. The fourteen-hour flight from Tokyo had left him drained and consumed by a pounding headache. The final thirty miles would require aspirin and caffeine.

The clerk, a young brunette woman, smiled unassumingly.

He'd never been in the Midwest, yet it had a comforting, familiar feeling. He placed his bottle of Coke, bag of chips, and aspirin on the counter.

Julius dug through a few Japanese yen in his pocket, and pulled out a ten dollar bill.

He slid back into his car, gulped down a couple aspirin with his Coke, and found his way onto Interstate 80 West. He merged into the heavy traffic, but traffic quickly thinned as he continued west. Rolling hills gave way to green fields, green pastures dotted with cows and a few trees. Green- and- white signs flashed by about every five to ten miles, announcing small towns tucked behind hills.

Julius was able to use the signs to tick off the distance he'd traveled—five, ten, fifteen, twenty-five. Anytime now he ought to see...Yes, an exit sign for Beetle River. And there were trees in this state. Tall green trees beside the Beetle River exit. His mobile phone buzzed and he pulled across to the shoulder of the exit ramp.

"Hey?" he answered.

"You're looking for Alberto Meister." It was Director Myer. "He's the kingpin that disappeared from Chicago."

"Okay, Director. You got it on the computer? I spent forty-eight hours losing the agent tailing me. Germany, Brussels, finally Paris at the Louvre. Forty-eight hours. Haven't had time to look." He ran his fingers through his hair.

"Yeah, it's all there. Everything's set up in the intel I'm sending. And look, thanks for taking this. You're the only one good enough to step in. All the other agents are in place, and it's good to go."

Julius felt sick. "Just get me the info."

"Contact me when you get your base up." The line went dead.

Only thirty-three years old and chaos, destruction, and despair haunted his every waking and sleeping hour.

Easing off the exit and then back onto the shoulder of the main road, he angled to get a better view of the town. He reached over the seat, grabbed his carry-on bag and rummaged for his binoculars. Through his binoculars he glassed over the small Midwest town sprawled on the hillside across the river bottom.

A tap on his side window made Julius slide his hand under his jacket to grasp the shoulder holstered Beretta. He semi-relaxed when his peripheral caught the smiling, wrinkled face of a sandy-haired man.

The man tapped again. Julius extended an index finger. "Just a minute." He slid his binoculars into their case and hit the window switch.

"Can I help you?"

"Looks like you have a tire going down. I've got an air bomb."

"What? I picked up this car half an hour ago. The tires were fine." Julius scouted the scenery. Only him and the old man. He opened his door and slid out. "Well, I'll be..." He stared at the sagging rear tire.

"You've got air?"

The wrinkles on the old man's face indicated a life of many weathered storms, and his lightly starched button down shirt and neat work slacks suggested the old man's age to be in his mid-seventies.

"You'd be surprised how many times this comes in handy." The old man stepped across to his pickup and pulled out an air tank. "Not many stations out here and it's a long walk if you're not prepared. Not a very forgiving place." He handed Julius the tank. "Like the Good Book says in Proverbs, 'Good understanding giveth favor. And the way of the transgressor is hard.'" The man squinted. "You're not from around here are you?"

"No. Out east." Julius squatted down and attached the hose to his tire.

"Beautiful country out east."

"Yes. Sure good you came along." Julius felt the side of his tire. "Do you have a tire tester?"

"Yep." The old man placed the device into Julius's waiting palm.

"Looks good here." Julius handed the tester back and stood. He whistled, looking over the sleek lines of the man's pickup.

"What a pickup. 1928 Ford in mint condition."

"I always wanted one of these buggies when I was young. Lots of space between me and being a young lad, but there's something to be said for getting what you want. Doesn't always happen."

"No. Seldom does." Julius smiled, but the words pulled at his heart.

"Still, God's always mindful of his children."

"You're a preacher?" Julius peered at him.

"Not hardly." The man snorted. "Well, I need to get going. Tell them hi at Mom and Pop's for Hiram McCormick."

"Thanks." Julius waved as Hiram backed his pickup around, and disappeared down the road.

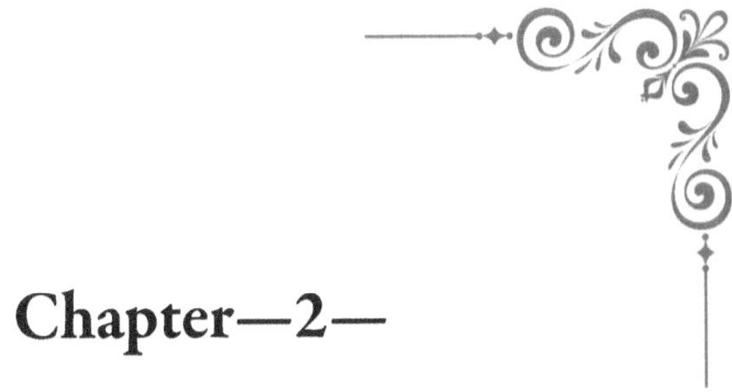

Chapter—2—

Julius dropped back into the white Buick Somerset. Something about Hiram resonated like a cloister bell down a long passageway. A familiar passageway. A passageway that, once you stepped into it, led you to a kind of heartache or homesickness

More than anything, he longed to sit in that orchard again eating green apples and salt. To run barefoot through the pasture where his family's milk cows would lift their complacent heads and stare at him. He wanted to splash in the creek, shouting at his brothers and his sisters....Over the past couple of years, as time sped forward, all of his journeys abroad just seemed to draw his heart closer to home. The only problem was, he could never really *go home*—either the boy or the orchard would be different.

Julius cradled his aching head a few seconds before he pulled the car back on the road. Just one more time, he reassured himself. *All I have to do is survive one more time. God, you'll have to carry me through this one.*

The hollow rumble of his tires on the broad brick street vibrated in his mind and brought his eyes back into focus. Yellow light shimmered through spring leaves of ancient trees along the main street of Beetle River. In the sun-flecked landscape, Julius could see that during its heyday, this town had seen plenty of action.

But today it existed in quiet, dilapidated, silence, like an old gray horse slumbering as it stood in the sunshine of the late spring morning—one that had seen better days and now bided its time.

How many residents lived here? Three hundred? He blew out a breath and scowled. They wouldn't send a detective of his caliber for little minnows, but how could a kingpin crime boss hide here? Everyone knew they chose big cities with lots of people, and lots of action where they could get lost amongst the crowds.

Mom and Pop's Café sat on the street corner, a single-story early-1900s vintage red-brick building with large plate-glass windows on either side of the heavy glass door. The antique sign read Good Eats—The Best For Miles. Julius pulled the Buick Somerset around to park nosed in along the sidewalk.

In the space beside him a man slammed the door of his tan pickup and stepped across the sidewalk to the cafe.

Julius followed the screen door banging shut behind him with a good solid whack. Motionless ceiling fans, a black-and-white checkerboard floor, gleaming canisters and spotless vinyl booths made Julius look for the jukebox. Had he left 1987 and stepped back into the fifties?

The man from the tan pickup continued to the end of the counter. "Howdy, Pop," he said to the stocky, gray-haired cook before throwing a leg over the last stool and settling down. "Bring me a cup of coffee, Becky. I'm supposed to meet Tom. He wants a bid on a project." He leaned both elbows on the counter; his straw cowboy hat shielded his face.

"Pretty busy?" She placed the steaming cup of coffee in front of him.

"Always." He cocked his head and pulled the cup toward him.

Julius sat at the opposite end of the counter. He absorbed the homey atmosphere as the aroma of bacon, eggs, and hash browns mingled with the scent of roast beef and mashed potatoes. His taste buds went into overtime, and his stomach audibly rumbled. A slight early morning coolness still hung in the air.

"May I help you?" A pleasant girl with an honest face, pulled a pen and order pad from her apron.

"A cup of coffee. And what's good to eat here, Becky?" Julius smiled.

Her oval brown eyes widened, apparently studying his now tan face, dark brown eyes, trimmed dark brown wig, beard, and mustache. "Everything's good. Just like the sign says."

"What would you suggest to a poor, weary traveler whose last meal was a cold croissant five hours ago, somewhere over Chicago?"

"You want breakfast or lunch?" Her pen poised mid-air.

Julius looked at the clock. "Eleven forty-five. Let's go with lunch."

"How about a hot roast beef sandwich, mashed potatoes, gravy, and vegetables du jour?"

"Vegetables?"

"English peas are in season..."

"Peas will be fine."

Becky turned, hung the order at the window and brought his coffee. "Cream? Sugar?"

"Thanks, black is fine." Julius spotted a section of the local newspaper on the counter and pulled it toward him, perusing the pages as he covertly observed the other customer. The man, hidden behind his own section of the paper, sipped his coffee. Julius noted from his blue jeans and work boots he worked outside at physical labor. The sleeves on his chambray shirt, rolled up to three-quarter-length, revealed tanned, muscular forearms. He had an excellent physical shape, no beer belly or even the hint of a paunch. And he had a white cowboy hat.

"Thanks," Julius put his paper down as Becky brought his food.

The first man turned as a new customer arrived, "Hey, Tom. How's it going?"

"Sorry I'm late," Tom said. "Had a cow calving. A first calf heifer."

"Haven't been here long. Just got my coffee. Becky, bring Tom some coffee." He picked up his cup and twitched his head toward the back. "We're going to a booth."

Julius glanced up as the man stood and turned to head toward the booth. It took all Julius' self-control not to choke. He looked away quickly, pretending to rescue his napkin from falling. He knew that face. A face like chiseled granite. Those eyes. Those sapphire blue eyes as cold as ice, or hot enough to burn a hole right through you. There could be no mistake. The family resemblance was far too strong. It was his dad's face from twenty years ago. But his father would be in his seventies now. But how? Questions pummeled his mind.

All of his family lived back in North Carolina. No one lived in the Midwest. No one. His father had three siblings—four but his older brother had died in the war. None lived here, but short of a doppelganger...that was the only explanation for a family member to be twelve hundred miles and fourteen years away from Julius's youth?

He fought as his mind wanted to slide back in time to when he had left home. The time of confusion and turmoil. He stared at his plate with unseeing eyes.

"Refill?" Becky approached with the coffee pot.

Julius held out his cup, thankful for the distraction.

"You just passin' through? I've never seen you around before."

"In a manner—" he sipped his coffee, buying time. "of speaking. I'm working on a book about small towns across America." He felt like someone had given him a sucker punch between the eyes. "And collecting stories and pictures. There's supposed to be a local Bed and Breakfast?"

"Bed and Breakfast—Mister?" She cocked her head to one side, waiting for a name.

"The name's Julius. Julius C. Armstrong."

"Pleased to meet ya' Mr. Armstrong. Let's see." She waggled her pen in the air. "You go out here to the end of the block—and three blocks, right to the edge of town—about a quarter of a mile down the road, maybe less. It's a big old house."

"About a stone's throw, then?"

"That'd be right." She smiled.

"Becky, we need a refill," Tom called.

"Sure, be right with you, Mr. Brooks." The waitress grabbed a fresh coffee pot and headed to the booth. "Oh, go on!" She came back laughing at their teasing.

"This food is excellent." Julius tried to lead into the nagging question in his mind. "By the way," jerking his head indicating the pair sitting at the booth, "who're those fellows?"

"Mister Brooks is in the overalls..." she stopped speaking as two pickup trucks clattered to a stop outside. "Say..." Her gaze moved toward the big front window. "If ya want dessert ya better order fast. Business picks up right directly. Some folks come just for the pie. We have some mighty fine pie."

The doors on the trucks slammed emphasizing her words.

He raised his right eyebrow. "What kind?"

"Today we have strawberry cream, chocolate, raspberry, cherry, and apple. All homemade."

"Cherry and a dollop of ice cream." His mouth watered as he waited.

Julius savored his pie and puzzled over the man in the cowboy hat. There could be no mistake. The question came at him again, how had that man come to be here?

As people surged into the restaurant, the noise level rose to a loud drone. The original pair, Tom Brooks and the cowboy hat, walked out the door as Julius scooped up the last bite of pie.

"Time to vamoose." He handed the money to the thin old woman at the register.

"Everything all right?" she asked in a gravelly voice.

"Real good, ma'am. Best food I've had in a long time."

"Glad to hear it. Pop don't want any complaints about his cookin'. " Her wrinkled face drew into a smile.

"Say, Hiram McCormick sends his regards," Julius remembered the old man's admonition.

"Hiram McCormick? The name doesn't ring a bell. Must be a friend of Pop's." She handed him change, and slid the register drawer shut. "You come back, soon."

"Thank you. I expect I will." He nodded his head and walked out.

He unlocked his car and found his carry-on bag. Rummaging in the side compartment, he produced a pair of walking shoes. "Been sittin' too long." He tied his shoes, and then stood, and got his bearings. "Okay, to the end of the block, then three blocks right to the edge of town." He moved through the directions until he arrived at the town's edge. He squinted at the house in the distance. "Hmm, closer to a mile I'd say." Julius hesitated but decided to walk it anyway.

He blotted his face with a handkerchief and slowed his pace as he reached the paved driveway, which led to a three-car garage that had what appeared an apartment above it. An open breezeway connected the garage to the house. His experienced eye told him the house had once been a medium-sized two-story farmhouse. Someone had invested time and money in stonework, additions, renovations, and landscaping. A five foot wrought iron fence surrounded a sizeable front lawn. *Wow, this place is gorgeous.* Julius never expected a bed and breakfast in this small town to be so luxurious. He strode up the driveway looking for the Bed and Breakfast sign. He opened the wrought iron gate and followed the broad stone path leading past a large screened in front porch, a bay window, and around a tower on the north corner of the house. *Still no sign. Should be here someplace.*

He continued along the path which led to a backyard gate framed with a trellis covered in leaves, and tiny rose blossoms.

Through the trellis lay a yard with raised beds of kitchen garden vegetables and herbs. Vivid flowers, scattered higgley-piggley among the plants, caught the eye. A sturdy maple tree dominated a patio, shading picnic tables and chairs. In the distance, pine trees stood sentry at the yard's perimeter, sheltering old-fashioned lilacs, flowering trees, and a children's play area.

The back screen door whooshed open and slammed shut, and a tall woman crunched down a pea-gravel path. Her large garden hat concealed most of her face, but her purposeful walk and the brandishing of her garden hoe contained a haunting memory.

Muttering in animated conversation, she leaned her hoe against a raised bed. "Oh, bother." She slipped off her sandal and shook it, releasing a shower of pea-gravel. Losing her balance, she inadvertently sat on the path with a loud crunch.

Julius swung the gate open and strode the short distance to where she sat. "You know, that's not a good place to sit." He spoke in a pleasant voice.

"Oh!" She gasped and clutched a hand over her heart. "What a Godsend! I thought you were Ruth! You see, I lost my dignity." She gave the appearance of searching for something on the ground. "But I guess it isn't down here." She shrugged and laughed. "If you would help me up." She held up her hands. "Before Ruth gets here, I would be especially grateful, kiddo. And don't talk too loud. Ruth gets somewhat excited when she finds me sitting in odd places."

As if on cue, a young woman's musical voice called out, "Mrs. M, where are you? Are you all right?"

"See what I mean?" she whispered as he grasped her hands and helped her stand.

"It'll be our secret." Years seemed to peel away as he helped her to her feet. The memory of the unblemished face of a younger woman playing patty cake with a baby took her place. The younger woman's hair, a corn silk yellow, fell in soft waves highlighted by the morning sun. "Everybody loves my baby, that's why I'm in love with you, pretty baby…" and her laughter mixed with a baby's coo as she finished the song. He shook his head slightly to clear the memory. The older woman returned as she spoke to someone.

"I'm right here, dearie," she called to the unseen Ruth. "And, yes, I'm all right. Just talking to this fine young gentleman." She dusted herself off and rearranged her simple cotton dress and apron into proper order.

"The name is Julius C. Armstrong." He gave her his pseudonym watching closely while he waited as she straightened her collar. She didn't seem to recognize him, but what did that prove?

"Amanda MacDonald—" Fighting with her unruly hat, she leaned on his arm as he helped her to one of the chairs under the maple tree. "Thank you, Mister Armstrong." She gave up on the hat and tossed it onto the picnic table.

"Here, let me help." He arranged the pillows then helped her settle into the chair. At the sound of light, quick footsteps crunching on the path behind him, he turned quickly. A young woman halted abruptly avoiding running into him by mere inches. His heart did crazy flip-flops when he gazed down into her brilliant blue eyes. *Miranda?* In his mind he blessed his thorough training. His mother had drilled her children often with the reprimand, 'Close your mouth; you're not a cod.'

Like a high-spirited filly, the young woman took a step back and stared at him.

"Ruth," Mrs. MacDonald gestured with her hand, "this is Julius C. Armstrong. Mr. Armstrong, this is my friend and cohort, Ruth O'Brien."

He veiled his eyes and fought the urge to call her name, he knew this was not Miranda. His thoughts were like confetti on New Year's Eve. *Dear God, not here, not now.*

"Pleased to make your acquaintance, ma'am," he said. With a slight nod and smile to cover his wildly scattered thoughts. Miranda had drowned. He knew she had drowned. He still had nightmares recalling the battered body of his sweetheart pulled from the swollen creek those many years ago.

"Ruth, do we have any iced tea in the fridge?" The older woman reached for her hat and fanned herself.

"I'm sure we do." Ruth's brows furrowed and she hesitated. "I'll go get some. Mr. Armstrong, would you care for some tea also?" Her tone had an icy, reserved manner.

"That would be great. It's a longer walk here than I expected."

The women stared at him, uncomprehending.

"Becky, at Mom and Pop's gave directions out here to the bed and breakfast.' She said I could see the house about half a block from the edge of town."

"Oh." The women chorused so closely, they could have been singing, and a dawning light replaced their blank expressions.

"I'll get the tea." Ruth retraced her steps with less reluctance.

"So, what's your business, kiddo?"

Julius backed up and sat in one of the many chairs scattered close to the picnic table. "I'm a freelance writer commissioned to do a book on small towns."

"Well, you sure came to the right town. They don't get a whole lot smaller than Beetle River, Mr. Armstrong. By the way, may I call you—Julius?"

"I would prefer that." He couldn't guess. Had she recognized him? She was always a bit of a rogue. Like the time he and Chuckie Malone had finagled a corn wagon onto the roof of the local feed store about two in the morning. Mr. Mueller, the owner had not been amused, until someone made the suggestion that Mueller use it as advertisement. Julius knew who that someone was. Saved his hide from a fate Julius could only imagine.

Ruth returned and placed a tray, holding three glasses and a pitcher of iced tea, on the picnic table. She poured one glass and then, with a simple dexterous move, wrapped the old woman's fingers around her glass in a motherly fashion. "Here's your tea."

Blind! The woman had maneuvered so well that he hadn't picked up on it.

"Thank you, Ruth. Julius says he's a writer doing a story on small towns. He's looking for a place to stay. Right, Julius?" She sipped her iced tea.

"How long will you be here?" Ruth asked with a slight frown.

"For two, maybe three weeks." The detective retrieved his hanky and blotted his brow. Was that why she hadn't recognized him? He couldn't imagine even blind she wouldn't know him. As a kid he could never fool her or his...dad? Where was his dad? He *might* be able to pull this off with his mom being blind, but his dad would know. Seventeen years—dear God don't let it be too late.

"Mr. Armstrong," Ruth said.

"Julius, ma'am." He returned his handkerchief to his pocket and ran his fingers through his hair.

"We don't allow drinking or smoking, and there isn't a TV." She frowned.

He raised an eyebrow and laughed, "Now that's a first. A business is trying to run customers away. And who told you I snore?"

"So, you don't have a problem with drinking, smoking, or unseemly behavior?" Mrs. MacDonald snickered.

"Only snoring." He smiled and shrugged. "I'm easy to get along with. I'm up early and go to bed early. Some people say my work is my life. Of course, that isn't true. Not quite anyway."

Mrs. MacDonald traced patterns in the moisture gathering on her glass. "I'm sure you want to know details."

AS THE THREESOME LOUNGED in the shade talking, Mrs. MacDonald answered Julius' questions about room rates, meals, schedules and other details, while Ruth sat quietly listening. Julius tried to get a feeling from the words and expressions. I don't think I'd want to play poker with either of these two.

"Would you like a ride back to your car?" Mrs. MacDonald asked.

"No," Julius said, "I haven't been able to work out lately. I can use the jog back."

"We'll need some time to get our accommodations in order. Michael should be coming along anytime now. Do you hear his old beater of a pickup, Ruth?"

"Yes." Ruth patted her friend's hand. "I think I can hear Sally Lu now." She turned to Julius. "If you don't mind riding in Michael's old pickup I'm sure he would run you into town."

THE HAIR ON THE BACK of his neck prickled as Ruth faced him. Julius felt her mentally probing places in his mind where not even he wanted to go. Memories of days gone by yapped in his thoughts. Only by exerting his willpower could he keep them at bay. In his youth there were people who were believed to have the power of discernment. People able to read the thoughts of others. He frowned in annoyance. *This is not possible.* "No, ma'am, I'll jog back to my car, and be back in about an hour. I want to drive around. Get a layout of the land." He stood and placed his glass back on the tray. —*What I want is to get out of here and refocus my brain.*

"Supper's at five-thirty." Slowly Mrs. MacDonald unfolded from her chair. "And," she called as his foot crunched on the pea gravel path.

He turned toward her. "Yes, ma'am?"

"You're going the wrong way."

"This way, Mr. Armstrong." Ruth turned in the opposite direction and pointed him toward the open breezeway connecting the house and garage. "About an hour?"

"About an hour." He swung into a smooth stride down the driveway then toward town.

He frowned as a pickup turned into the driveway he had just left. *Must be Michael.*

Chapter—3—

Time to pick up the pace, to drive some of the demons out of his mind. Breathe, breathe, stretch out the legs, expand the lungs, deep breath. No thinking allowed here, just auto-pilot as his feet pounded the ground. He slowed when his running shoes touched the concrete sidewalk. Still walking with a purpose he covered the few blocks back to his Buick, unlocked his car door and slid into his seat. Julius drove up the street to a small park where a few children played and parked close to the shelter house.

Now he could think after clearing his mind. He had needed that run to clear his head. In this one day, he had flown from one part of the earth to another—and from one lifetime to another. He didn't understand how this had happened. First the man so much like his own father at the restaurant, and Ruth, so much like his childhood sweetheart, Miranda. Lastly, Mrs. MacDonald. How the years had changed her. The last he had seen her, her hair was still corn silk yellow, but now it was white. As shimmering white as Christmas angel hair decorating the tree. His heart pained him as conviction grew to how much of the changes he saw there were due to his actions. What had brought them here, to this tiny, insignificant town in the middle of nowhere— twelve hundred miles and seventeen years from his childhood home? And where were his other siblings? What had happened to them? And where was his dad? Was he still alive?

The message of the old man, Hiram, echoed in his mind: Sometimes we don't get what we wish for, but God's still mindful of his children.

Well, that's all well and good, but where does that leave me? What to do? How can I possibly stay here and expect to carry this off? True, I've been in too many tight spots before. Actual live or die situations, like the time he was portraying an ambassador to…he couldn't remember the insignificant country, but it had an important part in the Middle East politics. He'd had a mind moment and forgot what language he was speaking. Just a moment, but it was a warning sign. Here, even if they recognized him, his family wouldn't be likely to shoot, torture or leave him for dead. No, he knew only his mother and Michael were here, and whoever the man at the restaurant was. It could be Lewis, his oldest brother. His age would be the closest to that man. What of the rest? Were they scattered like dust in the wind? What had he been thinking when he left? You can't just leave people behind. That totally went against everything he'd stood for all of these years. You never leave your brother…or sister behind. He visited the shelter house restroom, bought a fresh can of Coke, back at the car he got out his camera and prepared it for use. I can't just walk off. This case is set and ready to go, so let's do it. He glanced at his watch—I've got thirty minutes yet. Julius put his car in gear, backed out and headed up the street.

JULIUS UNFOLDED FROM the front seat of the Buick and stretched to work the kinks out of his joints. Retracing his earlier steps he crossed through the breezeway and followed the sound of whistling around to the backyard.

"Hello, there," he called out. The young man stopped whistling and looked up.

"I suppose you're the fellow that's staying upstairs?" The young man sat at one of the tables hulling strawberries as Julius approached. "I'd help you get your gear, but Mom has me busy here. Say, you don't happen to know how to hull strawberries do you?" He grinned. "By the way, my name is Michael," he half-stood and held out juice-stained fingers. "I'd shake your hand, but—"

"That's all right." Julius stuck his hands in his pockets and gazed down at the young man. "I'll excuse the oversight. My gear will keep, and the name is Julius. Know how to hull strawberries? I should say. Got an extra huller?"

"Yes. Mom was going to give me a hand, but she had to go tend to something else," Michael said, and pointed at the extra huller lying on the table.

With a burst of action, Julius seized a towel and tucked it into his belt as an apron and grabbed the extra huller off the table. "There isn't much left here. We should have the job done in jig-time between the two of us. Let me tell you about the time I worked as a waiter on a cruise ship..."

Being easy talkers, their conversation flowed, and tantalizing smells wafting from the house added speed to their work. They both looked up as Mrs. MacDonald joined them.

"Michael, putting a guest to work? Mr. Armstrong here will think we ought to pay him." Mrs. MacDonald good-naturedly chided.

"Mom, you always say treat friends like family. I'm just practicing what you teach."

"Aye, Michael, you are incorrigible." She shook her head.

Michael wiped his hands on a dish towel and grinned at Julius as they finished the last of the berries. "That means I'm wonderful. Come on—let's get your gear." He turned back toward his mom. "He's got time to clean up, doesn't he?"

"Sure. Get him settled into his room. Don't talk his ear off, and get right back. You hear?"

"Yes, ma'am," Michael winked at his new acquaintance. Julius wiped the berry juice from his hands then followed Michael through the breezeway back to his car.

Julius opened the trunk, and Michael grabbed a medium-sized suitcase with one hand and an overnight bag with the other. "You sure travel light."

Julius picked up the remaining case and a valise. "Habit." Something he'd learned in the military to travel light and fast. Julius followed as Michael led the way toward the garage, where they entered a stairwell from the breezeway to a small apartment over the garage. "Supper's in forty-five minutes?" He asked as they reached his room.

"Yes, sir." The young man set the luggage down and backed out the door.

Julius walked to the big east windows, and pulled open the deep burgundy drapes. His eyes skimmed the large yard on the south side of the driveway. Tall stately red maple trees flanked the front by the road as well as two weeping willow trees. There was a flower box with petunias and plantings of sunflowers nodding in the sunshine besides an old timey hand push garden cultivator used as a lawn ornament and several other scattered bushes. The front lawn was somewhat visible from his room, and all of it held an aura of elegant peaceful beauty.

With a sigh, Julius glanced at the ornate antique clock on the nightstand. Not an abundant amount of time, but sufficient. Setting his suitcase on the bed he found his kit and carried it to the bathroom. Placing the items in order on the bathroom shelf, pulling his shower cap out he prepared for his shower. His skin tone was semipermanent so he only needed a quick touch up after his shower. He splashed on cologne, ran his fingers through his hair, beard, and mustache with meticulous scrutiny. *Looks good.* He checked his shirt and buttoned his cuffs. Opening his military ARPA phone, he typed in; Bingo, and hit send. Tomorrow he would need to set up his computer. It was an exciting time to be part of the technology community. So many things happening, and as part of the military, Julius had equipment that wouldn't be available anywhere else for several years.

Exhausted, he sank into the overstuffed chair by the west window. A lazy breeze flowed through the room from window to window. He longed to be an ordinary Joe, raising a passel of children; to have no thoughts of life out there. No notions of troubles, or rumors of wars, or... His mind clouded, and questions swirled. Shock after shock had hit him today. The last one being Michael. How old had Michael been? Nine? Ten? And now he was so grown up. So mature, and—so good. Julius had been in this business too long. He'd seen every situation...well he thought he had. A weary sigh and he shook his head. If I leave, all of our work's down the tubes, and this evil crime ring walks. It needs to be brought to justice. He had a job to do, and the old man's words came to him, 'God's still mindful of his children.'

Drawn by the tantalizing aroma of baking garlic bread and frying beefsteak, Julius pulled on his boots, snatched his hat, and bolted down the stairs where singing voices led him out through the breezeway and to the back door of the house. A bass lead sang out, "Today is the day of salvation," and the sopranos echoed.

"Who is worthy to be saved?" Again the echo.

Julius hesitated at the back door. The singing reminded him of his youth when he and his siblings would sing the old time gospel songs as they washed and dried dishes. Or maybe someone had learned a new way of singing an old hymn and they'd try it out. Julius raised his hand to knock, but the door opened first.

"Well, come on in fella. Whatchya doin' out here?" Michael's eyes were wide in good-natured surprise. "The food's inside."

"Smells good." Julius dusted his boots on the mat as he entered. He stopped as his eyes met the simple elegance of the late afternoon sunlight sparkling on water glasses and, dancing across ironstone plates, the silverware and the dainty lace tablecloth. The tempting aroma of the food placed on the table reminded him that good food could fill the stomach, but a good atmosphere was needed to fill the soul. Despite his determination to remain unaffected, the ambiance was perfect. The longing for home washed over him and left him like a starfish stranded on the sand.

"You needn't knock, Mr. Julius." His hostess's gentle words brought him back to reality. "Just come on in."

Michael brought his Bible as they sat down for the meal. "Be merciful unto me, O God; for man would swallow me up: All the day long he fighting, oppresseth me... What time I am afraid, I will put my trust in thee," Michael finished reading the psalm, and then after the blessing, he declared, "Well, as my uncle used to say, 'Good bread, good meat, praise God, let's eat.'"

"Michael Hosea!" Mrs. MacDonald gasped as her fork clattered onto her plate. "Your uncle did not say that and neither should you!" She sat up indignantly in her chair.

Julius stifled a laugh as Michael dipped his head and attempted to look repentant. "Well, I kinda thought he said it." He shrugged and cleared his throat. "Must have been somebody else." He looked at his plate repressing a chortle.

Ruth's eyes twinkled with laughter as she passed a large bowl of lettuce salad. "Mr. Armstrong?" She spoke with a lofty tone.

"Umm—" He cleared his throat. "Julius, ma'am." He didn't dare look in her direction.

"Julius, would you care for some tossed salad?" Her tone carried exaggerated dignity.

"Thank you." He grasped the salad tongs and began to fill his salad bowl.

"How were the rest of your excursions?" Mrs. MacDonald passed the potatoes.

"The jog back to my car seemed shorter. I did some driving around. There should be some good photo shots. Beautiful country around here."

"Would you care for some more garlic bread?" Mrs. MacDonald asked him.

"You must have a good business here, ma'am. This food is excellent," Julius said polishing off the rest of his beef steak and laying his knife and fork across his plate.

"Thank you, Mr. Armstrong. We do a lot of cooking. I do hope you've saved room for dessert. Fresh strawberries and shortcake are coming up."

JULIUS SIGHED IN CONTENTMENT as he slid back from the table. Do not get comfortable here, he reminded himself. Comfort is relaxed, relaxed is dangerous. I can't let my guard down—

Michael's spoon clanked in his bowl. "I'm so stuffed I can hardly wiggle." He exhaled as the dishes began to disappear from the table.

"Two servings of strawberries, shortcake, and ice cream did seem a little much," Mrs. MacDonald said. "He's one of those disgusting people who can eat like a pig and never gain an ounce."

"That's because I work like a dog the rest of the day," Michael said.

"He does work hard." She ruffled his hair as she passed.

"Don't mess up my hair. I've spent hours getting it just right." He frowned and smoothed it back into place with embellished motions.

"You're a hoot. You haven't spent hours on your hair in your entire lifetime," she said.

Julius stood and picked up his plate. "Here, let me help."

"Oh, no you don't, Mr. Julius." Ruth removed the plate from his hands.

"Michael, show Mr. Armstrong around a bit, we'll finish out here," Mrs. MacDonald said.

"C'mon, Mister." Michael stood and slid his chair under the table.

Julius followed Michael into the spacious, modern kitchen. He gazed in wonder at the dark walnut cabinets and polished, gold flecked granite counter tops. "Wow." From the dark ceiling beams to the terra cotta floor tiles, the cavernous kitchen was saturated in rustic Spanish décor and seemed to contain a double of every appliance.

"The laundry room is through that door," Michael nodded toward a darkened room to his right. "We have the laundry room/mud room to leave our boots and wash our hands at the sink. That door exits to the breezeway, which will take you to your accommodations. From the kitchen, we come into the foyer." Michael motioned for Julius to follow him through the doorway opposite the one they had just come through. Michael stood back and motioned toward the kitchen. "The kitchen, laundry room, this foyer, the living room and the bedrooms over this part of the house," he pointed upstairs, "made up the original thirty-six by the twenty-four-foot farmhouse. When we remodeled we added the breezeway, garage, and all that is on the south, and everything else to the north of the living room..."

"You've put in a lot of work here." Julius stopped to examine the living room. "Look at that fireplace. My mother loved a fireplace, and that one is fascinating." Julius stroked his fingers over the large rough stones of the fireplace.

"Mom found the design out west. The stones are local."

"She helped design this? That'd be no small task, especially since she's—" Julius sputtered to a stop.

"She hasn't always been blind," Michael said. "She and my sister, Laura, helped with the work."

"I see. She maneuvers around so well, I just assumed..." Julius fished for the rest of the story.

Michael sidestepped so Julius could view the next area, but didn't add to his original comment. "The next room we call the book nook. It's the common library."

Julius stared. "As a child, this would have been heaven on earth." Julius walked into the nook, turned in a circle, and imagined lying across the area rug engrossed in a Hardy Boys, Little Britches, or Dickens novel on a winter's eve. It brought back the memories of trying to find time and a secluded spot to read. Sometimes he'd hide in the barn loft where the gray or calico tabby cats would curl up beside him. If all else failed he could at times find a few minutes by himself in the outhouse, but that wasn't a good get away.

Julius looked over the selection of the volumes on the right side shelves then walked by a bay window and comfy window seat to peruse the floor- to- ceiling bookshelves on the otherside. The room had the feel of a cozy chamber. Figurines and a few pictures added pleasant dashes of color. A deep- red leather loveseat flanked by two mismatched Queen Anne chairs bordered by elegant end tables made the room even more inviting.

"Off of the book nook, the tower is a separate alcove—it's used for entertaining small groups." Michael motioned at the raised platform with a baby grand piano and a scattering of chairs.

"This reminds me of an English Manor I once visited," Julius said.

"The next room in there is the office and research room." Michael moved past the door to the next room as he spoke.

Julius made a mental note as he followed Michael.

"Over here—" Michael indicated a large pocket door. "—is the formal dining room, and a small bathroom tucked beside the kitchen. And now you're at the back side of the kitchen." They stepped into the kitchen where Ruth and Mrs. MacDonald had just finished cleaning up.

"I've done some photography on Spanish homes. This ranks up there with some real classics—looks like something out of a magazine," Julius said.

Mrs. MacDonald shut a cupboard door and leaned against the counter. "As a bride, the first home I had was a cabin. The first married years, we didn't have running water. Our bathroom was a little room—about forty feet out the kitchen door at the end of a long path. Our children were half raised before we had what many people today would call necessities. But in time things became easier. Not better but easier. Water in a faucet doesn't make life better just different. As Charles Spurgeon wrote, 'Happiness does not consist of how much you have, but how much you enjoy'...."

A man's voice rang from the front door. "Where is everybody?"

"We're back here, Lewis." Mrs. MacDonald led the way toward the front door.

Julius thought about how nice it would be to exit to his accommodations as they filed toward the foyer and the front door, but of course that would never do. There was no way to avoid the man he recognized earlier from the café.

"This is my little big brother." Michael referred to the fact that he was the taller of the two. "Dad always said the longer we kids came, the taller we got."

"I may not be the tallest, but I'm still the oldest, wisest and best looking." Lewis joked.

Mrs. MacDonald held up a hand. "Lewis, this is our new renter, Julius Armstrong." She emphasized the word *renter*. "He'll be renting the gardener's apartment for three weeks. Julius, this is my eldest son, Lewis."

"Glad to meet you," Julius said with a handshake.

"Didn't I see you this morning at the café?" Lewis's eyes narrowed. "How long will you be here, and what's your business? Not to be nosy—just—curious."

"I'm a free-lance writer. The plan is two weeks. Probably three to finish up." With effort, Julius smiled. He could feel his heart beating erratically. Would he be able to pull this gig off? Would they recognize him? If they ever write a training manual, they should include a how to handle section on things like this.

"I see." Lewis hesitated as if mulling the explanation around. "I hope you enjoy your stay." Turning to his mom, he said, "That's funny, Mom. Laura's pretty good at making a dime, but she never thought of that source of income."

"He's got a point Mrs. M," Ruth said, and she and Michael laughed as if there was a hilarious joke.

"Well, anyway, I came over to tell Michael I need him to take the boys out and start moving fence tomorrow. I have a job putting in irrigation, but I need to move those sows."

Julius tucked that conversation with its apparent joke into a nook in his mind and then took advantage of the change in subject. "Glad to meet you, Lewis...and everyone."

He smiled and twisted with a slight bow to his hostess. "Thank you for your hospitality, but I've flown half-way around the world today. If you'd give me leave, I think I'll take up my hat and wish you goodnight."

"Good night, Mr. Armstrong," Mrs. MacDonald said.

"This way," Ruth led him to the laundry room door, "Like Michael said, you go through that door, across the breezeway to the stairs. Sleep well."

"Thank you...and good night."

Once upstairs in his room, he unhooked his case from its hiding place under the bed. Setting it on the small coffee table he opened and folded the screen into position. He was not unappreciative of its special design and function. A special military prototype, a one of a kind computer built to answer to his touch only. He could boot up briefly to check on the intel Director Myer was sending, but his battery wouldn't last long, and he was exhausted. Tomorrow he'd hook it up to a stable power source and attach it to a dish. After checking messages, he looked at some of the files, and then powered down and got ready for bed.

He was so ready for sleep, but thirty minutes later he lay wide-awake. Throwing the covers back, he rose, and, stepping across to the open window, he dropped into the over-stuffed chair. Lewis had left fifteen minutes before. Now, Julius watched the lights in the central house wink out and heard the chatter of Mrs. MacDonald, Michael, and Ruth as they migrated up to bed, leaving the lower house quiet.

His brows drew together as he sat brooding. The sparse lights of the serene countryside mocked him as they blinked across the darkness.

He held his head in his hands and groaned. *Oh Lord, what am I doing here? Missions like this don't happen... assignments don't embed the agents smack the middle of people who know you intimately. They don't expect you to carry on undercover as if you are strangers for three weeks. Trying to convince you these are just people.*

...I did read of an agent embedded in familiar territory time and again during World War II in France. He was recognized once. An old acquaintance identified his voice in a phone call.

The nerve strain of walking among the criminal elements, the not knowing if this day would be his last, it all made him old—and skeptical. He heaved a deep sigh and massaged his forehead.

Outside, frogs sang from a distance, and a solitary light shone upstairs in the house. Notes drifted from a piano and floated across the void. Pachelbel's "Canon in D" had always been one of his favorites. Tension eased from his heart and mind.

Tomorrow, he thought, *I'll deal with this tomorrow.*

Chapter—4—

Thursday, June 11<u>th</u>; Through the open window, Mrs. MacDonald heard the whispering of birds stirring with the dim morning light. In her mind she imagined the dark eastern sky turning different glorious hues moment by moment. Soon with the actual dawn, the sun would burst over the horizon just as Psalm nineteen declared; 'And rejoiceth as a strong man to run his course.'

She dressed, hung her nightclothes away, and smoothed the sheets and the coverlet into place. Her stockinged feet made no sound as she moved to a deep-purple Sausalito chair against the wall beside the pink vanity dressing table. She sat down, put on her headphones, and pressed Play on the tape recorder in order to listen to the recorded Bible reading. With her eyes closed she could feel movement as Ruth crossed to the window seat between the bone white Brittany antique vanity and the matching Brittany vanity in pale pink and gold. There was a slight pause as Ruth glanced out the window overlooking part of the front yard before sinking into the cushions, and burying her face in her arms.

Mrs. MacDonald's heart still ached at the memory of the loss of Ruth's mom. Forty-two—too young to be gone. The neighborhood had been shocked by the death. It was ruled as a heart attack, a natural death, but no one believed it. Philip Meecham, *he had no reason to be there*— he had called for an ambulance at the house from the O'Brien kitchen. Her mom had sent Ruth to her Grandfather's on an errand. If only Ruth had stayed home that day. If only...

After twenty minutes, Mrs. MacDonald pulled her headset off and closed the recorder. "Finished?" Ruth selected the brush from the dressing table. Mr. and Mrs. MacDonald had taken her into their home after that fateful morning. Mr. O'Brien had made the decision. So, Ruth took her personal items that she wanted from her home, but touched nothing else in the house. He closed up Diana and Ruth's house and, like a time capsule it was left as it was when her mom had been carried out.

"Laura and the girls did a fantastic job on this room," Ruth said as Mrs. MacDonald sat down on the vanity bench in front of the mirror.

"Yes, the hint of lavender in the paint and wall paper repeated in the furniture and accessories is perfect."

"I have a picture in my bedroom just like that one." Ruth began to quote, 'Heavenly Father up above, Fill our lives with peace and love. May angels watch o'er me through the night and wake me with the morning light. . ."

"If I should die before I wake, I pray dear Lord, my soul you'll take. That picture, at one time, hung in my room when I was young," Mrs. MacDonald finished.

"That is so precious. Do you believe in angels, Mrs. M.?

"Funny you should ask, Ruth. Just yesterday I was thinking on a story my Dad told about when we were moving from out home in the city to his Uncle's property in the mountains. Our car had broken down that night and we were stranded a few miles from our destination. A stranger happened by with a team and wagon and he helped get us to our property. With his help we got settled in for the night, a fire in the fireplace and some warm food cooked over the fire . . . as a torrential rain hit. He said his name was...that's what I was trying to remember. But when dad asked around no one in the area had any knowledge of him or anyone by his name. Dad said the man appeared to him one other time. Dad had stopped to chat with friends at the local mill when there was a huge explosion. No one knew how Dad made it out alive. Dad wasn't quite sure either, but he woke up lying in the grass. His last remembrance was of some Scotsman talking to him about cats." After a slight pause Mrs. MacDonald spoke again. "I believe in more than one kind of angel though. This last year would have been impossible without you."

"Friendship works both ways. Where would I be without you and Mr. MacDonald?" Ruth's delicate fingers removed tangles and slid through the long hair as she arranged the silvery white tresses that shimmered in the light. She slipped hairpins in to hold the plait in place then stood back to survey her handiwork. The older woman's hair still had enough wave and natural curl to compliment her large wide-set brown eyes, high cheekbones, and pleasant countenance. "Looks good." Ruth assessed the tall, slender older woman. Mrs. M was a combination of grandmother figure Ruth had never known, and the mom she had known. Stubborn and independent, Mrs. MacDonald had a knack for adventure that kept Ruth on her toes—and got them into unusual situations. Keeping Amanda MacDonald out of catastrophes must have taxed more than one guardian angel.

"You sit over there and I'll tend to your hair." Mrs. MacDonald picked up the brush and began to brush Ruth's abundant auburn mane. "I had a cousin whose hair grew almost to the floor, but her hair wasn't as pretty as yours."

"Grace is deceitful, and beauty is vain." Ruth smiled as she repeated her mother's admonition.

"Check your pocket, see if there's some false pride hiding in there. I haven't seen any lately." Mrs. MacDonald's fingers moved systematically through the long strands. "Describe Mr. Armstrong again, would you?" She became thoughtful as she waited for Ruth's words.

"Tall, muscular, and wiry. Dark brown hair and eyes, a neatly clipped beard and mustache. He could have a lopsided smile, but with the beard and mustache, it's hard to tell. He's thoughtful, hardworking, careful, and a sense of humor. I'd say he's about thirty-five, give or take."

The older woman pursed her lips weighing Ruth's words. "You've added some details. 'Thoughtful, hardworking, and careful?' What's that mean?"

"He asked to help clear the table, that's thoughtful. He didn't back down from helping Michael with the berries. No half-hearted berry huller."

"Careful? And how tall is tall?" the older woman began braiding and winding the long hair into a knot.

"He's almost as tall as Michael." Ruth frowned wondering at the word careful. "He seems honest, but ...he's...not...forthcoming. His mind is closed to me in some way." Ruth thought, creasing her brows.

"Don't frown, Ruth, it will give you wrinkles."

"How do you know I'm frowning?" Ruth's eyes widened as she realized she was frowning.

"Don't grimace, either." Mrs. MacDonald slid several pins into Ruth's hair.

"Honestly! I don't know... I think you have radar!"

"The blind don't see with their eyes they see with their heart."

Ruth gave her a quick hug, "Let's go, breakfast won't fix itself."

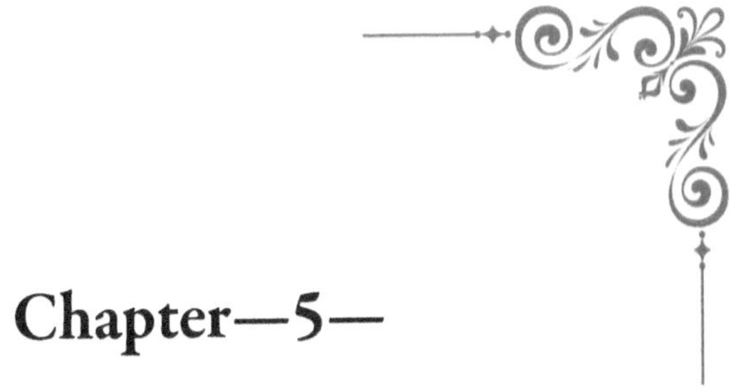

Chapter—5—

There was the familiar intense smell of sweat-drenched bodies, fear, and terror and smoke. Fire was burning all around, yet he continued his frantic search for his fellow team mate.

"Brooks!" He kicked open the door of the next room. In the far corner, Brooks sat propped up his rifle trained on the door.

"Thank God. Thank God," Robbie Brooks' voice shook with relief. "My right leg's broke, my left arm's useless..."

The far side of the roof caved in, sending flames and sparks in every direction.

"We're the last ones. I gotta get us out now." Julius bent, and, as gently as possible, he draped Brooks across his shoulders. The flames singed his eyebrows, smoke and falling debris made it impossible to breathe or see. He clutched his friend and his weapon, with only one thought—survive.

BOOM, BOOM, BOOM! SOUNDED under Julius's window as Sally Lu roared to life. Julius rolled off the bed and hit the floor, Beretta in hand. He searched the room and brought his senses into focus coming to grips with where he was. His heart, thudding against his ribs, began to calm. He holstered his gun and pulled himself to his knees. "Hey, what're you doing starting that beast at three in the morning?" he shouted out the window.

"Sorry, sir." Shamefaced, Michael switched off the engine.

Oh, man— Julius took a deep breath and ran his fingers through his hair. *What time is it? Was I sleeping or what! I'm usually up by now.* His mind continued to reel in confusion. *What day is it?* He crossed to the west window. "Hey," he spoke in a more subdued tone now as the young man appeared on the other side of the breezeway. "What time is it?"

"Six-fifteen—I'm sure sorry, sir."

"Yeah, yeah. Thanks." Julius rubbed his hands over his face. *That's fine—just wonderful.* In the bathroom, he splashed water on his face, rubbed the sleep out of his eyes, and stuck in his contacts. *That dream! If he'd only stop dreaming that dream!* He sighed and pulled on jeans, and a dark blue T-shirt. *And all those other dreams...* He strapped on his shoulder holster and weapon, slipped his vest over it and touched up his hair. He took a deep breath and ambled down the steps to the kitchen. *I gotta get a grip. Or else Julius Armstrong, detective extraordinaire will be ex-detective and in not a good way.*

He picked up the note propped on the kitchen counter. *"— Carafe has- coffee, help yourself."*

Julius found the mugs and poured a cup. Carrying it to the sunporch, he turned a heavy wooden chair so he could look out the windows, and sat. He inhaled his first draught of the potent liquid. With closed eyes he felt it seep through his body. *Oh, God, if only these dreams, and specters would stop.*

The spring inside his mind relaxed, and instinct began to take control. He opened his eyes and looking out the windows, he scanned the backyard and its surroundings. A path led between the pine trees on one side and a small orchard on the other. Beyond the grove, smudges of color indicated buildings. His observations of the surrounding area yesterday had shown him that on the back side of this piece of land lay pasture enclosed in a short line of hardwood trees.

He moved back into the kitchen to refill his mug and nonchalantly sorted through the desk area in the corner—a clean, neat workspace, with a few sticky notes hanging around. He picked up a clipboard and read, "Daily Menus" at the top. *Humph, don't need to read this. The smell of bacon, scrambled eggs, and*—he took a deep breath— *blueberry muffins already tell me the morning's fare.* He looked around, but didn't see anything. *Must be in the warming oven...*

He rifled through the pages. *Hmm, just menus.* Glancing out the window, he saw Mrs. MacDonald and Ruth in conversation, strolling up the path toward the house. He grabbed his mug and slipped back to the sunroom as he heard their footsteps in the breezeway. Their voices rose over the sound of running water as they washed their hands in the laundry room sink.

Mrs. MacDonald entered the sunporch. "Good morning. How are you this morning? Ruth, please grab me a mug of coffee?" The chair scraped lightly on the tile floor as she took a seat.

"I'm fine, ma'am," Julius said. "In spite of the jolt, Sally Lu gave me."

"Would you like a refill?" Ruth addressed Julius as she brought in the coffee pot. "Oh!" She stopped short, gazing out the window. "That beautiful cardinal is back!" She stooped and set the coffee pot down. Moving in measured steps, she spoke softly. "The sun is just touching parts of the backyard. Patches of light are illuminating the bird feeder in the maple tree."

Julius forgot his coffee as he watched the cameo of the older woman, with silvery white hair and subtle pink complexion, and the younger woman with her crown of brilliant auburn mane, and rose-tinted features. A knife twisted in his heart. Miranda had been a beauty, and the reminder of her was a sharp pain in his chest. On closer inspection, Miranda didn't resemble Ruth's peaceful, serene countenance, yet the likeness still came too close.

As Michael came whistling down the path, the shy cardinal flew off.

"Pardon the interruption," Mrs. MacDonald said to Julius. Ruth filled their mugs and left the room. "We've been watching that bird for some time."

Water splashed in the laundry room sink as Michael washed his hands.

"So, what about Sally Lu?" Mrs. MacDonald asked.

"I'm sure sorry about the racket this morning." Michael appeared in the doorway, straightening his shirt sleeves.

"Oh," Mrs. MacDonald said wryly, "I see."

"I should've been up." Julius shrugged.

As Ruth brought in plates and silverware, Mrs. MacDonald hopped up to excuse herself. "Well, I've left Martha to do all the serving."

"Just stay put. I'm not Martha, and you're not Mary," Ruth said, "Here, Michael set these around please." Handing the items to Michael, she left to fetch the food.

The table all set, and the food steaming hot, Julius sat back, observing Michael as he began reading: "In my distress, I cried unto Jehovah, And He answered me..." Michael continued reading until he cited Psalm 120, and then asked the blessing.

"Michael, would you come here?" Ruth placed her napkin beside her plate and started for the laundry room.

With fork halfway to his mouth, he stopped, replaced his fork on his plate.

Julius watched as Michael followed Ruth to the laundry room and chuckled even though he could only see Ruth's back as she held up a washcloth.

"Here—hold still, you've got a smudge right here." And she dabbed at the spot.

"What is it, Mr. Julius?" Mrs. MacDonald asked.

"Those two are about the same age, aren't they?"

"Four years difference. Like brother and sister—or best friends."

"I know it's none of my business, but—"

"He's still in college, and she's barely out of high school. Around here, we believe in courting, Mr. Armstrong."

"I did say it isn't any of my business." Julius leaned back with a slight narrowing of the eyes, watching their interaction. "But...they just look right together."

"In our current situation, there's no good time," Mrs. MacDonald said, her voice more gentle.

Julius thought on the answer. What was their current situation, and what did she mean? He waited as the pair returned to the table. "Where should I go to get some local history?" He helped himself to bacon from the platter, and blueberry muffins from the basket.

The trio answered in unison, "Mrs. Irving."

Julius plastered butter on his muffin. "And where do I find this Mrs. Irving? Is she the local librarian or historian?"

"Gossipmonger, Mr. Armstrong." Ruth smiled at his question. "She knows more about most people around here than they do themselves."

"She has the local Antique Mall on Main Street," Michael said, taking another bite of bacon and scrambled eggs.

"We are putting up strawberries this morning at Lewis and Donna's." Mrs. MacDonald said. "Lunch is at twelve-thirty. Fried chicken. Donna's fried chicken is superb—you don't want to miss it. When Mrs. Irving lets you go, come on over." She took a sip of coffee.

Julius looked at his watch. "Hmm, seven twenty. What time does the Antique Mall open?"

"Eight thirty. You have about an hour." Michael drained his coffee cup and pushed back from the table. "And I better get snapping. Places to go, things to do."

JULIUS PULLED HIS CASE from under the bed and carefully laid it on the nightstand. On the wall in back of the nightstand he located the phone jack and hooked his modem into it and set up his computer. Opening his west window he ran some wires and set up a temporary antenna. *Well, this connection will do for now.* Julius sent the note to Agent Shields—*Iron in the fire.* Shields will let Junco know I'm all right, and I should get a response by tonight. He hit a second button, and the computer started running information from Director Myer. The message came up; *We may need you to fly into Chicago concerning the group. Here's the dossier.* His gaze flicked over the data as it ran across the screen. First, a picture of his man Albertoo Meister and his activities. Okay, drugs, murder, theft, human trafficking, and? He lifted an eyebrow and with a quick glance, scanned the growing list. And it ties in here? How? Who?

Peaceful morning sounds of birds joyfully singing and calling to one another, feeding their clutch of babies echoed from the surrounding woods and trees. How would someone with a rap sheet like that hide in here? Good night! There goes the neighborhood. His mouth twisted into a sarcastic grimace.

Shutting his computer down, he found a new hiding place for his computer behind the nightstand, hanging the case temporarily on the frame. Camera, recorder, notebook, all ready to go. Julius checked off his list, grabbed his notebook and pen and thudded down the stairs. Ruth was backing a green Suburban out of the garage when he arrived at his Somerset.

Ruth stopped and rolled down her window. "We'll see you at twelve-thirty-ish. Lewis and Donna live in the big powder blue house over there." Ruth pointed across the section of farm land.

Hmm, how convenient. Just down the road..."Gotcha." Julius nodded. "See you there."

Chapter—6—

The front door of The Antique Mall was still locked, but Julius saw a bell and rang it. Waiting just a few minutes he heard the slow steps and then the blinds in the door raised and he heard fingers fumble with the lock. She still held the feather duster as she unlocked the door, the bell above it tinkled. "Hello there, young man. Are you looking for something or someone?" She arranged her spectacles and peered at the tall, slender young man squinting at her business sign.

"Both." Julius approached the sharp-faced, blue-haired bird of a woman as she scanned him head to foot. "Looking for stories—and someone by the name of Mrs. Irving."

"That's me." The proprietress held the door open. "I could be the oldest antique here." She laughed at her joke, sounding like a crackling piece of paper. "Some folks say I know everyone's business, and—" she added with a sly, knowing wink, "a little bit more."

"I'm looking for local stories," Julius said.

Mrs. Irving followed him silently for a few minutes as he looked around before she spoke. "I didn't catch your name."

"Julius C. Armstrong. I'm writing a book about small towns."

"You're not looking for antique hand held hair dryers, then," she said with a dry cackle. "Follow me," Mrs. Irving's shoes made a dull thudding noise on the uneven wooden floorboards as they wound through the aisles. "I have a display here at the back you might be interested in."

"Antique photos?" Julius paused and surveyed the back wall of the room. There were several wedding pictures of handsome couples in wedding attire displayed on the wall. Underneath the larger wedding photo there were a few family pictures in a display for each name. "Okay, this is what I'm talking about. Who are these folks?"

"That is Lawrence Anderson and his wife, Angela. This one over here—" she moved to another section of the display, "is Olan Christianson and his wife, Lainie. I've arranged them by family." she pointed to another area. "My late husband's family, Irving, and O'Brien." A whisper of a sigh escaped from her thin, wrinkled visage as she ran a feather duster over the pictures.

"Let's see here..." Mrs. Irving pointed to different pictures and told some family history about each. "Seven families settled the town. Anderson, Christianson, Thompson, all came to this country from the same place in Norway—they met up with Irving, Holmes, Smith and O'Brien on the east coast. The families formed a group out east looking for farm land out west." She seemed to linger over the last image of a tall, dapper man in a fashionable 1920's suit. He appeared to be in his twenties, as he leaned against the side of a stylish buggy with a sleek bay horse hitched to it.

"I came across an older gentleman yesterday," Julius said. "Name of Hiram McCormick. Don't see his family in here."

"McCormick? No, not anyone around here by that name. Might be up north, but not around here. Only O'Brien."

Mrs. Irving paused and then finished tucking the O'Brien picture back in its place.

The old woman had again said O'Brien with a slight sigh.

"Which ones would be the most interesting?" He pointed to the pictures.

"Hmm." She squinted, tapping her thin fingers on the table. "Well, of course, everyone has a story." She frowned. "The two most interesting would be Charlie Anderson and Pat O'Brien."

"What kind of fellows are those two?"

The old woman pounced like a chicken on a bug. "Charlie Anderson. Now if you want stories Charlie's the man," a smile danced across her wrinkled face. "He had a fall this February and is recovering at the retirement center. Here—here's a picture of Charlie and his wife Eleanor. She passed on about four years ago..."

Her tongue clicked against her teeth as she mulled over the second question. "And Pat O'Brien? He was quite a catch back in the day." She caught herself mid-sigh, but her eyes held a youthful sparkle. "Pat and Charlie! Those two loved a good time and had a knack for interesting escapades. A lot of good stories."

"Are these pictures then of Pat O'Brien? And who's with him here?"

"Yes, that's Pat, and his sweet wife, Priscilla. She came for a holiday visit and decided to stay...after she met Pat. She died quite a few years ago from a broken heart..."

"Broken heart?" Julius startled at Mrs. Irving's plain speech. "Does that mean Mr. O'Brien wasn't the catch he had appeared?"

"No, Pat was one of the most decent men around. Can't say that about that mean spirited, old...Ralph Meecham. He wanted Priscilla in the worst way, and she wouldn't have him. There's been rivalry and—on Ralph's part at least, hatred ever since. He spread lies and made their life as miserable as he could. Prissy was a dear soul and gentle, it finally weighed her down." Mrs. Irving dabbed away tears. "Pat and Prissy deserved each other. They were good people."

"Mind if I snap a few pictures?" Julius held up his camera.

"That's fine." She paused as Julius shot a few pictures.

"Pat's granddaughter, Jack's girl, I think her name's Ruth, took up with those new folks west of town. She isn't interested in any of the young fellas." Mrs. Irving fingered some of the photos back into their display places. "A few years ago someone tried to start tales about her. Some said it was old Ralph Meecham's grandson, Philip." Mrs. Irving nodded and winked. "She decked ole' Philip. Gave him a black eye, she did. Told him he wasn't man enough for her, and if he tried to start any more rumors about her, she'd give him worse the next time." Mrs. Irving harrumphed into her handkerchief to hide a snicker.

"New folks in town?"

"Their name's MacDonald," she said with a frown. "No one knows much about them. They just showed up one spring about ten years ago, bought some land, and dug in. They seem friendly enough. No one has a bad thing to say about them. Religious folks, but ... some folks use religion as a cover. They bought that old Herrington one-room schoolhouse. Used it to start a small 'non-denominational' church out there on the north side of town." Her face wore a shrewd disapproving frown.

"But I've never heard anything but good about them."

JULIUS TOOK A FEW MORE pictures of the family displays and Mrs. Irving. After he scanned his notebook, he flipped it shut and left Mrs. Irving's shop. Walking toward his car Mrs. Irving's words chased in his mind. A dangerous criminal in this community? "Ouch!" He knocked his head on the car frame. Humph! He rubbed his head and glanced at his watch.

He eyed the pickups in front of Mom and Pop's on the corner across the street. Maybe a cup of coffee would give him time to think—and eavesdrop on local conversations.

"Thanks," he said, as Becky brought his coffee and a giant cinnamon roll. The only other customers were three men sitting at the counter.

"So, Steve, how're your soybeans doin'?" The first farmer took a sip of coffee.

"They're up. You plant any corn this year?"

"Mostly corn. Only a hundred acres of beans this year. Think prices'll go up?"

"Hopeful. What about you, Jack?"

"Yeah, I've got everything in. Good thing I don't have to depend on my hobby ta support my living, though."

"My wife and I both work off the farm for our living." Steve took a gulp of coffee. "Shop doing good?"

"Decent, it does decent. Always someone needs something fixed or welded. How's your dad doing, Chuck?"

"Fine, should be home soon."

"Good, good." Jack shook his head.

"Did you hear about those stolen cattle?" Chuck asked.

"Sure did. Have they caught the devil that done it?" Steve said.

"Why'd they wait so long to report it?" Jack scratched his head.

"It happened after Memorial Day, I guess," Chuck said.

"You guys don't have the whole story." The cook stepped out of the kitchen.

"Okay, Pop, tell us how it goes." Steve laughed and pushed his hat back on his head. "More coffee here, Becky." He motioned to the waitress.

"Well, you know Danny and Michelle hired that Lenny kid." Pop began his story as he leaned back against a cooler. "He's been their hired man for a year. Lenny had some of Danny's cattle at his place there in the cattle lot. When Lenny took a four-day weekend on Memorial Day, Danny went over to check the cattle. There was a steer out, and the one gate wasn't chained as Danny liked, but it was a holiday, and he was in a hurry. A week later, when they were counting cattle to sell, there was about ten head missing."

"Hoo-ee! Ten head! That'd make a fella…"

"Hey guys," Becky called, "look who just pulled up."

Julius looked out the big front window as a young man stepped out of a flashy new red pickup, and an older man eased out of the passenger side. As the pair ambled toward the door, the third farmer stood. He pulled money out of his front jeans pocket, and spoke with a slight drawl. "Pop, I'm sure glad I don't own this business."

"Why's that Jack?" the cook asked.

He looked at the young waitress. Apparently choosing his words, he jerked his head vehemently in the direction of the two incoming men. "I wouldn't want to serve folks like that. Keep the change, Becky." He threw his money down and pushed out the door as the newcomers entered. The farmer paused and spat on the step. He stomped to his pickup, jerked the door open, and slammed the door behind him. He threw the pickup in gear, screeched out of his parking spot, and sped away.

Becky sighed and filled a glass with water. Walking to the front door, she washed the step.

Julius' eyes narrowed. *What gives?* He went to the register and paid. Then he hurried to his car, and retrieved his camera from the passenger seat. He began snapping pictures of Mrs. Irving's Antique Mall, another of the old depot, Mom and Pop's Café, the pickup trucks sitting out front, nonchalantly including a couple of license plates. Then he stepped back inside the café and took some pictures of Mom and Pop, and Becky, and the customers.

"Sure, I'll bring you some copies," he told Mom and Pop.

"Did ya' get settled into the Bed and Breakfast then?" Pop asked.

"Yes, I did." Julius stuffed his camera back in the case. The younger man of the two newcomers glared at him. "Well, I gotta run, or I'll be late for my next appointment. Thanks."

He threw his camera case into the passenger seat. "Ouch!" He whacked his head in his haste. Come on!" The starter ground, and the motor sputtered then roared. Julius backed out and shoved his foot to the floorboard. In his rearview mirror, he saw the red pickup backing out of its space.

At the top of the hill, Julius took a right on the first street he came to, went through the next intersection, then cranked a hard right to slide into the alley and lay low. The red pickup idled down the street he had just spun off of and screeched to a halt. The backup lights came on, and Julius gunned the motor and shot forward. Just out of the alley, he turned a hard right and taking the same street that had brought him there he went left, down another alley and nosed in behind a garbage dumpster.

"Oh, good Lord," he muttered as the red pickup crawled down the street in front of him. "How do you hide in a white car?" He backed up and pulled out of the alley. Back at Main Street, he chugged to the top of the hill and took a left turn. The street should turn to gravel up here, and an acre of trees grew on this side of town if yesterday's casing of Beetle River served him right.

Julius coasted into a growth of shrubs bordering what looked to be abandoned property. Some pink and white hydrangea bushes leaned against a broken trellis, and several clumps of orange daylilies peeked through the overgrown grass. With a bit of luck, he would be out of sight here. He rolled his window down and heard a motor humming up the street.

The sound died away in the distance. Julius let out his breath. He couldn't stay here, that pickup would be back. He backed out and continued down a rutted path that grew more narrow and overgrown. In the distance, Julius could see another gravel road intersect this one. He hesitated at the end of the forsaken road and looked both ways. Hearing nothing but birds and natural sounds, and seeing nothing moving, he pulled out onto the gravel road. His glance in the rearview mirror caught a shimmer of light behind him. His foot pushed the accelerator. "Come on, Nellie." The speed increased at a snail's pace.

"I think I could peddle faster than..." he muttered and his words broke off as he recognized the road. "Hallelujah, I was right."

A moving van with Trusty Delivery Service in large letters across the side sat backed up in the driveway of his newfound bed and breakfast. Julius turned on two wheels into the drive as a tan pickup approached from the front of him. He came to a stop between the house and the van and the tan truck pulled in and parked directly behind him.

Michael barreled out of the passenger side of the pickup and stormed up to Julius' side of the car. "I don't know if that's how you learned to drive, mister, but in our part of the world..."

Julius held up a hand and motioned back over his shoulder as the red pickup whizzed on past not slowing down.

Michael's eyes widened and he looked back at Julius. "That's pretty good for someone who hasn't been here for twenty-four hours. You always make friends so fast?"

"Sometimes I'm quicker than that." Julius closed his window and got out. "I thought I was supposed to meet you over there?"

"These folks weren't supposed to be here until tomorrow, but here they are." Michael turned as the driver of the pickup, a short woman with black curly hair, slid out and approached. "Donna, this is Julius Armstrong, Mom's stray that Lewis told you about. Julius, this is Lewis' wife, Donna."

"I'm sorry about having to cut in front of you, ma'am, but..."

"I'm glad I wasn't going any faster." She frowned but didn't turn away his apology. She turned to the delivery men. "We weren't expecting this delivery until tomorrow, but..." Distress showed in her large brown eyes. "Michael, check the door, please?" Her voice contained a soft southwestern accent.

Michael opened the wrought iron yard gate and walked to the entryway. "Voila," When he turned the door handle the door swung open.

"Ma'am, that door would not open. I tried, and Fred tried, and it would not budge." Greg, the largest delivery man said, turning bright red.

"Let's get this furniture unloaded." Fred frowned. "This is gonna put us behind and we'll miss our lunch."

Julius, Michael, and the two men unloaded several well-wrapped pieces of furniture and carried them upstairs.

The upstairs hadn't been part of the tour. Julius covertly studied the small bit he could see. It was a large room with books, an antique loveseat and a deep cushioned setae, but the real eye catcher was the baby-grand piano set in front of the floor to ceiling windows that overlooked the front yard. *Will this place never cease to amaze me? The money someone must have to do all of this!*

"We're sorry for the mix-up," Donna told the delivery men. "Why not come on over and have a bite of lunch? It will be late when you get back to Hermon."

"Well, now," the largest man surveyed his hostess, "if it isn't any trouble, I think we'll do that."

"Greg," Fred growled. "I don't want ta..."

"Who's driving?"

"Okay, okay. Have it your way." Fred threw up his hands, "If the boss says anything it'll be your hide." Fred slammed the passenger side door.

The smell of fried chicken, mashed potatoes and freshly baked cobbler dominated the air as they walked into Lewis and Donna's farmhouse.

Julius was seated at the large round table and after the blessing, he filled his plate as the food was passed. Various conversations hummed around as Julius put on his vacant look, and just listened.

"Hey, this is some good fried chicken, ain't it, Fred?" Greg finished his third helping of fried chicken and mashed potatoes.

"It sure is." Fred waved him away still talking.

"This peach cobbler is the best I've ever had." Greg pushed himself back from the table. "Sure enjoyed the meal. Thanks, for invitin' us, but we gotta be goin' now. Come on Fred."

"You know," Fred elbowed his companion as they walked to the door, "you were right. A real nice family."

Chapter—7—

"Come on. I have something to show you." As dishes and food disappeared from the table Mrs. MacDonald motioned for Julius to follow her.

"Lewis and his family have a nice place here." Julius stood at the back door and perused the large covered deck, complete with several scattered tables and a large area for grilling and entertaining. "They've put in a lot of work here. Do they help with your bed and breakfast?"

"They do have a nice place." She grasped the handrail and led down steps onto a pathway that threaded through trees and shrubs. "Every year there's a new project. For instance, some of the trees are bearing fruit, and some are just getting their feet settled." She waved her walking stick at several trees.

Julius inspected the pathway threading through trees and shrubs. "From the road, the landscape tricks the eye into believing that the house is set close to the hill. The deck, the walkway, the herb and vegetable garden, all this back here is hidden from view."

Emerging from a cluster of trees they were confronted with a vine covered courtyard. Mrs. MacDonald crossed the area and opened a round front door to a quaint cottage set in the side of the hill. She paused a moment, allowing her eyes to roam as if trying to feel his reaction. "So, what do you think?"

From the entryway his gaze wandered across the large light filled room. He cleared his throat. "Don't you suppose the three bears might come back and catch us unawares?"

"I think we're safe." She smiled and led him past a coat closet and into a cozy kitchen. "Have a seat, kiddo." She motioned toward a pleasant eating area just off the kitchen. "Since we just finished lunch," —she pulled a wrapped container out of the freezer—. "This will be for later.

Julius sat at the round table and looked out the large window. Mrs. MacDonald maneuvered with agile movements around the island between the eating area and the kitchen.

"So, what do you think?" She sat down looking directly at him.

"It's quite a comfortable hide-away."

"Like something out of Tolkien and...."

He nodded his head. "The inside appears larger than the outside. The cottage is invisible from the outside with the ivy, climbing roses and flowers reaching over the courtyard. And, yes, what at first glance looks like a small cubbyhole... this is quite large."

"Julius," she picked up a rattan coaster from the middle of the table and began pulling on the edges. "This is where I live—Ruth, Michael, and I are just house-sitting for Laura and her family. While I'm confessing, I should add we don't have a bed and breakfast establishment either. There is a regular, bona fide bed and breakfast south and east on the edge of town, but you went west and north. Smith's B&B is out of commission for at least a week. They had storm damage two weeks ago. However, if you feel cheated, or unhappy, with our arrangement, no one will hold it against you if you want to try the real bed and breakfast." She tossed the coaster a short way into the air and let it fall on the table.

Being blind, she could not see the smile that kept trying to break into a laugh. The laugh finally won. "Hoo, ha," Julius stopped to catch his breath. "Your daughter doesn't happen to be married to a Juan Alvarez-Gonzales does she?"

"Why—yes. That's his name." Her eyes grew wide with amazement. "How could you know that?"

"That was the name I heard the delivery man give." Julius wiped his eyes with his hanky.

"I'm glad you can laugh." Her face reddened. She picked up the coaster again and began pulling at it. "Well, now I have my confession made, come, help fill my bird feeders. I'm sure Michael has neglected them." She tossed the coaster aside and slid her chair back from the table. Crossing to the other side of the island she tugged a container from the pantry shelf. "And of course I'm helpless. Here's the bird feed."

"Ma'am," his voice held a note of laughter, "you are a lot of things. Right now, impatient maybe? Helpless isn't a term that describes you." He took the container of feed from her. "And I suppose that explains the joke."

Mrs. MacDonald walked to the enormous westerly window in the breakfast nook, touched the woodwork beside it, and what looked like a window slid open—as did Julius' mouth. She stepped out into the warm afternoon sunshine. "Close your mouth," she said, "you're not a flycatcher, and what joke was that?"

"Laura and her dime..."

JULIUS PULLED THE TOP off the first feeder and poured birdseed in. He now had a small portion of the story, but something here didn't fit. The amount of time, money, and the technology—"Doesn't living here and all of this cost a lot of money?" His eyes narrowed. "How do you manage?"

"It doesn't cost anymore to live here than it would cost elsewhere. We have our separate areas of work and support. Such as

Lewis Junior is putting in irrigation for another local farmer." Mrs. MacDonald held the container for Julius as he replaced the top. "Those of us here are retired. Michael's in school, Ruth at present is my paid companion. Juan has an antique furniture store. We combine work for the three households for a number of things. Monday morning, for example, the men will put up hay for the livestock this winter." She stopped and ran her fingers over some spearmint, broke off a leaf, and began chewing the herb as they ambled along the path.

"Juan Alvarez-Gonzales. That's not a name you run across in this part of the world. Is he from around here?"

"No, Laura and her first husband worked for several years in Spain before Lyle died. Juan was a local resident from Spain they had converted."

"From Spain? I find it odd that someone like Juan would move here?"

"Mission work in Spain was Lyle's dream, not Laura's. Being away from family was hard on her. One has to live somewhere. Juan maintains his estate in Spain and they divide their time between here and there. It fits with his import/export business. Afternoons are beginning to get warm." Mrs. MacDonald waited as Julius filled the last feeder. "Let's go get something to drink."

"HOW LONG HAVE YOU BEEN in this area of the country?" Julius watched as the birds landed on the feeder outside the window. He was finding it difficult to ask the question running in his mind, *where's dad?* No use putting it off, he decided. "Are you a widow? You've not mentioned..."

"Oh, no." She gasped, realizing her error. "Mac, is on a mission trip. He'll be back in two weeks. About the time you'll be leaving."

"So, why don't you kind of fill in some of the gaps here. If you don't mind. This is good sweet-tea, by the way." He took another sip as they sat at the table inside.

Swirling the ice cubes in her tea, the older woman took her time before she spoke. "It's no great secret, but our past is just that—past. We lost James twelve years ago. The police report called it a home burglary. One evening a man walked into where James and Lily lived. James was dozing in front of the TV, Lily was at an evening cleaning job. The man was looking for..." she shrugged, "something. Money? Drugs? Something. An altercation took place, and in the struggle, James fell, struck his head and died. The intruder told the authorities that Lily planned everything. Lily said he kept flirting with her at the restaurant where she worked, but she told him she was married. The jury convicted him and sent him off.

"After that, we were tired. We felt like we had run through a gauntlet and were beaten and bloody. Lewis Junior and Laura, were happily married by then and we were on good terms. Anna and Michael were still at home, but everyone else was gone. That man they locked up made it clear what he would do when he got released. We were prompted to change our names and leave home. We hung a US map on the wall and threw a dart. Here's where we landed."

"And—Lily? What became of her?"

"We were never able to get close to Lily during the years she and James were married. After James died, we went our separate ways. I don't know where she went." She stared at her tea. "I forgot those tea-cakes." She hopped up and went for the goodies.

"So, when are you going to bring your wife and daughter for a visit?" she asked as she carried the cakes to the table.

Alarmed at the question Julius' knee bumped the table and his tea spilled.

"Oh—how clumsy of me! How did I spill that tea? I'm so sorry!" She grabbed a napkin and dabbed at the tea.

"Here." He jumped up and grabbed paper towels off the roll. "It's my fault. Let me finish mopping."

"Hello, hello?" Ruth called through the front door.

"We're in here, honey— I can't believe I did that!" Mrs. Mac-Donald fretted.

Ruth brought a towel to dry the table then with careful tread, carried refills to the table.

"Did you come clean with Mr. Armstrong? Did he tell you what a deceiver you've been?" She settled on her chair and leaned forward. Resting her chin in the palm of her hand she smiled at Mrs. Mac-Donald.

"Ruth, you know I never told Mr. Armstrong anything deceitful or untrue." The older woman's pained expression looked like that of a child that is wrongfully accused.

"Well," Ruth raised her eyebrows and tilted her head sideways. "No, you didn't deceive Mr. Armstrong, but neither did you try to relieve him of his error."

AUBURN STRANDS CURLED around Ruth's forehead. *I don't know any girl more physically attractive than Ruth. She's no older than eighteen—at the most nineteen. How can she be content as a companion to Mrs. MacDonald?*

"I'm hoping that Mr. Armstrong has forgiven me. I am repentant—for his mistake."

Julius smirked. "All's well that ends well. I did make the mistake," he said then frowned. "But I never get directions wrong. Not even complicated ones." The frown lines deepened then he shrugged. "I guess there's a first time for everything."

"You've never had directions from Becky Anderson before." Ruth snickered. "She can confuse almost anyone. Strawberries are finished, the kitchen is cleaned up, and it's time for the chickens to go home." Ruth took her last bite of teacake.

"True, it's time to be going. Ruth and I are going back to Laura's. We'll we see you there after a bit?" Mrs. MacDonald carried the dishes to the sink.

His face wore a perplexed frown. "There's still quite a bit of afternoon left. Do you suppose anyone would mind if I took some photos?" Julius handed Ruth a tea cake to put in a baggie.

Mrs. MacDonald hesitated. "Ask Lewis. Perhaps Michael will show you around." She rinsed the cups and stacked them in the sink drainer. "Done," she said.

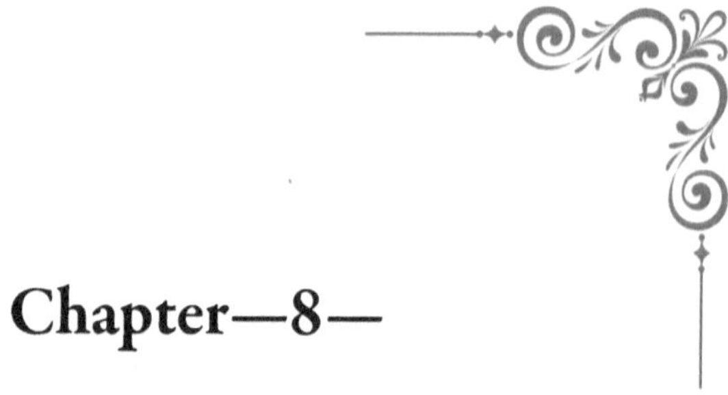

Chapter—8—

Julius changed film in his camera in the shade of the deck awning. "I need to get this film sent today. Where do I go?"

"Hermon's the closest place—about twenty minutes." Michael lounged in one of the chairs scattered across his brother's deck.

"Well, I gotta do what I gotta do. You want to ride along?"

"Sure." Michael stood. "I'm game. Let's take my vehicle though."

"What? You want to take Sally Lu all the way to Hermon?"

"No, we'll take my car. I only drive Sally Lu around here. She's a classic." He grinned at Julius. "I'll pull around, just hang on." He walked toward the garage. A minute later a silver Firebird pulled to a stop in front of where Julius waited.

Julius slid into the passenger seat of Michael's car. "I thought you said Sally Lu was a classic. I need to stop at the house and grab some stuff on the way by."

"Yeah, I need to change boots," Michael said.

"YOU LADIES ALWAYS FIND something to do." Julius walked into the kitchen as Ruth busied herself preparing supper. He glanced at the clock. "We have just enough time to get the film sent. If Michael hurries." He looked at the clock again.

"How did you convince Michael to get out his silver bullet?" Ruth asked.

"He didn't want to ride in my car." Julius grimaced. "It is getting painful." He rubbed a spot on his head.

"There's Michael. Oh, tut, tut. Being prideful?" Ruth teased as Michael came into the room.

"We are on a manly mission, and that calls for a manly machine, my lady. Wanna ride along?" He smiled at her.

"No, but remember the speed limit. And seatbelts. Our conscience is working over-time." Her face sobered.

"Yes, ma'am. Come on, old man." Michael sighed as he walked past Julius to the door.

Over the short ride to Hermon their friendly conversation brought back a longing for the years he'd missed and flooded Julius' mind as he rode shotgun. The mid-afternoon sun warmed a forgotten place in his heart.

"I only need to stop to overnight this. Any place else you want to go?" Julius motioned for Michael to pull into the parking lot of the large convenience store coming up.

"Not much time since we need to be back soon for supper, but let me think. Maybe someplace."

Julius approached the counter and shoved the film into the designated envelope. Then he filled in his contact information and dropped the envelope into the overnight slot.

"You must be in a hurry to show your boss your work?" Michael said as they walked back to the car. He popped open the trunk and put in a couple of sacks of ice.

"Yeah, rush deadline. Got to show the boss I'm busy."

A few blocks later Michael pulled into the parking lot of a local ice cream shop. "I want to stop and get some hot fudge sundaes for Mom and Ruth."

"Are you kidding?" Julius' eyes widened in astonishment. "Won't they melt before we get out of Hermon?"

"I've got this covered," Michael said. "I've got a cooler." He smirked. "And ice. Come help me carry stuff." The bell tinkled when they pushed open the door, and Michael led the way to the counter. "I'll take two hot fudge sundaes and two shakes. What kind of shake do you want, Julius? Two hot fudge Sundaes, a large cherry shake, and a large strawberry." Michael grinned at the young woman.

The waitress juggled his order, periodically peeking over at the tall, good looking blond. "That will be ten dollars and fifteen cents, please." Her voice dripped with sweetness as she beamed up at him.

He handed her ten dollars and fifteen cents. "Keep the change, Margie."

"Oh, aren't we cute," she said as the cash drawer dinged open.

"My mom thinks so." He winked at the young girl.

"I'll get the tip." Julius dropped two dollars on the counter. "Have a good day, Miss," he said with a nod.

"Thank you, sir." She smiled and picked up the tip.

Michael stopped fishing in his pocket. Picking up his shake and a Sundae, he said over his shoulder, "Thanks, Julius. Grab the others will you?"

"You shouldn't fluster the girls so." Julius stopped by the door where Michael waited.

Michael pushed out the door and held it for him. "Thanks for leaving a tip—I've got it in this pocket somewhere. Those girls don't take me serious. Besides, I never saw that girl before in my life."

"Why'd you call her Margie, if you didn't know her?"

"That's what name tags are for," Michael popped the trunk and placed the sundaes in the cooler.

"Could be enough ice?" Julius raised his eyebrows and stared into the cooler.

"Yep. Better-'n-nothing," Michael slid into the front seat and hit the ignition.

JULIUS LEANED BACK and relaxed as the scenery slid by. "What did Ruth say before we left?"

Michael sighed; as he slowed his car and put it on cruise. "This machine drives so smooth I lose track. That's one reason I don't drive this thing more often."

"One reason? And what's the other reason?"

"Driving it around here is like driving a big neon target. So, I just don't. It avoids problems."

"I don't have a pre-knowledge of the affairs around here," Julius spoke into the silence, taking a bite of his strawberry shake. "Is that our turn coming up?"

"Almost home." Michael's eyes were stormy. He smiled and waved as they passed a police car. "Why didn't you smile, Julius? He's taking our picture." Michael slowed and began to pull over.

"That police officer? What gives here?" He did a double -take and his eyes narrowed.

"Yep." The police lights came on in his rear-view mirror. "I figured I'd give him a reason this time."

"What in the hey-wired world?"

The officer approached. "Driver's license, please." They waited while the officer checked the document. "There isn't a violation. I thought your passenger side taillight wasn't working, but it's fine now. You might want to get it checked out anyway." The deputy handed the license back and sauntered back to his cruiser.

"At least that didn't take long, but what's the point?" Julius stroked his beard. "Law enforcement working overtime?" Something familiar about the man niggled at the back of his mind. The way he walked, perhaps? His voice? Or his face? "Is he local?"

"Yes. Officer Meecham." Michael's tone hinted at a history with the man. "Otherwise known as 'our conscience.'"

Julius closed one eye and looked sideways at Michael. "Surely you don't have a problem with law enforcement?"

"Law enforcement? Yeah, right! Law enforcement?" He spat the words as they pulled back onto the pavement, then turned left onto the gravel road toward home. "No, you don't have pre-knowledge of the affairs around here. If you're blessed, you won't have any knowledge. Most of our officers are upstanding, good people, but he's a bad plum."

"In what way?"

"Just be forewarned and stay clear of him. That's all."

JULIUS AND MICHAEL set the hot fudge sundaes on the kitchen counter.

"We stopped at Winnie's, and I brought sundaes." Michael set his shake on the counter. "We would have been here sooner, but—"

"We may have been later if you hadn't set your cruise," Julius said.

"Why's that?" Mrs. MacDonald savored the cold, creamy concoction.

Michael wrinkled his nose. "Ruth's warning."

"Ahh," Ruth raised her eyebrows and poked at the moat surrounding her mountain of ice cream.

"What warning?" Mrs. MacDonald said.

"Something about a conscience?" Julius answered.

"Oh," Mrs. MacDonald said. There was a long silence as the four of them focused on their treats. "So, I guess now that we've had dessert, let's have supper?" She cleaned the last of her ice cream out of the dish.

AS THEY ATE THEIR MEAL, the conversation lagged. It felt stunted, as if something evil lurked in the room.

"Did you get some good shots this afternoon?" Mrs. MacDonald asked.

"Yes, I got scenery shots, and we took pictures of the milk cows and the horses. Some good photos. I have a few frames left to finish off on this roll."

"There should be some good pictures in the orchard if you want to head out now before it gets dark. Michael has some chores left outside yet, and Ruth and I will be out directly." Mrs. MacDonald began stacking and carrying dishes into the kitchen, and Ruth followed with a soup tureen.

"YOU LADIES LOOK PICTURESQUE sitting on the bench framed by the trees." Julius snapped the last shot and rolled the film into its case. "I need to hook up a satellite connection. I can run it out the window and stick it up on the roof, if that will work?"

"That'll be fine," Mrs. MacDonald said.

"Mmm." Ruth inhaled the early evening aroma of the orchard. "What a lovely time of day."

The twilight shadows began their descent as Michael approached. "Might as well head back to the house," Julius said. Michael began singing a church song, as they strolled along the path and Mrs. MacDonald and Ruth joined in the chorus.

Julius savored the sound. It reminded him of more pleasant days.

As they approached the house the singing quieted.

"That was incredibly in synch. You must sing a lot together to blend so well."

"Singing is a sign of a joyful spirit," Ruth said.

"It's pleasant to listen to, but I think I'll take my queue from the sun and the chickens." He turned toward the breezeway.

"Goodnight," Michael and Ruth chorused.

"See you in the morning." Julius waved without turning as he walked ahead.

"God willing." Mrs. MacDonald said.

Chapter—9—

Julius lay across the bed staring at the ceiling. He needed time to gather his thoughts which seemed to run aimlessly in all directions.

I won't hear back on the film 'til tomorrow morning.

Back- up would be nice. That crook chose an odd place to hide. How could anyone get close to him without drawing attention? Wherever he was, he kept a low profile.

Back-up needs to be closer, but I can't bring them in closer. I can understand why this guy is out here.

What! Julius woke with a jerk. A chilling sweat pricked his skin in spite of the warm night. He rolled out of bed and sat in the chair. Closing his eyes, he heard Junko's cry as the water swept her away in the flood. His baby, Mai, called and reached out to him. Over it all, the sound of a loud droning. He shuddered reliving the nightmare.

He blotted the sweat from his face. Were Junko and Mai safe? His eyes narrowed. How did Mrs. MacDonald know he had a wife and daughter? His mind tormented him. He could break the rules just this once. He could contact Junco directly, but that would create a trail and put them in more danger—*what's that*? He straightened, straining his ears. There it was again. A small airplane flying low and close. Then quiet.

With a step, he entered the shadow of the curtains, peering in the direction of the sound. The bright light of the moon cast everything into black and white. A dark figure was sitting under the maple tree. Then another figure joined it, and yet another appeared from nowhere.

Julius shook his head. No matter what Mrs. Irving had insinuated he knew these were unassuming people. These were his people. But he knew even simple folks can become involved in ugly things.

What had Mrs. MacDonald said about losing her son? Someone looking for drugs or money?

Who was this Juan Alvarez-Gonzales? Why would he want to live here?

I'm letting personal feelings interfere. I must become detached.

After a few minutes the three figures disappeared into the house.

Silent as a nighthawk, Julius slipped down the steps, and through the laundry room. Crouching in the kitchen, he crept as close as he dared, every nerve a radar antennae, straining, listening to the three in the dark living room. He caught only an occasional word or phrase.

"Careful... don't know...funny. Comes yesterday ...now what?"

"need ask...afraid?"

Low murmuring and footsteps approached the kitchen.

"...every three weeks." Michael finished the sentence.

Julius ducked back into the laundry room, but the footsteps started up the stairs.

"Shall we check the doors?" Ruth stopped with the question.

Mrs. MacDonald paused, "No, that won't be necessary."

Julius exhaled slowly as the firm footsteps continued up the stairs. Time to earn the paycheck...beginning in the kitchen, he found little reminders on sticky notes stuck here and there on the refrigerator: innocent notes in neat handwriting. *Hmm?* Julius spied a memo tucked behind the others that said, "*Shipment, Friday, 12th.*" He looked at the clock on the wall. Two o'clock. That made today the morning of the twelfth. And here, he pulled out another scribbled note: "*Friday, 3rd.*" Curiouser and curiouser.

As he moved through the house, something chewed in the back of his mind. In the living room their coffee table book? A well-used Bible. The superb book room, with its inviting window seat bathed in cool shadows. On around to the tower room. Shaded by a red maple tree, it was darker yet.

The dining room was locked. With a little expertise, he finagled the lock and slid the door open. Shining his small flashlight around the room into the nooks and crannies, he checked through the sideboard, the linen closet, and several other pieces of furniture, and he perused the pictures hanging on the walls. There was a safe behind one painting, but nothing in it. He gazed out the large windows. The moonlight washed the side yard in an eerie glow. Beautiful room, picturesque scenery, expensive doodads—no wonder they locked these doors. He slid the doors shut locking them as he moved back to the office. The house appeared open except for two doors.

Everything looked like a showroom. The furnishings were expensive and impressive, and the house was decorated in impeccable taste. The art, the furnishings—everything could have been out of a magazine—they were just perfect. *Just perf. . . ah, that's what's odd. This is more like a museum than a home.*

Julius picked the lock, opened the office door and secured it behind him. What a bold contrast. All of the pictures that, in a normal house would be in the other rooms were here. Pictures of handsome looking babies, older children, wedding pictures, vacation pictures—all here.

Julius picked up and scrutinized an old photograph of a young, tall, fair-haired couple, Mr. and Mrs. MacDonald. Why is it impossible to think of old people as ever being young? Julius sighed. *What would he be like when he was sixty-four, or seventy?* The room bore the look of an ordinary office. File cabinets, office supplies, and commonplace things that you might find in a typical workplace. He snapped pictures with his mini-camera and sorted through invoices, and receipts ... what was this? He laid a yellow voucher on the desk and snapped a photo.

His heart caught when the door rattled. He switched off his small flashlight and folded into a cubbyhole. Military training was indispensable at times like these. Good thing he had locked the door.

"I'm sure I heard something," Ruth whispered as Michael switched on the light.

"We're all on edge, Ruth. I don't know what Mom was thinking."

"So right," she said.

Michael poked around, looking in some apparent spots. Julius hunkered into a small space.

"I guess I was just imagining things." Ruth backed out the door.

The room darkened, and the lock clicked. Julius's heartbeat returned to almost normal. An intense, quiet breath escaped his lips.

Whew! Too close! He inhaled another deep, sweet breath of air as their footsteps receded. Julius counted to a hundred before he eased out of his hiding spot. *Oh great,* he groaned at the sight of the receipt on the desk. He replaced the voucher in the file and checked around the room. Nothing else out of place. He crept out the door and locked it. Listening after every step, he stole back to his room. The brilliant moonlight still smiled down on the landscape. This time he slept well.

Chapter—10—

Friday, June 12th; Thank God, no dreams. Julius stretched, plumped the pillows up behind his head, and took a few minutes to peruse the luxurious room, and its furnishings. It's been years since I've slept in a bed as comfortable as this. Gardener's quarters, indeed. He dug in the drawer of the bedside table for the Bible he expected to be there. A scripture played in his mind, teasing his thoughts as he flipped the pages in search of words. As a child, his family had attended every Sunday church service and every midweek Bible study. As children, he and his siblings had memorized almost the entire Bible—one scripture at a time. Where was that verse? Something about taking care of things. Not in Psalms. . . ah, here in Proverbs "A righteous man regardeth the life of his beast; But the tender mercies of the wicked are cruel." If this was a provision for a gardener, these people cared even for their paid employees.

Julius snapped the Bible shut, pulled on a pair of jogging pants, and slipped on his running shoes. *Coffee.* He headed for the coffee pot full of the strong hot brew.

"Good morning." Julius nursed his coffee as Michael ambled through the sunroom. "Thanks for your help yesterday." He looked over the top of his mug at the young man. Michael looked frazzled. Dark circles under his eyes, his hair almost in order. Did his shirt look buttoned off one button? Julius hid a snicker. "I should be able to help on Sally Lu after dinner."

"If you know anything about engines, I'd welcome pointers." Michael rubbed a hand through his hair. "I'm on summer break. You'd think I'd have more free time. Monday we have hay bales to throw." He flexed a well-muscled arm.

"Yeah," Julius said, "it's been a long while since I've had that kind of manly exercise."

"You can just take pictures," Michael said

Was that a challenge? Julius wondered. He drained the last of the dark brown liquid from the mug and stood. "After I visit the little boys' room, I'm off for a jog. I'll be back in a little."

"Later then." Michael waved and sauntered toward the coffee pot.

What were they doing at that time of morning? What about the sticky notes? And how did she know he had a wife and daughter? He jogged down the road, the questions like thick fog wafting through his mind. He knew these people were what they seemed to be. Perhaps not so simple, but honest. Yet, underneath the calm, the sense of peaceful repose, there ran a ripple of something. What was it? What was the delivery due today that the sticky note was referring to? And why really would Mrs. MacDonald take in someone she thought was a total stranger? Unless somehow she knew who Julius was. Could she know? And even then how would she know about Junko and Mai?

The jogging began to clear his mind. But not for long, Julius heard a motor approaching in the distance and he promptly made a U-turn. Now is the time to hit my mile a minute...he increased his speed determined to outrun any chance of being caught on a dusty gravel road. His feet pounded faster and faster until he stopped inside the breezeway. He blotted his face. Good run. Julius froze. Ruth's voice in the distance grabbed his interest. He jogged through the orchard, tracing the sound. Nearing the exercise ring, he slowed to a walk.

"Mrs. MacDonald, Michael will string both of us up." Ruth stood at the corral fence by the small barn. "You're supposed to stay off the horses for these two weeks! If something else happens to you . . ."

Riding a chestnut gelding in the ring was the sixty-four-year-old blind woman.

"Honestly! You are worse than a child!" Ruth turned as Julius joined her. "Do you see how hard it is to keep her out of trouble?" Ruth rolled her eyes and groaned.

"She seems to be doing a fair job." Julius laughed. "It's a good thing she's helpless."

"Helpless?" Ruth's eyes widened, and she gasped. "I don't think she's ever been helpless. Oh, great, look—Here's Michael. We're caught like flies in the molasses jar. Pull that mule up, Mrs. M. Michael's coming across the pasture."

"No sense impugning the credentials of a good horse." Mrs. Mac-Donald slowed the gelding and Ruth backed the horse into position beside the mounting block. Mrs. MacDonald swung down and stood straightening her outfit as Michael rode up.

The look on Michael's face was of mixed incredulity. Julius could not decide if the young man wanted to laugh at his mother or throttle her.

"Sanchez is all ready for you to finish," the older woman said. "Ruth and I will just go back to the house and finish breakfast." She picked up the hoe leaning beside the gate. "Come, Ruth,"

The two young men watched as the ladies ambled up the path and disappeared. They heard the porch door whoosh open and shut.

Michael stared at Julius and shook his head. "I have been around that woman for twenty-four years, and she never ceases to amaze me," he said. "Do you ride? Swing up there on old Sanchez, and we'll take a go- round. Mom probably did a good warm-up already. We'll just finish them off."

Julius hesitated. "I don't usually ride in jogging pants, but I guess." He put a foot in the stirrup and launched into the saddle. "We just had a couple of Indian ponies when I was young."

"You rode when you were young?" Michael took the lead across the pasture.

"Nothing like these critters, but we sure had fun," Julius said.

They rode for about twenty minutes until Michael slowed his pace.

"LET'S WRAP THIS UP, and get on to breakfast." Dismounting at the barn gate, they led the horses into the lot.

Julius rubbed the tops of his thighs. "I need to put Horseback Riding 101 back on my exercise routine. My legs are out of shape."

Julius followed Michael to the house. "Say, I need to run up to my room for a moment. I'll be right back."

Julius stopped short at the top of the stairway. He pulled his Berretta out of its holster and dropped into a crouch. With caution, he pushed his door open. His eyes searched the room checking the small niches. Rising, he took a quick, light step toward the bathroom and flipped on the light. Nothing. A further search revealed a towel on the bathroom floor, his luggage tampered with, his camera film missing, one window screen askew, and a few minor things out of order. Rule number one; never let your guard down. The only film they had gotten was the unimportant pictures. He checked the drop from his window—probably not their route in or out. Julius holstered his weapon, and then went down the steps and through the breezeway to the front yard. He scouted the labyrinth of pathways around trees and flowers all of which led to the main route in front of the house. You could reach the road, but it would have to be over a five-foot wrought iron fence, or the long way around through the gate. As he searched inside the enclosure a patch of white caught his eye. Hearing footsteps on the pathway, Julius looked up to see Ruth hurrying toward him.

"We didn't hear you." Ruth told him.

"What's that?" He straightened up and dropped the white object, wrapped in his handkerchief, into his shirt pocket.

"We didn't hear you come through the kitchen. Michael just came in, but we didn't hear you come through." She explained again.

Julius shook his head still confused.

"You left the front door open?" She frowned with annoyance.

"I didn't go through the house. I went through the breezeway." He pulled at his bottom lip, and his eyes narrowed.

"But you left the front door. . ." Her eyes widened and they stared at each other.

RUTH HURRIED INSIDE and with light, quick steps rushed up the stairs, with Julius trailing behind. Mrs. MacDonald trailed behind as she heard movement continue through the upstairs.

"Oh, no!" Ruth gave a sudden cry.

"What is it?" Mrs. MacDonald arrived at the door of the room at the same time as Julius. The aroma of an earthy, flowery perfume drifted on the air.

"Most of my valuables are at the other house, but I had my brother Reuben's pinky ring on a chain, here on this jewelry tree. It's gone, and my perfume is knocked over. Someone has rummaged through the dressing table."

Sympathy stabbed at Julius' heart as he noticed the worried look in Mrs. MacDonald's eyes. "Maybe we should go downstairs and sort this out," he said.

"WHO WOULD RUMMAGE THROUGH Ruth's stuff? If I ever find out... for sure." Michael's face appeared foreboding as he shoveled sausage and scrambled eggs onto his plate. "I have an appointment that I'm late for."

"What were you looking for outside, Julius?" Ruth asked.

"Clues."

"What kind of clues?" asked Mrs. MacDonald. Her food grew cold while her fingers tore at the napkin in her hands.

"Clues as to who stole the film out of my camera case," Julius said.

All eating at the table ceased, and three pairs of eyes stared at him.

Julius saw the thoughts whir through Michael's mind; the young man's eyes became shrewd.

Recalling the prize in his pocket, Julius pulled it out. He opened the handkerchief wrapped around it. "I found this in the front yard by the fence," he said.

"What is it?" Mrs. MacDonald asked.

Ruth peered at it as if it were some loathsome creature. "It's a matchbook from the den of iniquity." She pulled it closer and used a butter knife to open the flap. "It's missing three matches and was dropped sometime this morning after the dew went off. We've never had burglars before, Mr. Armstrong."

Julius' eyes narrowed. "What else do you make of this?"

Her eyes held a faraway look as she replied, "I need more time."

THE MAN SORTED THROUGH the pictures. There were pictures of kids, cows, chickens, and even some stupid pigs, but the ones he wanted from Mom and Pop's Restaurant were not here. He snorted with disgust. That guy, whoever he was, must be smarter than he looked. But wait. The man stopped. His heart throbbed, his hands shook violently. Studying the pictures he held in his hand, a fire began to burn in his insides, slowly at first then with more intensity. He placed those few pictures on the dresser before him. They were worth more to him than the ones he had been looking for. He dumped everything else in the trash and tried to steady his hands as he picked up the last three pictures. Why? The fire leaped in his heart. Why is the only woman I want, someone I can't have? He gritted his teeth. There in an orchard wearing an everyday blue cotton dress. He saw in his mind her large eyes the color of a brilliant blue sunset, framed by her long dark lashes. He imagined her soft cheek, her hair.... Oh, God! Oh, God, why?

Chapter—11—

"I always get directions right. Yet here I am. As if God had stepped in and directed me," Julius said.

"So, you do believe in God?" Mrs. MacDonald lingered under the maple tree after breakfast was put away and the dishes cleaned up.

"The thief didn't get what he was looking for, but he realizes it isn't here," Julius pulled at his lower lip avoiding her question.

"I pray you are correct." Mrs. MacDonald looked up as Ruth joined them, "Do you have the lunch menus?"

"Yes, here are today's menus. It says chicken stir fry for lunch. What do you think? Do you have anything else in mind?" the young woman sat on the bench, the week's lists in one hand and her cup of tea in the other.

"No, chicken stir-fry sounds good to me," Mrs. MacDonald said as she rose from her chair. "I need to get the laundry out of Michael's room." She hurried off.

Ruth perused her lists, then after a short pause took a sip of her tea. "I wish we could back up and have last week this week."

"Why is that?"

"Nothing happened last week. We were blessed with a couple of late calves and a nice rain shower. Only one drive-by shooting."

"Drive-by shooting? Isn't that a bit unusual? I mean this isn't exactly the hood."

"People have the impression that out here in the country, everyone's peaceable, honest, and love their neighbor. Our neighbors overall are decent folks. However, human nature being what it is, not *all* people are good. We have our problems, but we tend to take care of them as best we can." Ruth shrugged. "Into each life adversity comes, we change the things we can, and trust God's timing for the rest."

SITTING AT HIS DESK, Julius drummed his fingers as he waited for the computer to load. The thief wanted the film, the pictures he'd taken at Mom and Pop's. And it had to involve the last two customers at the restaurant. Not rocket science, but he had some digging to do.

We change the things we can, and trust God's timing for the rest Ruth's words,' nagged at him as he rummaged for a pencil in the desk drawer in his room. Stuck in the back of the drawer he found a tear-stained photograph of a teenage girl, a baby, and a little boy approximately two years of age. The words on the back were blurred, but he did not need the writing. He carefully laid it aside.

He found the pencil and wrote down names and a few other facts he wanted to check out, based on Mrs. MacDonald's story from the day before. Finally, logged into his computer, he navigated to some articles from the local paper, Beetle River County Chronicle. There were some curious transactions recorded in the papers, which by themselves were nothing out of the ordinary. Lots of DUIs, and it seemed like drinkers and fighters went together. The detective tapped the fingers of his left hand while making a note of the number of references. There were also several arrests, many of which were the same offenders.

"Woman Found Dead of Heart attack," grabbed his attention: "Philip Meecham called for an ambulance Saturday morning after finding Ms. Diana O'Brien in a state of unconsciousness. By the time the paramedics arrived, Ms. O'Brien was unresponsive. She is survived by her estranged husband Jack O'Brien; a son, Reuben of Colorado; and a daughter Ruth, of the same address as the deceased." The paper date was November 3, a little over two and a half years earlier. He scribbled more information in his notebook. He checked through the files and pictures Director Meyer sent him, several of which he printed off to put on his detective board. The detective board was hidden behind the antique dressing screen. There were five pictures; Albertoo Meister, Philip, David, and Ralph Meecham, and Diana O'Brien. Julius looked at his watch and frowned. Still no message from Shields regarding Junco. This was not like her at all. They should have been out of Tokyo and into their safe lodgings by now. He glared at his computer shut it down, and then stood and stretched. *Need a break.*

"THIS AFTERNOON IS PLEASANT." Julius brought a glass of tea outside to sit with his hostess.

"A little more breeze would be nice." Mrs. MacDonald sat in the shade of the maple tree. Picking up a handful of fresh green beans out of her small basket she snipped them.

"I've wondered about parking my car out of view?" he said.

"We could move one of Juan's cars to Lewis' for a time."

"I think it might remove some of the problem." He put his glass on the picnic table.

"Maybe," she nodded.

"Mind if I join you?" Ruth sat beside her companion and spread her handwork on her lap. "I've been working on this for a present. I don't know if I'll ever get it done."

"That picture is very detailed." Julius leaned down and examined the work in progress. "I've seen large tapestries in museums. I have no idea how people have that much patience." There was a slight pause before he asked, "Do you know when Michael will return?"

"Soon, I should think." Ruth chose a skein of blue floss.

Julius spoke again, "I'm going into town this evening. I probably won't be back until ten thirty. Will that be a problem?"

"Shouldn't be. Will you be able to come to worship with us on Sunday?" Mrs. MacDonald asked.

"I'll put it on my docket. Oh, there's the prodigal now," Julius said as Sally Lu roared up the drive. "I told him I'd help work on Sally Lu today. I've got a few minutes now."

"Hey," Michael exclaimed as he burst through the breezeway, "guess what!" He dropped into a chair next to the table. "The Smith's Bed and Breakfast on the other side of town was ransacked last night." He stared at Julius.

"Oh, no!" the two women dropped their projects, eyes wide with shock.

"Oh, yes," Michael said.

"What happened?" the two questioned.

"Whoever did it didn't take anything, and it was just the guest room that was hit. Thankfully, there wasn't a guest." His eyes narrowed as he continued to stare at Julius.

"Seems to be a lot of burglars in this country." Julius scanned the treetops.

"Well, I never..." the older woman spoke. The two women picked up their projects and went back to work, shaking their heads over the news.

"Got time to work on Sally Lu?" Julius stood. "I'll leave my tea here and be back."

"I guess." Michael frowned, and trudged after Julius through the breezeway.

When they reached the pickup Michael lifted the hood.

"Look here," Julius demonstrated. "If ya just give it a few squirts of this." He sprayed some carb cleaner in the carburetor. "Then turn the screw on this side here to the left. That should do the trick. Sally

Lu should run much smoother now." He straightened up and wiped his hands on a clean grease rag. "Your mom and I talked about parking my car in the garage. But I probably won't be back until about ten-thirty tonight."

"Yeah, we'll take care of it." Michael frowned and looked away. Then sudden anger flamed in Michael's eyes, and he looked straight at Julius. "Who are you? And what are you doing here?"

"What do you mean, Michael? It's me—Julius. Julius C. Armstrong, a freelance writer, working on a book about small towns."

"In a pig's eye! Those burglaries? He's only harassed us from afar before. . . until you got here—"

"Cool down—friend," Julius said.

Chapter —12—

T he June evening had a pleasant feel. Julius observed the Friday evening traffic. People were looking for a good time, and Hermon had much to offer. The marquee in front of Frankie and Johnny's Superclub screamed, "Live Shows 8:30 and 10:00!" Julius idled through the busy parking lot, found a spot— not too close, not too far— and parked.

It took his eyes a short time to adjust to the dim light inside the establishment. He stopped at the, "Please Wait to Be Seated" sign.

"How many in your party?" the hostess asked.

"Just a single," he answered. "A quiet table would be desirable."

"Here you are, sir," she led him to a semi-private table overlooking the stage. "There will be someone with you in a few minutes." She handed him a menu.

"What would you recommend?" Julius asked the server as he looked over the menu.

"The ribeye's excellent. The shrimp is excellent. We don't have anything that's not noteworthy, sir."

"So you'd recommend the ribeye? I'll take that then. On the rare side. Baked potato with sour cream, and butter. Fried okra, and yes, tossed salad with the house dressing, please. What would I care to drink?" He repeated her question. "I'll just take a glass of soda water. Thank you." He handed her the menu.

He leaned back in his cubby hole and stretched his long legs out in front of him. The hostess, waitresses, and bartenders wore the same style outfits complete with the fringed vests, cowgirl or cowboy hats, and boots. The large bar, the glitz and glimmer, and the glittering people behind their fancy facades were part of the spangle and shine. Julius knew places like this. The lights were purposely dim, so people could see only what they were supposed to see. It hid the sad emptiness that lay behind the laughter of the crowd.

This is my world, he thought sarcastically. This is what I'm used to, and where I've been for far too long—deceit and charade. He glanced around the nightclub. Funny. To simple, religious people this would appear to be a 'den of iniquity.' He recalled Ruth's comment on the matches.

"Well, well," he murmured as he observed the same young buck from Mom and Pop's with what appeared to be a businessman, as they were seated close to the stage.

"Thank you." He moved back as the salad disappeared, and the main meal was placed in front of him.

"Mind if I join you, cowboy?"

Julius looked up to see a blonde haired woman smiling down at him. "No, ma'am—have a seat."

"My name's Angie. You're new here aren't you?" She looked him over with a deliberate gaze.

"Yes, ma'am," he said. "Would you like a drink?"

"That would be most kind. Just call me Angie."

Catching the attention of his waitress he told her, "Same as I've got, for the lady here." The waitress gave him a puzzled look but went for Angie's drink.

"Where you from?" Angie asked.

"Peoria. And are you from around here?" He finished his potato and cut a bite of his steak.

"Independence. Just moved here from Independence."

"I've never been to Independence," he made small talk for a few moments, continuing to work on his meal. He leaned forward and slipped a note under the napkin beside her glass.

"I have to forewarn you…" He started an explanation, but he was interrupted by the blaring music and the spotlight gleaming on the small stage.

"Ladies and gentlemen," the announcer came over the loudspeaker. "For your evening entertainment, right from Las Vegas—Ms. Louise Crabtree!" A curvaceous platinum blonde in a blue sequined dress pranced into the circle of light.

Too late to make himself heard, Angie raised the glass and took a sip.

If the music hadn't brought the conversation to a halt, her sputtering and choking would have.

"Cowboy!" she hissed, rising abruptly, "That ain't funny!" She stalked, away still clutching the napkin to her mouth.

"I've often found soda water good for the digestion," he said into the air as Angie slipped into the ladies room.

His eyes scanned the customers sitting up front by the entertainment. *Very cozy*, he thought, as he found where the two men were seated. A slim, brunette hostess sat beside the younger man. She touched his hand and whispered in his ear. He leaned toward her and with a laugh, whispered back.

A short time later, Angie reappeared, slipping quietly back in her seat. "I'd appreciate it if you'd warn me next time," she said with a smile that did not match her tone.

"Sorry, I tried, but the music's too loud," he smiled back in a friendly manner. "Find out about that name if you can. What about the two down there?"

"I'll get you some info on them. Will you be in again soon?" She leaned toward Julius and smiled.

"Should be, but not too soon. Got your schedule?" From a distance, it would look like they were carrying on a friendly conversation even as she slipped him a piece of paper. Julius watched the show for a short time, and then pushed back from the table. "Well, thank you for your time and company. I'll be looking for you next time I visit," he said with a wink.

"Good luck, cowboy."

"Was everything all right?" The cashier's manicured nails tapped on the keys.

"Yes, it was excellent. Thank you, ma'am." He paid for the meal, pulled his cowboy hat lower, and walked out into the warm night.

Finished here. Time to backtrack to the house. Julius turned on his blinker at the stop light.

Julius parked on the road a short way from the house. He had disabled the dome light and the other bells and whistles for silence. Now he slid out of his vehicle without sound. *Earning my wages,* he thought as he began to scout around. Sally Lu, as well as Lewis' pickup, sat in the driveway. *Still early*, he decided, looking at his watch in the scant light. Julius came around to the front of the house and stood concealed in the shadows, close to the window. He had a good view of Mrs. MacDonald, Ruth, Michael, and Lewis in the living room.

"... We value your thoughts, Ruth, on the turn of events." It was Lewis' voice. He wrinkled his brow, his voice held a tone of exasperation. "What in the world possessed you to take in a stranger, Mom?"

Mrs. MacDonald answered, "Matthew 25:35, 'I was a stranger, and ye took me in.'"

"Mother," he groaned. "With Meecham harassing us at every turn? And we don't know this guy."

"I'm not flippant, my son. He doesn't seem a stranger to me. I can't explain it, but it was the right thing to do." Her manner was subdued but earnest.

Michael said, "The burglar wasn't after Ruth's things. He was after Armstrong's film."

Ruth's words were cautious. "With Mr. Armstrong, I see two people. One person is friendly, easy to get to know, and honestly what he appears to be. The other one is cloaked, and keeps to himself."

"Ruth has hit her thumb with the hammer," Michael said. "Mr. Armstrong is friendly and easy to get to know, yet where's he from? Who's he working for? Does he have a family?"

"Mr. Armstrong isn't part of them. But whether he is an answer to our prayers, I don't know. "

Hmm, an answer to prayer. . .he had been called that on several occasions, but what were they praying for here? Considering some of the conversations of the past few days he had a few ideas. Julius put that information in his file of 'to be considered later since the conversation in the living room took a new turn.

"By the way." Ruth looked at Mrs. MacDonald. "What did you say to him yesterday just before I came in?"

"I don't remember," Mrs. MacDonald said. "Why?"

"I had just walked in the door, you were bringing the cakes to the table when he had an intense reaction to something you said. Which is why you spilled the tea."

"I asked him if he was going to bring his wife and daughter for a visit." Mrs. MacDonald said. "I didn't feel a reaction. That's why I was so confused."

Silence then, as Lewis, Michael, and Ruth exchanged frightened glances. Ruth touched Mrs. MacDonald's hand. In a soft voice, she asked, "Did he tell you he had a wife and daughter?"

"I don't remember that he did. No, I must have confused him with one of those deliverymen."

A mistake? Was that all it was? Even as a child he remembered times when his mother seemed on occasion to have knowledge from somewhere else she could never really explain. That explanation made sense to Julius and he would be more careful in the future.

"Anyone can make a mistake," Lewis comforted his mother. "Are you sure he doesn't have a wife and daughter?"

"Does he wear a wedding ring? How would I know if he has a wife, let alone a daughter?" She rested her cheek in the palm of her hand.

"How indeed, Mother," Lewis sighed as he rose to leave. "I need to be getting on home. Lots of things to do tomorrow. Your young man should be showing up at any time."

"I'm surprised he isn't here yet," Ruth said as they stood.

Even at this distance, Julius could see the look in her eyes. The same disturbing look that made Julius uncomfortable as if she were looking into his soul. The hair on the back of his neck prickled, and he shivered.

"Oh, Jehovah," Lewis led them in prayer, "Grant us peace, safety, and a shield against evil. We pray that those who are away from us will return safely. We pray that if this newcomer is an answer to our prayers, you will watch and keep him safe. And we pray this time of trouble will pass soon. In Jesus name."

They began a hymn:
All through the life that's mortal,
And when I pass death's portal,
Remember me O' Mighty One.

Chapter —13—

J ulius turned into the driveway as Lewis, Michael, and the women came out the front door.

"Picked up a different rental car?" Lewis asked as Julius rolled down his window to greet them.

"I did. The other one had issues, and life is too short," Julius said. "Maybe tomorrow I'll replace the six rolls of film I lost."

"It could be worse," Lewis said.

"That's right. Could've been." *If you only knew.*

"Do you think that Caprice will be better?" Michael surveyed the car. "I like the charcoal color, and there is a bit more head room."

"I do think it'll be better. And I think I'll hit the rack. These late nights." Julius smiled and eased the car into the garage. The burden of responsibility he carried for these simple folks weighed upon his heart. Julius parked his car. The biggest problem was, he couldn't afford personal ties. Becoming personally involved had cost him dearly in the past. He closed his heart to the pain for the suffering and loss of life that had touched his and left scars. It became too easy to mess up when you cared too deeply. And this time, he couldn't afford to mess up.

SATURDAY, JUNE 13th; Morning. Julius walked out of his dream in full desert combat gear into the gray pre-dawn light of his room.

At least it hadn't been a violent passion filled nightmare like so often occurred.

Oh, God, what do I do? Julius brooded. *The clock is ticking. Time is running like sunshine through a knot hole in the barn door. I haven't had word from Junco. It's too early to hear from the Director about the O'Brien house.* He weighed his options. *Smart move of O'Brien to seal it up until a proper investigation would be made. I've got to get in there.*

With silent tread, he made his way to the kitchen. Snuffling around, he found the coffee grounds, started the coffee, and then located the clipboard with menus. He grabbed some eggs from the fridge, chose a bowl from the cupboard, found a whisk and an egg separator, and began dividing the whites from the yolks. The stairs creaked with light footsteps as he began whipping the egg whites.

"Mr. Armstrong, what are you doing?" A shocked voice came from the area of the doorway.

"Your menu for this morning is waffles, bacon, fruits—whatever that means—and whipped cream. I've got the coffee covered, and I'm whipping the egg whites for the waffles. I figured I could be useful instead of just ornamental."

"He hasn't told you about the time he worked on a cruise ship?" Michael poked his head around the door frame.

"Apparently not." Ruth frowned.

"Well, let's get on this then." Mrs. MacDonald wafted into the kitchen behind Michael. "Ruth, you grab out the bacon. Mr. Julius, how far have you gotten?"

Julius switched off the mixer. "Coffee, and I've got egg whites here."

"You can either drink your coffee or go help Michael. Ruth and I have this covered."

"So, I've been relieved of duty?" He stepped back with a smile then turned to select a coffee mug.

With deft fingers Mrs. MacDonald found measuring spoons, baking powder, and salt. "Yes, at ease, Corporal," she said.

The title caught him like a blow to the chest. What did she know? Why did she keep making these odd statements if she didn't know? Were these off comments her way of trying to let him know she knew?

"I guess I'll give you a hand then?" He looked at Michael, as he controlled his reactions.

"That'll work." Michael sipped his coffee. "Too hot. I'm gonna let this cool." He set his mug on the counter. "Come on out when you're ready."

"I'm ready." Julius set his cup beside Michael's and followed him outside.

"DO YOU THINK HE'S AN answer to our prayers?" Ruth chose her words with care, as Mrs. MacDonald folded the egg whites into the waffle batter.

"Answers to prayers come in many different forms. I knew a man that prayed for his father-in-law for forty years before he saw him obey the gospel."

"That's true." Ruth said. "But we don't have forty years. I hoped beyond hope that when Juan visited with Chief Mallory about their dog getting shot, there might be some sort of action." She clicked on the stove and plunked the bacon into the frying pan.

"My dear girl, when your mamma died there should've been some sort of action. A person is much more precious than a dog."

"Yes, but—"

"No one has even been in to check your house to investigate." She shook her head. "Heart attack, indeed. We're all pretty sure your mother didn't have a heart attack."

"Yes, but while Sergeant Biles was head of the department, we knew how that would go. Him being on the take with David Meecham. Now that Chief Mallory has taken over, there is a chance for an honest investigation."

"You're right, Mallory comes with good credentials, and not because he's a friend of your dad. I do think we may get answers for both problems—yours and the rise in crime and the extortion racket in Hermon." The old woman poked the waffle out of the waffle iron. "You best be getting the cream out and whipped. They're coming up the path now, and you know they'll be hungry."

"I'VE BEEN WONDERING something." Julius paused by the maple tree in the backyard.

"What's that?" Michael gazed over where Julius looked.

"Where's the dog?"

"Just before Juan and the family left two weeks ago, their dog, Dulce was in the driveway when I pulled up to park. A car went by, I heard the shot, but didn't get the car or license number. Thank God the kids weren't out."

"That's your drive-by shooting?"

"One of them."

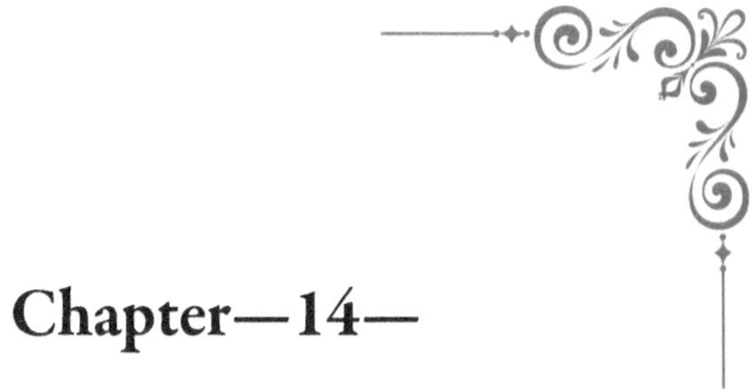

Chapter—14—

After breakfast Julius waited impatiently as his computer brought up information. His heart rate picked up as he read the dossier: Carlos Juan Alfonso Alvarez-Gonzales. Born 1937, one older sister, Sophia Isabella, one younger sister, Maria Teresa, and a younger brother Francisco Manuel. Juan worked— unofficially—for his government, and, at times, for the U. S. government. His wealth, title, and prestige gave him access to positions and people at high levels. He didn't need the import business; that was a cover. Four more pictures to go on his board.

Julius checked his watch. Waiting for info, he tapped his fingers irritably. There it is. The message popped onto the screen: 'No info from Shields and Nightingale. Local cold case, green light on house possibly linked to case.' Julius shut down the computer; and hooked his case back into its hiding place. He grabbed his kit for gathering evidence and his camera and bag. He checked his Berretta, grabbed a second clip, and stuck it in his vest pocket.

He slung his camera over his shoulder, and briskly walked out the back door and down the path. The morning reminded Julius of his growing- up years in the Blue Ridge Mountains. The verdant fresh green foliage, the birds twittering, and the damp earthy smell deluged his senses. The path led past the few buildings where the animals were stabled, and took him past a small cottage, that was shuttered and closed.

Standing at the end of the path in the shadow of an elm tree, Julius listened and watched. No movement, no sound, everything quiet. With caution, he crawled through the strands of barbed- wire fence. A small growth of hardwood trees stood a few paces away, and he ducked into its sheltering cover. Soon the thin protection of trees came to an end. He swept the gravel road with a glance both ways before scurrying from ditch to ditch, and then disappeared into a large grove.

A scant remnant of a pathway, choked with overgrown weeds and an occasional fallen branch, wound through the trees which led toward the back of the house. The lawn inside the fence surrounding the house had been mowed and kept tidy, but the grass on the outer side of the gravel driveway needed attention. Julius let himself in through the antique house gate. It latched shut behind him, as he set off to inspect the exterior of the house, snapping pictures as he went.

He pushed "Record" on his miniature tape recorder and began speaking. "Evidence starts here in the back yard as I follow the flagstone path. Picture one: Wooden back porch on a two- and- a-half-story Victorian-style farmhouse—stepping- stone path toward the porch, two wooden steps up onto the semi-enclosed porch. Neat porch, pegs, and hooks for coats, mats on floor in front of the door and one to the side for shoes and boots, two well-used wooden kitchen chairs, a metal pan (apparently used for feeding cat) orange cat (looking for food).

Julius, with a light touch and gloved hands picked the lock and soon stood inside a tidy comfortably sized kitchen. He locked the door behind him and looked the room over.

A clean porcelain cup and saucer in the dish drainer. The remnant of ancient coffee in the pot, a tea kettle half full of water. A towel and two pot holders had fallen on the floor, and cobwebs covered the flowered curtains adorning the two windows.

A door from the kitchen led into a decent-sized bathroom that doubled as a laundry room. Didn't look like anything was out of place here, either, but he took more pictures. There had been unusual activity in the dining room. The table sat scrunched against the wall at a unique angle. One porcelain cup on the table had been overturned, a negligible amount of dark brown liquid—possibly coffee, stained the table cloth. A smaller empty glass lay on its side. It looked to be a juice glass of some sort. A dining room chair was overturned as well, about two feet from the table situated against the colonnade. At some point, the fire in the living room stove had been stirred, as there were ashes on the floor, but the fire had burned itself out. He snapped a picture of a boot print in the ashes, measured it then compared it to the size of a mud print on the Oriental rug in the dining room. He scraped some ashes from the rug and put the remnants into an envelope, sealing and labeling it. Julius used his evidence vacuum to pick up some fine white powder from the colonnade, stepped out to take a few shots of the front porch, and then moved on upstairs.

The bedrooms looked unmolested with beds made up and clothes laid out in one room.

It was puzzling to Julius that no one, not even Ruth had mentioned Diana O'Brien's death. Mrs. Irving had mentioned it briefly, but then she had clammed up quickly. A thought brought him back to the kitchen. Julius took a picture of the floor in front of the door, and then kneeled down and examined the scant remains in the trashcan. He grabbed the small plastic sack, but as he wound it up two shadowy figures passed by the side window.

"I got over as fast as I could, Stu. Doesn't look like there's anyone else been here. We should be able to clean up any evidence and get out of here quick."

Julius stowed the sack with the rest of his evidence. Moving swiftly through the dining room and across to the front door, he opened the door that led to the porch and slipped out leaving the door open. He stashed the evidence behind the lounge which sat on one side of the door, opposite the two wicker chairs on the other side. The orange cat maybe had gotten tired of waiting for breakfast on the back porch, it was reclining on the chair nearest the door.

Julius stretched a fishing line across the top porch step and then crept down the three wooden steps hunkering in the bushes at the bottom, every nerve as taut as the fishing line.

"Earl, why is it you and me always...Hey, why's this front door open?"

Footsteps cross the dining room floor. The moment the screen door opened, Julius rustled the bushes.

"Somethun's in the...Hey! Catch that cat," Stu called as the cat sashayed into the house through the open screen door. "I'll check out the—" a tall, thin guy took two steps across the porch, but tripped on the top step and rolled down the cement sidewalk. "Watch that first step, Earl," he said.

Julius grabbed him by the nap of his shirt and drug him around to the side of the house. Snatching a chunk of tree limb, he knocked him on the head, and bound his hands and feet with a nylon rope from his bag, concealing himself on the other side of the house. He waited as more footsteps crossed the porch.

"You know I'm allergic to cats. Why'd ya send me after this idiot cat?" The orange cat yowled as Earl dangled it over the porch rail.

"Over here!" Julius imitated Stu's voice.

The man let the cat drop and walked down the steps. "What'd ya find?"

As he stepped around the side of the house, Julius gave him a karate chop to the neck. Earl went down like a sack of cement. It was short work to truss him up then return for the fishing line from the front steps. "What do I do with these two?" he said out loud. He grabbed his stuff and slipped into the grove of trees. He clicked on his pocket communicator, "Assistance needed at Diana O'Brien's address, 2016 Woodhue Road. Two vandals apprehended." He clicked it off.

Julius chose a tree close to where the two lay on the ground. Up he went climbing the smooth-barked tree. He settled in as a dark blue sedan pulled in the drive. Two men rolled out, and with guns drawn they scouted around the house.

He pulled out his pocket camera. Though their timely arrival made it appear as if they were responding to his message, these guys weren't acting like police. One fellow had a Panama hat on. He watched as their scouting ended as they stood over the two unconscious men under his perch.

"Whoever it was that called in must've just vanished. I don't see anyone around. No one came out of the grove."

"Could be still hiding. That place hasn't been cleaned out in years," One man twitched his head toward the grove of trees. "Maybe we should torch it. Get rid of everything. These two idiots, the house, the evidence. It'd all be taken care of." The man took a lighter and a piece of paper out of his pocket.

"You'd have to take them two out first." The first man nudged the tall, thin fellow with a hard boot to the ribs. The semi-unconscious man moaned.

"So, don't let me stop ya," the man with the lighter said.

Julius reached under his vest and slid out his weapon. Where were the police, and why had these yahoos shown up? Earl and Stu may be shady characters, but sending them into eternity wasn't that guy's job. Not today. Julius took aim as the man pulled out his gun.

A small car pulled into the drive, and Lighterman put his toys away posthaste. He jerked his head at the other man. "Go distract whoever that is," he said.

Goodnight! Julius groaned as Ruth slid out of the car. He could see a passenger and surmised it to be Mrs. MacDonald. Could this get any worse? The only thing he could do from this range would be to scare the bejeebers out of those clowns. He had been a sniper in the military, but not with a Berretta handgun.

Hand over hand he silently worked his way down the tree. He checked both ammunition clips in his vest pockets. No time to spare he wormed his way through the ditch along the front fence of the house. Julius rose up on his knees hidden by the tall grass. Peering at the yard, he listened and watched as Lighterman wandered over and joined his accomplice, Gunman, at the small car.

"We heard this place was for sale," Gunman said.

"You heard wrong," Ruth said.

"Maybe we got the wrong address. You own the place?" Lighterman said.

"My grandfather does. He doesn't like trespassers. You best be off, mister."

FROM THE PASSENGER seat, Mrs. MacDonald rolled down her window to listen. She didn't like what she heard. Those men's voices made her skin prickle. *All those years ago, when Mac and I practiced martial arts blindfolded it was just fun. I never thought I would use those principles in real life.* Reaching down, she nervously ran her hand along the floorboard. Nothing. *It has to be in here*, she fretted. *One more try. Ah, here it is. She inspected it quickly—safety's on, and it's loaded.* She hit the power switch and finished rolling down the window.

"Excuse me," she said out the window. No response. Ha, no one ever pays attention to old women. "Excuse me," she said in a louder voice. "Perhaps you know who John the Baptist is?"

FROM JULIUS' VANTAGE point it looked as if a handgun had appeared from the passenger side window, and although from where he hid in the grass he couldn't make out the words, someone speaking loudly. *Mrs. MacDonald* ? This is not the time to lose your sanity. Julius groaned and lined up a shot. If the men started roughing up the ladies, he had a bead on the Panama hat. It took every ounce of control he had to contain himself. His hand on his weapon did not shake, but his heart quivered.

"Hey!" A sudden shout came from the other side of the house. "Hey, we need some help here." Earl and Stu had just come to.

Lighterman took a step back. Julius knew this would not end well.

"John the Baptist had a mighty message! One that you should heed!" This time Mrs. MacDonald's voice rang out like a loud, clear bell. "Repent!" She shouted.

A shot rang out, and Lighterman's straw hat flew into the air. As Gunman drew his gun, another shot rang out, and the gun flew out of his hand. Julius flattened himself in the tall grass as a police vehicle pulled into the drive. He glanced at his watch. Noting the amount of time their arrival took, he guessed the police force had been really busy, or they had a snitch somewhere.

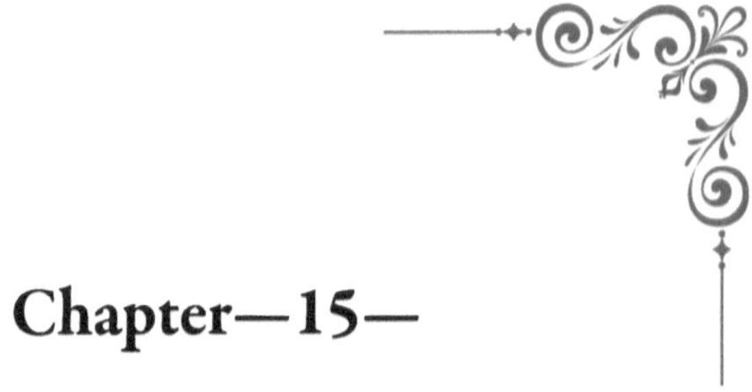

Chapter—15—

Julius picked up his shell casings, snaked back through the tall grass, and grabbed his camera case and paraphernalia. For all the long way home, he felt eyes watching him. Finally reaching the breezeway, he dashed up to his room and showered the dirt and sweat from his body, all the while ruminating on several questions. Why had they called in someone to 'mess up' the crime scene now?

Did someone know stuff they shouldn't? If so how much, and was his mission compromised? Why hadn't he heard from Junco?

What a morning in this quiet sleepy community. Julius rolled his eyes. *Good thing nothing ever happened here.*

Hot dog, that stings! Julius sprayed some disinfectant on the gash in his leg from the barbed wire fence, then applied gauze and tape. He stopped to listen as the car pulled into the driveway. Mrs. MacDonald and Ruth's excited voices chattered on their way inside.

"Where have you been?" Ruth asked as Julius came into the kitchen.

"I've been exercising, and gathering pictures. What have you two been up to?"

"I had to go over to Grandpa's. You'll never guess what happened." Ruth's eyes were wide as she gasped to catch her breath.

"I guess not. Never was much of a guesser. What happened?" He poured a cup of coffee and leaned against the counter.

"We took some stuff over to Grandpa, and I went by Mom's to feed Oliver the cat. There were two—"

"Four," Mrs. MacDonald said.

"Four, that's right," Ruth said, "but we only saw two at first. Two vandals at the house. They tried to pretend they were only there because the property was for sale—"

Julius feigned puzzlement, "I didn't know your Grandpa was selling your Mom's house?"

"He isn't." Ruth gave Julius a withering look. "It's complicated, but anyway, then Mrs. MacDonald here starts shooting, and the guy on the other side of the house started hollering."

"Wait, Ruth. It goes like this, Julius. We pulled in to feed the cat. These men come up like they're looking to buy property. Ruth tells them to leave about the time I pull my pistol out of my purse, and the other two, who are tied up begin to yell—"

"You have a pistol? Isn't that unusual?"

"It's a leftover from before my accident. I've only used it for target practice, but I guess I must have shot the hat off of one fella, and the gun out of the other guy's hand." She stopped with a confused look on her face. "Except, I didn't take the safety off, nor did I have my finger on the trigger."

Julius glanced at the clock. "Whoa, look at the time. Not to interrupt, but I need to slip into town."

JULIUS CHUCKLED AS he drove toward Herman. The look on Mrs. MacDonald's face when she'd tried to figure out how she had shot the man's hat off his head. They should soon find out from the police that she hadn't fired the gun, but for now he'd leave them to wonder without him. He pulled into the parking lot at the Herman Police Department and went inside. The young woman looked up as he approached the desk.

"May I help you?"

"I need to speak to Chief Mallory."

"He's busy right now. Can I take your name?"

"Julius C. Armstrong. I'd appreciate if you'd pass that on to him now."

"Sir, this being a Saturday—"

"Crime doesn't take a holiday, ma'am. I tell you what, just pass my name on, and if he's still too busy for a friend . . ." Julius winked.

"Oh, I didn't know." She pressed the buzzer. "Julius Armstrong here to see you, sir."

"Julius Armstrong? Send him right in," Mallory said.

"That door right there." She pointed.

"Thank you." The door opened as he approached. "Chief Mallory?" The door closed to the office, and Julius held out a hand.

Mallory shook Julius' hand. "Have a seat."

While they settled into their seats Julius observed Chief Mallory. The guy could have been the police officer poster model with his pre-cision- cut reddish-brown hair, no- nonsense brown eyes, and trim muscular physique.

Mallory leaned forward, resting his elbows and folding his hands on his desk. "What can I help you with."

"Two things. The police report file from November 3, 1985, on Ms. O'Brien's death, and I need a local telephone van Monday after-noon about 3:30 p.m. Can you get that for me?"

"I'll get you the report, but it'll have to be unofficial." Mallory's eyes narrowed. "You need me to get the van set up? What's going on?"

"I need to get into the Meecham house, and it must be someone that can be trusted implicitly." Julius opted not to answer the ques-tions on Mallory's face. "I need it in the O'Brien grove by Diana's house. The grove and the path are kind of overgrown, but drive it in and let it sit. Should be easy to hide it in there. I'll need it for about an hour and a half."

"You know ninety-nine percent of this police force is honest and reliable."

"Wouldn't deny that. Problem is that last one percent, now isn't it? And there has to be more than one on the pay."

"That's so. Things have changed since I've been here these last six months, but it all takes time. Say, what was going on out there this morning? I got some strange reports," Chief Mallory said.

"When the ladies got home before lunch they had a wild tale about four fellows over at the Diana O'Brien property. What did you hear on this end?" Julius asked.

"We got your call— excuse me, a call needing assistance with vandals at the said property at 9:08 and sent our officers out right away. When they arrived they found the young O'Brien woman, and an older woman—MacDonald I believe, with a bead on two shysters. The two men, from out of town, swore they thought the property was for sale, and they were looking at it to buy. We also found two trussed-up fellows, Stu Bingly and Earl Jacobs, who couldn't explain why they were there, or why and how they were tied up. It all seemed to be an orange cat's fault. We detained them but eventually had to let them go. The cat seemed innocent, but wouldn't talk."

Julius coughed into his handkerchief. "I see. That kind of sums it up, I guess." He caught the twinkle in the police chief's eye. "You say the call came in at 9:08?"

"That's what's on the log. I'll call dispatch. You can check with them. Oh. . . and I'll check for that police report on Diana O'Brien's death. Just a minute." Chief Mallory walked to a bank of file cabinets along one wall. After a few minutes, he came back with the report. "You know it wasn't listed as suspicious, don't you?"

"Heart attack is what I read. Isn't that unusual for someone that young?"

"Yes and no. Not if there's a family history. And not if you don't want to investigate."

"Yeah, that's what I'd think. Well, thanks." Julius tucked the file in his briefcase and stood. "If you'd have that van Monday I'd 'preciate it. I'll be in touch."

Julius closed the door behind him and walked to the front desk. "Dispatch?"

The petite brunette officer looked up at Julius' question and motioned. "Down that hall, first door on the right."

Julius knocked on the door and entered.

A middle-aged, balding man looked up from where he sat at the control panel. "Can I help you?"

"Chief sent me. Were you here this morning?"

"No, Marcy's on duty in the morning. I have the afternoon shift. Why?"

"I needed to ask about a call that came in this morning about…" Julius hesitated and scratched his forehead. "I don't remember, 8:30 or 9:30 I think."

"Let me check the log." The man ran his finger down the times. "We have a call about 8 a.m., another at 9:08, but nothing in between."

"Thanks," Julius said.

JULIUS DROPPED INTO his car and glanced at the clock on his dashboard. One o'clock. He pulled into the A&W drive- in. "One root beer float," he said into the mic. Julius leaned back and savored his float. He checked his pager phone, he had sent this morning's call at 8:48, twenty minutes before dispatch had posted it. *Have to find out who Marcy from morning dispatch is.*

His mind wandered back to another A&W root beer stand from his youth. As a young kid, he sat scooping ice cream from his float as his brother's wife took her scheduled break. He liked to come in the afternoon after football practice, and listen to her talk while he waited for his brother to get off work. She never said anything noteworthy, but she was kind of funny. "I don't much care for that cigarette," he said to her once.

She squinted through the smoke at him. "Don't you think smoking makes me look mature?" She raised her nose a tad bit higher and turned her face so he could see her profile.

"No, it makes you look like a little kid trying on her mom's lipstick or something. And it stinks."

"You should try it. You'd look debonair."

"I'd look dead. That's what my folks'd do to me." He took a big drink of his root beer.

"No, you wouldn't. They wouldn't have to know. All the guys that are cool smoke."

"That list'll have to not include me. Thanks, but no thanks," he said. He knew he couldn't keep it from his father. That guy knew everything. He had eyes everywhere.

"Don't you wanna be cool?"

"No," he said.

"Well, your folks don't like me anyway." She assumed a pouty look.

"That's not true. My folks like everybody." He stopped eating his float. "Why wouldn't they like you?"

"I'm not lying. It's because I'm part Cherokee."

"You're kidding? That blond hair and blue eyes sure had me fooled."

"Tom, my brother, has black hair and brown eyes."

"Isn't he a step-brother?"

"Hi guy," his brother slid into the seat across from him. "Need a ride home?"

"Wouldn't turn it down. Goin' my way?"

"Will be if I give you a ride. Man, that thing stinks, woman!" his brother squashed her cigarette out in the tray.

"Well, I gotta get back to work anyhow..." She stuck her tongue out at her husband before leaving.

THAT CONVERSATION HAD remained in his mind for years. He'd never thought of his parents like that before. Julius smirked at the thought of when he did try smoking sometime after that. He was right, he couldn't keep it from his father, but it didn't turn out the way he'd expected. In hindsight there had been other times when his brother's wife instigated like that. It always caused friction in some way. The conflict finally got to him. He wasn't quite eighteen when he signed up for the military, but he had to get away. Letters from family had come regularly at first, but after boot camp, they came less often. He still received a package each year on birthdays and holidays. After his time was up, he chose to disappear. When he met and married Junco, his sister-in-law's words haunted him with what if's? He'd never thought his parents were prejudiced, but what if? Fourteen years I've wasted. Fourteen years lost. Maybe not wasted, but lost. Fourteen years. All because of a little snit who was playing games.

"Thanks," he said as the young waitress picked up his tray. He backed out, and then pulled in to over-night his next roll of film, then set off to turn in his evidence bags to another agent.

Chapter—16—

S unday, June 14th; The grass sparkled with light dew that glorious June morning. Julius followed the MacDonald car into the parking lot in front of a small, white country-church building. He crawled out of his car and joined the three companions.

"Nice spot. Not quite in town— close, but not far." Julius pursed his lips and observed the building and its surroundings.

"We like it here," Michael said.

"And what a fresh morning." Ruth took a deep breath. They turned and walked up the steps.

"Thanks," Julius said as Michael held open the door. Once inside, it became clear that this structure was a remodeled country schoolhouse. Bits and pieces of memory sifted through Julius, as he remembered the similar one- room school- house of his past where his education had begun.

"Hello there." A short, rotund man of middle age, and a woman of similar age stepped up to greet him in the foyer.

Michael stepped forward. "Alberto, this is our house guest, Julius Armstrong. Julius, this is Mr. Alberto Heide —and his wife, Wilma." He introduced the couple.

Mr. Heide extended his hand, "So, where ya from, Mr. Armstrong, and what brings you here?"

"I'm from out east." Julius shook hands with the couple. "I'm a freelance writer."

"Freelance, huh? You going to be here long?"

"Only a couple of weeks." Julius watched as others began to arrive.

"The Heide's live just a couple of miles east of here. Their son-in-law here, farms with them." Michael indicated a newly arrived young couple.

"Michael, come help with these screens," Ruth called from the front of the building.

"I guess we'll go open the windows, okay, Dora?" Michael asked one of the little girls who came in. Her pigtails bobbed, and she smiled. He took her hand, and they went to help Ruth. As they slid screens in the opened windows, fresh morning air filled the building.

A tall, serious young man in a plain navy- blue suit shook Julius' hand. "I'm Brother Paul Wilson. It's good to meet friends of the MacDonald's. You say you're here for a short time?"

"Yes, just a short time. Are you the preacher here?"

"My wife, Maria, and I are here for the summer." The thin, sandy-haired man indicated a tiny dark-haired woman with two children that joined him.

"Pleased to meet you. Are these your children?" He smiled, remembering why he did not like these encounters.

"Yes, we have two children, Hannah and Daniel." Maria's words tumbled out with a charming accent. "We would like to have maybe four like Mr. and Mrs. MacDonald." Her face became rosy in embarrassment. "Do you have a family, Mr. Armstrong?"

"I'm here alone ma'am— how long will you be here?"

"At least through August. This will be our second summer to work here." She paused before finishing. "Paul has completed his schooling, and we're looking for a permanent congregation."

After a few moments of meet and greet, everyone found their places. Ruth took the smaller children, and Michael led the older ones to their Bible classes. The adults stayed in the auditorium.

"Ask for the old paths...." Brother Wilson read verse one of Jeremiah chapter six.

Julius thought of grand cathedrals, magnificent monuments, and the countries he had been in, and the sites he witnessed during his life. How many beautiful shrines? How many churches were more interested in tributes for themselves, or getting numbers into their buildings rather than getting people into heaven? He sighed, and opened the pew Bible and followed along.

Julius observed the small, simple congregation as the people of varied ages settled into their pews. The light from the east windows highlighted the faces of each person. From older parents and grandparents to younger parents and children. There was a quiet and respectful aura as the small children sat tucked into their parent's arms.

Alberto Heide favored his left leg as he stumped to the front of the auditorium.

"The first song this morning, 'Saints Lift Your Voices,' song number seven please."

Pages whispered while everyone found the correct song. Like the calm before the storm, there seemed to be gathering strength.

Alberto raised his hand, and with a downbeat began, "There is none like him..."

Julius closed his eyes and joined in as the simple melody washed over him. Not any man-made artificial accompaniment could ever equal the beauty of God made human voice raised in praise toward the creator. His spirit soared as the simple songs were raised heavenward.

"We need to be strengthened with all power according to the might of His glory. We need to Give Thanks to the Father, who made us meet to be partakers of the inheritance of the Saints of Light. And who delivered us out of the power of darkness and translated us into the kingdom of the Son of His Love." Brother Wilson quoted as he brought his lesson to a close.

At the end of the lesson, Julius stood beside Michael as they sang, "Will you come... Will you come with your poor broken heart?"

At the final amen, Julius stepped out into the aisle after Ruth and Mrs. MacDonald passed. They made slow progress toward the exit as they stopped to talk. Nearing the back pew, Julius noticed a middle-aged woman with dyed red hair and penciled- on eyebrows stop and whisper to a boy on the bench who had come in after the service began. His torn blue jeans and holey tennis shoes looked out of place.

"Ruth?" The woman beckoned to her.

"Thank you, Ethel." Ruth sat beside the boy. "How's your mom, Billy?"

"She's sick in bed, Miss Ruth." His blue-gray eyes were huge in his thin dirt-smeared face.

" and can't take care of Lollie and the baby. I don't know what to do." He stopped and wiped his face with a dirty sleeve. "She can't get up. I'm afraid—" Billy began to sob, his skinny body shook with spasms. Ruth wrapped her arms around him as if to hold him together.

"There, there, now," she said.

"She's so sick. And Dad's been away for days. Mmmiss Rrruth," he sniffled and wiped his face on his sleeve again.

"I need to drop some things off at the potluck on the way to see about your momma. We'll throw your bike in the trunk. You ride with us. Okay?"

"Here." Julius handed Ruth his clean handkerchief. She dabbed at Billy's face then gave Billy the hankie.

"Miss Ruth." He blew his nose; there was only a slight tremor in his voice. "Are you an angel of the Lord?" He peered into her face.

"No, just a servant." She smiled at his innocent question.

"If you're a servant, them angels must be somethin.'" This time he used his shirt sleeve and the handkerchief.

Ruth's face flamed bright red. "I'm sure they are, Billy."

"Everyone has gone on to set up the potluck, Ruth," Michael came in from the foyer.

"Good, we're ready to leave too. You and Mrs. M, run on. If Julius doesn't mind, Billy and I can ride with him."

"It works for me." Julius shrugged.

"All right, Ruth," Michael said.

"I just need to grab my Bible." Ruth surveyed the auditorium, "—my purse, and a bulletin." She ushered Billy out the door.

HE SAT ALONG THE COUNTRY road behind the scraggly trees and the few bushes that gave him cover. His eyes narrowed. He leaned closer to the windshield as the activity in front of the church increased. *Soon*— his emotions ran riot, and his pulse quickened. *She should appear. They should be leaving any time now. What is taking so long?* He scowled and leaned in closer yet. *Where is she?*

Finally! There she is, but—someone is always with her! Why's she have that low-life Marsh kid with her? Disgust rose in his throat and threatened to choke him. *And who is that fellow she's with now? That other blond jerk left with his mother, but someone else has taken his place. "I don't know who..."* He leaned farther forward, frowned and glared as the charcoal gray car drove away. *Why? Why!* With an angry jerk, he shoved his car into gear and drove toward home.

"So where you been? Pining over that O'Brien girl again?" The older man scowled and cursed as the young man slammed into the house.

The young man's eyes narrowed, "Leave me alone." He answered glaring at the man.

"Them O'Briens! Their women have been a particular pain far too long. You pine over her—you know she's not for you. Just forget her!" He cursed again, "I told ya to get rid of them two women long ago. You only did half the job. Git rid of her." His voice became a primeval growl.

"And I told you to leave me alone." The younger man glared in return.

Chapter—17—

"Just follow Michael up that drive there," Ruth said. "Our Sunday potluck's are on a revolving schedule." Julius, Ruth, and Billy were the last to pull up the drive at the Cole's country cottage where the potluck was being held that Sunday. Joe had the grill warmed up, and the tantalizing aroma of barbeque floated on the breeze.

"Man, does that smell good!" Julius exclaimed as he parked.

Ruth hopped out of his passenger's seat. "I'll be back," she said and hurried off.

Julius rolled down the windows and turned off the car. He turned to look at Billy in the backseat. "My stomach is rubbing against my backbone. How about you?" The detective wanted to ease the turmoil in the boy's blue-gray eyes. Julius retrieved a box of doughnuts from the back seat beside Billy. He took one and offered the box to the boy. Billy eyed the donuts, hesitating. "Suit yourself," Julius said, " but when I was in the military, I learned to eat when I had a chance. Didn't always know when another opportunity would come along." Julius bit into a chocolate jelly-filled doughnut.

At the word, *military* Billy's face lit up. "You were a soldier, mister?"

"I was a Marine. Four whole years," Julius said.

Billy selected a doughnut. "You're older than my dad." He spoke around a mouthful of cream filling.

"Is that so?" Julius finished chewing and took another bite.

"My dad was in the Army." Billy sat up a bit taller, his face shining with pride. Then the light faded out of his face, "but sometimes it makes him forget Mom and me and Lollie and the baby."

Julius forced his last bite of doughnut down, and wrapped his last half of doughnut in a napkin leaving it in the ashtray. For some reason he was full.

Ruth poked her head in through the open car window and looked at Billy. "After we have a prayer, we'll go take care of your momma." She opened the door, and Billy jumped out. "If she has to go to the hospital you children can spend the day with Lewis."

"DO YOU THINK BROTHER Paul and the Heides will be back soon from taking Mrs. Marsh to the hospital?" Julius bent down to pick up a stray Styrofoam cup as they cleaned up from pot luck.

"It's hard to say. They might keep her overnight." Lewis set down a large dish swathed in padding. "By the way, I've been meaning to tell you, I have an old plat book at home. It shows who owns what land, and who lives where. That might help navigate the countryside for your book writing assignment."

"Great. You going straight home? I'll follow you and pick it up."

Julius stopped at the end of Lewis' driveway and studied the newly acquired plat book before pulling onto the road. He traced the road with his forefinger around to the south and west and read the names from the book. Pat and Priscilla O'Brien, and further around here Sean and Genevieve O'Brien and a grade 'B' road right here. How convenient. Back around on this mile is listed under Jack and Diana O'Brien, where Ruth, her mother, and brother lived.

Julius folded the plat book into the console and slid the car into gear. He stopped in front of the O'Brien house he had visited the day before. Like a painting you've seen at too close a quarters, it helped to back up and get a distant look. A two-story farmhouse with fresh white paint and green trim at the windows gave it a charming look. The crisp gingerbread doodles curled around the eaves and embellished the porch. However, that didn't disguise the fact that no one lived here. The neat lawn inside the picket fence emphasized the appearance of a monument marker. He put the car in gear and drove on.

The field on the north of the grade B road is listed under O'Brien, but right smack next to it is a parcel listed under Meecham.

Julius followed a convoluted route first north and then further west where the name in the book read David Meecham. He stopped about a fourth of a mile short from the house and slipped into the cover of the trees and bushes along the road and between the fence rows. He pulled out his binoculars and did a once over of the area.

Meecham's house sat on a swell of land across a field of young corn. There was a cut of land where a dry creek bed ran catty-cornered taking a jog around between the corn and pasture in back of the house. Julius took special note of the house and outbuildings and several vehicles that came and left. Not glamorous work, but necessary for laying out a plan. Better than the exciting side that consisted of being shot at, or attacked. That possibility came tomorrow, Monday.

AFTER EVENING CHURCH service, Julius followed Lewis out the door to the parking lot. "Thanks for lending me that plat book. How's Mrs. Marsh doing?"

"They were rehydrating Mrs. Marsh and getting some nutrients back into her system," Lewis said. "They should be getting back soon and we'll take the kids back later."

Michael leaned against the hood of his car. "Mom and Ruth and I will stop by the Marsh's to see if they're home."

"You going to be back to the house soon?" Julius called to Michael.

"The ladies have been cleaning up at the Marsh's this afternoon, so this shouldn't take long."

"Well, I'm heading back to my room," Julius said.

JULIUS SWUNG DOWN FROM the roof and climbed back in the west window on his room. He just finished wiring his small disk into place when Michael puttered up the drive. It had been intense a few moments ago as he pushed to get things hooked up, but in spite of the interruptions, his base had become established.

"Okay," he spoke into his phone, "It's up. How's my reception?"

"Good—and good," the voice on the other end said. "We'll get those pictures out to you shortly, and contacts."

"I'm ready." Julius folded his gear away and stashed it back in its case. With a sigh, he glanced at his watch. *Need a break. Oww... I don't remember ever being this sore after horseback riding in my life.* Julius groaned and stretched his aching muscles. He eased down the stairs and through the breezeway.

Mrs. MacDonald sorted laundry as he passed. "Help yourself to the coffee pot. We should have some rolls to go with it," she said.

"You must have read my mind." Julius moved slowly through the laundry room.

"Are you up to throwing bales tomorrow?" Michael laughed as Julius gimped into the sunroom.

"Tomorrow I meet some of the residents at the retirement center."

"Mom does the retirement center after lunch at two o'clock. Throwing bales won't take over a couple of hours in the morning."

"I've used muscles this week I forgot I had. Throwing bales should finish me off."

Ruth came in with a plate of old-fashioned cinnamon rolls. "Say, Georgie Porgy, Michael and I usually ride on Sunday evenings, but he has to write some letters. You up for a horseback ride?"

Julius groaned. "Don't you guys ever stop?"

"It's the only solution to ease the pain." Ruth smiled as she handed out rolls and plates.

"I do need to write letters. After we polish off these cinnamon rolls, we can saddle those fat lazy horses while Ruth changes into her riding gear." Michael popped a bite in his mouth.

JULIUS AND RUTH LOPED the horses across the pasture and stopped at the farm drive. "Grade B road like that one," she pointed to the road in back of her mother's house, "is a fancy name for a dirt road," Ruth said. "There are a number of them. That's where we do most of our riding. Lead up that way along the shoulder of the road, and then go right on the next Grade B." She motioned with her riding quirt.

The horses were eager to go, and once they reached the Grade B road, they galloped with abandon savoring their freedom. Their riders enjoyed their own private world as the trees on either side formed a green canopy overhead. The sound of the silver peeper frogs singing, the smell of the growing corn mingling with the fresh-cut hay in the early evening created a dreamlike charm.

"You're quite an accomplished rider," Julius said as the horses slowed, content, at last, to step along side by side.

"My brother, Reuben and I had ponies in our younger days, but I didn't appreciate riding until Mrs. M. She says I possess a natural ability." Ruth pulled her horse to a stop. "If we go much farther north, we go toward Meecham's." She grimaced. Her horse shook his head and rattled his bridle as if saying 'No!' She turned south. "If we go to the south, we can go around past my Aunt Genevieve's.

"Mom, Reuben, and I lived over there." She pointed across the field. With a deft flip of her quirt, she flicked a fly buzzing around her horse's ears. There was a small path just inside the fence that led down to a stream. They followed it to the stream, and the horses dipped their muzzles into the cold water.

Back on the road, Ruth continued her description. "Aunt Genevieve lives here during the late spring and until November. She's been on a cruise and won't be back until July this year," Ruth said as they rode by a two-story farmhouse framed by old cottonwood trees. "Dad's been farming their place since Uncle died. He's tried to encourage one of Uncle Sean's boys to come back and take over the farm."

"Your uncle must have been young when he died," Julius said.

"He hadn't ever been robust. He got sick as a child, and it took his health. He married his childhood sweetheart."

"How many children did they have?"

"Three. Two boys and a girl."

"That must have been nice to have cousins so close."

"They were quite a bit older than we were. Dad joined the military, and of course, Uncle Sean couldn't pass a physical. He married Aunt Genevieve right after graduation."

"I see. So his kids would have been almost ten years older than Reuben and you?"

"Yes, the boys were twins —Allen and Tim— then the girl came last. She was so pretty—took after the O'Brien side. Except she had brown eyes and auburn hair. The boys took after Aunt Genevieve's family."

"So the boys weren't pretty."

Ruth laughed, "I didn't mean that. The boys were good looking. They had blond hair like Aunt Genevieve and blue eyes like Uncle Sean. But Dee was drop-dead gorgeous."

The gentle rhythm of the horses' steps gave a feeling of comfort. Julius observed that Ruth radiated a quiet, pleasant, personality and a natural exquisiteness. Many young women sought outward beauty, often with paint and powder. However, youthful innocence contained a charm all the art of industry could not reproduce.

"So, the O'Brien population dwindled. You're the only one left in town?"

"Allen went off to med school; Tim went to Canada, and Dee to California. Reuben went into the military, but I'm content here. Dad, Grandpa, and now the MacDonalds—This is my home. I haven't heard from Reuben, but maybe twice since Mom's funeral."

"I'm sorry." Julius caught Ruth's quiet, thoughtful face in his peripheral sight. "I heard about your Mom having a heart attack."

Ruth took a deep breath. "It's like the giraffe in the trees. Everyone knows, but it's too dangerous to talk about."

The horses touched noses and the creak of the saddles as they eased along appeared to soothe Ruth's spirit. Julius chose to remain silent, hoping that would encourage Ruth to speak out.

"Our world became Mom, Reuben, and I in that house after mom and dad's argument." She pointed in the general direction. "And Dad moved out and went to live with Grandpa. When I was almost eleven, Mr. and Mrs. MacDonald started a Bible study with Mom, and we began attending church. Dad started teaching Reuben and me martial arts and spending time with us. As Mom changed Reuben and I hoped for reconciliation between Mom and Dad. It looked like there was a real possibility.

"Then in high school, Phil Meecham tried to blackmail me saying he'd cause problems for my family unless I played his game. Grandpa told me to confront him in public, and that's what I did."

Julius cleared his throat. "Did it work?" The gathering shadows settled across the countryside as he thought about Mrs. Irving's story.

"There've been no more verbal threats, but Meecham's still out there. To this day I can't do anything without his shadow following me. The Meecham family, like a fat spider, always seems to be lurking in dark places ready to pounce." Ruth busied herself by smoothing her horse's mane.

"After Mom was killed, Mr. and Mrs. MacDonald took me in. I've been there ever since."

"Killed? I thought she had a heart attack?"

"That's what the police report said, but no one believes it. I hope those men the other day didn't mess things up." She frowned.

"Mess things up? How so?"

"Everyone knew Police Chief Biles was in cahoots with David and Ralph Meecham, Phil's dad and grandpa. Phil called for the ambulance for mom. Dad knew there wasn't going to be an honest investigation, so Dad closed the house up. He thought about hiring a PI..."

"You think it was Meecham?"

"It would point that way, and the whole community thinks so."

"And he did threaten you. . ."

Ruth nodded, but remained silent.

"How well do you know Phil Meecham? He wasn't a police officer then?"

"He's about four years older than I am. Not too long after he graduated from high school he began working toward becoming a policeman, taking classes and stuff. How well do I know him? I've grown up around Phil."

"Yes, but we can grow up as a bosom friend and still not know a person."

"True." Ruth sighed. "I used to feel sorry for him. He was like a pawn in a chess game. Expendable. Not valued, not loved."

They arrived back at the farm drive; the full moon wove a web of light around them. Night creatures rustled and whispered in the twilight. All of creation seemed drawn together in the same struggle of survival. The hoot of an owl sounded, and the silent shadow of a night bird slid over them. Julius knew this story would be finished in its own time.

Chapter—18—

In the darkening stable, they quickly removed saddles and bridles. Amid the pleasant aromas of hay and grain, they finished settling their horses in for the night and closed the shed doors.

"Thanks for listening," Ruth said as they walked toward the back of the house.

"It helps to sort things out." He smiled, and, with a flourish, held the door for Ruth. "After you."

"I thought you were lost." Michael said as Julius entered the living room. "I was about to send out the troops."

"No, not lost, but the ride was pleasant. There's some beautiful country out here, and I had a much prettier companion this time around." Julius grinned at Michael.

"I'm sure that's so..."

"Come on, Uncle Michael!" Lewis' three boys called. "We wanna finish this game."

"Okay, okay," Michael turned back to the Sorry game board.

"Anyone for more popcorn?" Ruth brought in a large roaster pan full and several small bowls.

"Thank you." Julius accepted his popcorn and watched Michael and the boys, arguing, moaning, groaning, with glee depending on the moment and each turn of events. Julius took a handful of the fluffy white kernels. "Excellent popcorn, Ruth."

He turned to Lewis, who was sitting in an overstuffed chair. "So, how're things going?"

"Thank you." Lewis refilled his bowl of popcorn and turned to Julius. "We just took the Marsh kids home and put them to bed. Gretchen—Mrs. Marsh is looking much better."

"What's this about Mr. MacDonald coming home next week?" Julius said.

"Yes, he's on a Mission trip that will be over next Friday. He'll start home midafternoon Saturday," Lewis said.

Michael rolled over on the floor and sat up. "Sorry, boys, no more chances to win. I beat you all three games fair and square." He dismissed them with a wave of his hand.

"Ah, c'mon Uncle Michael! Just one more game!" they chorused.

"Nope. Go eat your popcorn and cry quietly." He turned back to face Lewis and Julius and threw a piece of popcorn up into the air and caught it in his mouth. He grinned and tried the stunt again.

"Some days, brother." Lewis gave Michael a one-eyed frown.

"I know, I know," Michael laughed. "I'm teaching the boys to be unique."

"Boys, finish up your popcorn. We need to be going before you become too unique." Lewis shook his head and rose to his feet.

"It's time for me to wrap it up too." Julius finished his popcorn and stood. "Tomorrow's a long day. Good night."

"Good night, kiddo," Mrs. MacDonald called as he left the room.

"Good night." The others chorused.

He walked out the breezeway into the evening shadows. The moon brought out a restless spirit within him, and rumpled his tired mind. With no particular destination, he chose a random path and followed it toward the front fence. In the distance the fields and land looked level and flat. Julius snorted. Just try walking across that flat land, and you would find creeks, bogs, dips, and hollows. This simple life was like that. It had its ups and downs with no level playing fields. Ruth had her share of sorrows. Michael, an easy-going, likable kid on the surface, was easy going and likeable, but he was also more. A scripture came to his mind: "Though he was a Son, yet learned obedience by the things which he suffered." Michael had the strength of character that trials would burnish to a brilliant hue adding depth, and passion.

The soft breeze whispering through the trees brought smells and sounds of early summer. The peepers around the pond and crickets all were night sounds of peace and harmony. He stopped and leaned on the fence. Somewhere in the distance, a police siren sounded out of place. The city lights of Hermon, although not visible themselves, caused a bright glow on the horizon.

A shower and bed sound good. He sighed. Junko and Mai—I wish I were home...*what am I thinking, I wish they were here*. Where could they be and why hadn't he heard from Junco? He closed his eyes and pictured, Junko, her long black hair that smelled like jasmine and orange blossoms. His arms ached to hold little Mai and rock her to sleep. He turned toward the breezeway and climbed the steps to his room. The warm water from the shower rolled stress from his body, but the pain remained in his heart.

Julius readied for bed and then sat on the floor with his computer. A small light illuminated his detective board. He tapped in codes searching through the database on his computer. He began to receive information, then arrange pictures into groups. Loose strands of Ruth's story and other pieces of the puzzle flitted through his mind. He continued arranging pictures in groups; these were Chicago people with the missing Meister at the top. An older man, well groomed who apparently enjoyed the finer things of life. Although he was past his glory days and no longer in his jet-set time. The guess would be that the contact here was probably the Meecham group, but the how, who and why was missing. Clarke and Holiday was a money laundering front supported by Meister. Adam Clarke had bought out his partner's interest a couple years ago, when the old man Holiday suddenly died in a rather suspicious accident. "*This is who you'll be investigating this week in Chicago,"* the note from Director Meyer informed him.

As images floated across his mind and screen his heart ached with yearning. *Where have the years gone? I feel like a hundred and three, instead of thirty-three. Is it true you have to travel around the world to come home, or am I just confusing old sayings?*

A message appeared: "Searching, no Song Bird, or Little Parrot yet." With a groan, he shut down the computer, stowed it into its hiding place, snapped out his small light, and slipped into bed. Julius had to get some sleep. . . he relaxed as the first notes of "Moonlight Sonata" floated into the night.

Chapter—19—

M onday, June, 15th; The next morning, Julius took his mug of coffee outside and sat under the maple tree, as the silent messengers of the sun appeared in the eastern sky. Mrs. MacDonald and Ruth in quiet conversation sauntered along the path toward the house.

"We'll have breakfast ready in a few minutes," Ruth said as they passed.

"I'm just getting started, no hurry," Julius said.

Mrs. MacDonald leaned her hoe against the side of the house, and they were swallowed up as the door shut behind them. The smell of the sausage and pancakes wafted on the breeze bringing buried memories to the surface. The heart ache and the yearning returned from the night before as he fingered his mug. He sighed and looked up as he heard footsteps on the path.

"Hey," Michael said, "Bring your mug inside and let's eat. It's about time to head to Lewis.'"

"MIND IF I TAKE SOME pictures while you hitch up?" Julius asked.

"Do you get paid by the picture?" Lewis said.

"I take a lot of pictures for this job." Julius checked the settings on his camera and snapped pictures of the wagon and some of the helpers while he waited. Watching Lewis bring the enormous matched pair of Percheron horses out and back them into their places, Julius wound up a roll of film. Changing the old roll for a new one, he stashed the old in his case just before Lewis raised his voice.

"Listen up! While this information is for Julius, our greenhorn, it will serve as a reminder for everyone else. I drive the team, and we have a couple of stackers on the wagon. The rest—"

Greenhorn! Julius thought without humor—if he only knew. Lewis finished his instructions, and amid light-hearted camaraderie, everyone climbed on the large wagon jostling along behind the team of gigantic horses. Lewis pulled to a stop when they reached the field. Everyone slid off and fanned out to their places, except the designated stackers.

"Giddyup there—C'mon Dolly, Pete!" Lewis shook the reins. The pair leaned into the harness, the steel wheels creaked, and they moved like clockwork, as the tug chains jangled. The shouts and noises of men and beasts mixed in the mid-morning air.

Michael and Julius jumped off and found a spot next to the bales. Michael readied one of his hay hooks as Lewis drove the team toward them. "This is how you do it, now, Julius." He swung his hook, lodging it into a bale, and dragging it a short distance, and as the wagon started rolling by him, he launched the other hook embedding it into the other side of the bale. Then lifting and with an easy movement heaving the bale onto the wagon.

"Okay, you old city slicker, let's see what you're made of," Michael shouted as the wagon rolled in Julius's direction.

This isn't my first rodeo either. City slicker indeed. Julius hooked the bale with one hook, and drug it a short distance. Instead of using the second hook, he swung the one hundred pound bale around with a single fluid motion. *A precise timing in this dance makes all the difference in delivery*—and Julius, with a flick of his wrist, heaved his bale up onto the wagon. It landed precisely where he had intended, right at the feet of the first stacker.

Chapter—20—

“I think we should have timed hay loading and retirement center on two different days. I'm going to rest for a bit while you get a shower and clean up.” Mrs. MacDonald said as Julius pulled into the driveway. “I'm just not as spry as I used to be.”

“What's wrong with you? You've only been up since five-thirty, and it's now one o'clock. At sixty-four I hope I'm as ornery as you.” Julius turned the engine off and brushed his fingers through his hair and beard. “I've got hay in my hair, in my shirt, and I'm going to have to hurry to get ready. What time are we supposed to be at the retirement center?” He looked at the clock as they entered the house through the breezeway.

“You have half an hour. We want to be there by two.” Mrs. MacDonald opened the closet in the entryway and put her purse on the shelf. “I'll put my feet up and wait in here. Everything's ready to go when you are.”

Julius' sixth sense tingled. “That'll be fine.” He called out then moved without sound looking into the nooks of the rooms as he went.

“What is it?” Mrs. MacDonald whispered as she felt his movements. She cocked her head to one side and turned slightly at the living room entrance.

In the silence, Julius and Mrs. MacDonald stood a few feet apart. “Wait here,” he whispered.

Julius slipped out the breezeway door and, glancing down the driveway he scanned the road toward town. There in the distance a dark figure of a man moved slightly. In a flash, he sprinted back through the breezeway. The garden gate blew, unlatched in the wind. The pea gravel crunched under his feet as he tore down the path and flew out the gate. Beyond the barbed-wire fence, a man was running toward the end of the pasture at a goodly pace. If only Julius could catch up before the runner disappeared into the trees. He pushed his speed to the limit. He came to the fence and vaulted over it, but broke stride when he came down on the other side. The figure slipped into the trees.

Goodnight! Now I have to get back over that blasted fence! During the adrenaline rush vaulting over the barbed wire fence hadn't been a problem. Now without the adrenaline, the picture looked different. Jogging down the fence row toward a corner post with a gate, he heard a bullet being chambered. That sent a tingle up his spine and recharged his adrenaline.

Julius changed directions at a dead run, zigzagging toward the trees. A shot rang out, and something whizzed by his ear. He broke his running pattern just as another shot rang out. Dirt and grass spit into the air where he would have been. At last, he reached the safety of the trees, and another shot rang out, again where he had been, spitting more dirt and grass.

A surprised bawl came from the trees and the crunch of twigs, branches and underbrush sounded as a body scrambled through the brush toward the road at the other side of the trees.

Julius stood under the cover of the trees as the sound of a vehicle door slammed, and a vehicle zipped away down the road. Examining the ground, Julius scouted around. Dropping to one knee, he studied the shell casings and wrapped them in his handkerchief.

"That could have ended worse," he said as he returned to the orchard path where Mrs. MacDonald was waiting.

"All's well that ends well. So they say." Mrs. MacDonald spoke from the cover of trees.

Julius blotted the sweat from his face with his sleeve. "That was close."

"I should say. Not many folks run *at* someone shooting at them."

"I left my stuff in my camera bag, but I won't be caught without my credit card again. I'll go get ready for our visit. Do you need to call someone? Don't know where those yahoos came from."

"They won't be back today, but I'll call Lewis. You wouldn't think out here we'd be troubled with this stuff. It's a sad day, and there went my nap. You'll have to hurry now."

JULIUS PUSHED OPEN the glass door, and they walked into the retirement center.

"Hi there," a woman waved as they entered. "I'm just making the coffee. I'll be right with you." she repositioned the coffee maker.

Mrs. MacDonald set her cake on the counter and went to speak to an older woman sitting at a table. Julius leaned on the counter.

A few seconds later the woman who had greeted them approached Julius. "With Mr. Mac gone on his mission trip, I didn't know if anyone would be able to come," she said. "They've been coming for close to ten years now, and even though the MacDonalds are newcomers, nobody holds that against them." I'm Sheila she held out her hand. "You related to the MacDonalds?"

Julius shook her hand. "They're graciously hosting me for the short time I'll be here," Julius said. He watched as Mrs. MacDonald circulated around the room and spoke to several people before she sat at the piano and began to play some older, favorite songs. The aides helped several residents to the lunch room. Sheila took it upon herself to introduce the five women and four men to Julius.

He took special note of the last two names. Charlie Anderson: (What had Mrs. Irving said about Charlie? He was recovering from something?) and Ralph Meecham (How is he related to Phil Meecham? What had Ruth said about Ralph last night?)

Once everyone was settled, Mrs. MacDonald began to play old favorites and several of the residents sang lustily along.

"I'll have to come back next week for entertainment," Charlie chuckled. "I haven't had this much fun in years. How about I bring my accordion, Amanda?"

"By all means, Charlie, come back and bring your accordion." Mrs. MacDonald laughed.

"How long is that husband of yours going to be gone?" Charlie asked.

"Two more weeks. Do you miss him?" She turned from the piano keys.

Charlie guffawed and slapped his knee, "Amanda, I was thinkin' I'm gonna need some help when I go home, maybe I could convince you to come and keep house for me."

"This woman's taken, Charlie—but you should have someone coming in to clean."

"Chuck has it set up. How about if you'n Mac come over for a visit?"

"That would be more like it," Mrs. MacDonald said.

"So's this one of your boys?" Charlie asked.

"Charlie, this is Mr. Julius C. Armstrong. He's doing a story on small towns, and he's looking for some local color."

"Local color?" Charlie's face lit up. "Turn your machine on there and get this one." He waited until Julius had everything set up then told his story. "About sixty years ago when I was still a feisty young man, me an' Pat—that's Pat O'Brien for the record—we helped old man Williamson move his outhouse..." Charlie paused and rubbed his chin. His audience already knew the story, and most of them were wearing smirks.

"How good of you, Charlie." His story caught Mrs. MacDonald's interest. "When I was growing up, some people in our neighborhood moved theirs every few years—"

"Well, Mr. Williamson took exception to our generous help. It was about twelve midnight, and he happened to be sitting in it."

Too late Mrs. MacDonald saw it coming. "Charlie, you old unrepentant sinner!" She gasped in mock horror. "I'm going to go get the cake and coffee set out. Julius, you'll have to take care of this fellow. He's probably got more local color than you have recorder." She walked to the counter and began cutting the cake, and sliding it onto plates.

"You have such good looking children," the twins Bertha and Bernice exclaimed as the snapshots were passed around. "This picture here—" Bernice held up a picture of Ruth. "This is Pat's granddaughter isn't it? She looks so much like him." The two older women whispered together and laughed.

Bertha continued where her sister left off. "Such a delightfully handsome man. Bernice and I tried everything—well not quite everything." She blinked and fluffed up the collar on her dress. "But everything within decent bounds, to get his attention." The women both sighed.

Julius smiled remembering Mrs. Irving's remarks about female antics.

"Then he married Prissy." Their faces drew into a pout.

"Remember the time of that..." Bernice said.

"That epidemic?" Bertha finished the thought. "Prissy came in and nursed half of the town through it. She was worn out. It's no wonder she got sick herself."

"Was that when they lost their baby girl?" Bernice asked.

"No, they lost little Rose the year before—" Bertha stopped speaking. They turned and glared at Ralph Meecham.

"Enough. It's too sweet." Ralph Meecham said after chasing every crumb of his second piece of cake. "And the coffee's too salty." He drained the last of his third refill as he sat alone at the end of the table, scowling and ill-tempered. "No, I don't want to see those photos." He pushed them away. "Especially not O'Brien's granddaughter. Too much O'Brien—baah!" He rose with haste and shuffled down the hall to his room. One overall strap hung behind, and a red farmer hanky dangled halfway out of his back pocket.

"IT'S BEEN GOOD TALKING to you." Julius packed up his recorder beside where Charlie relaxed finishing his coffee. Mrs. Mac-Donald busied herself chatting with Sheila and picking up her belongings.

The steel-gray haired man smiled up at him, "The MacDonald family are good folks. Amanda's got spunk. Her affliction may slow her down, but not much."

"Her husband must be quite a fellow, too," Julius said.

"He sure is. They're two peas in a pod." Charlie said handing Sheila his plate and cup.

"You going home soon then?" Julius asked.

"Yes, I am. Tomorrow to be exact," Charlie said.

"I met an old fellow about your age a few days ago. Did you ever know of someone by the name of Hiram McCormick? He'd a been tall, maybe red-haired, well-built fellow."

"No, never knew any McCormicks around here. I know a couple of fellows would fit the description, but not by that name." Charlie shook his head.

"Ready Julius?" Mrs. MacDonald called from the doorway.

"Sure am." He shook hands with Charlie, "glad to make your acquaintance, sir. Maybe I'll see you around since you're going home."

"You never know," Charlie said with a nod. "Us old codgers show up in strange places, and at odd times."

"HERE, I'LL LET YOU have the box with the cake crumbs." Mrs. MacDonald laughed as Julius opened the car door and she slid into the passenger side.

Julius dropped into the driver's seat, cranked the starter, and backed his car around. "Charlie sure is full of stories, isn't he?" Julius said with a chuckle.

"He sure is. Quite a contrast to Mr. Meecham. It's sad how many people are like Ralph Meecham. God sends so many blessings on everyone, but they get so wrapped up with everyday living that they don't even stop to say thank you. Ingratitude is a horrible sin."

"Ingratitude—I'd never thought about it." Julius waited at the stop sign while a pickup passed.

"The love of money is a root of all kinds of evil, and ingratitude is a root of evil also." Mrs. MacDonald frowned and fingered the handle on her purse. "We all should be grateful, but we want to do it our way. Or we just want to do what we want to do. Regardless of the consequences to ourselves, or to others. We think everything should be democratic—like we should get to vote on things. Why do we think God needs our opinion? How absurd, how absolutely blasphemous." She shook her head.

"That's a different way of looking at it," Julius said, relieved they were back to the garage. He switched off the engine. "I'm going to be out and about for a few hours."

"You need to be careful." Mrs. MacDonald's face puckered into a doubtful look. "I know those fellows are long gone, but. . ." She hesitated then clamped her mouth into a thin line and let the subject drop. "You have your job to do and don't need an old woman telling you something. I've got some things to do to prepare for supper. I'm rather surprised Ruth isn't home now, but when she gets back, I'm going to take a short nap." Mrs. MacDonald spoke over her shoulder as she climbed out of the passenger seat, and retrieved her articles.

"Here, let me get those. You don't need to be so stubborn and independent." His tone carried a light-hearted note, but his face wore a frown.

"I'm surprised at you, young man. Of course, I have to be stubborn and independent. It's who I am. And let me tell you—" her face relaxed into a smile "Go ahead, and get my stuff, I'm just teasing, but don't frown it'll give you bad wrinkles. And close your mouth."

Julius self-consciously closed his mouth and smiled. "You are the most cantankerous person I know."

"Can't be true, but maybe pretty close." She laughed as she walked toward the breezeway. "If you want to take a bottle of water with you, we have some insulated containers. It'll snap on your belt."

"I'll set this stuff on the counter before I go get the rest of my gear. Some water would be handy."

"I'll get it ready." She put her purse on the counter beside the cake container.

"Thanks. I'd appreciate it." Silently, Julius took the stairs to his room two at a time. He dropped into a crouch and shoved open the door. Scanning the interior of the room everything looked normal. Still cautious, he checked out the bathroom. Assured that all was clear, he pulled out his carry bag, checked through the items, snapped it shut, and headed for the door and for his afternoon assignment.

"I know we have more bottles, but couldn't find but one container. Will this do?" Mrs. MacDonald heard him enter the kitchen and indicated an insulated bottle sitting on the counter.

"That'll be fine, ma'am. I'll see you in a few hours." Julius picked his camera from the counter, and the insulated pink bottle with the picture of a little pony on the front and hurried out the door. *The bad guys better watch out, I'm armed and dangerous.* He rolled his eyes at the thought. *It wouldn't do any good to worry Mrs. MacDonald—of course, being blind, she wouldn't know, but a pink pony?*

Julius scouted around taking a circuitous route to the back of the property. As he worked his way through the trees that bordered the pasture and the road he stopped to listen. Only nature sounds filled the air. Still wary, he checked the length of road both ways with a scope and paused for several minutes. An overgrown grove of trees enveloped the empty O'Brien farmhouse on three sides. He quickly slipped out of the cover of the trees, across the gravel road, and into the safety of the O'Brien grove of trees. With stealthy tread, he moved through the underbrush until he reached the overgrown driveway in from the grade B, or dirt road.

The telephone service truck was parked on the north side of O'Brien's property concealed off the dirt road on the overgrown lane in the grove of trees. His right hand checked his weapon. He released the safety. Those yahoos the other day had been watching Earl and Stu. They could be waiting now. Ever vigilant, he scouted around. From behind a nearby tree, Julius inspected the truck. He stood close enough after a short time he slipped across a few steps to the back. With a prayer, he opened the service doors and stepped up and inside.

He emerged fifteen minutes later in a black and tan telephone company uniform. He took the picture off the clipboard and slipped it onto his shirt pocket. New identity, new day. It's more challenging to apply a disguise over a disguise. He had lightened up the skin tone, taken out the brown contacts, given himself a flatter nose, the hat would cover the hair color, the beard was a bit touchy. He checked the badge against his makeup job. Not bad for the few minutes, and conditions he had to work in.

Julius backed out of the drive and stopped again. One more look in the mirror to ensure that he appeared like the guy in the photo he'd been given—some guy by the name of Joe Smith—a new employee of *Co-op Telephone Company*. He repositioned the cap then drove the light blue van sporting the title, *Co-op Telephone* off the dirt road, onto the gravel road then over a mile. He stopped by a telephone pole at an intersection. He surveyed the countryside. A heavy sigh escaped his dry lips. He took a swallow from his water. When he put it back in the cup holder, he covered it with a shirt and turned his attention to the work at hand. *Like the saying goes, here's one for the Gipper—or maybe not. Duty calls. Lives hang on me completing this job—successfully.*

He hooked his harness around the pole and like a monkey he shinnied up to the top. After looking busy for a short interval, he did his work of adding a disrupter. *Now for the finishing touch.*

Julius drove at a crawl down the gravel drive toward a white two-story farmhouse with a red roof. Short brown grass covered the landscape, giving it a barren, dry look. Julius could see evidence of several doggie landmines scattered more than occasionally across the lawn, and in the center sat a dog house. As he approached the front door, a Great Dane woke from his slumber. Foaming, chomping, and barking wildly the dog hit the end of his chain. Julius fished in his pocket, pulled out a doggie treat, and hoped for the best as he tossed it in the direction of the offended animal. The dog did not take the bait. Undaunted, Julius continued to the porch, knocked on the door and waited; all the while the dog fought the chain snarling and barking. From inside the house, a chorus of sounds erupted.

Oh, great, more dogs, but these sound like ankle biters.

The door opened, and he looked down at a small pudgy girl wearing a pink gingham apron and wielding a spatula in her left hand. "Can I help you, mister?"

"Well, now I don't know. Are you the lady of the house?" *This is sure a strange turn of events. There aren't supposed to be any youngsters here.*

The little girl giggled, "No, I'll go get my momma. Just you wait." She turned and ran back across the living room to what must have been the kitchen, shouting as she went, "Mom, mom."

"I'm coming, Nancy. Just give me a minute."

Three ankle biters were jumping and yapping for all they were worth on the other side of the screen door. A young woman's voice spoke to the child as they came back toward the door. From what he could see, it looked like a typical living room, just a bit messy.

"Hello, can I help you?" A blonde woman in her mid-twenties peered out at him from a dim interior. "Would you dumb dogs, hush up?" She tried scooting them out of the way with her bare foot. "I'm sorry, they just make more noise. Hush up, Dixie! She's the leader," she said.

"Those little dogs don't bother me near like that one in the yard, ma'am," He said with a smile. "My name's Joe Smith, and I work for the telephone company. We've had complaints about some phones in the area not working. Can you tell me if your house phones are all working?"

"I don't actually live here. This is my uncle's house, and we're do-ing some cleaning for him. The ones downstairs are working, but I don't know about upstairs."

"Who's at the door, Melody?" A male voice shouted down the stairs.

She turned and raised her voice. "Some guy from the telephone company."

"Tell him we don't need any more work on the phones. They were just out last week, and everything's fine!"

"You've heard it from the source then." She turned back and smiled at Julius.

"I guess I have now. Here. —Here's my card. Just put it by the phone, if you ever need anything give me a call." And as an afterthought, he handed an extra card to the little girl. "Would you like your very own card, Miss?" He smiled. "And have a great day."

He walked back by the Great Dane. The dog still chomped and foamed and fought the chain. Julius stepped up into his service truck, backed around. He glanced in his rearview mirror. The Great Dane stopped straining at the chain and now sniffed at the doggie treat before gobbling it up. A slight smirk crossed his face before he cruised out the driveway.

"Whew! That went better than I thought it would." After a haphazard course down a couple different roads, he took another drink of water and idled down the O'Brien's dirt road and coasted the van into its original spot nestled in the brush of the O'Brien's grove. When he opened the door, sounds of a hammer rang out from a busy carpenter working up around the house. He took his water bottle and slipped into the back of the truck. Using the water, he wiped off his Joe Smith disguise. He replaced the brown contacts and changed back into his blue jeans and a blue shirt. He cracked open the back door and listened. The hammering continued up at the house. He slid out. With a casual air, he stopped to snap a random picture along the dirt road, crossed the gravel road into the field opposite the O'Brien acreage, and followed the fence row to the Meecham property just north of the O'Brien field. He took more pictures of the Meecham field then turned back and retraced his path back to cross into Juan and Laura's trees and pasture.

He breathed a sigh of relief as he reached the cover of the trees. *It seemed like a lifetime since noon. A little more investigating out here, and I should be due at the house for supper.*

Chapter—21—

At dinner, Julius took the food as it passed, and filling his plate, he listened to the others chatter. "How's been your day, Ruth?" Michael asked.

"Mr. Marsh came home about two o'clock this morning while Lila and Joe were sitting with Gretchen. He slept until about one this afternoon. After that, he got up and talked to Gretchen—briefly then went to town. Ethel and I sat with Gretchen until Mr. Marsh came back from town. He came clattering back, sober, in good spirits, and their cupboards aren't bare anymore."

"That's great!" Michael took the slaw Ruth handed him.

"I'm glad it's the end of the day. Time to eat and relax," Mrs. MacDonald said as food was passed around the table. "Here, Julius, have some fruit salad. How was business at Juan's store, Michael?"

"Pretty lively for the first two hours—then slowed down. Pass the rolls, please?"

"It's good to be home." Ruth handed Michael the bread and butter. "The Marshes live close to the park, and the children are accustomed to playing at the park whenever they feel like it. Ethel and I weren't comfortable with that, so I went with Billie and Lollie to the park, and Ethel stayed at the house with Gretchen and the baby. Here, Julius, have some fresh broccoli?" Ruth passed the bowl.

"We all should be grateful, but we want to do it our way. Or..." the earlier conversation niggled at the back of Julius's mind a short time later, as he sat pondering in the shade of the maple tree. He cupped his head in his hands reflecting as the conversation played and replayed: *"We want to do what we want to do, regardless of the consequences to ourselves, or to others."* In the background, the trio sang, "I'll Fly Away. Oh, God." He groaned and rubbed his hands over his face. "I wish I could... I just wish I could." *"Everything should be democratic... Why do we think God needs our opinion?"*

The door closed as Michael came out. "So, what's up?" he asked.

"Just thinking."

"Mom says she sees things more clearly now than before she was blind." Michael sat at the picnic table and propped his foot against a chair.

"How'd it happen?" Julius asked.

"A year ago September, she and Lewis' boys were out horseback riding during the late summer. A pheasant flew up in front of her horse. The horse shied away from the bird. She had her left foot out of the stirrup. A rock in her boot, or something. When the horse shied, she slid off and hit her head. The doctors said it isn't permanent blindness, and she's certain her sight is coming back. So far the doctor says it's not measurable if it is." He shrugged. "She's accepted it better than I would've expected. Only occasionally does she kick at the goads. When Dad's home they ride the horses, and she still has her music."

"Are you ready to go, kiddo?" The screen door whooshed shut as Ruth stumped down the steps.

"Surely, girlie." Michael shed his serious tone of a moment before.

"Aw, Michael, you're a nut." She rolled her eyes at him.

"Thank you, for the compliment, my dear." He stood and turned to Julius. "Are you going to be around for a while this evening?"

"I intend to be."

"Not that she needs watching, but it never hurts to have someone handy."

"Yeah, I'll be here," Julius said. "Gotcha covered." He wandered back into the house as Michael and Ruth left.

"JULIUS C. ARMSTRONG, what are you doing?" Mrs. MacDonald demanded with a jump.

"I'm coming in to talk to you. What are you doing?"

"Just resting my eyes. That's what they call it, even when they're snoring at fifty decibels. My, you did give me a start though." She fanned herself with a paper. "Ruth just started me on this crochet pattern, but now I've messed up." She frowned and tried to straighten the yarn out. "I suppose Ruth and Michael have gone and you are left here to keep me company. You poor thing." She continued still fingering the yarn she could not see.

"Ruth and Michael are gone, but I'm not poor, thank you very much. Here, let me look at that pattern. I used to know something about such things." He took the pattern, and by holding the pattern in one hand, he looked over the yarn and the work that had been done. "No," he said. "You're still right. Here's the color you need." He took her hands and guiding them, re-established where she was in the pattern.

"I'm surprised at you, young man." The white-haired woman smiled.

"Why's that?"

"Most young men wouldn't own up to knowing anything about crocheting."

"Well, it isn't common knowledge at work, ma'am."

"Does your wife crochet?" she asked.

Julius sighed, his face twisted in anguish. "No, but she likes crafts."

"I'm surprised that you would remember then."

"Remember what?"

"How to crochet."

Julius' face puckered in a troubled frown.

"My friend," Mrs. MacDonald began with a slight hesitation on the word friend. Laying her crochet work down with care, she took his large, strong hand in both of her careworn ones. "God's purpose does not fall to the ground. He does not purpose in vain."

"How could you people have any place in my purpose?" Julius' voice wavered as he struggled for control. "There are things I can't tell you. I seem to have stumbled onto you folks. I wish—" He paused to swallow the goose egg lodged in his throat. "As God is my witness, I wish I could un-stumble. My business puts your lives at risk. Our earlier altercation may have to do with your previous run-ins. Or not...but I must finish my affairs here."

"What's wrong, my—Julius?"

"My whole life is one big risk. I've been running and running, and now? I don't know. I have no choice except to continue."

"Are you finished with your task?" Her face grew gray and pained.

"No."

"Would you leave your task unfinished?"

He bowed his head over their clasped hands and shut his eyes. "No," he whispered.

Running her fingers soft as silk over the top of his sinewy power-ful hand her voice almost a whisper. "When God opens a door you're supposed to walk through it. We've been in danger here — Ruth, her family, and friends continue to be tormented no matter what or where your affairs. If you were called here to us, there is a reason." She squeezed his hand then picked up her work where she left off.

"I DIDN'T WALK THROUGH the door. God picked me up and threw me." Julius sat down and watched his hostess crocheting: *a young man, a young woman, and an old blind woman. Against an unscrupulous, ruthless enemy? And Junco and Mai—what about them?*

She stopped crocheting at the end of the row. "God's judges have often been destitute, weaponless, and against impossible odds. I will pray for your family…and don't frown. It will give you bad wrinkles." Her hands continued where she left off.

"Are you sure you can't see?" His eyes narrowed and searched her face as his frown deepened.

"No, I don't see, with my eyes…"

"But the blind don't see with their eyes, they see with their heart." Ruth finished the sentence coming in followed by Michael.

"All's quiet on the Northern front." Michael stood beside his mother's chair.

"You have to be careful with her." Ruth smiled at Julius. "She reads minds and hearts easier than most people read books."

"Yeah." Michael grinned. "As a little boy I could hardly think of doing something naughty, but what she had me by the nap of the neck and headed for the woodshed."

"After the first few little books, it becomes easier and easier." Mrs. MacDonald dismissed their chatter with a nod and continued crocheting. "What's going on tomorrow, Michael?"

"Not much, Mum." His thoughts were somewhere else as his fingers ruffled through his hair mimicking his older brother. "I've got to be at the store most of the day. Anything you need from Hermon?"

"Donna, Ruth, and I will be going shopping sometime this week. I'm just sorting plans…"

"Well, I'm going for a drive." Julius stood up. "I don't expect to be gone long, just long enough to blow the cobwebs out. I'll see you all later." Julius headed for the breezeway.

He backed his car out of the garage and idled down the driveway, and cruised into Beetle River. *Pretty quiet. Nothing happening here—except a dog chasing a black and white cat across several yards, some young punks smoking cigarettes lounging on the steps to an old apartment building.* He turned the corner and had to touch his brakes to slow down to miss the same dog chasing the same cat across the street in front of him. All the businesses were closed now except the R&R Pub. He drove out south of town headed west. *Not even a dog chasing a cat out here.*

Julius spied an old blue pickup truck along the shoulder of the road, a jack propped up on one side. Some guy in faded blue jeans peered down at a flat tire.

Pulling up beside the man Julius called out the passenger side window, "Need some help?"

"Yeah, guess so."

As the fellow straightened, Julius noted a physically fit, tall, well-built man in his early fifties. Julius recognized him as the same fellow he had seen at Mom, and Pop's the other morning. The one who had spit on the step.

"My spare seems to 'uv went down too. I need to run up the road yonder to my place and get some more air in it." He motioned with his free hand. He took his hat off scratched his head and slapped the cap back on. "I'd 'preciate it if you'd give me a lift that far."

"I can do that. Throw your tire in back there. I'm in no hurry."

The man threw the tire in the trunk and came around and folded into the passenger seat. "Thanks," he said. "You're new around here aren't you?"

"Yeah, Julius C. Armstrong." He reached his hand across.

"Jack. Jack O'Brien." The older man nodded at the introduction and grasped his hand. "I don't know how come that tire went flat, but I don't figure how my spare's down also. Glad you came along. It's not far, but bumping a tire down a gravel road isn't great entertainment. I've heard about your book project. You find much for a story in Beetle River?"

"When my publisher sent me here, I thought, that guy's nuts. But as they say, every person has a story, and towns have theirs as well."

"I heard you're staying over at the MacDonalds?"

"That's me."

"Seem to be good folks... how do you know them?" Jack asked.

"Well, it's kind of a long story. Let's just say I got lost in the desert."

"I've done that before too." The laugh lines crinkled around Mr. O'Brien's eyes. "Say, just pull down the drive here and back up there beside the shop." He motioned to a large pole-frame building as they pulled into the drive. "I'll just run the hose from the compressor to the tire in the trunk, and we'll soon be on our way."

"THANKS FOR YOUR HELP, Mr. Armstrong," He said a few minutes later as they pulled back onto the road.

"Just call me Julius."

"Julius. It would've taken me a lot—well, I'll be!" Jack scowled. As they approached his pickup, a lone figure lounged against the driver side door like a hungry snake looking for its frog. "Look who's here. The devil himself. I sure 'preciate your help, but no sense you gettin' the wrong side a' the law. Might as well skedaddle." His scowl deepened as they pulled up beside his vehicle.

"You may need some more help. I'll stick around just in case." Julius switched off his engine and opened his door.

"Suit yourself. It's always welcome to have someone coverin' your back." Jack shot a quizzical glance over his shoulder as he climbed out.

From all that Julius had heard about Officer Philip Meecham, a person would think the man to be a ten-foot ogre. In Julius' estimation, he stood less than six-foot and appeared a trim good looking, dark-haired young man, even out of uniform.

Julius slid out, shut his door, and watched as Mr. O'Brien sauntered to the back of the car, hefted his tire out of the trunk, and rolled it over to where his pickup waited. He ignored the person leaning against his pickup door as he began to replace the tire.

"O'Brien," Meecham spoke in a cocky tone of voice. "O'Brien, why don't you get something better than this old rust bucket?"

"Same reason you don't get a brain." Jack drawled his reply without looking up. "I don't have a mind to."

Julius watched Meecham's jaw muscle twitch with anger.

"Who's your friend?" Meecham swallowed, ignoring the insult.

"You writin' a book?" Jack needled.

"No. Who's your friend, O'Brien?" He gritted his teeth.

"Ask him. He's got a tongue, Meecham." Jack spit like he had something unpleasant in his mouth. The spittle sent a small puff of dust onto Meecham's polished boot as it landed in the dust just at the tip.

Phil Meecham's eyes narrowed as he looked down his nose. "It's time you O'Briens stop living in the dark ages. You need to wake up to who's in control here." His eyes narrowed more, and he scrutinized Julius, who relaxed against the trunk of his car. "You. You're the fellow that took those pictures the other day." He smiled. "What's your name, mister?" He barked.

Julius stood up straight and all but saluted. "Julius Caesar, sir!" He bellowed in his best military fashion.

"One of these days, O'Brien, you're gonna push your luck too far! I don't know who you are mister—but I will find out. Count on it buddy!" He growled as he jerked the door open and flung himself into his pickup. The vehicle roared to life, the tires spun out and spewed gravel.

"That wasn't very nice a' him." Jack looked up at Julius, admiration in his voice. "Now you done it."

"Did it." Julius corrected O'Brien's grammar. "Now you did it,"

"Yeah, I guess I did it too, didn't I?" Mr. O'Brien gave the lug nuts the last turn, stood, and they both laughed.

Chapter—22—

Tuesday, June 16th; "So how'd your jog go this morning?" Mrs. MacDonald asked Julius after breakfast the next morning.

"Fine. In a couple of weeks though I'm going to have to hit the course. Not good to get lazy." He considered the chase from the day before.

"This is the day we're shopping in Hermon. Too bad you don't have business in Hermon about twelve o'clock this afternoon."

"If a person had business in Hermon, where exactly would he want to find himself at twelve noon?"

"Over on Orchard Street at a little restaurant called Tweedle Dum's. We reserve a table when we go shopping. It's quiet, and it's near Juan's store. Did you get your photos replaced?"

"Mostly. I'm off to the café for some local color now. What time are you leaving for town?"

"Ruth and I are just waiting for Donna to come to pick us up. Most stores don't open until nine." She sighed and frowned. "That makes it mid-afternoon before we get home."

"But a woman has to do what she has to do, right?" Ruth, adorned in a lacy pale green dress, rustled through the doorway.

"You look lovely this morning, Ruth." The older woman took a deep breath. "Is that a new fragrance you're wearing? It smells heavenly."

"She always tells me that I look nice. I could be in curlers and a robe—"

"Ruth doesn't wear curlers, and a robe doesn't rustle, and she does look lovely, doesn't she, Mr. Armstrong?"

Julius assessed the subject with narrowed eyes and tilted his head to one side. "As my daddy used to say, like frosting on a cake."

An involuntary gasp escaped from the older woman.

"What's wrong?" Ruth turned in alarm.

"Oh, nothing." Mrs. MacDonald said waving her away. "Just an ache and a pain we old folks get of a sudden."

"If Mr. Julius Caesar is going to get in on the local gossip he'd better get going," Ruth said.

"Hmm. Been talking to your dad?" He took note of her light-hearted tone. The sorrow in her eyes took a different note even as she smiled her answer.

THE CAR PUTTERED DOWN the driveway, and he turned toward town. His thoughts were of his girls—Junko and Mai, his Little Parrot. Would they love this place and these people? Things were so different from the hustle and noise of the city. He drew his thoughts back to the present with an effort as he pulled up and parked beside an old blue pickup—the same one he had helped with last evening.

Dishes rattled, cups clattered in their saucers, and Mom and Pop's bustled with activity. Several familiar voices called a greeting as Julius walked in. What a difference a week made. News traveled fast, and his reputation had gone before him. And as the scriptures said, had made a place at the table for him. He sat at his usual booth.

"There you go Mr. Julius C.," Becky said with a broad grin as she brought his usual coffee and placed it on the table in front of him.

Half an hour of chit chat and people began to drift off to their businesses.

"You're quite the hero." On her break, Becky brought her pop over and slid into the booth.

"Yeah?"

"Sure 'nuff. How'd you come up with that reply so quick? Julius Caesar—ha, ha!" She smirked and took a sip.

"That's my name."

"What?" Becky squawked and choked in surprise.

"Julius Caesar Armstrong. That's my handle."

"No way." Her mouth fell open. "Well, knock me over with a feather!" She laughed and slapped the table as he nodded his head. "No wonder it came so natural! How in the world did you get a name like that?"

"It's my daddy's fault. When he first saw my mom, he said 'I came, I saw, I conquered,' and she said, Julius Caesar?"

"Oh, go on!" She cried in exasperation. Picking up her glass, she swiveled out of the booth. "I can't believe a word of it!" She hee-hawed all the way back to the front of the café.

"I gotta be goin'," Jack said to the other two farmers sitting with him at the counter. He reached into his pocket. "Places to go, things to do, folks to…"

Becky interrupted, "Hey, guys, look."

Julius looked out the window as the shiny red pickup parked out front and David and Phil Meecham climbed out.

"Pop, I'm sure glad I don't own this business. Keep the change, Becky." Jack threw the money on the counter.

"Yeah, Jack," Pop rumbled from the kitchen. "I hear ya.'"

"Say, Mr. O'Brien—" Julius jumped to his feet and tossed his money on the table. "Let me go first."

"Sure, you go first—Julius." Jack guffawed and slapped him on the back.

Chapter—23—

A half an hour back at his room, Julius pulled pictures and identities off his computer and put them on his detective board. Some were from yesterday's picking up hay. He still had some unidentified characters, but they were coming together. Time to head out for lunch—he backed out of the garage and turned toward Hermon and Tweedle Dum's. He pulled into the corner parking space under one of the shade trees. He rolled down his window and the fresh morning air assailed his nose. Mentally he ticked off some items on his to do list; he had rented a post office box, his base was operational, and his team was in place. Still no word from Junco. He fidgeted. Yet, as Mrs. MacDonald said, he couldn't walk off his post here. He looked through more of the pictures he had received from headquarters. This last batch of pictures had a photo of Gunman identified as Frank Wilde. Lighterman was known as Gary Young, both from Chicago. They seemed to be in the pay of Meister and Clarke. He drummed his fingers on the car door, mulling the information over in his mind. Juan began receiving threats about the same time Meister, a known extortioner had disappeared. Meister, Wilde and Young had to be connected in this.

Julius grabbed the copy of yesterday's local newspaper from his passenger seat and thumbed through several pages. Then he went back to read individual articles. Nothing of note on the front page. Some foreign ambassadors visiting local farms, touring factories. A write up about the effects of the earthquake last week—Not much on the second page either. A small article on the third page caught his eye: Washington, D.C. Body found on sidewalk. Pennsylvania Avenue N.W., Special Agent Davison Shields, fighting for her life, beaten during an apparent attempted robbery...with shaking hands, Julius turned to the personal ads. He scanned the notices. Nothing here, just regular entries, except, wait . . . God help us. He sat stunned unable to move.

Like water trickling through a hole in the dam, thought slowly seeped back. Julius saw a dark green Taurus pull into the parking lot. Ah, finally, here they are. Donna parked on the other side of the lot, and the three ladies and two of Lewis's boys clambered out and ambled into the entrance.

Later, I'll deal with this later. Julius checked his Beretta and slid it into his holster. He buttoned his sports jacket and slipped out of his car as Michael drove up in a Lincoln Mark VII.

Julius leaned against the corner of the building until Michael joined him. "You clean up pretty good."

"It's a job requirement." Michael held the door for Julius. "You got roped into lunch too?"

"It's a job requirement. That's a pretty slick looking car."

"Yeah, it's Juan's company car. I only drive it when I'm working at the store. Under duress."

"Why's that?" Julius picked up a copy of the daily paper from the newsrack, his mind and actions were on autopilot as they waited to be seated.

"Anyone who looks like they have something is a target to some unmentionable parties. People related to Ruth, or friends of the O'Brien family are in double jeopardy."

Julius solemnly nodded his understanding, but his mind wanted to read the article about Shields, and any other article relating to it. He dare not read it until he was alone, but turning it off and focusing elsewhere was difficult.

At some point I'll probably need to trust Michael with some information. Julius looked at Michael. "You going to be at the store all afternoon?"

"Until 5:00."

"I have some errands to finish here in town after lunch, but I'll stop in before going home," Julius said as the hostess approached.

Michael turned to the hostess, "We're part of the MacDonald reservation." Then he turned back to Julius. "I'll be there."

JULIUS WAITED IN A secluded spot on the hill above a shelter house at the park. He glanced at his watch. Late, his contact was late. The newspaper lay within reaching distance. Not now. He pushed the temptation away as a police cruiser glided through the park. He glanced at his watch again. Late by a few minutes could be excused, but ten minutes was beyond his limit. He put the car in motion and headed toward the store. Two streets from the park he glanced in his rear view mirror. Every turn he made a young blonde woman in the white Ford followed. Hmm. Not here, not now. This is supposed to be an easy case. Okay, okay! Why would this one be any easier than any other? He whipped into the car wash. The front door began to open as a car exited from the rear. He followed under the front door with barely enough room and scooted out the back door as the front door closed leaving the white Ford on the other side. He would be long gone before they realized what happened. He pulled into the alley at an auto repair shop and parked among several vehicles and slipped across the alley and into the back door to Juan's store.

"LISTEN, MR. GONZALES won't be back for another three weeks. If you need to speak to him, it'll have to wait." Michael's voice was impatient.

Julius's ears perked up, and he finagled around for a better view of the situation. *Two men. I could take care of them, but... I can't blow my cover. Unless it's an absolute necessity...* he strained to hear.

"No, sir, I'm not authorized to pay you anything, and I will not," Michael said.

"We can make it very uncomfortable for you," The big guy said in a smooth voice.

"Let me make myself very clear. This is not my store. I am not authorized to pay you or anyone else any amount of money. And I'm not going to pay you. If you don't get out of this store now, I will call the police. Do I make myself clear?" Michael had sat on the edge of a desk, but now he stood to his full height, towering above both of the men.

"Accidents happen, you know. You have a nice store here. A nice car—a pretty face, we could change that for you," the big man did all of the talking in an intimidating voice.

"You have a really big mouth, and I could take care of that for you," Michael said.

"Marty," the other guy spoke at last. "We'll come back like he suggested."

"Okay, Harry." With a long look at Michael, he finished the conversation. "Pass on the message to your boss, little man." They turned and walked out the front door.

Julius slipped to the window in time to write down a plate number, then returned to where Michael stood phone in hand, dialing. "Just a minute," Julius said and disconnected the call.

Michael turned, his blue eyes blazing, and pulled back his fist. "Don't tell me..."

Julius threw up a hand. "I said, just a minute." He punched some numbers into his own Arpa phone, and spoke into it. "Plate number, 4590JS, tan Chevy Impala," he said. "Just pulled out from Imports Magnifique, heading north. Two men, both in sports coats and fedora hats. Pick them up. I need a fingerprint expert here at the Imports store now. Use the back door. Out." He turned to Michael, "Go lock that front door and change the sign. No one uses it until we fingerprint it. And don't you touch anything those two may have touched."

"YOU'LL HAVE TO PRETEND you didn't see any of this, Michael."

"Sorry, I almost punched you…" Michael looked stunned and relieved.

"A temper isn't a good thing. It makes a person too apt to do something foolish. Now, you might begin by telling me anything you know." They had moved to the darkened office by the back door, and were watching as several officers went about gathering info in the front store.

"These fellows aren't local. They showed up maybe two months ago and started harassing Juan," Michael said. "This doesn't seem to be connected to Meecham's business."

"You need to be careful. These folks make David and Phil Meecham look like nice guys. I catch a flight out tomorrow morning. I'll be back Friday afternoon. Don't take any chances. Here's my number. Can you memorize it?"

Michael looked at the number and laughed. "Yeah, I can do that. That's funny."

"My boss has a sense of humor." Julius hesitated at the back door. "I'm on my way back to the house. If you need me, you've got my number."

"Got it, double-oh-seven." Michael snorted as the alley door shut behind Julius.

LATER IN HIS ROOM, Julius pulled out the newspaper and scanned through the personal ads. Nothing here. Which page was that? He turned the page. Halfway down the middle column, he stopped. *Songbird and sparrow, three more days...* He memorized the rest of the information.

After supper, Julius sat in an outside chair and leaned against the maple tree. Neither he nor Michael had told the ladies about the incident at the store, although he had told Michael about the shooting incident the day before. While the piano music drifted from the house; some of Schumann, Liszt, Chopin, Beethoven, Mozart, and lesser-known artists, the darkness crept in and settled around him. Ingratitude—the words from Mrs. MacDonald weighed heavy upon his heart and mind. Julius closed his eyes, breathing deep of the fragrance from the multitude of trees in the orchard. Most orchards had some similarities, some things in common. Yet this flatland orchard was missing so many things. Julius' heart ached. The bittersweet memories flowed over and around him, even as he recognized that the orchard was different, and the boy that he had once been would never be the same.

Julius's ears picked up the hint of a car motor, a soft shushed car door somewhere close. He heard scuffling coming along the driveway and drawing near. His nerves tightened. He slid his hand under his vest. A shadow, unaware of Julius, lurched ever so slightly and fumbled for the chair by the table. Julius relaxed. Whoever it was did not pose a threat. After an exceptionally stunning piece of music, Julius broke the silence. "Maybe they should charge admission."

The shadow jumped, startled. "What? Where are you?" He stammered and looked for the speaker.

Julius recognized the voice. "Where have you been, Kid, and why are you here now?"

Still unsure of the speaker's location, the shadow's shaky voice answered, "My life's messed up." After a slight pause, he continued. "I don't even know where I am. What about you?"

"I know where you are, and I'm here on business. What's up in your life besides being messed up?" In the darkness both forms blended into the tree.

"I'm about as far down as a man can get. My wife left me. No money, no food, I've smoked my last cigarette..." His words trailed off.

"Man, I'd say! You reek, Kid!" Julius wrinkled his face at the stench. "You had enough money for booze didn't you?"

"At some time I did. I don't know what day it is, or-or how I got here."

"I could use some close back up with this job, but..." Julius thought about his discovery about Davison. "No, I should just send you on home. This isn't pretty here, and you're not in any shape for that." Julius' heart turned to lead. How had this happened? How had a person so full of life and hope become a wretched drunk? "I can't risk it. I wish I could trust you—"

"I wish —I wish I could be— but things have become my master that I didn't see coming. I can only promise to do my best," the shadow said.

Julius heard the snuffle and what he guessed to be a movement of wiping his nose. A war raged within him. Lives depend on this going right. Dare I risk it? Stake success on a drunk trying to dry out? Two voices fought, pulling him in different directions. *I can't fail. I've never failed.* And the other voice, *I can't leave him behind. We don't leave our wounded behind.*

"To do their best is all we can ask of anyone." Julius looked around. Had someone else spoken? Only he and I here— and that sounded like me talking.

"Wait, I'll be back." The dim light from the back of the house swallowed Julius up as he disappeared through the door. The light winked briefly as he returned. "Here." He thrust a plate of reheated leftovers, a spoon, and paper napkin at his companion.

"Thanks, man."

The spoon scraped against the plate, and the man wiped his face and hands with the paper napkin.

"That's the first *real food*, I've had in so long I can't even remember."

"You can shower and clean up in my room, catch some sleep. In the morning I'll find you a different place to stay."

As they came to the foot of the stairs to Julius' room, the music ended. Julius could hear the faint sound of crying. With a grim look of determination, he climbed the steps.

WEDNESDAY, JUNE 17th; Julius waited until after the Bible reading and prayer the next morning. "I told Michael yesterday I'll be gone for a few days. And I must apologize to you, Ma'am. Last night I found it necessary to offer your hospitality to an acquaintance. I am hopeful that if I ask you to trust me in this, and forgive my inability to bring this acquaintance to you at this time, you will do so."

Mrs. MacDonald frowned and tapped her spoon on her cup. "I assume you didn't have to let on. We wouldn't be any the wiser?"

"You assume correctly. We are leaving this morning. I will add some extra money for his night's stay if that's a problem. I won't be back until Saturday."

Michael frowned, but neither he nor Ruth spoke.

"You are taking this person with you, then? He won't be coming back here?"

"I am taking this person with me, and no, he won't be coming back here—without your knowledge."

Mrs. MacDonald's eyes appeared to focus on her coffee cup as if looking for guidance. "The money's no problem. We'll see you Saturday."

"Thank you, Ma'am." He hadn't realized that he held his breath.

"I WILL LEAVE THIS CAR with you. I have an account at that store."

"Humpf," his companion mumbled around a sausage and biscuit. "This is good, but I can't finish it, just the coffee." He picked up the cup and warmed his hands.

"Let's get you a motel room, and we'll pick you up something to wear. I'll try to help you get your bearings before I call a cab and make tracks for my flight. Now, remember, the name's 'Julius C. Armstrong' as in 'Julius Caesar.' Got it? There are a few simple jobs on the list I gave you."

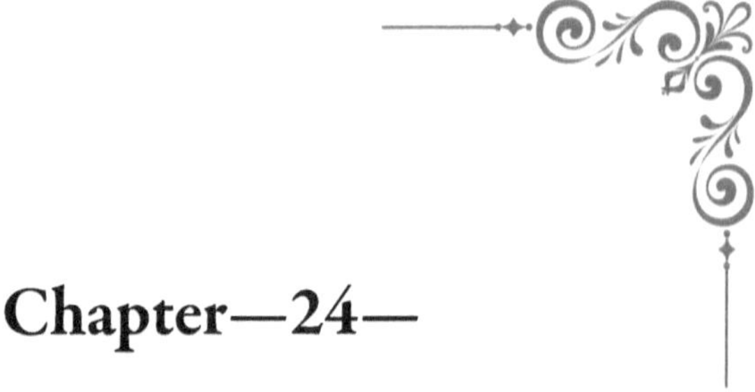

Chapter—24—

Julius settled into his seat on the small courier plane and slid the small suit-case and a satchel into the back with the items the courier was delivering, but his computer-case he left on his lap. "With a wing and a prayer," he sighed.

"Sir, it won't take a long time to get to our destination," the young pilot said.

"Just glad you're going my way," Julius said.

"No problem. It was just me and Bertha here. I've got another route that'll bring me back on Saturday morning. Just meet me back at the hangar."

"That'll be good," Julius shouted back over the engine noise. "I'll see you early Saturday morning."

At the small airport Julius made a short stop at the restroom in order to make a few changes to his clothes and disguise, leaving Julius behind for a while. A plain unmarked car was waiting for him.

Julius sat in the back seat next to a familiar face. "Hello, Bob. Thanks for setting this up for me,"

Bob frowned and shook his head. "This is a break from protocol. If things go bad—we've already lost Snowman, we can't afford to lose you on this case."

"But you haven't been able to find Junko and Mai? How's Shields doing?"

"She'll make it—but it was pretty close. But this smells of a trap, Armstrong. I don't like it. You should let us handle it. There is one more option where Shields could have hidden them…"

"I have to do what I have to do. Those people won't fall for anything less than the real McCoy."

"I hear ya, but your back-up is pretty shaky in this town. Since the main operation is in the mid-west it's shaky and thin here."

"It'll be alright. I've never failed you in the past. I'll be at Clarke and Holiday's first thing in the morning," Julius collected his few items and got out of the car. "Thanks for the ride."

He walked into the cheap hotel stopped at the desk and picked up his key. Once in his room, Julius threw himself into the battered overstuffed chair, set up his computer and ran the information. Half an hour later he opened his door a crack. No sound in the hall, he opened the door and peered out. *Empty.* He shuffled from his room looking like a grungy street bum. He pulled a formless stained hat onto his unkempt hair and took the stairs down to the service entry. He slid out the door and into the alley.

He looked carefully as he ambled out and onto the street. After two blocks he stopped to rummage in his baggy coat pockets and leaned against the building under the awning of the corner business. With an idle glance, Julius looked up and down the street in both directions.

The door to the business opened. "Get out of here. We don't want no panhandlers beggin' for money here!" The man growled and shook his fist.

"I ain't no panhandler, I'm lookin' for a job."

"A job? Who's going to hire a dirtbag like you? Get out of here!" The man gave Julius a shove.

"Don't touch the merchandise, man!" He brushed imaginary dust off his rumpled jacket as he and his feet got in the same step. He continued two blocks until he reached Joe's Diner.

The bell on the door tinkled, and he shuffled over to a table. He glanced at a middle-aged man in a business suit sitting with his back to the wall at the table next to the window.

Julius dropped into a chair his back to the wall, at a table next to the businessman who was peering at the morning paper. A college-aged black woman was sitting at the counter reading a textbook. The bell tinkled again as a young twenty-something man entered and sat at the counter. "Coffee and a ham sandwich," the young man said.

The waitress brought the man at the counter his order then came around to Julius. "Can I help you," she said.

Julius grungy fingers pushed some quarters into a pile, "Coffee and a roll, ma'am," he said.

He watched the waitress walk behind the counter for his order. *Couldn't be over 25, but life has dealt her a tough hand looking at the worry lines on her face. Choices. How many times do the choices we make turn our lives into joy, or misery? And then we blame it on others.* "Thanks." He reached for the coffee she placed in front of him. "Cream and sugar'll be fine." He shoveled sugar into his cup, and stirred, careful not to spill.

"I'm looking for someone to help with a job," the man in the business suit held the paper toward the waitress. "If you know any-one looking for work, here's the address. It pays well." He slid his chair back.

"I'll pass the word, sir," she said. "This address here?" She pointed to the paper.

"I've circled it right there," he said following to the register. "Keep the change." He picked up his ticket. The door tinkled behind him as he left.

"I need a coffee to go," the man at the counter fished for money in his pocket. "And do you have a bag for my sandwich? I got to get to work," he said with a quick glance at his watch.

The waitress left the paper on the counter and busied herself at the register as both the young man and student left.

"Miss, what kind of job's he got there?" Julius asked when she brought a refill.

"Mister, if I was you, I'd steer clear of that man." The waitress whispered.

Julius and the waitress glanced out the big plate glass window. The businessman loitered outside speaking briefly to a street punk.

"Everyone he deals with ends up iced." She rolled her big brown eyes. "Mighty suspicious. If you ask me." She handed him the paper.

"I'd sure like to have some money. I just got back into town."

"Don't believe I've seen you around before. I know all the regulars."

"I like warmer weather I go south in the fall and winter—then my sister took sick. Went to help her for a few weeks. Don't remember seeing you before either." He rubbed a hand over his chin.

LOCAL GOSSIP AND LOCAL restaurants go together like ham and beans. Julius stuffed the newspaper into an inside pocket on the right side of his baggy coat before he lumbered out the door of the diner to head back to his hotel.

A few blocks down a punk leaned against a building next to an alleyway entrance. "You got a cigarette, man?" the punk said.

"Minute." Julius stopped shuffling and fumbled in his coat sleeve. Through veiled eyes, he scanned his surroundings. The punk had vacant unfocused eyes, but Julius sensed danger. The reflections in the business window showed two men coming from behind, and one coming from the side. The waitress's warning ran through his mind. There was no time to dwell on it. "Sorry." He turned, and sidestepped between two parked cars and had just enough time to shuffle into the street and beyond the car rolling toward him. The driver laid on the horn and shouted unrepeatable greetings out the window, missing him by a narrow inch. The other vehicle coming from the opposite direction repeated the first driver's actions and similar words. It was enough time and distraction. He crossed the street and disappeared into the deli. *They would be coming.*

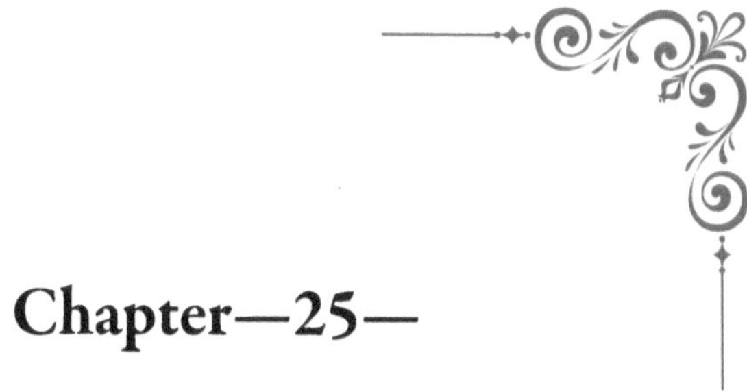

Chapter—25—

Julius ducked his head and pulled off the non-descript hat as he pushed open the deli door. At the same time, he pulled the rumpled coat off, turned it inside out, and draped it over his arm all in one smooth movement. He buttoned the dark blue vest into place, pulled a collar out from around the neckline, and dusted the leather shoes by wiping them on the back of his pant legs. Within seconds his appearance had changed. Anyone looking for an older grungy street bum would not find it in him.

The deli, a cozy, bright establishment contained a small seating area with fifteen tables on the right hand, a counter with two cooks preparing selections on the other side. A deli case on the left containing a number of mouth-watering choices beckoned.

"Can I help you?" One of the two servers looked up as she restocked the sugar, salt and pepper containers and approached from his left.

"I'm looking for the men's room." He stood straight and tall.

"Certainly. Back down that way and to your left." She motioned toward the back of the building.

"Thank you." He nodded and strode back to the men's room where she had indicated. He heard the front door open as he shut the bathroom door behind him.

Julius combed his hair, scrubbed the dirt off his hands, placed his brown contacts in their holder in his pocket. They wouldn't be looking for blue eyes. Brushed his black hair back neat and spruced up his attire. He looked in the mirror as a once over, stood up as tall as possible. Footsteps approached the lavatory door, someone knocked.

"Just a moment." He opened the door. "Pardon me." He walked past two of his pursuers who waited impatiently on the other side of the door. With intense scrutiny, they looked him up and down then beyond him into the restroom. Without looking back, he walked to the counter and stood in line.

"Nice day out." He spoke in a polite manner to the chunky bald headed man in front of him.

"Yes, it is." The man nodded at the cook who handed him a corned-beef on rye sandwich and onion rings. "Thank you."

"I'll take a croissant, and some ham and cream cheese—and those onion rings look good. I'd like some of those as well." Julius spoke to the cook, keeping track of the two hooligans out of the corner of his eye. "Are you in town for the convention?" He asked the man as they waited for the rest of their food.

"No, I work two blocks north of here in real-estate. You're here for the convention?" The man asked.

Julius watched the two ruffians scan the deli for the street bum. Their eyes flickered over several couples sitting at the tables, and the few people standing in line along with himself at the counter, but no street bum. The taller of the men leaned over and whispered something to his companion. The other man shrugged, they looked one more time then turned and left.

The bald man took his selections down to the cashier. Julius bent over as if to pick up something off of the floor. He pulled a ten dollar bill out of a pocket inside of his shoe, slid his tray down to the cashier and handed him the ten, and the cashier returned the two quarters. "Thank you." He pocketed his change.

Julius sat down at a table across from his new acquaintance. "So, you're in real estate, then?" He asked after a brief pause. He took a bite of his croissant and let the guy talk. With just a few questions here and now he kept the man talking about his job and golfing for thirty minutes. Julius gauged his meal down to his last onion ring. He glanced at the clock on the wall.

"Oh, hey, it's been interesting to talk to you, but I need to get going. Hope all goes well with your ventures."

"Good talking to you. I need to get back to work too. Here's my card if you're ever looking in the area."

Julius waited at the light, and then went two blocks off course, caught a taxi. He slid into the back seat. "I need to kill some time. I've got an appointment in ten minutes at this address, but I don't want to look too eager. You know what I mean?" Julius handed the driver a card with his hotel address written on it.

"Sure, mister, I can do that." The driver eased into traffic and drove a few blocks around the area.

As the driver wove through traffic Julius kept a watch out for a tail. It looked all clear, no one followed him. At just the right minute, the cab pulled up in front of the hotel.

"Thanks, and keep the change." Julius handed the man his fare and climbed out. Walking into the hotel, he nodded to the guy at the desk and proceeded on to the elevator. He punched the button and waited, looked at the clock behind the counter and punched the button a second time. At last, he heard it chugging to a stop, and the door jerked open. He stepped in and held the door for a gray-haired gentleman.

"Thanks." The man nodded at him and sauntered into the elevator. "Third floor please."

"Man, this thing is slow. I've seen a dead skunk move faster than this." Julius reached over and punched number three.

The aged man snorted his agreement as the elevator chugged up to the second floor. With a few shaky jerks, the door opened. Julius stepped out into the hall. The elevator sighed and the door shut behind him. With a quick look at his surroundings, he could hear loud voices in a room close to his, but he saw no one. The floor creaked with each footfall. Julius unlocked his door and flipped on the light. A quick once over and he ducked into the room. A search showed everything as he had left it.

Newspaper. Where's that newspaper? He rummaged through his jacket pocket. Taking a clean sheet of writing paper, he began systematically pulling the code out of the ad. Songbird and chick in cage. If you want to see them alive meet at... *Hmpf! Well...* He copied the address out.

"I'll need a cab in about half an hour—yes, yes, at the Listering Hotel. Thank you." He hung up the phone. *Now for a quick shower, and I'm off again. I've been gone from this work too long—and not long enough.* With a sigh, he turned on the water and worked some of the shampoo into his black hair. When he emerged from the shower, he left the disguise behind. The black hair and dark brown skin had disappeared. Soon a tanned athletic man with light brown hair and mustache stood in his place. He looked in the mirror as he pushed the last button through the button hole on his light blue shirt, straightened the belt on his tan trousers, and topped it all with a sports coat. He slipped his Berretta nine millimeter in his shoulder holster and buttoned his jacket. He picked up his few carry items. From habit, he checked the hall before slipping out his door. As his door shut, two men emerged from three doors to the left of his. Their voices were raised as they continued to argue. He watched them in the chrome fixtures on the lights as they waved their hands in exuberant conversation, following him until they got to the stairs.

He could hear them as they walked down the stairs. Their wrangling grated on Julius' nerves. He had a sense of unrest. He scrutinized the rundown hallway with wary eyes. A shabby green and gold-flecked carpet covered the floor. Hall lights, most of which gave out a feeble glow underscored the need for new wall paneling in several areas. Julius reached the elevator, and with a slight turn he positioned himself sideways watching doors. He leaned forward and punched the elevator button. The elevator labored to rise as his gaze zeroed in on room number 217. A quick maneuver and he sprinted like a gazelle back toward the stairwell. A muffled shot thudded into the wall panel where he had been standing, and another whizzed into the wall behind the stairs. He leaped down several stairs to the landing. He heard steps pounding down the hall, as he turned to the second set of steps. One of the arguing men showed through the window on the door at the bottom of the stairs in the first story hallway, but now he was quiet. Was the guy alone? Julius would soon know. Down the next set of stairs he flew and jerked the door open.

"Hey!" the man stepped in front of him.

"Sorry, fellas. No time for chit chat." Julius kneed him and pushed him into his accomplice. They both landed in front of the landing door.

Another room door opened as he rushed toward the outside door. *Goodnight, who keeps these guys coming?*

A woman started out the door, but he pushed her back in and kept going. Whoever was behind him could start shooting. No reason an innocent —or otherwise—person should get shot. He hit the outside door and flew around the side of the building.

Slowing to a casual saunter at the front of the hotel, he slid into the waiting cab.

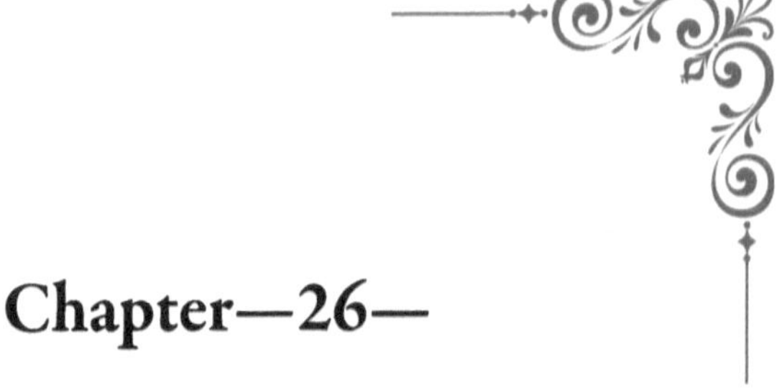

Chapter—26—

"Here's the address," Julius handed the paper with the address to the driver and bent down as if looking for something by his feet. The taxi driver pulled smoothly into traffic. If he noticed the men standing in front of the hotel looking up and down the sidewalk, he never missed a beat. Julius straightened up and caught his breath. "I'll need you to wait. It shouldn't take me long."

The driver watched the traffic around him. "You're not from around here I take it?"

"That's right." Julius shook his head.

"There's no sense me waitin' at that address. People that go there never come out again. Just so you know."

"Thanks for the word. I've got no choice. Tell you what, here's your fare. How about you wait twenty minutes? If I'm not back, take this message." Julius stopped talking. Scribbling a message on a sheet of paper, he slid it into an envelope, sealed and addressed it. "and my belongings to the Drake. Leave them at the front desk."

"Everybody's got a choice, Mr...You'd trust a cabbie?" The man slid the note into an inside pocket in his jacket. "What's to keep me from selling your stuff to the folks in that building you're going to? They'd pay well, I'll bet."

"That's probably right, but I'm a better bet than they are. You're just as likely to get a ticket nowhere on their route."

"I'll wait fifteen minutes. Across the street by the Snack Shop on the corner." After finagling through traffic, the driver pulled up on a side street by an old brick building in a poor section of town. He reached over and hit his timer.

"Fifteen minutes." Julius slid out and disappeared into the alley. He pressed his body against the brick wall and looked toward the other end. Nothing, no movement, no sound either inside or outside the building, just ominous silence hung in the air. There was an old set of fire escape stairs, and a couple of windows open just a crack. Julius moved along the wall to the door, and with a light, careful touch tried the latch. *Are those windows open to tempt me to enter there, or deter me from going in there? I'm not overthinking this one.* He slipped the pick in the lock and opened the door.

The metal door closed behind him with a click as if locking from some unknown source. He stood in the darkness, pressed against the inside wall, his heart thudding against his ribs, his breathing shallow. He perused the large darkened room that at one time had been a clothing business. There were a few sewing machines along the far wall in front of an office with glass windows. Across the room, there were a few cubbyholes tucked under metal stairs to the second story.

With a slow movement he reached down with his right hand. Picking up the dilapidated wooden chair he skidded it across the floor. A spotlight beamed on and highlighted the chair in the middle of the room.

"Congratulations, I'm glad you made it, Agent Chameleon. We've been waiting a long time," a smooth deep voice spoke from somewhere up above. The light began to circulate around the room. "You might as well come out. We will find you, and there is no way out—as the taxi driver told you. No one ever comes out of here alive."

Julius took a deep breath, and his heart rate evened out. He'd been through this before, the question was could he do it again? *Breathing, just focus on breathing. Don't close my eyes.*

"We have your possessions, your case. All we need are your passwords and your codes. If you give us those we'll kill you quickly, otherwise...it will be messy." The light continued to play around the room. Several times it came close to the edges of his shoes, but he remained motionless and in the shadows.

"We are patient, but you can't remain immobile forever."

Julius heard a scrabbling sound come from the area of one of the cubbyhole rooms. He knew that sound. He hated rats with more than a passion. They were merciless, wily rodents and ugly beasts. He could hear them, more than one, beginning from the room they came with scurrying feet. He watched as a shadow moved across the floor toward him. *Just a matter of time. And the light continues to circulate. So, where to go from here?*

Continuing to scan the room, his eyes the only things that moved, he measured the distance between his position and the stairs. He felt a movement across his foot. Another object stopped at his feet. He could see it rise up on its hind feet as if to climb up and investigate. *Not today, Buster.* With a very slight movement of his toe, he encouraged the varmint to move along. The mass of bodies had thinned out as they continued to surge toward the other end of the room. One larger body began snarling and pushing. After a particularly vicious attack that left one of the rats gurgling out its last breath, the beast turned its attention to Julius.

Julius, waiting his muscles tense, as the snarling rodent neared his spot. At the right distance, he cocked his leg and sent the angry animal sailing in the opposite direction of the stairs. It landed with a solid thump semi-senseless, the light focusing on it. At the same moment Julius leaped to the end of the pack, and in a mad dash, threw himself over the stair railing and several feet up the stairs. Silent as possible he finished the rest of the steps and found himself at the open door to the room with the open windows he had observed from the alley. Julius stepped into the room.

"You made it," the voice said. "As I said before, we can do this with or without mess. They got a bit too rough with Shields. I have a new assistant. He's just learning the ropes."

The creepy voice made Julius sick. The laugh had a hollow sound that sent shivers up and down his back. There was just a mask. *Probably just to give an eerie effect. An unnerving ploy.* The figure was tallish and well dressed. Someone stood in the background. *Waiting for his cue, I suppose.* Julius's eyes narrowed.

"We've heard about you—you've dodged my best agents." The voice stopped, he inspected Julius from head to foot. "Don't look like much on the outside...Got just enough from Agent Shields to know about Songbird and chick." Again he cackled. "Too bad for you," he repeated. "Now if you'll just give me the passwords and codes. We'll skip to the end."

"What if I don't have passwords and codes? What if I'm just a carrier? What if the titles, Songbird, and chick, don't mean anything to me?"

"Don't be coy. Modesty doesn't suit the occasion. You'll be songbird by the time we're finished." He twitched his head toward Julius, and the man from the background came forward.

Julius relaxed his muscles. Watching as the man, with a cocky, confident smile came at him. A large muscular man, dark hair, narrow eyes, he moved easy on his feet. *Probably done some boxing,* Julius analyzed. *There's more than one move in this dance.*

"Aren't you Al from down at the club?" Julius said.

"You stupid— I don't know you from nowhere." The guy paused for a second.

The question, used as a momentary distraction, gave Julius the time for his move. He whirled and struck the man with a body slam that sent the much bigger man flying backward through the window, to the pavement below. Julius began to turn back when a pinprick caught him just above the collar, and his world became fuzzy.

"You didn't think it'd be that easy, did you?" The creepy voice barely whispered, and the eerie laugh echoed.

"THE FEAR OF JEHOVAH is the beginning of knowledge, But the foolish despise wisdom..." Julius heard his voice reciting. Memories sifted into his mind in the gathering darkness. He struggled to move his left arm. He lay on a hard surface. No matter what he tried, his body either would not or could not respond. His eyes were the only thing that would move. He looked at his surroundings as best he could. *Same building and same room.* He strained to hear or feel the presence or breathing of someone else. This is one nightmare I wish I could wake from. I wish it were a dream. *One thing I ask, oh, God, don't let me betray anyone.*

Torture had always been something he had done to himself. After being shot he'd drug himself over rough, barren wilderness. Or when the ledge he stood on gave way. After falling farther than he wanted to remember, he and his fellow platoon member crawled through enemy territory farther than he wanted to remember. Today torture took on a new meaning. A tingling began in his fingers and toes...

"Now we'll get on with your information, Agent."

A slow warmth ebbed into his body. He could not tell if the Creep, as he began to think of the person, had just come in, or if he'd been there all along.

"If you'll just co-operate, we'll be on our way. Otherwise, we do have ways of helping you remember."

"I don't even get a last meal? That's not a sporting affair."

"It's a stupid practice. To waste food on someone whose next stop is death."

"I'm not hungry anyway. But shouldn't I be able to face my accuser?"

"Stop stalling. Password first, then code!"

"I need to sit up...get some circulation back in my brain," Julius said.

"Don't get comfortable," the voice said, and pressure holding him in place released him.

"Pencil and paper. I'll write you the password." He flexed his left hand.

"What do you take me for? a fool?" the voice spat out. "The password without the code is useless."

"First things first. My computer is set up for me. No one else in the world can operate it."

"You're stalling."

"Believe what you want. Take me out, and you'll never get what's in that machine."

"It's true, boss." a different voice spoke from the shadows. "As far as I can tell. This computer won't respond to my entries."

The Creep glowered at Julius but handed him a pencil and paper. "Don't cross me. I might just change my mind about making it quick."

Julius wrote down a password and handed it to the Creep, who gave it to the guy with the computer.

"It's up, boss, but this is gonna take a while at this rate."

The Creep looked at his watch. "I'll be back. I've got other things to attend to. Get those codes." He scowled. "I'll send Red in." Turning at the door, and with a jerk of his head, he indicated Julius. "You two watch him. He's dangerous."

The feeling had returned, but the lack of co-ordination still lingered. Julius continued to flex his muscles and stimulate blood flow.

"I need those codes," the man with his computer case glanced at him.

"I have to put those in myself..."

"Not possible. You gotta stay there," the technician continued watching the screen. "Just give them to me."

"Chan eil aon chànan gu leòr."

"What...what language is that?" Technician man stared, his mouth hanging open.

"It's... I told you I'd need to put them in," Julius said.

"What do we have here?" A short, ginger-haired man scowled down at Julius.

"This guy's pulling a fast one—or trying to," the man with Julius's case stared hard at Julius.

"We don't have time for stupid," the second man said. "Ell is gone. Just you and me. We can get rid of him. Tell the boss he didn't make it."

"You did that with the last guy. It won't fly this time. This one's too important."

"We'll just pick it out of him then." Red grinned and held up a pocket knife.

"It's simple. My case will only respond to me. If I can't leave this spot, bring it here," Julius said.

"It's a trap," the man named Red said. "Aren't you one of those computer geeks that can do anything? Just do it."

"I've never seen this before. He says this case is person sensitive, and it'll only respond to him— it'll only work for him."

"Then give it to him, you idiot."

Julius watched as Red's hair and complexion became the same color. He had them in a tight spot. *It was a good idea when we set it up, but...*

"I don't have a choice." The technician stood. He dawdled between the two choices. "I don't know. The boss—" Against his better judgment he set the case where Julius could work it.

Julius, his left hand running swiftly over the board worked his charm.

"What are you doing?" the Creep's voice entered the doorway.

"It's person sensitive, Boss. Only he can..."

"It's a trick!"

"No. Look." A look of relief spread across the tech's face.

"Very few people choose their own death." Julius handed the case back to the technician.

"What?" The relief was replaced by horror.

"You didn't think it'd be that easy, did you?" Julius' eyes narrowed, his world slowed.

"HIRAM?"

"Yes, Lord?"

"The Lad's in trouble."

"How do the forces of darkness always seem to find him, Lord?"

"He needs an Ebenezer."

"Aye, Lord. Grace—and a stone of help."

JULIUS WATCHED AS TIME slowed around him. He could see the tech staring at the case as files flipped across the screen. Red stood with his mouth open but made no sound. The Creep/Boss also stood rooted in one spot. His voice in slow motion, one long drawn out word—"No!"

Julius could see himself sitting on a chair; he could feel a sense of finality. Then he heard a voice echoing around him.

"Laddie, Laddie..."

Where have I heard that voice before?

"I canna always be pullin' ye out of these situations. Didna I tell ya, the way of the transgressor is hard?"

That's where I've heard it. "Hiram? McCormick?"

"Tha's me, Laddie. You know you've made some pretty wild choices—Only a cat has nine lives, and your name's not Tom."

"Cuidich mi, O Tighearna mo Dhè: O sàbhail mi a rèir do thrò-cair," Julius said.

"Yes, God will hear," Hiram said. "Now I've got to get ye outa here."

And I bet that cab is gone... Julius' world went blank.

AN OLD MAN WITH AN arm around a much younger man swaggered into the hotel. He stopped at the desk and picked up a key.

"Had a wee bit too much of the bottle," he said with a wink at the clerk. They continued to walk to the elevator singing in a delightful Scottish brogue. He punched the button, the elevator dinged, and the door opened. As the elevator sped to the third floor, he stopped singing. *I've never had to sing for two people before.* "Wake up, Laddie," he said as the room door shut behind them.

He unloaded Julius on the bed in the darkening room and watched the city lights wink on as the sun sank below the horizon. Hiram ran some cool water on a clean washcloth and applied it to his patient's face. After several gentle dabs with the cloth, Julius began to wake from his stupor.

"Aye, Laddie, Nightingale and Little Parrot are safe. Stop worrying about them. That one was too close. God isn't finished wi' ye yet, but..."

"What's that?" Julius shook his head. He thought he heard someone speaking. He groaned and sat on the edge of the bed. *Where in this world am I? I feel like I've been ground up and spit out again. I hurt too much to be dead.* Things seeped into his consciousness little by little. He knew where he should be. He remembered the cabbie putting his envelope in his coat pocket. "Oh, God, help me." *Wait.* He switched on the television.

"So what happened here? You say you live just down the street?" Julius squinted at the television as the local reporters stood on the street as close as they dared to a massive fire, flames billowing into the evening sky.

"I'd just sat down to watch the tube when this huge explosion rocked the entire neighborhood. I live two blocks down, and it knocked me out of my chair, pictures off the walls. I don't know what it was, but man it was big. Kaboom! It was big. Glad I was inside. Most everybody was inside. This part of the neighborhood is abandoned, only the Snack Shop on the corner. Too bad about the snack shop. But man, it was..."

Julius flipped the channel. Same picture, different reporters.

"Hello, this is your man on the street. We're down here where there's just been a tremendous explosion. Police say there were at least four bodies, badly burned, none alive."

With an effort Julius rolled himself over and up off the bed. With small agonizing steps he made his way to his suitcase and rummaged through it. Most of the clothes were here, but no computer/electronics case. *Goodnight— I'm in the right place where I'm supposed to be, but I have no idea how I got here.* He ran his hands through his hair. *Where's that jacket with the newspaper? Aha!* Searching through the pages, he found the information, took note then tore the paper into shreds and flushed them down the toilet. Pulling out a Bible he searched a few chapters in Proverbs.

Here it is in Proverbs thirteen verse one: "A wise son heareth his father's instruction, But a scoffer heareth not rebuke." He read down through Proverbs thirteen verse fifteen, "Good understanding giveth favor, But the way of the transgressor is hard."

Oh, God, how many times have I refused to hear my father's instruction? I walked away from everything I'd been taught. So sure I knew better how to live my life. My life isn't worth a paper nickel. Memory, like an asleep foot reviving began to return. *What about Mrs. MacDonald, Michael, Ruth, and now the newest member of the team, the Kid,? If the Runner can follow my line back, they are in danger.*

Thankfully Junco and Mai were safe. The Creep didn't know what the code meant. Shields hadn't compromised anything. Exhaustion washed over him. He switched off the light and curled up on the couch.

Chapter —27—

Thursday, June 18<u>th</u>; The sharp sound of the phone jangling beat against Julius' ears. With a groan, he crawled across the floor.

"Hello?" He imitated a female voice.

After a slight pause, "This is the desk. May I speak to Mr. McLaglin?"

He checked his hotel ticket then answered in the same female voice, "One moment."

"Hello?" Julius changed his voice and answered.

"Mr. McLaglin, our instructions were to give you a wakeup call at 6:00 A. M. There're a couple of packages for you at the desk. Would you like for us to bring that up?"

"Yes, please." He hung up and ran his hands over his face. With careful movements, he stretched and noted his surroundings. *Can't believe I'm so stiff and sore.* He stretched and exercised his muscles, limbering up his actions. Limping over to the breakfast nook, Julius sorted through the various selections. He ran water into the carafe and started a pot of coffee.

At a knock and, "Front desk." He peered through the peephole in the door.

"Thank you." he opened the door to take the packages. "You having a good morning?"

"Gets better from here on. My shift's about over." The young man smiled at Julius. "Get in a fight last night, mister? Your friend that you came in with didn't mention that."

"Friend? What'd he look like?"

"Tall white-haired Scottish gentleman. Well dressed, well spoken. Liked his accent." The desk clerk stopped with a chortle. "Had a good singing voice...He stopped got the key, said you'd had 'a wee bit too much of the bottle,' and then took up singing some song I've never heard before. I've got a tonic might help bring you back on your feet. I'll send it up before I leave."

"Thanks. I've got coffee ready. Should do the trick." Julius shut the door and turned back into the room.

The packages must be from Bob. He turned the packages one way then the other. *A note attached.* He tore it open and read:

Your own computer? Irreplaceable. This new one will have to do. Don't know how you're not dead. Several bad hombres are gone with that explosion. That was some explosion. I'm assuming you lost your Beretta as well. You'll have to pick up on your own anything else that was lost. Appointment at Clarke and Holiday's this morning at 9:00 sharp. The info is included in the file.

Julius studied the dossier again. Adam Clarke had paid John Holiday's widow a tidy sum for her share after Mr. Holiday had passed away. On the surface, everything looked to be a bona fide business, but things didn't match up.

So that's Mr. and Mrs. Adam Clarke? And this is the deceased Mr. Holiday. The wives, the families of both of them. He flipped through the information. *Wow...* His heart did a double beat. Lily? *That had to be her. She doesn't have a twin. My, my, I'd say she's outgrown her small town roots. They used to call her scrawny, but now?* She had learned how to dress to an advantage. He examined the picture in detail. *Should be interesting.*

HE SAT IN THE OFFICE of Clarke and Holiday and thumbed through his briefcase of papers. Julius could feel her eyes stray back to him as if there was a magnet glued there and she couldn't look away.

She picked up the phone as it rang, "Clarke and Holiday. Just one moment." She pushed a button to transfer the call. Delia Rusche looked away.

The intercom squawked to life. "Send in Mr. McLaglin."

"Mr. Clarke will see you now, Sir."

Her pretense of filling out paperwork didn't fool him. He could see her watch through veiled lids as he picked up his briefcase. "Thank you, Ms. Rusche." He read her name off of the name plate on her desk as he passed into Mr. Clarke's office.

A SHORT FORTY-FIVE minutes later the office door opened as Julius left. "All right." Adam Clarke's voice was congenial in tone, but very insincere. His hands remained firmly stuck in his smart black trouser pockets as he jangled his keys and coins. Julius could see through him like a well-polished window.

"We'll get those financial records and papers. I'll have my secretary get that information right away and see you at three o'clock this afternoon."

"Three o'clock." Julius disguised as McLaglin picked up a black fedora hat. He disappeared, after closing the outer door behind him. The only thing left was the steady cadence of his boots along the length of the hall and down the stairs.

SUNLIGHT GREETED JULIUS, disguised as McLaglin as he stepped out the door. Julius was feeling like a 1940 style film noire detective as he pulled his fedora down and walked the few steps to his company car. "Just sit tight a few," he told his driver, as he slid into the passenger seat. Julius pictured Adam Clarke making some phone calls and preparing to fly to his island home. From the dossier he had received, Julius recognized Clarke's wife entering the door he had just come from.

"Hey," he answered his phone. "Yeah, Clarke's wife just arrived. When I showed up this morning it was to put him in panic mode. They always make mistakes in panic mode. Your assignment is to tail them. They'll probably be taking their own plane. Our agent at the airport will contact you when they file their flight schedule, but don't assume their flight plan is set. You need to stick with them and don't let them out of your sight. If they do get to their plane, you do have back up to arrest them, but. . . Here they come. Gotta go—bye." He clicked his phone off and sat watching. "Just wait. We will need to follow the secretary in a few minutes," he told his driver. They watched Mr. and Mrs. Clarke get into a cab, and pull into traffic, and the other agents parked down the street that Julius had just put on alert pulled out and followed them.

"I don't know how much info you've got on this secretary, Delia Rusche," The other agent said. "I've had to follow her already on different occasions. She's witty and friendly, likes to flirt and is pretty with enough charm that she catches most men's eye."

"I've seen her picture," Julius said with a non-comital shrug.

"Unless I miss my guess, she's got ulterior motives for staying in Clarke's employment."

"Other than hoping to meet the right man—a man with money, but not exceptionally bright?" Julius smirked.

"Yes. Clarke doesn't pay her enough for what she spends. He may be smart enough to be second man on this totem pole, but he's not smart enough to see she's on the take. Probably a rival gang. Delia comes across as somewhere between a dumb blonde and a good old pal. . ."

"There she is. I think Clarke left her to clean up his mess while he attempts to get away," Julius surmised. The two agents watched as she caught a cab, and then they followed her into traffic.

"WELL, YOU ARE RIGHT, Kimmel." Julius glanced at his watch.

"How's that?" The other agent asked.

"We've followed Delia to three of the most expensive stores in this city, and all within the space of three hours. Clarke is going to have one grand bill from that spending spree."

"Serve him right," Kimmel said as they followed Delia back to the office.

"Why's that?"

"Leaving the poor girl to face the music and all that."

"He hasn't gotten where he is because of his compassion. He takes his orders directly from Meister." Julius had observed his partner for the few hours they had been following Delia/ Lily. Julius had a feeling that agent Kimmel might have feelings for Adam Clarke's secretary. "Park as close to where we were this morning as you can. I'm going to go back for my appointment with Clarke. We're sure he won't be there, and after her—actions I think I have a date for this evening."

"Yeah, it looks to be a long night," Kimmel said.

"That it does," Julius said as Kimmel parked.

PROMPTLY AT THREE O'CLOCK, Julius still in disguise as McLaglin did a rewind of the morning actions. The street door opened, boots on the stairs, boots in the hall, the door opened and Mr. McLaglin appeared in the office.

She looked up from her busy work, "I'm sorry, Mr. McLaglin, Mr. Clarke had an emergency." Her eyes were large and sympathetic.

"Mr. Clarke has an account at a local Italian Restaurant. Since you're the last appointment for this afternoon, we could catch some supper, and I could show you the sights. If you are free?" She smiled demurely as she glanced at his left hand.

JULIUS HADN'T EXPECTED Adam Clarke to be here. Mr. Clarke was someone else's problem now. Clarke's secretary's invitation fit into his plans like a missing piece of the puzzle.

"I'm flattered that you would drop your plans for me, Ms. Rusche, but I wouldn't want to interrupt any of your previous engagements."

"Please call me Delia. No, no inconvenience. I didn't have any plans. Just microwave pizza for one. I'd love to have an excuse for an evening out. I'll just make a few phone calls first."

She really has honed her skills. "When you're ready then." He waited, leaning on the door jamb while she put away her books, made her phone calls, and picked up her purse.

"Oh, just a moment." She slipped out of her office pumps, and into her heels. "The taxi should be ready when we get down to the street," she murmured as he took her elbow.

At the restaurant, Julius sipped his water and glanced at Delia. This case couldn't be more twisted. Where had the years gone? Years ago he had thought of himself as a kid brother to her.

"How long will you be in Chicago?" Delia sipped her wine.

"Not long. I'm called to quite a few different places." He leaned back as the waiter placed the shrimp cocktail in front of him. "One time I had a buddy that lived in Taiwan. He says Mitch, let's go shrimping. I told him, Mike, you're off the beam. I've only got a few hours..." Julius began a litany of stories that dated back to his military service years. He had to change the names of course, and never gave dates or real times, only long ago stories meant to entertain. His stories lasted from the shrimp cocktail all the way through the steak.

"Mr. McLaglin, I've never heard so many hilarious stories in my entire life." Delia dabbed her eyes with her napkin. "I haven't laughed so much, or so hard, ever!"

"Call me Mitch. How providential that you were able to come tonight. I'm sure Mr. Clarke wouldn't be as congenial." *The burden she carries she has chosen. There are no guarantees even if given a new chance she'll use it well, but I'll try, for old time's sake.* He gave an inward sigh. "Thank you," Julius said as the waiter placed the dish of spumoni ice cream front and center before him. He picked up the spoon and asked, "Are you married?" He indicated the rings on her left hand.

"I'm a widow." She frowned, avoiding his eyes. Picking up her spoon she attacked her dessert.

"I'm sorry. Just recently?"

"Not recently, but ..." She frowned. "You haven't had any wine."

"No, I'll stick to water—I'm allergic to alcohol." *And she has consumed enough for both of us.*

Smiling in a cozy manner, she reached over and covered his hand with her soft fingers. "I do find you charming. I haven't enjoyed an evening so much in a very long time."

"I'm glad you have enjoyed yourself." His napkin slid to the floor, and he removed his hand from hers to retrieve it. "Are you finished?"

"Yes, I do believe I am." She blotted her lips lightly with her napkin. She swayed when she stood. "I'm not sure that I can make it to my apartment."

"No worry." He grasped her elbow to help steady her. "I'll take care of it." They walked out through the dimly lit restaurant, and he helped her into the cab. Delia had looked smug as the taxi pulled into traffic, but now she appeared to shrink into herself.

The taxi nosed to the curb a short time later. Julius stepped out then helped Delia out.

"This isn't even close to where I live!" She looked around in bewilderment.

"I thought maybe we would see some of those sights you talked about." He ushered her into the little coffee house.

"The beguiled is beguiling." She allowed him to guide her to a small table.

Julius ordered a latte. "You must have an interesting job, Delia. How long have you worked at Clarke and Holiday?"

"It's a job," she said without emotion. "I've been there two and a half years. I'm looking for something different. Adam keeps telling me how unhappy he is at home. He's going to leave his wife then we can get married. One thing or another always gets in the way." She leaned her cheek on the palm of her soft manicured hand and sighed. "What to do?"

"I have some suggestions, but first... Here's a question." Removing an old picture from his pocket, he laid it on the table in front of her.

She studied the picture of a thin young girl standing beside a tall young blond man.

Julius watched her eyes narrow somewhat. She handed the picture back. She gazed into her cup for what felt like an eternity. "Cute couple."

"Lily?" Discomfort floated across her face like whipped cream across hot chocolate.

"Who are you, and what do you want?" She sat back in her chair, her eyes narrowed at the sound of a name she hadn't used in ten years. Her eyes searched his face again. "There is something familiar about your face. Should I know you?"

"I mean you no harm. I'm a friend." He could see an uneasy feeling, a fear in the depths of her eyes.

A cynical haze came over her. It made her lovely features cold and bitter. "I don't have any friends. Adam Clarke thinks I'm stupid enough to believe his lies. However, I get paid well, and I do meet some interesting people. So, until something better comes along..." She shrugged and swirled the last of her coffee around in the bottom of her cup.

Taking some bills out of his pocket, Julius threw them on the table. "The time has come. Let's go." He firmly grasped her elbow and escorted her outside. "Taxi!" he called.

"I want to know who you are, and where we are going." She pulled back from him.

"We are going somewhere to talk privately." The taxi stopped at the curb.

"What if I don't want to go?"

"— but you do." Julius' words were amiable, and he held the door open for her.

She shrugged a shoulder. "Maybe you're right." She slid into the cab.

JULIUS SLID IN AND watched his companion's pale, drawn face.

"How did you come by the name Delia Rusche, Lily?" Julius asked. She stared at him, her eyes large. He wasn't sure she was going to answer.

"Mom. She always liked her Great Aunt's name," she mumbled in a resigned hollow voice. "It changed everything."

"What's that?" he asked.

"James's death changed everything. My lawyer insisted I change my name, leave town—my whole life changed. I'd never been away from my home town before. Mom had always been a manipulating person. She changed. We both lived with fear."

"Fear is a hard thing to live with..." Julius said quietly.

"Fear and guilt. No matter where I go, the constant specter of the guilt is right here." She patted the seat beside her. "I killed James, just as sure as if . . . I honestly didn't see it coming. Bill Amery. . ." She shuddered and stopped speaking.

As the vehicle edged in toward the curb, she stared up at the beautiful hotel with beautiful lights, its promise of comfort, maybe even peace at the end of the journey. *At least it's a lovely hotel.* Her words were muddled. It had been a long day, and she had drunk too much wine.

Julius opened the cab door and helped Delia out. Standing on the sidewalk she clung to his arm. Somewhere she had decided that she could trust him like a friend. Sadly, Julius thought, *God knows she needs one.* Without speaking, he stopped and picked up the key at the desk then they took the elevator to the third floor. He held the door for her.

"This is nice—very nice." She stood inside the door a minute before she kicked her heels off, walked across the plush carpet and sat deep into the overstuffed Davenport. Fluffing up the pillows she made herself comfortable on the couch.

Julius pushed a button for the electric fire in the fireplace as Delia fished in her purse and pulled out her gold cigarette case. She snapped it open, selected a cigarette and clicked the catch shut. She lit the cigarette and inhaled deeply as she eyed the rich surroundings. "Very nice."

"Would you like something to drink?" Julius asked.

"No, I think I'm drank out." She took another puff on her cigarette. She puzzled over this Mitch McLaglin. Some of his mannerisms seemed familiar, but no one in her life had the name Mitch. Did she know him? Maybe, but not by this name. Fear prickled up her neck and across her scalp. Someone this good looking she would have remembered. She took note that he chose the overstuffed chair situated against the wall which gave him a panorama view of the hotel suite. He lounged back, stretching out his long legs. Delia knew why Adam Clarke had chosen her for his secretary, but Mr. Clarke didn't know why she had chosen to work for his company. A warning siren should have screamed at her when Mr. Clarke had mentioned this man as a government man.

"Lily, I want some answers, and I have something valuable for you in return. Tell me about this picture."

Julius could see the questions flit across her pale and drained face. What did he want? What was his angle? She weighed her options. "I don't know what you want."

"Let's start with who are the people in the picture?"

"You know the answers, Mitch—or whoever you really are. I'm the girl—Lily Fleur. Look how scrawny I was? In those days I could pass for fifteen—sometimes younger. The young man is James Mac-Donald. We were at his folks' place. One of his kid brothers took the picture." Her face lit up and softened as she spoke. "When I first met James—" A peaceful aura washed over her. "I thought he looked just like what God must look like. His red-gold hair like a crown, and those beautiful blue eyes? My heart did handsprings. I loved him, and his family. They were so warm and friendly. I saw what they had, and I wanted it. They weren't at all like my fragmented unhappy family. James didn't need a signature at twenty-one, but my mom signed for me. In two months I would've been eighteen anyway." She closed her eyes, and the cigarette smoke rose in lazy wisps.

Julius cleared his throat. "And then?"

"Well—" She paused and took a slow drag on her cigarette then blew the smoke into the air. "My god had feet of clay, and mom would ferret out any problem. She helped me see the feet of clay in the rest of his family too."

"How very kind of her." Julius' face appeared the same, except for a glint in his eyes.

Delia slipped into a world of her own. "I found I could disrupt the whole family. The older kids didn't fall for my game. The others? They never saw how I did it." She smirked. "I hated them all, the goody-two-shoes family—a church-going bunch of goody-goodies.

Then Bill Amery, the donut delivery man from Good Olde Bakery came along. I played him too. He kept flirting with me. I let him plot and scheme. But, one afternoon . . .late afternoon, while I worked at my afterhours cleaning job, Bill stormed into the house. James had fallen asleep watching television. During the fight, James fell, hit his head on the coffee table, and died. The neighbors heard the ruckus and called the police. It was over before I got home."

JULIUS WATCHED HER face turn hard and spiteful. All the paint in the world wouldn't make it beautiful. His heart ached for this lost soul, for the sorrow she had caused innocent people, for so much loss.

She started to laugh, but her hollow laughter turned to weeping then to uncontrolled sobbing. Julius pulled several tissues out of the complimentary box and handed them to her.

She blew her nose and wiped her eyes. "James is the only person I ever loved. I killed him. I killed the baby. I have wished so many times I had died." More tears gushed down her cheeks. She sobbed and rocked back and forth. "James, oh, James."

She cried out the years of sorrow and pain. At last, the tears stopped, and she quieted with only an occasional moan and sniffle.

Julius' face softened. "I will be more generous to you than you have been." He leaned forward. "Lily, look at me—" His voice commanded to rivet her attention.

Her eyes stared into his, growing larger then narrower. A slow seeming recognition warmed her face. "Eyes—I do know you, but ..." she sucked in a breath.

"It isn't important now. Just trust me." His features retained a blank appearance, his voice remained controlled. "You must follow my instructions exactly. Stay in this room. Do not contact Adam Clarke. When I walk out of here, within minutes, someone, a new agent, will be here. They will take care of you. We need you to verify information, and obtain necessary records for us. You have no choice except to co-operate, but you will be taken care of. Don't try to help Mr. Clarke, or it will be ugly." He stood and walked to where his few bags were stored in the dresser. "By the way, the goody-two-shoes family wishes you well."

"Wait. Don't leave me. Who—" Her tear stained face darkened with panic.

"Just a friend." He spoke over his shoulder and walked to the door. He turned at the door and looked back, his voice a sad echo. "Just a friend." The door closed behind him. From the hotel, he walked into the early gray predawn.

Chapter—28—

Friday, June 19<u>th</u>: "Good morning." Julius climbed into the seat of the waiting plane.

"Good morning, Sir. Just finished pre-trip we'll be off, as soon as you get settled," the pilot said.

"Good, I'm ready to be somewhere else," Julius said.

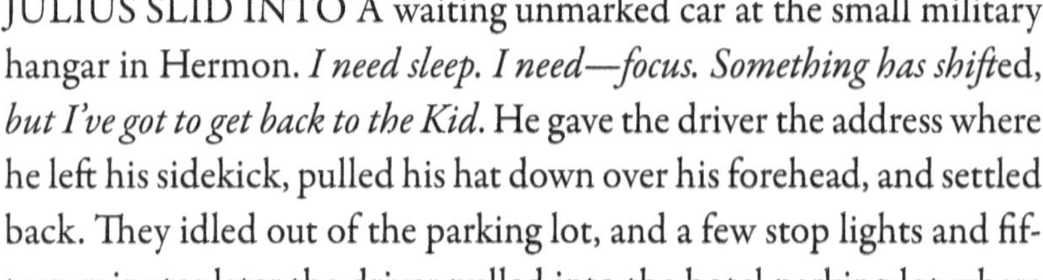

JULIUS SLID INTO A waiting unmarked car at the small military hangar in Hermon. *I need sleep. I need—focus. Something has shifted, but I've got to get back to the Kid.* He gave the driver the address where he left his sidekick, pulled his hat down over his forehead, and settled back. They idled out of the parking lot, and a few stop lights and fifteen minutes later the driver pulled into the hotel parking lot where two days and a lifetime before he had left the Kid.

"Thanks," Julius said. Slamming the car door, he sauntered to the motel room door. After several low taps on the door to the room, he slid his key in the lock. The room looked like a fight scene. A half-dressed body twisted in sheet and blanket sprawled half on, half off the bed. "Oh, God! Don't let him be..." his heart almost stopped as he reached out and touched the pale wan face...it was still warm. "Praise be! Hey, wake up," he grabbed the shoulder and gave it a vigorous shake. Julius ducked as the Kid came up swinging. "Hey, man, no fighting in here! This is a respectable establishment!"

At the sound of Julius' voice, the young man flopped back on the bed with a groan. "Oh, man—I dreamt the devil had me and had his fingers around my throat." He sat up and ran his hands through his wild blond hair. "I've had it bad. You don't happen to have a cigarette on you?" He looked at Julius.

"Sorry, kid, I gave them up somewhere back in the desert."

"I want a cigarette so bad and..." His hands shook as he ran them over his face. "I feel like I'm gonna' unload lunch." He tried to scramble out of the bed sheets.

"Wait." Julius untangled the blanket and the sheets from the body. "I think you're good now." He grasped his arm to help him stand. "You look bad. I've never seen you look so rough unless it was the time you almost drowned. I'm back now."

They made it to the bathroom in time for his companion to retch into the stool. Julius handed him a warm wet washcloth. "Did you get the list completed for me?"

"I did the best I could." The Kid ran the cloth over his face.

"Get your shower, Seth. I've got a bit of business to do." Julius shut the bathroom door, picked up his new case, and set it up. The screen lit up, and his eyes scanned the information. *Thank God. They had shown up on schedule. Delia had been disoriented at first but did co-operate. She gave them account numbers, financial records, all the info they needed and more. She should be out of danger now and heading for a safe house.*

His mind wanted to wander. It wanted to go back and catch up, to file what Lily had told him into perspective. The ocean of sorrow wanted to wash over him and drown him, but not now. He pushed it away. *There would be time when they finished this case. There would be time when he grew old. There would be time...but what if he didn't, and what if there wasn't?* He pushed the thoughts away. *Would there be a time when it didn't matter? He only had now—now was what mattered.*

He needed the key to this case. This name went nowhere. Meister. Meister, but it only appeared there in the records. How did it tie in over at Beetle River? He squinted at the screen.

"Hey, Jo, what's up?" The Kid sauntered out of the bathroom, towel drying his hair, another white towel wrapped around his waist.

"Julius, Seth. Remember—Julius. I'm working. There's some soda crackers and soda." Julius shrugged toward the desk as he took some notes.

His companion found the soda and crackers, and then perched on the edge of his chair. "Hey, that's cool. Julius. Fill me in. What are you doing with that?" He pulled his chair closer and sat down. Leaning forward he skimmed over the screen and crunched on the crackers. "What is this? I've never seen anything like it—well, on a sci-fi show."

"Where've you been? This is 1987 you know." Julius didn't take his eyes off the images as they flicked across the screen. He tapped in some more numbers and letters, and the images changed.

"I've worked in computers and electronics, but, man, this is way crazy." The kid's eyes almost bugged out.

"There's this name here." Julius pointed to the screen. "It appears in New York in the late 1800s, dies out—or disappears. It appears here in Chicago in the early 1900s, and the same thing happens here. It has resurfaced, but it doesn't go anywhere, and it doesn't..." Julius stopped speaking and watched as the kid finished the package of crackers.

"What is it, Jo—I mean Julius?" He took a sip of the soda.

"Places to go and things to do. I've made a reservation for us." Julius shut his computer down and packed it away. "Get some clothes on. Good night, Seth, if you got any less body on those bones, you wouldn't even have skin." Julius picked up the phone and punched in a number.

What a blessing I came across the kid. If I can pull him out of this muck he's stuck in he's worth his weight in gold. He's got me beat hands down...they thought I was smart. Julius gave a snort.

Julius hung up the phone. "The breakfast bar is closed. Let's just catch a sandwich on our way. That is if you're up to eating." He waited as his sidekick buttoned up a blue summer shirt, and combed his hair. "While you were in the shower, I phoned for accommodations at a Bed and Breakfast, in Beetle River. I have several other things on the ticket for today as well. We'll come back for your car when we're finished."

Once in the car, Julius pulled into traffic and headed north. "We'll try Walt's Coffee & Cream here." Julius pulled into a local diner and parked beside a police cruiser.

"Well, that's a switch. I remember when you and Chuckie Malone would stay as far away from Officer Jimmbo..."

"Yeah, yeah. I remember me an Chuckie too, but lives and people change." Julius rolled out of his side of the car.

"Apparently they do. Chuckie Malone's working in law enforcement back home."

"Is that so? We'll take a trip back memory lane when we're done here." Julius held the door for his sidekick.

They walked down a line of booths past two policemen. Julius nodded at Chief Mallory but kept walking to a booth in the back of the building next to the exit sign. "It's almost lunchtime, Kid, what sounds good?" Julius picked up a menu from the salt and pepper keeper.

"Toast and jelly?"

"How about a cheese sandwich?" Julius suggested.

"Okay, and a side of fries."

"Ready to order?" A chunky young woman with short brown hair placed two glasses of water on the table.

"Two cheese sandwiches, two orders of fries, one coffee, and one orange juice," Julius rattled off their order.

"Do you know where you are yet?" Julius asked as they waited on their order.

"Not really. Somewhere in the Midwest. People talk differently here than where we come from. I didn't socialize much while you were gone."

"That's wise, and you're right. We're in the Midwest. I suppose you don't know how or why you're here?"

"No, but I suppose you're gonna tell me, right?"

"I don't know how or why, but I can kind of shed some light on the situation. Does the name Gonzales mean anything to you?" Julius asked.

"Laura married a man— Juan Alvarez-Gonzales."

"Bingo. You're on top of things, Kid." The waitress brought their food, and after a moment of prayer, they ate in silence.

"I was going down for the count. Whoever drove me out here had to be an old friend of the family."

"And a good friend. Do you know how far this is from home?"

"A far piece?"

"Would you like more coffee?" The waitress interrupted.

"Thank you, yes." Julius held out his cup. "Anything else you'd like, Seth?" Julius asked.

"I'm good," he said with his characteristic lazy smile.

"Here's your ticket." She slid his ticket onto the table. "Have a good day, and come back again."

Julius picked up the bill. He pocketed a white slip of paper from underneath the ticket. "Keep the change." He handed the money to the waitress, and the bell tinkled as they walked out.

"Well, what's the paper?" the sidekick asked.

"Just sit tight. It'll be clear in a minute." Julius glanced at the white paper and backed out of the parking spot. He meandered through town with no apparent destination.

"What do you keep looking for, Jo? A tail?"

"What luck, I have a different rental. Two days ago I was tailed, but I'm not in the same car. You need to be careful if you drive the other rental though."

"Oh great. Cops and robbers. Which are we?"

"It depends." Julius drove down the tree-lined street and slowed. Turning down an alley, he pulled into a repair garage. The large double doors closed behind them. "Today we're the good guys."

"Hello," Julius closed his door as Chief Mallory approached.

"Armstrong." Mallory nodded. "Who's this?" He looked the tall, skinny, strung out kid up and down.

"Call him Matthew. He's back up." Julius grinned.

Police Chief Mallory led the way back to the office. Once inside, behind the closed door he motioned for them to sit down. "Matthew there could stand twice in the same spot and still not have a shadow—Julius Caesar?" Mallory grinned and sank down in the office chair. "A few days ago your favorite patrolman pulled everything he could find on Julius Caesar Armstrong."

"Didn't find anything, my records are sealed." Julius gave him a one-eyed smirk.

"But I'd stay clear of Philip Meecham. We don't want to sour the deal now."

"We're gonna need a better method of contact. I'll not come back to the station. Until it's all over that is."

"I've got my own mobile phone and a direct number to you. That should help in that area. I've got another couple of men—and a woman on a special team set up now as well. That should speed up and smooth operations too," Mallory said.

"What happened to my man on Wednesday? He didn't show, and I was tailed when I left our meeting spot," Julius said. "And the two goons at Import Magnifique."

"We can't put out a missing person on your contact. We've had crime in Hermon there's no denying that, but it hasn't been highly organized. We've been tracking it within the few months since my election. We've had several shop owners, including Mr. Gonzales, who've come forward with complaints. People threatening, demanding a payment or else something—same old tricks we've heard of from Al Capone and gangsters. It sounds like some organization's trying to muscle up the game here in Hermon. This pattern started a couple of months ago. When Mr. Gonzales reported his contact with these suspects, he had talked to other local business owners, but they are afraid to speak out publicly. Your Wednesday contact was going to turn over some info he had. My special team picked up the two men you called in and turned them over to your agents," Mallory said.

"If we get any info from those two, we'll see if our undercover op ties them with something bigger. Did you look over the pictures I sent you? Anyone familiar in the bunch?" Julius asked.

"There were a couple from your Monday's hay throwing that are a maybe. How about your undercover agents at Frankie and Johnnies?" Mallory asked.

"That group of pics were probably too far up the chain. I've got another group of pics that should be closer to the set up operations. The guys on the street operations. Here's the file on them." Julius handed Mallory a file folder.

"Thanks, this from this week?"

"Yes, fresh off the press. Frank Wilde and Gary Young. They're from Chicago. We're running their info as well."

"Good enough. We'll get right on it," Mallory said.

"I'm going to need that telephone van again. This week is rolling up. I've got a list of items for Friday as well." Julius took out a sheet of paper and handed it to Mallory.

"I turned evidence over to my team on the Diana O'Brien case. It will be reopened." Julius said.

"That case was before my time," Mallory said. "but the facts never did add up."

"Local people think Philip Meecham did it. What kind of an officer is he?" Julius asked.

"That's what's odd. He does a fair job. Not many complaints on him from anyone else ...except O'Brien's and their friends," Mallory said.

"I think there may be a surprise in this one," Julius frowned. "A&W a good drop?"

"It'll work once anyway. We'll set up each drop as we come to it—Is that his cover?" Mallory nodded toward the Kid.

"That's just him." Julius could see that his Seth had spaced out.

"He looks stressed." Mallory frowned. "This is too big for somebody..."

"He'll make it," Julius reassured himself and Sergeant Mallory as he watched a confused blank look slide across the Kid's face.

"Are you two speaking a foreign language?" The Kid asked.

Julius picked up his hat. "Let's get moving."

"We'll be in touch," Sergeant Mallory said.

"MATTHEW? WHAT'S UP with Matthew?" Seth asked.

"Survival. If you go by your name, Seth, you'll blow our cover. Not just yours." After a few minutes, Julius pulled into the parking lot at the mall.

"I see. For how long?"

"For a week. I'll fill you in later." Julius parked and turned to his companion. "I'll go in first. Here's my watch. After ten minutes you come in. I'll be reading a paper by that entrance. Go on down the left-hand side of the mall. Look casual. There's a small Asian restaurant almost at the end. Go into the restaurant, and tell the hostess you're looking for William. Follow her, and wait for me. Got it?"

"Yeah." Seth shook his head.

"Repeat it then."

"You go in. Ten minutes later I come in. You're by the door. I walk down the left side of the mall to a restaurant, and I ask for Will."

"What kind of restaurant?"

"Asian?"

"And you're looking for William." Julius felt the stress rising.

"Okay, okay. I have it. Asian restaurant—looking for William. Like William the Conqueror."

Julius slammed the car door and sauntered to the entrance. He bought a paper and a pastry from one of the vendors clustered at the entry. Sitting at the table with a view of the parking lot, he drank his coffee. He appeared to read the newspaper with an occasional bite of his pastry. *Maybe the kid couldn't handle this. What if he couldn't follow simple directions…*Ten minutes, eleven, twelve, thirteen—*where's that kid? Come on, Seth. There—the car door opened and the Kid slid out.* Julius watched as Seth rambled toward the entrance. Julius's heart skipped a beat. Where had those two men come from? Unaware of being followed, Seth ambled toward the mall doors. With those two tailing him, he would not make it to the doors.

Julius spied the security guard just a few feet away. "Those goons are going to mug that guy out there."

The security guard stepped through the front doors. "Hey, you! Young man! There's a message for you." He waved.

The two goons melted in among the parked cars.

"Yes, Sir? Where's my message?" Seth said when he got to the door.

"That man over there—" The guard turned to where Julius had sat. "The guy over there alerted me that there were two men following you , but he's gone. Look, he knocked over his coffee."

Walking to the small round table, Seth read the message, 'What thou doest, do quickly'. He picked up the mess and threw it into the trash can. Forgetting to look casual, he moved ahead of the few mall walkers as if it were a race. He glanced at the hieroglyphics on the Asian restaurant window and ducked inside.

"May I help you?" The tiny hostess spoke with a heavy accent.

"I'm looking for William." He tried to look casual as he twitched a glance over first one shoulder then the other.

"Please to come dis way." She led him swiftly to the other end of the establishment, turned down the hall, and motioned. "Stand here." He stood in front of the picture at the end of the hall. The hostess pushed a panel, and the whole wall swung around. In the dark, he felt rather than saw a presence standing beside him.

"Are you William?" He asked.

"Not hardly. Take off your sunglasses, dude," Julius said. "I see you got my message."

"I'm here." The Kid removed his sunglasses with a trembling hand.

"How did you miss those clowns closing in on you?"

"Man, I'm just surviving right now. Like, one foot up, one foot down." He shook his head to clear the fog out of his mind.

"That's what I'm concerned about." The elevator stopped, and they stepped out into an underground parking garage. Julius pushed the button on a key fob, a black non-descript car beeped, and the lights came on. "Here's our ride for the day." Julius and his companion slid into the front seat. "There are several rehab centers scattered around the country. I found this one patterned after a ryokan.

A Japanese inn for the Samurai. You need healing. We should both profit from a few hours R and R. It'll take us about forty-five minutes. Just relax and enjoy the ride," Julius said.

SETH PULLED HIS BALL cap down over his eyes while Julius drove the quiet forty-five minutes to the center. The wind in his hair and the sunshine on his face was enough encouragement to lull him into a peaceful sleep. Julius pulled in and parked and as they approached the stone building, an attendant met them and led them over a small bridge to a private entrance. Once inside, a gracious young woman in a kimono greeted them and led them to a private room.

Swathed in towels, Julius led the way down a hall to another room. "These people have knowledge of herbal healing. We are booked for three hours." They stepped inside, and the door slid shut.

THREE HOURS LATER JULIUS began to reapply his disguise in the mirror at the rehab center. "After Miranda drowned life spiraled out of control. God stood on one hand, and what I thought I wanted lay on the other. Chaos swarmed around me."

"Life isn't quite as simple as we believed when we were growing up." Seth pulled his blond hair into a ponytail.

"It wasn't—Miranda was so beautiful, so free-spirited. She had been warned...we all had been warned, not to use that log as a footbridge. She would do what she wanted," Julius said.

"In some ways, her death forced us all to grow up, but you were kinda like her beau so it hit you harder."

"Kinda? Miranda had our life all planned out. Where we would live, even what curtains she wanted..." Julius smiled at the memory. "Only now can I find some peace in the memories. At that point, confusion and turmoil came into our lives. I began running and fighting, literally and figuratively. Ever wonder why I was such an athlete?"

"They still have the pictures down at the diner, Jo. The ones where you took the football from one goal post to the other? That was a shadow to grow up under..." Seth finished pulling on his belt.

"The quarreling got worse and I couldn't stand the fighting. Fourteen years ago I walked—no I ran away. I've been running and fighting ever since. I needed today as much as you did." Julius inhaled the perfumed air. The tensions eased away as he finished dressing.

They walked into a big room where the keeper of the center, an old man, rustled in like a gentle breeze in the leaves. "Konichiwa, Julius-san." He bowed.

"Konichiwa." Julius returned the gesture.

"Have we helped as you wished?" The keeper asked.

"Yes, and we thank you," Julius said.

"You must come back for a proper visit," the old man said.

"We will, sir," Julius replied.

"I WISH I MAY: I WISH I might." Seth inhaled deeply of the late afternoon air and plopped down on the stone wall in front of the car.

"So, how do you feel?" Julius sat down beside him.

"Wait." Seth lowered his head into his hands. "My feelings are so strong, so overwhelming, and so alive! Being baptized into the Lord's family close to twenty years ago, I had this same beautiful feeling. But somewhere things blurred. Not because I couldn't tell right from wrong or good from evil, but I started making decisions based on what I wanted. I wanted a lazy man's salvation. Something you don't really have to commit to. I haven't felt so clean since that day I confessed Jesus as the Son of God and came up from the watery grave of baptism. I feel the providence of God and His power in my life. It's just pure joy."

"Providence!" Julius snorted. "Deuteronomy 29:29 'The secret things belong unto Jehovah our God; but the things that are revealed belong unto us.' I can't tell you how many unexplained circumstances in this past two weeks have come together as if planned. It hasn't been pure joy, but it's been amazing." Julius sat quiet for a minute, then with a sad quiet smile he turned to Seth, "Well, I hate to say it but it's time to go, kiddo."

The rosy glow in the west punctuated by the first few glittering stars reflected the peace and contentment of the two young men as they journeyed back to town and pulled into the same underground parking garage they had left from.

"The miles back seem shorter," Julius said as they walked back to an elevator.

"This service elevator's purty neat, Jo, and it doesn't even show—" Seth glanced around as they walked out of the dressing room in the men's clothing store. "How did we get here?"

"Gotta know your way around." Julius grinned. "We'll split up here and you go back down the left side, while I go down the right side here. Wait for me in the shadows at the front of the mall. I'll be right there."

Julius walked out the front doors of the mall and a figure from the shadows joined him. "Weather's pleasant," Julius said as they sauntered toward the car.

"Yes it is. What's that?" Seth asked as Julius pulled a slip of paper from under the car wipers.

Julius read the paper then stuck it in his pocket. "My stuff is waiting. We'll pick up the other rental car at the motel then you follow me to your bed and breakfast."

Chapter—29—

After stopping at the motel, Seth followed Julius through city traffic. On the outskirts of Hermon Julius pulled into a park-n-ride and rummaged in the back of an old pickup truck. Julius hoisted a covered bulky item out of the truck box and placed it in the trunk of the charcoal colored car. They were almost to Beetle River when a police car appeared and dawdled along behind them all the way to the Beetle River Bed and Breakfast. The police car idled past them when they pulled up to the bed and breakfast and parked.

"Hello." Julius extended his hand as they came up the steps to the porch.

A smallish, balding man stood and returned the gesture. "Hi there, I'm Olan Smith, the fellow you spoke to on the phone. This is my wife, Rheba." A plump woman with white hair sat on the porch in a rocking chair.

"Julius C. Armstrong. Pleased to meet you." He nodded. "My assistant, Matthew Hastings. He's here to help with some of the technical stuff."

"Come on in. Rheba just took some scones out of the oven."

"So, you're THE Julius Caesar?" Rheba led the way to a table in the cozy kitchen.

"Yeah, that's me," Julius laughed.

"How's the book comin'?" Olan poured coffee. "Have a seat." He gestured toward the kitchen chairs around the table.

"There's a lot more to a book than meets the eye," Julius said.

"Yeah, and so much going on that you can't put in a book." Olan frowned as he set their mugs down in front of them. "You want some cream and sugar?"

"No, I'm fine. What about you?" Julius turned to Seth.

"I'm fine," the Kid said.

"It's getting' worse." Rheba stirred her coffee. Her face wore a worried frown.

"Is that so?" Julius feigned surprise as he reached for a scone.

"Not two hours ago Jack O'Brien stopped at the carry out to get fuel and a pop. A quarter of a mile down the road guess who pulled him over?" Olan's eyes narrowed.

"You don't say." Julius dropped his scone in surprise.

"Meecham conveniently 'found' some stuff in the back of Jack's pick up. Jack said any fool could have thrown it in the back of his pickup, at the gas station, or since for that matter. He didn't know where it came from. If that O'Brien has nothing else, he's got nerve." Olan shook his head.

"I can vouch for that." Julius took a sip of his coffee.

"While they were arguing about it, a friend of Jack's drove up. Police Chief Mallory. Meecham's boss."

Rheba turned to Seth. "Folks don't care for Officer Meecham."

Olan lowered his voice, "Some folks are afraid of him. There's rumors..."

"Enough of that now. Another scone...and some jelly? Coffee's hot, have another cup." She passed the tray and shifted to a safer subject. "Our boys are both towheads. Like you, young man." She pointed to Seth. "It's the Anderson genes. Olan's mamma's an Anderson, and if you wander back far enough, I'm a second cousin on my daddy's side."

"You folks have a nice place here," Julius sat back in his chair. "How'd you come to have a second house just like the big house?"

"They're called grandparents' houses," Rheba said. "In the old days, the kids would keep the big main house. The parents would have a separate house—like that one, or several rooms of their own built onto the main house."

"Interesting. Would you mind if I take some pictures some time? I don't know what will get used. The editor sorts through the pictures, but..."

"Anytime," Olan said.

"Time to get him settled in." Julius shook hands with Olan and Rheba. "Come on, grab your stuff, buddy, time's awastin.'"

"I'll get the key, while you all get your stuff. We had to do some remodeling after a storm three weeks ago. Just got it done..." Olan said.

"Thanks," Seth took the key from Olan and they turned toward the small house next door.

"So, what do you think?" Julius set the suitcase down at the door and looked around the compact house. "Kitchen, bedroom, living room—for one or two people it'd be fine."

"Matthew Hastings?" Seth said.

"Matthew is your middle name, and I like Hastings from Poirot..."

"Okay, Hercule."

"You should see my phone number," Julius grinned at Seth. "First, let me set this up, and I'll start filling you in on this case." Julius uncovered an item he had fished from the back of the pickup and began to hook it up to the antennae already in place on the house. Making sure all the curtains were closed, he hooked his computer into the system and brought up pictures and files. "Here's some of what's going on," he said as Seth pulled up and perched on the edge of a living room chair. "This name of a second rate crook, Alberto Meister, appears in New York in late 1899. He's a runner for a big-time boss. He disappears but re-appears here in Chicago ten years later when Chicago racketeer, Big Jim Colosimo brings his nephew from New York to do some dirty work for him. That's in 1910, but Meister disappears again here. The dude must be about 25 when he resurfaced, but it doesn't go anywhere. It just dies out."

"If he dies out that's good, right?

"It can't be the same guy, but the name's back, first in Chicago, and they think he has a link here. And it's the same old racket—crime. Everything it touches turns to an ugly stinking mess. We picked up some men that were boot jacking Alvarez-Gonzales, but they're only the tip of what we're looking for. We picked up more of the ring just hours ago in Chicago. The noose is tightening. This should be over by Saturday morning, but I should have warned you between now and then this is dangerous. You can just sit this one out until everything's finished if you want. You're not in too far."

"I told you I'm here. We'll do this together, J-Julius. What about this stuff here?"

"I don't think these two cases go together, but this is a puzzle. A young police officer—you may remember the name Phil Meecham?"

"I heard the name."

"Yes, Olan and Rheba just mentioned him trying to arrest Ruth's father. His family has had a quarrel with the O'Brien family for quite a few years now. He's been stalking young Ruth O'Brien. After her mother's death she moved in with..." Julius brought up some more pictures. "MacDonalds." There was a loud thud, and Julius turned to gaze down at Seth. "What are you sitting on the floor for, fella?"

"I didn't know. I was asked if I wanted to move with them, but I was floundering and I guess, that's where I wanted to be. Besides, someone needed to stay and take care of Sis." Seth shrugged. "I didn't have a location or a name."

"I didn't think you knew, and they don't go by another name, but you see why I can't fail, Seth. Too much, and too many depend on me."

"You've never been good with failure, Jo. We'll do this." Seth's gaze met and locked with Julius'. "And how did you end up here?"

"I'm still trying to figure that out, but I'll fill that in later." Julius turned back to his screen. "Back to Miss O'Brien. Her mother died two, going on three years ago in November. The police report called it a heart attack, a natural cause of death. Remember Phil Meecham? He was the one who called for an ambulance, the one who found Diana O'Brien."

"That's pretty fishy if you ask me." Seth sat back on the edge of his chair. "What was he doing there?"

"He has no alibi as to why he was there, and it looks like a cover-up took place. There's a new sheriff in town—literally. His name's Mallory. The old one, Prescott Biles, was in cahoots with the Meecham family, but the new guy isn't playing their game."

"Mallory? That the guy at the repair garage today?"

"Yes, and it gets more convoluted. In Phil Meecham's statement, he says he believed it was murder."

"Why would he do that and incriminate himself?"

"He says he didn't do it. He came to the back door, heard sounds of a struggle of some sort, and when he went into the dining room Diana O'Brien was in the last throes of gasping her last breath."

"Oh, yeah, right...so, what do you think?"

"I don't think this story is over yet. He could be telling the truth." Julius shut down the computer and closed it up. "I'm going to take the charcoal Caprice. It's set up for me, and God forbid you should show up on their radar."

"Thanks."

"Welcome—I'll be over tomorrow. Just have odds and ends to work on. If you want to come to Church Sunday, I'll show you where the church house is. But you'll have to stay under the scope. Slip in and out without notice. You can see how important it is, but we will be done by next week or die trying."

"Tomorrow then," Seth said as Julius shut the front door behind him.

"HELLO, HELLO." A SHORT time later Julius walked into the Alvarez-Gonzales kitchen from the breezeway, and tossed his hat on the counter by the wall.

"So the wanderer returns. You're back early." Ruth put a plate in the dishwasher and straightened up. "Have you eaten? How about a ham sandwich?"

"Wonderful. What a day—what a battle." Julius threw a leg over the stool and dropped down.

"Mayo?" Ruth stood with knife poised above the jar.

"Please, and a dash of Dijon if you have it."

She placed the sandwich and a glass of tea on the counter. Sitting across from him she rested her chin in the palm of her left hand and drew invisible patterns on the countertop in front of her.

"In a battle, huh?" she asked not looking up.

"I used to believe the idea of good versus evil to be an over-blown church thing. But life has knocked that out of me. Some things are good and right, and some things are plain evil." Julius's mind drifted back to the night a young woman lay dying. *He could feel her thin desperate fingers clutching his sleeve with her remaining strength. He listened as his interpreter spoke. 'Take my children. For God's sake save my children.'*

He zipped the baby into his jacket, the little girl he tucked under his arm. He ran in the night toward the helicopter as gunfire rolled in the dust after his steps. It was against protocol, but he ran for their lives. Somehow he flung the girl and his interpreter into the open maw of the copter and rolled himself and the baby in last. Julius flinched remembering the bullet that caught him in the thigh. He picked up Michael's Bible as it lay on the counter and read John one verse five, "'And the light shineth in the darkness; and the darkness apprehended it not.' Evil is still trying to destroy Him, and all that is good. It's a battle. And too many soldiers are sleeping." He gently closed the book.

Sitting in the mellow light of the kitchen on that warm summer evening they could hear an occasional insect thud against the sunroom window screen. It was a simple country evening as the piano from upstairs accompanied the night time music from the outside.

Ruth stopped drawing her invisible patterns and looked up at Julius. "You surprise me." Looking back down at the counter she weighed her words. "Honestly, I know Julius isn't your real name. I don't know what your real name is. I don't trust anything I can see about you. But I trust you. Your words are true. This isn't a game. We're called to pray according to God's purpose. I feel, as Christians, we ought to be prostrate before God praying with all our might." She looked him squarely in the eye. "Officer Meecham tried to arrest my dad this evening for drugs." She shook her head.

"What is the problem between your two families?" Julius pinched his bottom lip between his thumb and forefinger in thought.

"The Meecham family has a problem with the world." Ruth heaved a sigh.

"Maybe so." Julius puzzled. "Except this problem is personal." He ran through the pieces in his mind. Meecham trailed and harassed Ruth, her father, her friends. He stalked her every step, and each day became more aggressive. Julius knew where it would end, unless...

"All I have is pieces." He held up a hand and bowed his head for a minute, and then resumed. "Something's missing in this puzzle."

"I could talk to Grandpa—you should talk to him?" Ruth said.

"I could give it a go." He chewed each bite of his sandwich as he pondered. "Well, it's been a long day, and tomorrow will come soon enough. Thanks for the sandwich. See you in the morning." *Whew, he thought, well I couldn't very well confirm or deny that statement of hers. Just one more brick in the wall that Ruth and Mom are both special people.*

<u>SUNDAY, JUNE 21st</u>; "Your appearance at church this morning went well. I wouldn't have known you were there except the look on the preacher's face when you slipped in. And then he looked kind of perplexed when we sat down after the last song. Must've been when you left." Julius and Seth were concealed under cover of a few overgrown trees Sunday afternoon surveying the Meecham farmstead.

"Prob'ly." Seth pushed his hat further back on his head. "This morning I noticed a car parked south of the church building on that dirt road. It was still there when I left. I circled around and watched him from south of his position. After he left I lit out for the B and B."

"What'd he drive?"

"A sharp black Mustang."

"Hmm," Julius muttered.

"What?"

"Just talking. I missed a good pot luck." Julius peered through the binoculars at the Meecham farmstead.

"You need to be taking care... Wait! That's the car." Seth hissed.

"Don't come unglued, Kid," Julius whispered. "That's Officer Meecham." He handed Seth the binoculars. Julius squinted as a dark-haired young man threw his cigarette out the window of the sleek black car. He stepped out into the gravel driveway, squashing the cigarette. He was distracted by something in his hand as he sauntered toward the house. He ambled up the porch steps and slid the item into his shirt pocket.

"Oh. That's him." Seth raised his eyebrows and handed the binoculars back.

"Come on back to the car." Julius led the way through the scrubby roadside trees.

"Ruth—we'll call her, Nell—like in the cartoon. This fellow Meecham—we'll call him Snidely Whiplash, he's trailing our Fair Nell."

"Are you Dudley Do Right?"

"It breaks down there." Julius opened his car door. "Next week will be very busy. Tomorrow I'll need to go into the lions' den and continue getting it set up for the end game. Today I need to get equipment sorted, put together and ready." The car slid out of cover and on down the road. "I would like some pictures of the Smith's Bed and Breakfast," he looked at his watch, "before evening services."

MONDAY, JUNE 22nd; Julius slapped the plat book on the table as the Monday morning sunlight filtered into the kitchenette at Smith's Bed and Breakfast. He pulled out his pencil. "Here's the plan. We are here. We'll take your car and come down this way. Turn after we pass Pat and Jack O'Brien's house and go by this other house, to the dirt road in back of Diana's." Julius traced the road in the plat book. "To here by the O'Brien grove. Slow down but don't stop. I'll roll out at this drive." He tapped his finger on the map. "Drive around here, across from the empty house. Park in the trees and wait. It'll take me a short while to pick up the telephone van and get into disguise. Probably take me about ten minutes before I get back for you. Be ready for me."

"So far so good," Seth said.

"I'll carry you to here at the corner by the telephone pole south of Meecham's house. You wait ten minutes. I should be in the house by then. Climb the pole. On the right-hand side of the pole, you will see a box like this." Julius held up a small palm sized black box then put it on the desk in front of them. "Bring the one that's there back to me."

"Got it."

"Let's go." Julius ushered Seth out to the car.

Seth followed instructions and slowed as Julius opened his car door. "I'll bring the telephone van around in about ten." Julius slid out the door and slipped into the grove.

"You do a really good job with those disguises," Seth said as Julius dropped him by the telephone pole. "Ten more minutes?"

"Yes, ten minutes. It'll probably take me twenty minutes in all," Julius stopped briefly, then drove down to the gravel driveway and up to the house. A '69 Dodge Charger sat parked close to the residence.

That has been a flashy car at one time. Looks a bit abused now, though. Julius took note of the license plate; picked up the clipboard, and checked his supply of doggy treats. He walked carefully across the barren front yard. The Great Dane barked and snarled at the end of the chain.

Julius, only inches from being torn to pieces, walked on by. With an imperceptible flick, a doggy treat landed in front of the dog, but the dog continued to snarl and snap. Near the door, Julius heard two men's voices raised in a heated argument. *Hmm. Interesting.* He reached over and rang the doorbell.

He pushed the bell again, and the voices stopped. Quiet prevailed. On the third ring, footsteps approached from inside the house. The door opened first a crack, and then wider as the young blonde woman recognized his uniform.

"Telephone company, ma'am." He nodded and touched his cap.

"Yes, I remember you. We called this morning. We're having some problems."

"That's what Ralph from the desk told me. What kind of problems are you experiencing?" *That expression on her face—was it relief?— Or something else?*

"The phone in the kitchen has a lot of static on it. I'm so glad you left your card, Mr. Smith."

Julius followed her through the foyer into the kitchen. *Someone needs to do a bit of redecorating here. Even I know the '70's look is outdated.*

"Are you baking cookies again today?" He asked as the little girl looked up from the sink where she rinsed dishes.

"I'm helping wash dishes now." She smiled.

There's something not right. The little girl's lips smiled, but her eyes said something else. "Washing dishes? That's a big job for a little girl."

"Oh, it's not hard. We come to Uncle's house every week to help clean—Mom and me. This week we have to come twice."

"But you'd much rather be the baker than the bottle washer, huh?" He smiled at the child. He turned back to the woman. "I better fix that phone for you."

"Yes," the child said, "Uncle gets very angry when the phone isn't working—and so does Mr. Grumpypants..."

"Nancy—"

The little girl's face contorted into a funny grimace. Hiding his smile, Julius picked the receiver off the hook where it hung on the wall. He could hear the static and appeared to work on the mouth piece. He screwed the mouthpiece off, inserted the bug, and then replaced the piece.

"I think this should work better now." He backed up against the refrigerator. "Do you have any other phones besides this one?" He distracted the mother's attention. With his left hand, he removed the first magnetic phone card he had given them from off the refrigerator, changing it as he spoke for a new one. "I ought to check them if you do, and the box outside."

"In the living room, and..." The young woman hesitated. "I'll ask." She walked to the stairs. "Phil? Philip?" She called softly.

"What is it, Mel?" Philip Meecham buttoned his shirt cuffs as he met her halfway down the steps.

"The guy from the phone company's here. He wants to know if the phones upstairs are working."

"They're fine." He scowled at Julius who tinkered with the phone jack in the living room.

"I need to check the outside box where it comes into the house if the rest are working." Julius stood and walked to the bottom of the stairs.

"Check the outside box if you need to, not upstairs. That should be enough." Meecham's face scrunched into a scowl.

"I don't want to have to make another trip," Julius said.

"I know all the employees of the company. I've never seen you before." Phil Meecham's eyes narrowed.

"I'm Bill Farley's son-in-law." Julius looked at his clipboard. "Got a couple of other calls. I'll check that box, and get out of your way." He kept his manner pleasant and businesslike and turned toward the door.

When Julius entered the house, the Great Dane stopped his noise and snuffled up his treat. Now that Julius reappeared the dog's racket began again. Julius walked around to the back of the house to where the cables and box hung attached to the wall. He eyeballed the wires, strode back to his service truck and retrieved a ladder. He took five minutes at the top of the ladder. Julius attached another bug and peered in the window. Not much to see, but he snapped a few pictures with his tiny camera. He climbed down and carried the ladder back to the truck. He tossed the dog another treat on his way by. As Julius backed around, he squinted into his mirror. *They must not feed that mutt, or maybe he's just a sucker for treats.* The dog stopped barking and snuffled up the delicacy. Julius pulled out of the driveway and turned back toward the corner.

Back at the corner, Julius slowed down to a crawl giving Seth time to jump in.

"Interesting on this end." Seth settled into the seat.

"How's that?"

"You went in the front door, and some tall, lanky fellow came slinking out the back, got in that Dodge Charger and left."

"I noticed the car was gone. Here—" Julius pulled over long enough to hook up a small device that plugged into the cigarette lighter holder, and turned the clipboard into a small computer. "Flip that over and plug that in here." He handed Seth the clipboard and license plate number. "—punch those in and see who and what comes up."

Seth was quiet a few minutes while he followed instructions and then waited. "This is crazy cool! The name that comes up is a William T. Marsh. And here's a pic of his driver's license, address, the whole shebang." Seth's eyes were golf balls as he stared at the screen.

"You techi-nutcase." Julius chuckled. "And close your mouth, Kid, you're not a cod. What's the address there?"

"Six-zero-seven Walnut Avenue, Beetle-River."

"Wait in the trees by your car. I'll be back in ten. We'll go find W.T Marsh."

Chapter—30—

"There's never a dull moment with you, Jo—Julius. What are we cruising down this busy main street containing five pickup trucks parked at the local pub?"

"Keep your eyes open, and watch your side of the street, I'll watch my side." Julius turned left and counted the house numbers up the next block.

At the end of the block, Julius stopped and mulled over which direction to take. He turned right and drove slow.

"I'd be better at this game if I knew what I'm looking for—Oh! I see it! Six zero seven—and there's the '69 Charger."

"I knew you'd come through." Julius made a right turn, and pulled in toward the curb surrounding the park. "Did you get the house number? Check it and make sure it's the right one."

"Yepper, that's it. What now?"

"I had a clue, but right now I'm out of ideas." Julius shut off the engine and tapped his fingers on the steering wheel.

"I have an idea." Seth pulled out a couple of sandwiches. "Rheba sent me a couple of sandwiches. She's trying to fatten me up." He grinned. "Let's go sit at the table over there, and think on our predicament. I haven't eaten since brunch, you know."

"I'll go grab us a couple of sodas from up at the shelter house." Julius sprinted up the sidewalk to where the park bathrooms and vending machines were situated. He pushed the button and the can rolled out of the machine. He put his money in and hit it again, and picked up the second can. He looked over the selections of candy bars, chips, and crackers pulled the lever, and a couple of candy bars slid out. Turning as Seth walked up behind him, he handed Seth his soda and candy bar.

"Thanks." Seth stuffed the candy in his shirt pocket and opened his can. "I've spent a lot of time in parks like this." He took a sip and looked around.

"Probably more time than you should have." Julius opened his soda.

"I'll say. I'm glad that time's over."

They sat down at a picnic table, and after a short prayer, they ate their food in silence, watching nothing in particular.

"You have any kids?" Julius asked.

"No. No children." Seth stared at his candy bar, pain etched across his face.

"Didn't mean to pry—" Julius turned as voices broke the silence and a family walked down the sidewalk toward them.

"Hi there, mister!" came a familiar voice.

"Billy, how're ya doing?" Julius held out a hand to the youngster.

"I'm doin' better-n-better. Mr. Armstrong this is my Dad and Mom. We're gonna have a picnic in the park."

"Julius C. Armstrong." Julius stood and greeted Billy's parents. "I've met Billy from church. And this is—Matthew Hastings, my co-worker."

"My wife, Gretchen, and I'm William. Good to meet you as well. I've heard some about you, Mr. Armstrong. So, you're friends to them—" he hesitated trying to recall names.

"MacDonald—and O'Briens." His wife helped him out.

"Yeah, that's right—Lewis. He came along and gave me some help one time. I had a dead battery, no fuel. He gave me a jump, and...yeah, he helped me out. Good folks." He nodded and paced around in one spot as he spoke.

"Well, enjoy your picnic. We're just soaking in some down time before moving on for the day," Julius said.

"Thanks, man. We'll do that. Just gonna burn a few dogs, toast some marshmallows, watch the kids play. Nothin' fancy you know." The family moved on closer to the playground and set out their charcoal, and supplies. The children ran off to the swings.

Julius and Seth exchanged puzzled glances while they munched on their sandwiches. "I don't know." Julius shrugged. "We found him and are in the right place at the right time, but now what do we do with it?"

"I don't know either, but I have a theory," Seth said and finished his candy bar and soda.

"I can hardly wait. What is it, Kid?"

"When in doubt, go to the john."

"Go to the—? Oh, good night. Well, if you gotta go, I guess. I probably need to take advantage while we're here."

Up at the shelter house, Julius dried his hands on the towel then waited at the door. "I think we'll just get in our little car, and head out. I don't want to intrude on their family time. I don't think walking up and saying— we know what you're involved in, and if you co-operate we can get you out of your trouble, as being a great introduction." Julius pushed the door open and stopped. "Wait." He held up a hand, and listened. "Sounds like an argument or a fight."

"Probably something we don't want to be a part of," Seth mumbled as he followed Julius out toward the shouting.

Julius sauntered across the space, coming up behind three burly men jostling Mr. Marsh.

Gretchen, tears streaming down her face, huddled between her kids and the three men who stood in a circle around her husband, shouting and prodding at him.

"I'm out. Don't want nothin' to do with it." William kept repeating.

"You can't get out. You knew what out would mean, when you got in. There ain't no way out for you." The biggest burly man poked his fist at William. "No way out." He repeated.

"Hey, hey." Julius continued toward the group, Seth close behind. "What's this ruckus about? Can't a fellow even have a peaceful evening in the park?"

"Butt out pipsqueak, this ain't your fight."

"I've been told that before. Didn't work then either. Leave this guy alone. Can't you see he's having some family time? Look there, you've got his wife and his kids scared. That's just wrong."

"I told you to butt out. I'm not going to warn you again." The big burly man growled and turned toward Julius.

"Oh, wait a minute." Julius held up a hand, backed up. "Here, Hastings, you keep this." He handed something to Seth then turned back to the others. "Okay, now. What were you saying?"

"I said, 'butt out or else—'" The big man took three strides toward Julius.

Julius hit him with a side kick to the gut and an elbow to the diaphragm. The other two stopped mid-stride and began to back away when their leader went down. Julius drew his Berretta out from under his vest. "I'd stop right there, fellas. Don't move another step, or you're dead. I want your hands up, and sit on this bench until your ride shows up."

"What do you mean their ride shows up?" Seth's eyes widened as confusion washed across his face.

"Don't worry, Kid. Just hang on. About five minutes, and you'll know. Mr. Marsh, just burn your dogs and mallows. Don't give these folks no mind."

Seth scratched his head. "Well, William, if Julius says carry on—here let me help." Seth checked the charcoal on the grill and loaded a few hot dogs on. "They'll be getting warmed up here pretty soon. Ya got some chips? Get your chips out." He encouraged

Gretchen. William started to move, stiff at first; Gretchen still huddled over her children.

"Hey, keep your hands up, fellas. Pretend this is a new exercise class." Julius spoke as the captives' arms began to sag. "Here's your ride now, come to take you away." Two unmarked cars pulled up. Two plainclothes policemen corralled two of the crooks, while Julius holstered his weapon.

"Come on, guy." Julius began to shake the third crook. "Hey, hey...here you go." Once the crook woke up, Julius helped him into a car. Then they pulled away.

William's jaw dropped almost to his collar bone as he stood with Julius and Seth. A look of wonder covered his face, his eyes large, he stared at the tail lights. He turned to Julius. "Who are you?" His eyes narrowed and lasered into Julius. "Who are you?" His voice faltered with fear.

"Let's just say, maybe there is a way out for you. That is if you want to take it. You want to talk?"

TUESDAY, JUNE 23rd; And so it was a day later that William Marsh found himself sitting outside David Meecham's farmhouse as part of a sting operation. He felt his heart pummeling in his chest. He looked every now and again to make sure it didn't show through his shirt. He never thought of himself as a hero; never wanted to be a hero. Well, there may have been times when he and his cousin Frank played cops and robbers, or the times he'd watched Roy Rodgers, or Lone Ranger, or some of those super-hero-inspiring shows—but not anytime in recent history. Hero? Not for him. His motto? Make it out alive.

His father had been in the military and wanted his son to follow in his footsteps. William hadn't done anything spectacular during his time in the military, just went along to get along. He had served his term, not brought shame on himself, or his family, and made it out alive.

How had he come to this point in his life? Twenty-eight years old, married eight years and three children? The years had vanished in a fog. Here he sat, preparing to do a thing so contrary to his nature if someone asked if it could be him, he would have called them a liar.

He wiped his fingers through his straw brown hair pushing it out of his eyes. *I need a haircut.* He wiped it out again. He took a deep breath and pushed the car door open. He checked his shirt. Yeah, it's tucked in. He slammed the door shut, and stalked toward the house. The stench from the dog pooh in the front yard made him wrinkle his nose, as the Great Dane began his cacophony of barking. Between the large teeth on one side of the path, and dog pooh on the other side, a person didn't want to stray from the well-beaten track. When he reached the front door, he rang the doorbell and waited. A calm feeling washed over him as he leaned against the door jam. *It won't last, I know the minute someone answers the door, I'll hyperventilate. I'll pass out, and they'll find these wires under my shirt. Talk about being dead, that's what I'll be—*

The door whooshed open. "Come on in. I thought you weren't coming back?" The petite blond looked him up and down with contempt and stood aside for him to enter.

William T. hiccupped and stood up straight. "I've had a change of mind. The boss sent some persuasion yesterday. I've been thinking, I might be willing—if maybe the price is in my favor." He walked in and across the entryway following her toward the kitchen.

"Yeah, price. That's a game changer. Everyone can be bought for a price, can't they?" Her pleasant face twisted into a sarcastic grimace.

"Don't you get snotty with me. I know you don't come out here for nothing. And not all of it's pristine." His eyes narrowed.

Melody sighed. "I had hoped that maybe one of us would break out of here. Get clear of this—this house of corruption. When you left the other day, I thought maybe you'd make it."

William noticed her red-rimmed eyes, and the tear streaks down her cheeks. "Why don't you get out? Surely, you're not tied here. He's your uncle for Pete's sakes. He wouldn't get rough with you?"

"He wouldn't?" She snorted. "Family ties don't mean anything to him. He'd kill his own mother if it were of benefit. I might get by with Phil, but not—shh, here he comes." She turned and busied herself wiping the counter and putting dishes away.

William crossed his arms over his chest and leaned against the wall that jutted out between the kitchen and the utility room. He looked serene on the outside, but his heart and stomach were having a fistfight, and he didn't think either of them would win. He couldn't take the chance to look at the young woman who busied herself with household tasks. In his mind's eye, he still saw her red-rimmed eyes. *Had she lost hope? How had she gotten sucked into this? She had a decent job in Hermon and a little girl. Life's tough enough and for a young single mother? That's where the stick is. And once you're sucked in, there's no way out.*

"So, you want a new deal." The man's steel blue eyes made William feel like a lump of dirt lying on the floor.

"Uncle David, I'm finished here. Nancy and I are going to take off now," Melody said.

"I'll see you tomorrow then." He turned his attention to his niece.

"Tomorrow? No, I thought we were done for the week." She recoiled as if struck, and her face and voice registered surprise.

"I need you to come back once more this week. If not tomorrow, the next day."

"But, I have to work a shift tomorrow at the store, and half a day on the day after. I had an appointment on Friday—"

"I need you to come back one more day. You decide and let me know."

"I'll check my schedule." Agitation and anger flared on Melody's face. She snatched her keys and purse and marched toward the door. "Nancy?"

Chapter—31—

William heard her sandals click across the linoleum at the door, he heard the door open and close behind them. *Oh, God. Oh, God, help. Why did I ever agree to this? I'm dead. I'm not getting out of here alive. I'm too young to die, God. I've got a wife and kids—*

"So, you want a new deal." Those steel blue eyes moved back to focus on him.

"Well, I, uh, I…I got a wife and kids." William stammered his last thought.

"So, is this a new wife? New kids?" Steel eyes asked.

"No, no, same old wife—same old kids—" *Wait, did he just say that?* "Sick, my wife's been sick." He couldn't think fast on the spur of the moment. His new acquaintance, Julius what's his name, had covered this part about if someone asked why. "Yeah, wife's been sick."

"You've been with us now how many years?" Steel eyes stepped back and stroked his chin.

"Four years, boss. Four years I've been with you. Done you a good job too." *William T. you gotta get a grip. Right now your ducks're just paddlin' all over the pond. Make it out alive, remember?* "Yeah, a good job. Never asked for nothing more, but my wife's been sick. And the kids are growing." To stand in one spot was a different habit to William, and only by the power of some unknown source did he remain in one place holding up the wall.

"We can do you a better deal, I think. I'll get an okay from the man upstairs. I have another package along with the one you didn't take yesterday. Your sick wife ought to feel better with that."

"Better, she's getting better." William wondered why this man made him so nervous. A vision of a young woman and her hopeless voice echoed in his head. *I thought maybe you'd make it out.* "Get your stuff boss..."

"Wait by the front door," Steel eyes said.

"Sure." William dawdled toward the door, his head lowered and turned at a slight angle. He tried to see behind, listening as he went. The boss hadn't followed him toward the stairs. He had gone through a door and down some steps to the basement.

William inspected the living room. *What are these fellows working for? It's clean, but there isn't a television, no sound system, even the decorations stink. Carpet? Old. Curtains, paint, everything, old.* The voices in his head quieted for the time being. His toe tapped on the linoleum as the minutes ticked by. He began to hum that country song *Too Old to Die Young* by Moe Bandy. *Maybe he would head back to Charlotte. He didn't even remember how he'd got here.* Odd, the soft thump of footsteps upstairs. He heard a faint sound of music, voices from a television as an upstairs door opened and closed. Footsteps in the upstairs hall, and then the tap of steps down the stairs. He glanced at his watch. *It had taken all of fifteen minutes—and how had the boss gone from the basement to upstairs? Who could be the person upstairs? What had the boss meant by talk to the man upstairs?* The voices in his head had been replaced, but William didn't know if he liked the new ones.

"Here. And there's a bonus once that's delivered. Get your wife some flowers." Steel eyes handed over the stuff. "Tell them there'll be a new shipment Saturday."

"Will do, Boss." As William took the boxes, a chill traveled over him. *Do not trust him*, a new voice echoed in his mind. "Oops!" The box slipped in his hands, but he caught it in time.

"Careful." Steel eyes barked and opened the front door for him.

"Thanks." William couldn't get out the door fast enough. He retraced his steps to his car, opened the trunk, put the parcels in, and slammed it shut. His gaze kept darting around from side to side. *Gotta get out of here.* Ran through his mind over and over again. He slid into his '69 Dodge Charger, backed around and put his foot down on the accelerator. *It may be banged up and somewhat abused, but this baby can still move*—he slowed at the end of the driveway. He made a right turn, and drove a few miles around to where he was supposed to meet up with his new helper. He pulled into a field driveway and parked.

The two cops, as William had dubbed them, blended in so well with the scenery, William did not see them until they stood up and came toward his car.

"You did very well, my man." Julius did a check of the recorder. "You're still good to go. Here, put this on." He handed William a bullet-proof vest.

William's eyes took on a glassy appearance. "Bulletproof vest?" The words pushed themselves out of his dry lips.

"Yeah. The first part of this journey you weren't in danger. Unless I miss my guess one of those packages has some directions in them. This vest will do the trick. We'll follow you into town and hole up in the empty building across the alley—won't let you out of our sight."

"Better be in Frankie's. Across the alley won't do no good," William groaned.

Julius weighed his options. "Don't worry we'll take care of it. Where's the office? Describe how and where you go."

"I tap three times at the exit door, pause, and tap three times again. The door opens, and I go to my left through another door and down the hall. There are two dressing rooms for the entertainers. The third door is to Marley's office. That's my door. I knock and enter. He checks the packages. I pass him any info, he gives me my money, and I leave."

"Okay, I see how it goes. I'll have it covered. Let's roll then. William T. you're first, we'll be right behind."

WILLIAM TUCKED HIS shirt in over his new security wear, slid into his front seat, and drove out of the tree and brush cover along the dirt road. He hadn't been out of sight long enough to arouse any suspicions, in case anyone kept watch. *I can't even imagine I'm doing this. Reminds me of those cops and robbers TV shows. Nobody will ever believe this—maybe that's a good thing—if I come out alive.*

After an uneventful drive into Hermon, he pulled into a parking space toward the back of Frankie and Johnnie's where the staff would park. He had watched for his tail for the full twenty miles from Beetle River. However, that Julius must be pretty good, or he'd lost him. He frowned. *Go in, or wait?* It was getting late—his heart and stomach were doing their fist fight again. *I can't stand this. I don't know how I got sucked into any of it.*

He got out of his car and stalked to the back door. Still fuming inside, he knocked on the door like always, it opened as always. A new guy waited for him inside and led him down the hall. He tapped on the officedoor.

"Come in." Marley's voice was gruff.

"What's with the new guy?" William handed Marley the stuff.

Marley scowled at him, "Kevin, Crowly, and Bernie left town. Up and left. No word, just gone." Marley opened the first package with care, checked over the contents, then proceeded with the second one.

"Yeah, boss says there'll be a shipment Saturday." *You're dead. You know this vest isn't going to work—either that or they'll use a knife, or knock me on the head. What are you doing here? Where did those two backups go? Probably had a flat tire. You're a sittin' duck...* The voices had returned with a penchant.

"I guess you have a bonus coming." Marley finished checking the second package. "I'll get it for you." He reached into his desk and pulled out an envelope removed some money, and gave the envelope to William. "Here you go. Should be in order."

William looked at the envelope in his hands then stuck it in his shirt pocket. "Thanks." He turned to find the new guy blocked his retreat.

"Sorry, fella. Nothing personal, you know." The man smiled as he said it.

William heard the two shots from the .45 caliber gun, saw the flame spit from the barrel, felt the impact as it hit his body full force at close range. *You're gonna die—* was the last voice he heard.

Chapter —32—

"William, William T." Julius poured cold water on the man's face. With a light, brisk touch slapped his face. "Wake up, guy."

William's eyes rolled around, not opening. "I'm dead."

"Wake up, Bill."

"William not Bill." He sat up, blinking at the unfamiliar room.

"Yeah, and you're not dead either. You look a little rough though. You'll have a bruise where the bullet hit the vest."

William held his head in his hands and groaned. "It'll be a long time before that episode leaves my mind. I'll have nightmares for years." He shook his head. "I can't believe I'm not dead. How'd I get outta there alive?" He put a hand to his forehead, then to his chest.

"You did a great job, my man. When that bullet left the gun and struck your vest, you passed out cold. Went down like a rock. All our man, the new man? All he had to do was catch you when you fell like you were dead, and carry you out. Nobody's the wiser. Told you we wouldn't let you out of our sight."

"Good God—you mean?"

"Well, yes, God is good. And the new guy? Very convenient that those other three fellows disappeared yesterday. You need a drink of water? Coffee? There's a soda if you want?" Julius offered.

"Yeah, I need a drink—"

Julius' brows shot up, "Now, Billy told me you've sworn off that stuff."

"I guess so. Soda pop will do, I guess." William sat up and took a slurp out of the can. "It'll do." He ran a hand over his brow, and through his straw-colored mop of hair. "I don't know if I'm up to this, man. Where we go from here?" He finished off the can.

"You and your family are going to disappear for a few days. Can't have you walking around like you're alive when you're supposed to be dead. I've already taken care of your family. There's a little cabin by Bear Creek Lake." Julius winked and smiled. "Won't be easy, but you can do some fishing and have a little downtime."

"What about my job at the concrete plant? Duke won't be none too happy."

"Don't worry, it'll be fine. We've got Duke covered, and you can't do anything familiar."

"Like what?"

"Grocery stores are out. Laundry mat, home. Don't drive your car. There'll be someone nearby that will help you with any of those things. We can't take a chance for things to go awry at this point."

"I'm stunned. This has happened so fast. I guess I'll have to go along with it. Nothing else to do. My wife and kids are all right?" For once the voices in his head didn't have anything to add to the conversation.

"We had someone help Gretchen get a few clothes and personal care products in suitcases. They will be here shortly. I set it up yesterday."

"Thanks, man. We appreciate that. I have somethings I need to tell you before I leave. It may be important, or not, but—"

"That's the time. You tell me what you have, and we'll sort it out."

"THIS HAS BEEN A DAY and a night. I think the key in large part is tied up in that house." Julius stabbed at the air with a blueberry turnover, as he and Seth sat in Seth's room at the Smith's Bed and

Breakfast looking out the window at the ribbon of road in front of the establishment. "William says there's someone upstairs. Someone who likes opera, old movies, and smokes cigars. None of those things describe the Meechams I have come to know. Philip smokes Marlboros, Ralph used to chew, and Phil's old man, David, doesn't do either smoking or chewing. Maybe that's why he's so mean."

"Yeah, and you were told the upstairs is off limits. And it's good to know that there's a passage somehow from the basement to the upstairs."

"These are pretty good turnovers. You ever have any more leftovers like these I'll take them." Julius sat quiet munching his pastry. "Tomorrow's a pretty full day too. I probably won't make it over until just before lunch."

"Too bad nothing's going on in this little town."

"Have you checked out the library? Addy Thompson's Antique Mall, or the local gossip center?"

"No, maybe I'll try wandering the local street tomorrow," Seth said as Julius took a sip of his tea.

"Bwaha," it sprayed back into the cup, and Julius wiped his mouth. "Kid, somebody ought to slap you upside the head—that was pretty good though. Wander the local street. Goodnight, I need to head out." He stuck the rest of the turnover in his mouth and finished off his tea. "Tomorrow—"he said with a wave.

Chapter—33—

Wednesday, June 24th; Just after breakfast Julius' car rolled up the gravel drive and parked at the Pat O'Brien farmstead. He picked up his camera bag complete with notebook and recorder and slid out. The weathered ornate hand gate swung open when he squeezed the latch and let himself into the yard. Walking on a brick path up to the house he observed his surroundings. The remnants of well-tended flower beds, now gone to seed, lay like ghosts of the past. It would be difficult to pinpoint which was the predominant style Queen Anne, or the white mid-west farmhouse. However, the three-story home with an unusual stylishness and the added embellishments spoke of a master builder.

He walked up the four steps to the wide front porch that ran the length of the front and disappeared around the right side of the house. His boots echoed on the porch boards, his knock at the ornamental wooden screen door resonated then died away. This had been quite a home that now whispered of love and care from the past. The neat and tidy lawn showed regular upkeep, but no extras: no frills that spoke of a woman's touch. He knocked again and listened to quiet, slow footsteps approach from the back of the house. After they reached the front door, Julius could feel eyes observing him. The door opened a crack.

"What do you want?" a rough voice asked.

"Sir, I'm a friend of your granddaughter, Ruth."

The door opened a little wider. "Yes?" The voice came again, not quite so harsh.

"Ruth suggested you might be able to help."

The door opened to reveal Pat O'Brien somewhat stooped, yet still above average in height, his auburn hair had faded to a sandy blond. He stood solid and unmovable as he inspected Julius from head to toe. Goosebumps ran up Julius' scalp as the old man picked up the shot-gun and motioned for Julius to follow.

"A body can't be too careful these days." He stumped back through the house.

They passed a large fireplace in the entry room and into a large dining area. Both rooms were furnished in an elegant, but antique fashion. The door to the kitchen swung on a hinge. This looked to be where the old man spent most of his time. Julius wondered how he would ever get this silent man to talk. This was no Charlie Anderson with a ready tale to tell.

"What a pleasant room." Julius stood at the kitchen door looking out the row of open windows. Light, fresh air and bird song filtered into the large kitchen. The trees not far from the back door shaded this area and kept it fresh.

"That it is." Pat O'Brien motioned for Julius to sit down opposite the remnants of a breakfast of oatmeal, poached eggs, toast, jam, and coffee. "All that's left is toast, jam, and coffee, but you're welcome to share."

"No, sir, I didn't come to interrupt your breakfast. Ruth suggested this would be a good time to catch you at home."

"You like some coffee?"

"Yes, sir, that would be fine."

Mr. O'Brien moved his plate and bowl over to the sink and brought a cup of coffee. Motioning to a lazy Susan in the middle of the table he said, "Sugar's there, would you like some cream?"

"No thank you, this will be sufficient," Julius said. "I have a puzzle to solve. Maybe you could help." Julius frowned.

"What's the puzzle?" Pat O'Brien's blue eyes were as piercing as his granddaughter's.

"Ruth says that Meechams have it in for the world. Ralph Meecham does seem to be an unpleasant old stinker."

"That's a little mild." Pat O'Brien gave a rusty laugh, "You could say that and more."

"He may be unpleasant, and Meechams may have it in for the world in general, but there's something between the Meechams and the O'Briens."

"Come with me." Pat O'Brien put his coffee cup in the saucer and walked to the swinging kitchen door. His work boots thumped across the polished floors as Julius followed him through the dining room. Tucked behind and beneath the lavish stairway, stood an unobtrusive door. Mr. O'Brien unlocked the door which swung open on well-oiled hinges.

Julius gazed around the tidy room. It sparkled with the light and brilliance of a thousand rainbows from a skylight. His eyes were drawn to a portrait of an unpretentious child-like woman of about eighteen. Blond hair coiffed to resemble the waves of the fashionable bob, but with a bun and topped with a pearl hair ornament. She wore a pastel rose-colored silk gown trimmed with a sizeable amount of lace.

"Priscilla." Pat O'Brien confirmed what Julius had guessed. "Prissy made the rest of us seem like imitations. Cheap plastic flowers compared to a real fragrant rose." The old man's face wore a stoic expression. He handed Julius a well-kept album and gave names to the pictures as Julius thumbed through the pages. "We had four children. The twins, John, the one everyone calls Jack, and Sean was the oldest. Robbie, then our baby Rose."

Mr. O'Brien retrieved a hanky from a back pocket. He locked the door and led the way back to the kitchen as he wiped his nose.

"More coffee?" Pat O'Brien held the coffee pot toward Julius.

"Yes, thank you."

Mr. O'Brien poured their coffee then settled back. "My heart stopped, and my life began the day Priscilla stepped off the train at the Beetle River depot."

Julius chuckled. "So, you got the girl?"

"It made Ralph mad. You'd not know it now, but back then he could be quite handsome. But Ralph Meecham had a bitter spirit, and Prissy saw through his outward appearance. Age hasn't improved his character. He married a gentlewoman, and pretty, but not overly bright. Priscilla tried to be neighborly to Dolly, but Ralph wouldn't allow it. Time didn't heal his bitterness."

"Some people are like that." Julius leaned back in his chair. "They could have life on a silver platter, and still find a rock in the oyster."

"Yes, and Ralph more than most. Back then when folks got sick neighbors would pitch in. Priscilla was one to help wherever needed and there were three years of sickness right together. In 1951 the community was stricken. Then in '52, our baby Rose died. That broke our hearts. By the time influenza hit our community again in '53 Priscilla became sick nursing other folks. I've heard say the good die young. She died much too young."

"But there's still something missing. Did your problems with Meecham begin with Priscilla?" Julius tapped his spoon on his saucer.

"Ralph wasn't pleasant in grade school. Kind of a loner," Pat said.

"How many children did Ralph and his wife have?"

"There were three: two girls and a boy. The girls left as soon as they could. They couldn't stand the overbearing old coot. The son, David, was a quiet boy, not a thing like his dad. Ralph pushed David around like he had Dolly. David's wife couldn't stand Ralph either.

She and David just had one son, Phil. Funny that Ralph took to Phil. Sad that he made him into someone like himself. Maybe because Phil's ma ran off and married again."

"Ralph felt sorry for his little grandson?"

"No, it reminded Ralph of his childhood." Pat stirred more cream into his coffee. "You know, I'd forgotten. Ed and Martha Meecham couldn't have any children of their own, and they dearly loved and wanted children. Ed's sister had a child, but her man left her. What to do with the boy? Her brother and his wife wanted children, and she didn't. It seemed providential. Everyone got what they wanted—except Ralph. His ma didn't want him, and his pa didn't live far enough away."

"So, Ed and Martha adopted him?"

"No, that's part of what made it hard on him. He just took their name."

"Why so?" Julius's eyes narrowed.

Pat O'Brien cackled. "Some years later his natural Pa ran for some kind of political office. Everyone knew him. Men that run off and leave their women and children weren't looked on kindly. They called him Meister, the shyster."

"Mr. O'Brien—" Julius jumped up and pumped Pat's hand. "I have enjoyed our visit. You have a beautiful granddaughter, a wonderful son, and thank you for your help. Too bad I can't give you a reward. Maybe in heaven."

"What in the—" Pat O'Brien stammered.

JULIUS PULLED UP TO the Bed and Breakfast and glanced at his watch as Seth sauntered down the front steps.

"I thought maybe you'd forgotten me." Seth opened the car door and dropped into the passenger seat.

"Not so, Kid. Ya have lunch?" asked Julius.

"Rheba fixed Reuben sandwiches. If I keep eating maybe my breeches will quit sliding off." He grinned and patted his stomach.

"I have some errands. Since you've had lunch, we'll just head to Hermon." Pulling out onto the pavement they turned toward the city.

"Oh, look," Julius said as a police car pulled in behind them. He went through a mental checklist. When the police light began to flash, Julius slowed, pulled over, and stopped. "It's Snidely Whiplash."

"Huh?"

"Snidely Whiplash." Julius put emphasis on his words. "But don't stare."

"Oh?" Seth turned and stared as the officer approached.

"Good afternoon, officer. Is something wrong?" Julius asked.

"Just a routine check, Armstrong. License please."

Julius handed him his license, and Meecham checked it over. Officer Philip Meecham proceeded to do an equipment check.

"Everything appears to be in order." Meecham handed the license back. "You going to be around much longer? Don't you have enough pictures for your book yet?"

"I'll be leaving after church Sunday, but," Julius leaned back and stretched his long legs. "I've grown fond of some of the folks around here." He watched in the mirror as the officer's eyes narrowed.

"Yeah, you can go now." Meecham scowled.

Seth looked over his shoulder as Julius pulled back onto the road. "Snidely Whiplash, huh. Was Fair Nell at church?"

"Yes, she sat right in front of Michael and me."

"The one with the gorgeous auburn hair?"

"That's the one." Julius glanced in his mirror. *Good, the police car went the other way.*

"If the face looked as stunning as the back of her head, it's no wonder Snidely's attracted. I was going to ask who the dude you were sitting beside was. So, that's Michael?"

"Yep." Julius shot a side look at Seth. "Been a long time."

"Too long." Seth examined his fingers. "Where do the years go, Jo. What were we thinking?"

"I don't know. No use crying over lost time. Only four more days."

"Tears in a bottle." A shadow passed over Seth's face, and his eyes held a disturbed look.

JULIUS PULLED INTO the Hermon city park beside a beat-up black Fiesta. "You can stay here, or you can come." Julius got out and walked toward the shelter house.

Seth quick stepped until he caught up. "Can't be much help if I don't know what's goin' on."

Julius stopped for a drink at the water fountain on the edge of some trees. "Chief Mallory, you must be pretty good at camouflage," Julius said in a low voice.

"Yeah, I look a lot like a tree." Mallory laughed. "We're running through the stuff you sent us. We've identified a couple of people from those pictures you gave me. We've got it set up for the bust. We've got one leaker identified."

"Frank Wilde and Gary Young from the Chicago area are on the loose, and Bingley and Jacobs as well. They can still wreak havoc. The rising harassment in the community bothers me. Friday-Saturday morning there is a special drop, That's our target," Julius said.

"Other businesses have been threatened. One owner was beaten and robbed. The men threatening Michael MacDonald at Imports Magnifique were picked up and put in the pokey. Takes out two. You're right though those other nut jobs, Wilde and Young, have got records a mile long. And Meecham in cahoots with the other side makes it tricky. I've pulled in help from trusted men in surrounding departments for the sting out at Meecham's field, and I don't know how we're going to pull that off. I can't do that for day to day ops."

"We're narrowing down the playing field for whoever is trying to muscle in. I've got some leads. We'll be in touch."

JULIUS AND SETH PULLED into the parking lot at Frankie and Johnny's.

"This is some place!" Seth gazed around at the foyer.

"Yeah? Don't get too comfortable, Kid." Julius frowned at him.

"Yeah, yeah...I hear ya." He muttered and examined the carpet.

"Party of how many?" The hostess asked as she pulled out the menus. She led the way to the little corner table in the unobtrusive spot situated behind a planter with some tall ivy—the perfect spot for observing the scenery below. They placed their orders and waited.

"Hi there, cowboy." Angie greeted Julius as a server placed their salads on the table.

"Matt this is Angie."

"He and I have already kind of met, when he brought your message last week." She pulled up her chair.

"Do you want a coke?" Julius asked her.

"What? No soda water?" She laughed into her napkin.

Julius motioned for the waitress. "I'll take a 7-Up here."

Angie made a space for her 7-Up as the waitress placed it in front of her. "Thank you, Patty." She turned back to Julius and winked.

"Don't look now—" Julius whispered. "Snidely Whiplash."

"Ow!" Seth rubbed his leg. "What'd ya kick me for?"

"I might as well tell him to stare," Julius said to Angie. "He only follows directions that tell him to do what he wants to do." Julius looked over at Seth. "I see Snidely is not alone tonight."

Seth turned just enough to see Phil Meecham and a well-dressed middle-aged man seated at a table close to the stage. A brunette hostess sat with Snidely.

"What do you know about those two?" Julius twitched his eyebrows at the two men. He didn't look up, but pushed his salad bowl back and chewed on a breadstick.

"The younger one is a regular. He comes in three to four times a week. The other one I've never seen before. The younger fella has a special status. Brings in different guys. Something to do with his business. Usually Genie there is paired off with him. She says he's odd," Angie murmured as she took a sip of her drink.

"How's that?" Julius smiled at Angie giving any onlooker a sociable impression.

"He's moody. He can go from being friendly to antagonistic, or vice versa in a matter of minutes, and no rhyme or reason to it. He's taken to wearing a tiny gold ring on a chain. Genie commented on it a few days ago, and he threatened her."

"Say, you want something to eat, a salad, a dessert, or something? You look lonely sitting with just a soda." Julius patted her hand.

"We aren't allowed to eat out here. We're supposed to encourage patrons to relax and spend more on drinks and other stuff." She raised her eyebrows.

"Thank you, Patty." Julius smiled as the waitress brought their seafood specials. "So, what's the word on the street?" He signaled for Angie to talk while he ate. To anyone listening it was a normal conversation.

"I'm glad that your aunt is feeling better." Julius winked as he finished, pushed his empty plate forward, and leaned back in thought. He ruminated on the information. "Lots going on." He leaned forward to pick up his glass of water. With a sleight of hand, he picked up the piece of paper she had slipped under his napkin. "What's the show this week? Anything good?"

"Ms. Crabtree left yesterday, and none too soon I can tell you. That woman got on my one last nerve. We have a magician this week. He and an assistant. He's a middle-aged fellow. They look good under the lights, but they drink too much and are...cheap. She isn't as old as he is, but that lifestyle tells on a woman."

"We won't be able to catch the show." Julius pushed his chair back from the table. The lights dimmed as the show began.

"Have a good evening then," Angie whispered.

"See you next time." Julius smiled at Angie. They threaded their way toward the cash register as a dark-haired man in a tuxedo burst onto the stage, and his act began.

"Thank you, ma'am. Yes, the meal was excellent," Julius leaned in and spoke loud over the drumroll as the show progressed.

They turned to leave, but a loud blare of music grabbed their attention. Both Julius and Seth stopped and stared at the stage. A puff of smoke, a stunning red-haired siren in a blue sequined bathing suit, materialized so close to the front tables the patrons could have reached out and touched her. Meecham jumped up and pushed away spilling glasses, food, and everything on the table, creating instantaneous chaos. His eyes were harsh and hard, his face carved out of stone, as he shoved out of the restaurant. The restaurant door had not closed when Julius heard a car door slam and an engine roar to life. Someone jammed a shift, grinding through the gears. Tires squealed and spun out as it sped away from the parking lot.

"Did you get pictures?" Julius whispered to Seth.

"Yep, gotcha covered." Seth slipped a small camera into his pocket.

"Good." The two walked to the car then drove toward Beetle River. "I'll let you out at your place. I need to scout around before calling it a night."

"You don't need my expertise?"

"I'll be less conspicuous by myself."

"In the morning then." Seth closed the car door and waved as he walked to his room.

Julius drove out west of Beetle River. The way Philip Meecham looked when he left Frankie and Johnny's he wasn't on his way home. Julius slowed, coming up beside Meecham's abandoned car south of Juan's house. Now, which way? Julius drove on around to the copse of trees at the back of Laura and Juan's pasture. He left his car and moved swift and silent through the trees and across the pasture toward the house. He had become quite familiar with this route. Julius stood in the shadow at the back of the house. He could sense Philip Meecham's presence—his spine tingled.

HOW HAD HE COME TO this spot? Philip Meecham sat beside the driveway, his head in his hands. The cheap red-headed woman popping up in front of him would be etched in his memory forever. His head ached, and memories bombarded his mind. His first day in second grade he told his Grandfather about the beautiful red-haired girl. His Grandfather's hate filled the space as he shook his fist and spoke. "O'Briens. You stay away from them, they're trouble." *Why is life so complicated?*

He saw the good things she did, and wondered, how could she be so beautiful and good...and bad? And the time Billy Barton tripped *him,* and he tore a hole in the knee of his jeans. Ruth asked him, "Your momma can patch 'em can't she?". She didn't know he didn't have a momma. And the day Grandma had whispered, "Priscilla O'Brien was a sweet, decent person. Ruth and her brother aren't bad." Philip remembered the fear in her eyes. She died a short time after that. And who had started those rumors about him and Ruth? Now someone went with her everywhere. He shivered. He felt chilled somehow, even in the warmth of the night.

Laughter and music inside the house drew him toward the front window. *Even as a captive, she can enjoy singing and laughter. Here I am free, but there has never been singing and laughing for me.* A bitter taste filled his mouth, and anger filled his heart.

Just once! He crept as close as he dared to the window. There, a few feet away the light shimmered around her. She became a heavenly apparition standing in the beautiful room. Philip Meecham wanted to share that moment, to share her touch. She raised her hand to the young man's shoulder who stood in the room with her and spoke to him. Philip's eyes narrowed. Anger and jealousy seethed and fermented within him. He couldn't tear his eyes away. *I'll get you! I swear.*

Crouching in the shadows, he strained forward, every nerve focusing on the scene before him—suddenly, he was jerked farther back into the shadows. He grabbed at his neck, clawing to free himself of the choking grip. Choking, he couldn't make a sound. Darker and darker, the world grew dark. He faded from consciousness.

Half an hour later he woke to the touch of cold metal as he lay across the hood of his car.

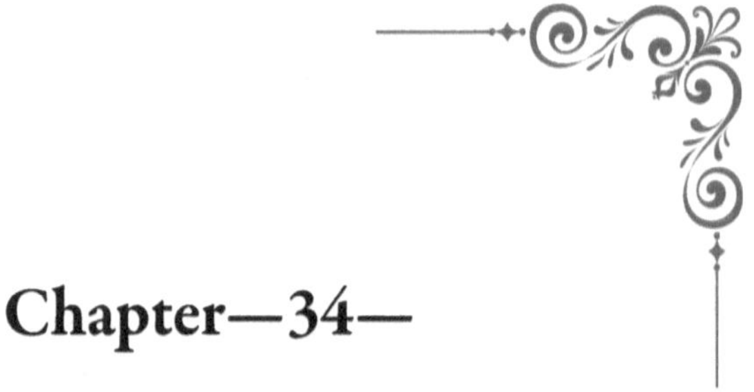

Chapter—34—

After depositing Meecham across the hood of the black Mustang, then retrieving his own car, he slowly tread up the steps to his room. Back at his room Julius rolled up his shirt sleeve and examined the wounds on his arm. He washed off the gashes and sprayed disinfectant on the welts. *At least I haven't been shot this time around. Shot at but no connection.* He flicked off the light and sat in the chair by the open window. *Saturday and this will be all over.* The look on Meecham's face at Frankie's gave him chills. He slid onto the floor by his bed and pulled his electronics out. He had a theory.

THURSDAY, JUNE 25th; Julius sat drinking his morning coffee on the sunporch. The last two weeks weighed on his mind. The Ladies' voices chattered at each other as they finished up breakfast, and Michael strode up the path toward the house. Julius's senses seemed heightened as Michael washed up at the sink whistling an old tune.

"What's life look like when you're done here? Got another book to work on?" Michael asked as he sat down at the table with Julius.

"I don't know what it will look like, but there's always one more story."

"You told Lewis you'd be done by Saturday? You think this'll be done by then?" Michael's eyes narrowed, and he lowered his voice.

Julius put a finger to his lips. "I'll stop by the store later."

With a nod, Michael said, "I'll sure be glad when Juan and Laura get back…"

"And Mac," Mrs. MacDonald brought in plates followed by Ruth bringing food.

"You gals sure do a great job on meals, but I'm not going to make it back for supper this evening," Julius said.

"Why ever not?" Mrs. MacDonald asked.

"Business. Always business." Julius shook his head.

THE BELL ABOVE THE door tinkled, and Michael acknowledged Julius. "I'll be right with you, soon as we're finished here."

"No problem." *This is sure better than the last time I was here.* Julius began to survey the wares. *Nothing cheap here. The quality of merchandise would draw clientele of discerning tastes and deep pockets.*

"I'll contact Juan, and see what he can find for you. They'll be back in a couple of weeks," Michael told the customer. He turned to Julius as the last customer walked out to his car.

"Quite a nice little establishment," Julius said.

"For a small store, Juan and Laura do a brisk business. If a person is searching for a specific item, antique or just hard to locate —Juan can find it if anyone can. I, however, feel like a frog out of the pond here." Michael adjusted his tie.

"You carry it off suitably."

"Thank you," Michael looked at him with anticipation.

"A certain officer pulled me over on the way out of town yesterday."

"Oh, now how did you rate that?" Michael asked raising his eyebrows. "You have moved into the 'to be harassed category' with the rest of us?"

"He wanted me to know he knows who I am."

"I hope he's not too sure of himself—Frankie and Johnny's again?"

"Other business tonight. But you need to be careful. Our favorite officer isn't the only challenge, remember."

"Yes, I remember. I thought of closing the store for a few days. Have any good answers for me?" Michael ran his finger along the beveled edge on an antique frame before glancing at Julius.

"Yeah, close down until Monday. Better safe than sorry."

Michael nodded in agreement. "You think this will be over Monday?"

"Yes. I'm going to let you in on this. I think you and Ruth can help us with this case."

"How so?" Michael asked.

"When I arrived, I was looking for someone named Alberto Meister. I'm sure I found him, just need one more foray into forbidden territory, but, I'm also needing local information about David and Phil Meecham's day to day operation. I know you two have been collecting information."

"That's true. What do you need to know?" Michael sat down at the desk.

"Tell me what you know. We're setting up a sting for Friday morning early. . ."

"David has been the real boss for—I'd say five or six years. Ralph has been in the care center for two years. They've been trying to move Phil in to replace Ralph, and even though Phil isn't my favorite person, I'm not convinced his heart is in the business."

"How's that?" Julius sat in the chair across from Michael.

"I just get that feeling. It's during these full moons that the plane brings in a big load of drugs and sometimes passengers too. David takes care of the day to day work. Phil just annoys the local populace, mostly. There's a small crew stationed out at the field where the plane drops every full moon. Phil is stationed at one end of the dirt road, David at the actual site, and then some locals like Stu and Earl."

"When you say small, about how many besides David and Phil?"

"Six at most. This last month has been hard on the crew."

"How's that?" Julius asked.

"They've had some of the old crew disappear. No explanation. So, new people have come in."

"How's this tie with Frankie and Johnny's?"

"They're major distributors."

"Sounds good. Now, for a couple of questions not related to that subject that you might be able to answer?" Julius said.

"I'll try."

"Do you know Ruth's, Aunt Genevieve?"

"Yeah, I've met her on several occasions. She's a pleasant person. Has a few more aches and pains than she knows what to do with," Michael said with a smile.

"What about her kids. Do you know them at all?"

"Can't say that I do. Ruth says her cousin, Dee is a real stunner. I know I've never met her. The two boys, I'm pretty sure I've never met them either. Why?"

"Curiosity I guess. So, they've not been back here since you've been here?"

"They've probably been back, I just don't remember them."

"What about for Diana's funeral?"

"Dee was in the hospital at the time and couldn't make it. The brother in med school couldn't make it either, but come to think of it, yeah, the other brother flew home. I can't put a face to him though. Ruth has pictures I'm sure."

"Thanks, that's a good idea. I'll ask her. Well, places to go, things to do. Drive careful and keep that number handy." Julius straightened up from leaning against a china hutch.

Julius opened the door and crunching across the parking lot strode out into the early evening. He slid into the driver's seat. "It's a frustrating feeling when I have to tell people to shut down and run," he said. "That makes me angry. Good people ought not to suffer like this," Julius said to Seth as he wheeled the car around and cruised down the street.

A short time later Julius pulled into the gas station and around to the air machine. "Need to check the tires," he said stopping beside an old beat up VW Volkswagen. He engaged the long-haired hippie in a short conversation, and then took over checking his tires.

"What now?" Seth said when Julius got back in.

"Need to finish up some last minute plans. I'll fill you in on my new info as we head for our meet up. . ."

"SO, WHAT'S NEW?" MALLORY asked as Julius and Seth joined him at the repair garage.

"We need two stings tomorrow," Julius said. "First one at Frankie and Johnny's. We've made some in roads into the usual workers by arresting several of their goons and Meecham is short staffed on the ground. William T. told me there's been an increase in packages and stuff going into the supper club, and there'll be another one before the moonlight plane tomorrow night as well. The plane is supposed to land—for a few minutes too."

"Our resources are tight too. How many agents do you have here? "Mallory asked.

"We have three at the club and five at large. That doesn't include the Kid here." Julius pointed at Seth. "Or Michael MacDonald and I know he'll be there."

"Untrained? You think that's wise?"

"He and Ruth have been extremely helpful. . . Here, let me draw this out—I'll send the Kid and Michael in the front of the Supper club like customers. They'll signal Angie to let me in the back door. I'll keep a lookout for the packages, when they come in the Kid will start a distraction, police called and no one will suspect, anything."

Mallory chewed on the end of his pencil and studied Seth, who had shed his hat and glasses for the moment. "Well, what do you think, Kid?"

"I've always been good at eating and causing distractions, so being a customer won't be a problem, and neither will the last part." He grinned.

"Okay. What's the second part?" Mallory's brow furrowed.

"We'll need to get out of town and set up at the field north of O'Brien's. Michael says Philip is parked at one end of this dirt road." Julius found a blank piece of paper and drew a map of the area. "Road here, O'Brien's own this eighty acre field here, and the next field is Meecham's right here. That's where the plane air drops packages, or in some cases it lands. David Meecham is here to meet the plane, and there is one maybe two other people to help it land . . ."

"That one's gonna be the hard one," Mallory said. "You've got to have enough net to bring them in, but not too much for them to slip through."

"Exactly, and there isn't lots of cover anywhere close, just a few scraggly trees and bushes."

"Ya think maybe William could identify some of the regulars on the drops?" Seth asked.

"Whoa, almost forgot you were here, Kid. That's a good idea. We might be able to replace one or two of them. . ." Julius said.

"And check on the plane, where it's coming from, where it would be going," Seth said.

"Sounds like we better get moving." Mallory stood. "We don't have much time left. Did you find your big man?"

"I think so. I have one more scouting trip into the unknown, but I have a good idea."

"Tomorrow, then," Mallory tipped his hat.

SETH PICKED UP TWO candy bars and sauntered up to the checkout at the Molly Mart convenience store. He leaned against the counter as Julius paid for fuel. "Who would've thought we'd see gasoline this high?"

"Yeah, but look at the price of everything else?" Julius said as they walked to the car. "Come on, Kid. One more errand before..."

"What's that noise?" Seth looked around the front seat as they climbed back in the Chevy.

"That's my—hold on." Julius punched in numbers. "I'd hoped we'd never need this. Give me co-ordinates as we go, and hang on." He handed Seth a pathfinder.

"I know you go North, you go north out of town...Do you know how many centuries it's been since I've used one of these things?" Seth frowned and stared over the compass.

"Probably about twelve years, if my reckoning is correct."

"That's about right. North ten then west six. I don't think we can get there from here. Unless you're flying a plane. North again four."

"We better be able to get there," Julius began to slow as he neared the site. "I think Michael's life depends on it."

"There's a car in the field, and lights on the road. They're leaving!"

Julius shoved the lever into park and sprang out of the Impala. Pulling his Beretta from its holster, he fired at the tail light speeding down the road away from them. "I'm sure I had a hit, but I need to radio this in to the police," he shouted, holstered his weapon and pulled out his radio. "Rollover, car in a field," he said giving the location as Seth and he slid down the bank, into the ditch and crawled over the broken barb wire fence. "One occupant ...no passengers. Out." Julius finished his call.

A police car with flashing lights screeched to a halt behind Julius's car. "Oh, great!" Seth groaned as Officer Phil Meecham flew out his door.

"I've called for an ambulance. They're on their way. Is anyone hurt? " Meecham shouted as he slid down the bank, and made his way to the scene.

"Careful there," Julius said. "The wires are loose. The car must have rolled through the fence. We just arrived. The Mark VII landed on its wheels but must have rolled more than once to get that far into the farm field. The one occupant looks unconscious."

Wedging his right foot against the side of the vehicle, and giving a terrific wrench Officer Meecham managed to yank the door open. Careful to not nudge the body, he turned off the engine. "I don't smell gas, but better check anyway." He called over his shoulder as he checked vital signs.

"I can smell gas over here, but the tank on this side is wedged into the dirt, and the tire's flat on the back passenger side," Julius said.

"I need some help then. We better get him out. His pulse is good, but breathing is shallow. Something's knocked him on the head. There's bleeding on the right side of the forehead. Gentle now." Meecham unlatched the seatbelt, and they began to slide Michael out.

"You catch the legs there, Kid, and help support the rest of the body," Julius said.

"Here's the ambulance," Seth said as flashing lights rolled up followed by a police cruiser.

"Need to get this guy out now. There's a gasoline leak." Officer Meecham beckoned to the paramedics bringing the gurney.

"Thanks for your help, Officer. You did well," Julius said.

"That's some way to end a shift, I can tell ya."

"What happened?" Chief Mallory looked at Officer Meecham.

"I arrived second. I heard the call come in. I was about a mile away and responded," Officer Meecham said.

"Meet me at the station so we can make our report," Chief Mallory said.

"Ten-four, Chief," Meecham scrambled out of the field.

"What happened on your end?" Mallory turned to Julius.

"I'll have to make a statement later. We were on our way out of town when we came across this rollover. There was another car here on the road, but as we approached they took off."

"Hmm, suspicious," Mallory said.

"Yes, it is. I believe it's missing at least one taillight. Keep a watch at local garages."

"We can do that. Do you know who the person in the rollover is?"

"Michael MacDonald, coming home from Imports there in Hermon. We'll catch you later. We've got some calls to make. And need to get to the hospital. "

As Julius and Seth walked to their car, Mallory caught up with them. "I'll talk to you at the hospital chapel."

"Okay, later." Julius slid into his seat and buckled his seat belt.

JULIUS HANDED HIS PHONE to Seth as they pulled back onto the road. "Call Lewis, tell him what's happened, and we'll meet him at the hospital. We're not far from the hospital here, less than fifteen minutes."

After the phone call, Seth hung up. "That was a different Philip Meecham than the one that pulled you over."

"Sure shocked the socks off of me. Gives me something to think on. Angie reported he has an alter persona. I don't know if that was it, or something else, but wow. You'll have to make yourself scarce when Lewis shows up," a few traffic lights later Julius pulled into the parking lot.

"I figured. At least I can find out how Michael's doing."

"Michael MacDonald?" Julius asked at the emergency room desk.

"Down the hall, take a right, and first door on your left." The man at the desk said.

They made their way down the hall, and Julius stuck his head in the door. "Can we come in?"

"Yeah, he's good," the nurse said as she finished patching the injury on Michael's forehead.

Julius pushed in while Seth pulled his hat down low on his head hiding his face and scrunched down on a chair inside the door.

"I see you're awake. We were concerned." Julius stood beside the bed where Michael lay.

"Yeah, I got knocked on the head, probably flying debris. They've taken some x-rays, but don't think there's anything serious. It's Mac-Donald constitution. Strong as an ox," Michael said.

"We called Lewis when we left the accident scene. Didn't want to upset the others. You'll need to make a statement to the police." Julius said when the nurse left the room. "And we'll need to have a private talk as well."

Seth caught Julius' glance and with a nod mouthed the word 'chapel', and slipped out of the room. A minute later the doors burst open, and the rest of the family hustled in.

"No, I'm alright. You guys don't need to get all excited. Like they say, all's well that ends well." Michael tried to quiet their fears. "I closed the store early. After you were there, Julius, I couldn't get in focus."

"What happened?" Lewis asked.

"I rolled the car. That's what someone told me, and something—probably flying debris hit me on the head. Knocked me out.

I didn't come to until they were wheeling me in through the ER entrance. I, I need to make a statement to the police, but I'll want some time to collect my thoughts before I say anything."

"The dust was just settling when we pulled up. The car's totaled, but like Michael said, it could have been worse. I called it in and had just slid down the bank when a police cruiser pulled up. He called for an ambulance and backup," Julius said.

THE DOOR OPENED AND a tall dark haired man greeted the family. "Hello, my name is Doctor Irving. I've had time to look over the x-rays. Yes, there are some bruised ribs, but what we thought was flying debris . . . might have been something else. We'll have to take another look at the scene." The doctor in his best bedside manner reassured the group assembled in the room. "Whatever it was, it doesn't look like he sustained any lasting effects from it. He'll need to be cautious for several weeks. I'll have the nurse prepare a room, and…"

"Oh, no. No, no." Michael with careful movements sat up. "I don't know where my hat went, but I'm taking it and going home."

"I recommend that you stay over-night for observation, young man." the doctor looked down his nose as he spoke.

"I appreciate your excellent recommendation, but like I said, I'm going home and observe from there."

"It's okay, doctor," Mrs. MacDonald said. "We'll keep an eye on him."

"This is highly unusual, but I can't keep him here against his wishes," he said with a shrug.

"I'm going to let you folks take care of this fellow. I had an appointment that I need to keep. I think you lost your hat somewhere in the desert, fella. But do not go back after it tonight." Julius stopped at the door and waited. "You do hear me, right?"

"Yes, sir," Michael said.

"THAT WAS TOO CLOSE," Julius joined Seth in the chapel.

"Boy howdy, you can say that again." Seth wiped a hand over his face. "When are you supposed to meet Mallory?"

"Let's move to a darker area. He should be joining us."

"That had to be some kind of ride," Seth whispered to Julius. "Reminds me of that dumb joke."

"Joke?"

"Yeah, you know, the preacher driving home one evening swerves to avoid an inebriated man stumbling down the road. The preacher ends up in the ditch, and the man rushes up and asks if he's all right..."

"And the preacher says, yes, the Lord was riding with me. And the drunk says, you better let him come with me. You're gonna kill him driving like that. Is that the one?" Julius asked.

"Yeah, that's it. Not really funny in this instance, but that's what it reminds me of."

They turned as the chapel doors opened. "What happened out there?" Mallory positioned himself out of sight.

"Haven't had time to question Michael in private, but the vehicle on the road had been chasing him."

"How can you tell that?"

"Tire tracks in the gravel. I doubt with all the activity anything can be gleaned from it now, but we were first on the scene. If we hadn't come when we did there's no telling what devilment would've happened."

"Shush, someone coming," Seth hissed.

Mallory pressed further into the corner behind a curtain, as Julius and Seth hunkered down on the floor under the back pew.

"You don't know what you're talking about, there's no one in here." An unidentified man's voice growled.

"I saw Chief Mallory come in here." A higher pitched voice whined. "You could turn on the lights…"

"You're a fool. There aren't any ceiling lights. This is a chapel, you idiot."

"I'm tellin' ya I saw…"

"And I'm tellin' you there ain't nobody here." They turned and left.

"Close. Too close. Good thing your hearing's so good," Julius crawled out from under the pew. "Mallory, I need to gather some more evidence, but I have a suspect in the Diana O'Brien murder case."

"So, it is murder?" Mallory said from the corner.

"There're a few things that are a puzzlement yet, but, yeah."

Chapter—35—

F riday, June 26<u>th</u>;"You sure don't let the grass grow under your feet, Jo. After that hike across the field, I'm feeling like I'm worse than outa shape." Seth gasped for breath early the next morning.

"I've got to get evidence out of here, and it has to be off the record." Julius stared up and down the side of the house then crunched down the path toward a side window.

"I've been accused of lots of things but never breaking and entering. At least this early in the morning no one else will be up...you're sure no one's home? This door isn't locked," Seth said turning the porch door latch. His eyes widened, and the color drained from his face as the door swung open.

"No, I come over twice daily to check the property when my sister-in-law is gone. What business do you have here at this hour, young man?" Jack O'Brien scowled at him.

Seth closed his mouth and swallowed before he answered. "Well, mister—" His mind went into overdrive. *Did Julius say this was an O'Brien's home? Something about a sister-in-law?* "My partner and I were here talking to your sister-in-law about putting on a new roof and maybe some siding awhile back." He looked around, but Julius had disappeared. *Great. This isn't supposed to happen. Things could get real here.*

"This early in the morning?" Jack's eyes narrowed, and he gave him a one-eyed look.

"Like they say, early bird gets the snail."

A puzzled look crossed Jack O'Brien's face. "My sister-in-law won't be back for two weeks. You'll have to come back then. Are you from this area?"

"No. My boss is looking to expand his business up this way."

"Where's your partner?"

"He's doing some figuring," Seth said with a vague wave. "If she won't be back for a couple of weeks, we'll come back then. Thanks for your time." He touched the brim of his hat and turned to walk away.

"Young man," Jack said.

"Yes, sir?" He turned back.

"My dad and I've been thinking about siding and a new roof as well. How long you be in the area, and do you guarantee your work?"

"How long depends on how much market we find work-wise, and yes, sir, we do guarantee our work. We aim to provide quality work customers can live with, and that we can be proud of. I'm kind of booked up with customer estimates until... " He stopped to consider. "I think about Tuesday afternoon this coming week. If you want I could stop over and do a free estimate for you?"

"We live back around at the house in that grove over there. Do you need an address? A name?"

"Give me your name and address. I'll put it in my records when I get back to the truck."

"My dad's name is Pat O'Brien, address 122 Sloan Avenue."

"Okay, Pat O'Brien, 122 Sloan Avenue—I'll put it down for 2:00 Tuesday afternoon. Have a good day, sir."

"WHAT WERE YOU THINKING, Kid?" Julius asked as they hunkered down in the grove behind the house. "You suppose he won't notice you didn't have a truck?"

"What could I do? My fearless partner abandoned me, and I had to think fast," Seth said with a shrug. "He sure wouldn't like it if I'd said, well, we came to break into this house and my partner..."

"What are you going to do Tuesday at 2:00?"

"Going to drop by Pat O'Brien's and give him some estimates. If Gwen and I move up here, I'll have to have work, and siding and roofing is what I know."

Julius watched as Jack O'Brien's pickup backed out of the driveway and drove back around toward his home. "You've got a point. I need to get that information out of there. You can stay here and keep an eye out this time. Here's the talkie," Julius handed him the hand-held communicator before he headed for the house.

Julius closed and locked the porch door, looking behind, he marked where Seth sat waiting amongst the trees in back of the house. Julius turned back to the job at hand. The house was neat and well kept. *Sure hope it's not too neat and clean.* Quickly he began scouting out the rooms. Apparently, Aunt Genevieve lived mostly down stairs, that was where her bedroom was, and the three other occasional occupant's rooms had been upstairs. He did his job efficiently and was just finishing his last room upstairs when the walkie talkie sputtered to life.

"Julius," Seth's voice hissed into the walkie talkie. "Julius?"

"Yes?" It squawked back at him.

"He's back. Mr. O'Brien just pulled back into the drive."

"Thanks."

Julius had become an escape artist back in his younger years when he and his co-conspirator, Chuckie Malone, had to dodge not just the local sheriff, Archie Daniels, but other hazards like their rivals, the Sage brothers. Julius gave Mr. O'Brien enough time to unlock the back door and enter. *Timing it just right he dropped to the ground from the upstairs front corner window, and then disappeared around the other side of the garage.* He slipped around and watched from the grove of trees as Mr. O'Brien came out and locked the back door and left.

"That was sure close," Julius spoke and stepped out from behind a tree.

"Hot dog!" Seth said with a jump. "A little warning would have helped, Jo. I mean, where did you come from? I didn't see you make your escape."

"I stopped announcing my flight schedule somewhere in the desert, Kid. It usually isn't healthy." Julius grinned at his companion.

"I've had my binoculars on the scenery ever since you left, you sly dog."

"Let's go. Things to do, places to go." Julius set the pace back across the field, and back to the car they had left in the grove behind Diana O'Brien's house.

"YOU KNOW, JO, I'M JUST not in the same shape I used to be." Seth fell into the passenger seat holding his side. "What's this?" He held up a pink pony water bottle.

"Hmm, probably means Mr. O'Brien's not so dumb, I guess." Julius looked at the pink pony water bottle. "Throw that in the back. We'll run this evidence in to be processed then there are a few odds and ends to tie up." He turned the car toward Hermon. "We'll drive by Juan's car and scout around in the daylight as well. The doctor's report questioned whether Michael was hit by debris or a bullet scrape."

"HOW ABOUT A ROOT BEER float to tide us over?" Julius said after their errands were run. "I know they've had lunch back at the house, so we may be out until supper. We were successful all the way around this morning, so only half a day left to go."

"Sounds like a plan, Jo. Doesn't that A&W bring back a memory?"

"Sure does," Julius said as he pulled in and parked.

"I never in a million years would have dreamed we would be cops and robbers in the distant future though. Thanks." Seth took his float and began to slurp it up.

"Today should be Mrs. MacDonald's doctor's visit. Michael and Ruth should be the only ones at home except maybe Lewis's boys."

"Lewis and Donna had one baby when they left home. Now they have three boys?" Seth asked as the waiter picked up their tray.

"Three good kids, in spite of Michael's unique influence." Julius chuckled at a memory.

"I'm not sure how to proceed from here. I don't want to spring your presence on everyone, and certainly not too fast, but . . . " Julius let his sentence dangle as he pulled in the driveway.

"YOU WERE UP AND GONE early. We got your note," Ruth said as Julius came in through the laundry room into the kitchen.

"Yes, there's lots to do today. Ruth, I'd like to introduce my newest side-kick, Seth."

"He was with you the other night right?"

"Yes, and he's going to have to be with me tonight. So we're going to be working as a team. I didn't want to surprise you later when we need to be focused. How's Michael doing?"

"Constitution of an ox. That's why Lewis took the boys with him, to keep Michael from doing Michael things." She rolled her eyes. "Hello, Seth." Ruth gave a reserved nod in the direction of a cowboy hat, a beard, and sunglasses who had followed Julius into the kitchen.

"Howdy," Seth said with a nod.

"Ruth, I need to ask you a few quick questions," Julius said.

"Quick questions? Sure."

"Your cousins— One's a doctor, one lives in Canada, and the girl lives in California?"

"Yes, somewhat. Allen is in the last stages of the doctor thing," Ruth said with hesitation.

"The boys are twins, but not identical?"

"No, not identical."

"They don't come home often?"

"No, Aunt Genevieve splits her time between here and Dee's. Tim came back for Mom's funeral."

"What color is your Aunt Genevieve's hair?"

"Huh?" Ruth had a confused look before she answered. "It's been prematurely grey. She dies it kind of a Champaign blond. That was her natural color. The worry with Sean's health..."

"So sad when people die so young," Julius said. "Did you kids ever use that backfield between your houses?" Julius asked.

"Dee used to come that way and visit Mom often. She was such a pretty, sweet young girl. I liked Dee. She's much more social than I am. She was good company for Mom. They would play cards. . . but the boys didn't come over."

"Thanks. That pretty well answers my questions. Could those horses use some exercise this evening?"

"After supper, right?" Ruth raised an eyebrow at him.

"I need to do some preliminary set up, and some snooping around—Yes, after supper."

"Have you had lunch? It won't be, but a jiffy and I can have a quick lunch. Would you like beef stroganoff or Chinese?" Ruth asked.

"Stroganoff will work."

"We plan leftovers to put in the freezer for quick meals like this." She slid a couple of plates into the microwave. Pouring two glasses of tea, she brought them to the counter. "Will iced tea—oh, my—" her eyes went wide, and she gasped. Ruth put the glasses down abruptly. "What are you going to do with him? He can't wear the hat and glasses all the time, and..."

"Well, I need his help, but since this book should be finished and wrapped up tonight . . .He can be himself tomorrow. I don't know where he'll go from there."

The microwave dinged, and Ruth placed the food on the counter. "I...I need to...I'm going to work on the garden while you two eat." Ruth left them to eat and scooted out the door.

"Seth, I think you've traumatized the lady. Maybe you should put your hat and glasses back on."

"I have that effect on women. She'll get used to it."

Julius snickered and shook his head. They finished eating, and put their dishes by the sink. "Let's grab a refill on tea and go sit outside. There's a pleasant breeze."

Ruth had a basket of lettuce and summer squash dripping in the shade ready for supper. She picked up a bunch of radishes to wash when Julius sat down at the picnic table.

"Are you ready for a horseback ride this evening?" Julius continued his conversation with Seth. "Supper's about five?"

"Five or five-thirty. The days Mrs. MacDonald goes to the doctor I fix a simple supper. She's pretty tired when they get back." Ruth's brows were pulled together, her face wore a frown. She spoke slowly. "You remember Mr. MacDonald gets back on Sunday?"

"Yes, I remember." Julius could see that something bothered Ruth.

"What about him?" She motioned toward Seth.

"I have a name." Seth scowled.

"I'm sorry. It's just such a shock." Ruth apologized. Wiping her wet hands on her apron, she extended her hand in greeting. "Hello, my name is Ruth; I'm pleased to meet you, Mr. Seth."

"And you as well, miss Ruth." He gave a firm handshake, his honest blue eyes bored into hers.

Looking back at Julius, she continued her thoughts. "What will we do with Seth until we go for our ride? Do you ride?" Her eyes were large.

"I don't know if I could face a horse or not." Seth grimaced. "I'm sure I'd end up on my—" He had a thoughtful pause, "fanny."

"Come on, fella, it isn't any further down to the ground from the back of a horse now than ten years ago." Julius laughed at him.

"That's what you think."

Julius frowned and scrutinized Seth. "He needs to lay low, but I need his help."

"Even Michael would know. Mrs. MacDonald is blind, but she has already guessed."

The color drained from Seth's face. "Blind?"

"I'm sorry. I didn't think. I've had time to get used to it. She fell off a horse and hit her head. It's been nearly a year now."

"That's what her doctor's visits are for," Ruth said.

"God knows how many years I've spent in my own selfish world. I only cared about what I've wanted. Only cared about what made me happy." Seth's eyes teared up.

Ruth reached out and squeezed his hand.

"The doctors hold out hope that her sight is returning," Julius said.

"I'm crying for myself. For how stupid, selfish, and blind I've been. I ought to walk away...just forget it. I don't need to add burden to burden." He wiped at the tears with a shirt sleeve.

"That would be selfish." Julius' face registered disgust. "Look at yourself, Kid. Self-pity—that's what it is. Remember, a burden shared is a load lightened, a joy shared is happiness increased." He handed Seth a handkerchief.

"You're right, I'm still selfish." Seth wiped his face and blew his nose.

Ruth gazed into the distance. She picked up a scrub brush and resumed washing radishes. "Someone has written, it is better to have loved and lost than to never have loved at all. I suppose that's true, but the losing gets pretty tough sometimes."

Julius frowned and looked at Seth. "Come on, Kid, I'm drained. I think I'll go upstairs for a nap." He stood and stretched. "I don't think anyone will mind if he stays here for a few hours. Do you?"

Ruth looked the newcomer up and down and shook her head. "No, I see why you had him stay the other night. I see why Mrs. MacDonald didn't protest. It's my guess she knows who you are, Mr. Julius, and she knows who he is."

"When he showed up it was a serendipity moment that has been helpful to me, but it had nothing to do with me. Once I get this mission done he'll be free to 'fess' up and tell his story. But it has to come after I'm finished," Julius said as he and Seth took their glasses into the house.

SETH SLEPT AS A FAN whirred. The air moved from one window to the other, birds in their nests napped, and the crickets were singing.

It felt like a lazy summer afternoon as Julius looked over his detective board and its pictures. First picture, Alfred Meister; second picture the group at Holiday and Clarke; third group, pictures of helpers at the hay wagon; then the others of Greg and what's his name, and the guys at Imports the other day, and . . . . *Better get some rest*. He collapsed on the rug. *Friday night— this will be a long night.* Part of his mind drifted off to sleep, but the other part remained watchful. A trick he'd learned on the battlefield somewhere in the desert. He woke up at the slamming of a car door.

Chapter—36—

"This is it, Jo," Seth said as they ambled out through the breezeway and sat under the maple tree. Seth was situated on the far side of the tree, out of sight of the house, and Julius leaned up against the picnic table.

"Your right, we either win or lose—tonight. I need to talk to Michael. You stay put. We'll get some supper out to you in a bit," Julius said.

Julius walked into the sunporch and sat. He could hear Mrs. M and Ruth walking in the front entryway.

"I am so excited, Ruth," Mrs. MacDonald said. "I am supposed to go back next Friday after Mac comes home. I'm sure that I can see colors and objects."

"We'll pray." Ruth walked Mrs. MacDonald to the recliner.

"You lie down until Michael comes in for supper. Everything is ready." Ruth shook out a light cover as her friend lay back in the easy chair. Ruth patted Mrs. MacDonald's arm and tucked the cover closer around her. "Julius asked to go for a ride this evening."

"So much rests on our trust in him." Mrs. MacDonald's face was drawn and grey.

"It'll be alright." Ruth massaged the tiredness out of her friend's shoulders. "For once you need to listen to your heart." She listened as Sally Lu idled up the drive. "There's Michael. Stay put and relax. It'll take about ten minutes to get everything on the table, and for Michael to get washed up."

"I wish these issues were resolved," Mrs. MacDonald said. "And no matter what the conflict, at some point we need closure."

Ruth walked into the kitchen and set the dish of lasagna on the kitchen counter. She could hear Michael washing and drying his hands at the sink. His whistling stopped as he paused in the doorway. "What's wrong?" He walked into the kitchen.

Ruth blew at a wisp of hair that tickled her cheek.

Michael smiled at her, and with a gentle touch brushed it out of her eyes and tucked it behind her ear. "You look weary. What is it, my lady?"

"You forgot my hot fudge sundae, Sir Lancelot." She dodged his question.

"Your forgiveness I implore, next time I'll bring you a dozen hot fudge sundaes." He leaned against the counter and smiled at her.

With a quick intake of breath she looked up at him, and her eyes widened in horror. "Michael. You wouldn't—what would I do with a dozen hot fudge sundaes?"

"Well, my lady, what do you do with one hot fudge sundae?" He continued to smile.

"I could never eat a dozen hot fudge sundaes, you goose," she scolded with a smile.

"Maybe you would have to share." He winked.

"Aye, Michael." She laughed with him.

Julius sat on the sunporch. What a good-looking pair those two are. Oh, to be young, in love, and to have your entire future ahead. But I never see any of the usual romantic overtures. Ruth wears only a class ring on her right hand. They act like best friends, not lovers. Yet, when I think on it, what better foundation for a lifetime together?

Michael turned and noticed Julius. "Supper time—Are you ready to eat?"

"Sure am—I had a short nap, and now I'm hungry. How 'bout ya'll?"

"I'll set the lasagna on, and fetch the salad. If you could grab the tea and glasses? Then I'll go get Mrs. MacDonald," Ruth said.

MICHAEL FOUND A SELECTION in his Bible and prepared to read. The ladies joined them, and he read I Corinthians chapter thirteen and finished with a prayer:

"Almighty God, we pray your blessings not only on our food at this time, but on our lives as well. Be a shield unto us by day and by night. May our business be your business now and forever. In the name of Jesus, Amen."

"Why don't you take that other fellow something to eat?" Michael asked as he filled his plate.

"I can take him a plate." Ruth slid back from the table.

"He could come in." Mrs. MacDonald's face brightened.

"Not now, tomorrow." Julius' brow furrowed, but his tone softened as he noticed the fallen countenance of his hostess. What did she guess? What did she know? It was plain she knew more than she said. "I'll not beat around the bushes. All three of you, Mrs. M, Michael, and Ruth have more than skin in this game. And tonight's the night when it all comes to fruition. You all know this is when they make their drop, so this isn't a revelation to you. I need a less conspicuous way to get close to my subjects at hand. Ruth and my side–kick out there need to observe. If I don't come out I'll need them to report. Michael, I don't know what you're up for after your accident yesterday?"

"After all we've done these last few years, tailing them, gathering info on their operation, I don't want to stay behind." Michael frowned.

"I should have plenty of time to get in and get out of where I need to go. You stay here until we get back." Julius turned toward him. "That doctor said for you to take it easy and rest. We'll take it from there when we get back."

The horses stomped flies, waiting patiently as Julius and Seth finished tightening cinches on the saddles. The stirrups fell into place as Ruth breathlessly appeared.

"Ready?" Julius questioned as he held her horse.

"I'm ready." She gathered the reins in her left hand. "What about Seth?" She stopped.

"I'm cool, dude." He grabbed the saddle horn and swung into the saddle ignoring the stirrups.

"Well, I guess so." Ruth blinked in astonishment. "Pardon me if I just mount in the normal manner." She slid her boot into the stirrup and swung into the saddle.

"You know—" Julius spoke with a sarcastic tone, "You will probably be sorry for that tomorrow, Kid." He followed Ruth's example and swung onto his horse.

"Oh, I forgot to tell Michael and Mrs. MacDonald something." Ruth pulled her horse to a quick stop. "I won't be but a jiffy." She swung down in a flash and rushed back up the path.

"It's impressive to see an animal you can ground tie." Seth lounged in the saddle as they waited.

"We trained most of ours as well." Julius leaned forward, arms crossed on the saddle horn.

"Yeah, except old Bess. Remember the time you stopped for something—and she ended up running almost home." Seth laughed.

"Yeah, I remember. —Good night, what was that?" Julius straightened upright looking at the end of the pasture beyond the shed.

"I'd say gunshots or a car backfire from over that-a-way." Seth waved in the direction of the road at the end of the pasture.

"You wait for Ruth. Follow me when she gets back." Julius wheeled his horse around and kicked him into a run.

Chapter—37—

The horse beneath him and the wind in his face reminded Julius of days long gone. Growing up in those Appalachian Mountains, running free and unfettered he had learned things most people didn't. His good physical condition, the ability to think fast, and the voice some called intuition were a boon to impel him into the positions he had achieved. These things were second nature to him. Like a dancer that always knows the next step, these things had kept him alive numerous times. Some people called it luck, he called it Providence. His father called it God.

Julius slowed his mount at the farm drive and observed the road. No traffic coming from the south, from the north he could see dust rising from a vehicle traveling away from him. He turned the gelding, Sanchez, and at an easy walk-jog down the road, Julius and horse followed the trail as it settled marking where the vehicle had gone. The track ended after several miles, but he followed the tire tracks over the road. He stopped at a small group of shrubs and trees.

His hunch told him the tires would end at the Meecham farmhouse, but how to get closer? His eyes scanned the layout of the house and yard. His best bet would be the cut of land with the dry creek bed. It ran all the way from the culvert in the ditch before him around between the field and pasture in back of the house. It would be the long way around, but he should be out of sight. The only open space butted up close behind the bit of a windbreak outlined against the sky. Skeletons of several outbuildings; a barn, a machine shed, and a few common structures surrounded the house itself. It could have been by choice or just dumb luck, but that pasture would make it difficult to get close to the residence unseen.

He dismounted and led the horse into the tall grass at the end of the bean row. After what he deemed a far enough distance Julius tied the reins up and left them around the saddle horn. *Don't want to fasten him down. I'll let him choose. Seth and Ruth should be here soon.* "Good boy, Sanchez." He ran his hand down the horse's neck and patted his withers. He turned back to the ditch and hunkered down crawling to the culvert that joined the two sides of the deep cut. Julius followed the cut along until he could look out and see the middle tree in the windbreak.

About fifty feet of open ground between this field and the windbreak. He dropped on his belly and crawled out of the creek bed. *Not much fence between fields only pieces here and there. Shouldn't have trouble sliding through. Ouch! Just have to watch for barbed wire in the grass.* He managed to work through the fence and across the pasture to the cover of the few trees in the windbreak. He had one wicked gash from the barbed wire, but just one. He wrapped his handkerchief around his arm as he rested. Too bad he'd left the binoculars with Seth.

It was not dusk yet, but there were a few lights on in the second story. From where he stood it did not look like anyone was downstairs in the kitchen area. Careful not to make a sound Julius crouched and followed in the shadows of the buildings down to the back of the house and scrunched under a window to the back door. With caution, he straightened enough to peer into the dark kitchen.

Julius tried the door. What luck—unlocked. Careful and noiseless he turned the knob and opened it ever so slight a crack and listened. No sound downstairs. Silent as a snake on a rock he crept in. Television sounds came from upstairs, and radio from another room also upstairs. Walking to the basement door, he opened it a crack and listened. *No sounds— guess I'll see what's down here.* He slipped through the door into the darkness and waited for his eyes to adjust then snapped his flashlight on and followed the stream of light down the basement stairs. Flicking the beam of light around the small room Julius spied a light switch over by some ancient wooden shelves. The light illuminated the room, but there were no other stairs than the ones he had come down. *Well, William, where are those steps?* His eyes scanned every nook and cranny before he ran his fingers around the wooden frame of the shelves. Tapping lightly down the edge he found what he looked for and tripped the latch. The shelves swung toward him opening up a large whole new room. *This is what I'm talking about...* He gazed around the room in wonder. *This is where they keep their goods, and over there is the staircase.* He switched the light on in this new room, switched the light off in the first room, and closed the hidden door. Using his small pocket camera, he took some pictures then crept up the stairs. Opening the door a gap he listened and tried to get his bearings. The stairs had led to a large walk-in closet in the middle of a vast hall. There were six doors, and all of them were closed. Two of them had sounds coming from them.

What to do now? Julius checked his watch. *Philip will be getting off work in about an hour, I better step this up. That leaves the old man, David, and Mr. Grumpypants, as the little girl had named him. The radio has country music, and the television sounds like a sitcom. Let's check out the sitcom.*

The carpet in the hall was an old runner patterned with floral swirls, the board floor underneath creaked ever so slight. He heard movement in the radio room and ducked behind the stair wall for the stairs. The person ambled out of the room as the country music got louder and into the bathroom, the door next to the radio room. Julius moved to the bedroom next to the sitcom room and opened the door a slight crack. He peered through the gap and judged the room was used as a storeroom. The fellow in the bathroom flushed the stool. Julius slipped into the storeroom. He shined his light around the room illuminating extra pieces of furniture and other objects. He stepped over to the window which opened *over a porch.* With careful movements, Julius opened the window and crawled out. As he scrunched across to the open window, where the sitcom grew much louder. *The person must be deaf, but at least they won't hear me.* He peered around the window casing at the person in the room. An old man slumped in the chair across from the television. He was situated where he could watch the television, the door, and the window. *Humph lot of good it did... from the look of blood that stained the left side of his face, Mr. Albertoo Meister is dead.* Julius cased the porch roof and secured the area outside of the room best he could, hopeful the sniper was gone. Then he slid in through the open window. He pulled the window shade down and quickly began gathering evidence.

RUTH MOUNTED AND REINED her horse around turning it so that she could look at Seth. "What is our mission now without our fearless leader?"

"He said to follow him when you came out. I imagine he hasn't changed his mind. The first half's easy." Seth waved a hand in the air. "He went over that fence, and across the hay field to the drive over yonder. When we get to the road, we'll go single file. I'll go first."

"Let's not go over the fence. Sanchez is a jumper. Esmerelda and Don Quixote are not."

"Fine. We can take the gate." Seth grinned.

They loped easily across the hay field and stopped at the road. "This way." Seth pointed and began following the horse tracks in the dirt along the road. They watched the ground with silent intensity as they tracked for the next thirty minutes. "Around this corner, and I betcha I know where it leads. What do you think?"

"I don't want to go that way."

"What?" Seth pulled his horse to a stop and turned to look at her. "What about the challenge?"

"Didn't say I wouldn't go that way. Said I didn't want to."

"Oh." He turned back to following the tracks.

"So—" He reined his horse to a stop. "This is where the hoof prints on the road stop, but look." He pointed to some crushed grass, and in the earth of the farm drive several fresh prints of horse hooves. "He's left the road and mushed his way through the grass there." Seth dismounted and began to lead his horse into the grass along the field.

"Quick. I hear a motor coming!" Ruth pushed in beside Seth.

"No cover here—"

"It sounded like Grandpa's pickup anyway." She rolled her eyes and sighed.

"And that leads us to the third horse." He pointed at Sanchez. The contented horse pulled his head up from where he stood grazing in the tall grass. Chomping and slobbering he shook his head, his bridle rattling.

"Back to our problem. The cut is the only decent cover, and it goes down and around the back way. He should come out in back of there." He squinted in the direction of the windbreak. "I have a job to do—but I've got a plan."

BACK AT THE BARN, THEY hurriedly unsaddled, and unbridled all three horses. Seth closed the barn door. "Ruth, you get the items from the house, and I'll pop up to Julius's room and change clothes."

"It's as plain as egg on your shirt," She said as Seth held the gate for her. "Julius needs you to help him finish what he's doing—but you think this plan of yours will work?"

"It will get me up close to the house, anyway." Seth raised his eyebrows at her as they walked up the path to the house.

Ruth stopped short on the path. "What's that?" They could hear strident unfriendly voices at the front of the house.

"I'll go check." Seth sprinted toward the house.

"SHE'S WANTED FOR QUESTIONING." Meecham's eyes narrowed as he confronted Michael and Mrs. MacDonald. Seth stood in the shadows and watched the confrontation.

"She's not here," Michael spoke through gritted teeth, his hands clenched into hard knots. "If you would like to check, I'm sure you know your way around." His eyes challenged. "Don't know when she'll return."

Mrs. MacDonald stood behind Michael, a restraining hand on his sleeve.

Meecham outweighed Michael by twenty-five pounds, but that was all the advantage he held. Michael's physical work had toned and hardened his muscles, and he towered above Meecham by five inches.

"That's alright." Meecham drug the words out. "I'll be back later." He acted as if he wanted Michael to throw a punch. He half turned toward his patrol car.

Michael's foot began to move forward, his fist balled up tighter. "Michael. Stop." Mrs. MacDonald's voice was a furtive whisper while Meecham sauntered toward his squad car. He settled into the driver's side. They watched as the police car lazed down the road toward town. No one spoke. The silence hung thick. Scripture out of Revelation popped into Mrs. M's head— *And when he opened the seventh*

seal, there followed a silence in heaven about the space of half-an-hour.
"But I don't have half-an-hour," She had spoken out loud without knowing it.

"What's that?" Michael turned.

"We don't have half-an-hour, Michael." Ruth came forward out of the breezeway, distracting Michael's gaze. "You go, now," She spoke to Seth, and gave him a nudge toward the steps to Julius's room. "Go. I'll get what we need from the kitchen." She turned to Michael, "Julius is in trouble. We're going to go get him out."

"Who's we?" Michael still felt rocked to his core.

"Julius's side-kick and I, and right now our job is getting Julius out of danger."

Michael shook his head to clear his mind. "I'll take mom over to Lewis. She can stay there. Where do I need to go?"

"You stay over there until we come back with Julius. Come on." She urged Michael and Mrs. MacDonald into the house. "I need to grab some stuff from inside."

"Waiting won't be easy," Michael said as Ruth followed them to the kitchen. "I'll give you an hour before I call in reinforcements." He stopped and stared as Ruth rummaged in the cupboards. "Ruth, what are you doing with those little boxes of cereal?" His face twisted in unbelief, and his eyes widened.

"We've got it covered." She grabbed a baseball cap off the hat pegs and pulled it down on her head and hurried out the door.

"Ready?" Seth waited for her.

Ruth looked twice and then looked again. "Whoa, you look different." She turned him around and inspected him from head to toe. Seth's slicked back hair was pulled up under an Indiana Jones Fedora. He had changed from blue jeans into semi-dress slacks, a button-down shirt, a tie, and a lightweight jacket. A pair of large framed glasses finished the disguise. He carried a clipboard and pen.

"You get the stuff from the kitchen? Daylight's wastin.'"

"Come on then." She nudged Seth with her elbow. "They don't do surveys at night. We better get there before it gets any later."

I'D SAY THIS IS THE guy I've been looking for. Mr. Meister himself, but someone else got to him first. I'll send someone back for him. I'm finished in here. Got all the evidence I need. Julius slid out of the sitcom room and back onto the little porch as he heard a door slam, and voices raised.

"I won't, no I won't," a female voice cried out. "Let me go."

The sound of a fist hitting flesh and the woman's protests stopped.

"That's what we needed. Is she dead? What will we do with the body?"

"Won't tell the boss. I'll dump the body in the basement for now. We'll take care of it later. You get her car out of here. Good she didn't have the kid tonight. Dirty business that."

"If I take the car how will I get back?"

"I'll pick you up. Just leave it over by the Anderson place. I'll pick you up in about twenty minutes."

"Anderson? He run me out of this part of the county. That Charlie Anderson told me what he'd do to me if he ever caught me—"

"Oh, lighten up, Stu. He's in the old folks' center. Won't know you're around."

"You're sure?"

"Good thing she's not heavier. Go on now."

Julius strained to hear the sounds. Someone entered the front door, the other man crossed the gravel. Julius overheard a car door. *Better retrace my steps and find out what's going on.* He found his way back to the closet and searched for the latch back to the stairs. *There doesn't seem to be a way back. Guess I'll have to go through the house.*

The stairs down to the living room were solid, and the noises came from the basement. Julius crept toward the back kitchen door. *I'll wait till they're gone and come back for the woman*—Too late he felt a movement behind him just before a porcelain pitcher shattered over his head.

"Tonight of all nights." Earl clomped up the stairs and pushed the door open. He scratched his head and stared down at the body on the floor. "I'll gag and tie this fellow up. Guess I'd better drag him down with the other body. You clean this mess up while I . . ." He began dragging the body down the stairs.

Julius heard the conversation and someone moving close by, but he was still groggy. A dim flashlight on the stairs gave enough light he could just make out a man kneeling close by him holding something. He felt a rope being wound around his hands. Unconsciously he kept his wrists as far apart as he could, as the fellow pulled on the cord. The man slogged a gag in Julius's mouth then stood up and dusted his hands off. Julius watched through narrowed lids as the man busied himself at the woman's side.

"No pulse—bad rap that. Stu will be facing murder charges if the cops find out. The boss won't like it. If you're gonna kill someone don't get caught," the man muttered as he walked up the steps. Julius's brain whirled.

"What's goin' on?" Julius heard more conversation from the doorway at the top of the steps.

"Your young woman. We took care of it. I'll be headin' off now. Shipment comes in tonight?"

"Yeah, and you need to get moving..." The door shut and the conversation petered out.

Survive, just one more time. Julius stifled a groan. His head ached, he couldn't reach up, but he figured he'd find more than a lump from the whack on his skull. Sweat poured down his face as he strained at the knots. He had his wrists rubbed raw, and sweat ran into the bloody wounds, but the knots loosened. Just a few more minutes and the rope between his hands and feet fell away. Next, he worked at the ones on his wrists. Footsteps crossed the kitchen, and the basement door opened. A small crack of light showed in the darkness. He used his teeth and pulled at the knot as he tried feverishly to finish freeing his hands.

"What're you doing? Get out of here. There's nothing down there you need." Julius heard a man's voice growl before the door shut.

Whew, he let out his breath in a whoosh. At last, the knots on his hands fell away. *Amateurs, glad they didn't check my pockets or frisk for anything.* Julius felt for his flashlight. Drawing it from his pocket, he located the young woman's body and checked for a heartbeat. *Hmm, I don't think you're dead, Melody, but it's a close call. Let's get out of here and get you to a hospital.* He scooped her up and put her over his shoulder. *Not the most elegant manner, but it'll have to work.* He started up the steps.

Julius paused at the top step. He could hear someone moving about in the kitchen. He opened the door a sliver and peaked out. He squinted to make out the reflection in the polished white refrigerator. Yes, someone sat at the small kitchen table.

Hot doggie, what to do now? I can't duke it out while carrying this woman across my shoulders. I don't want to spring the trap now before we gather in the net—

There was a pounding on the front door and the man at the table slapped down his newspaper. His fork clattered on his plate when the doorbell rang. "What would that be?" He growled a curse and stomped out of the kitchen.

Julius heard a familiar voice at the front door, as David Meecham opened it.

Thank you, Lord Jesus. Julius breathed a prayer, slipped out the basement door, across to the back door. Locked, he groaned, *Oh Lord, help*. He scrabbled at the latch.

Chapter—38—

His heart beat wild and erratic. The weight of the gun felt like a ball and chain in Seth's waistband as he walked toward the house. Taking notes from Julius in the past, he had several doggie treats in his jacket pocket. He pulled one out and tossed it at the Great Dane, who snarled threats at him from his length of chain. Seth cautiously ventured through the landmine territory and pounded on the door. When he noticed a doorbell, he hit that as well. It sent out a loud sound. Seth perused the outside of the house as he listened to the movement inside coming toward the front door. He glanced back where Ruth sat hunkered down in the car. In her ball cap, she could have been anyone. The door yanked open, and Seth looked down into a pair of steel blue eyes. Chills spread through his body.

"Good evening." Seth touched the brim of his cap. "My name's Ignatius Hornswaggle, and I'm taking a survey." Seth's eyes widened as from his vantage point Julius appeared through a doorway, a body slung over his shoulders. *Good heavens!* "Pardon me, what did you say?" He looked back at the steel blue eyes.

"I said I'm not interested," David Meecham said.

"Oh, but wait—" Seth stuck the toe of his boot in the door as Julius tried to open the back door. "You haven't seen the—look, I have free samples. Just take my survey. " He stalled for time as he pulled a small box of nondescript cereal out of a bag that dangled from his arm.

If the man's face had been a newspaper stamped in bold type it wouldn't have been any easier to read as Steel Eyes stared at Seth. "Are you an idiot, or a fool?" he said it in a low voice, like an earthquake gathering power.

"How about a free sample of shampoo?" *Good, Julius disappeared out the back door.*

Steel Eyes grabbed a wad of Seth's shirt as he growled at him, "What is it about I'm not interested that you didn't understand?"

"You don't have to get personal." Seth pried the man's fingers from out of his shirt. "I didn't know you wanted the toothpaste. Good night, and good evening." He turned and walked toward his car.

The man cursed after him.

Seth heard the house door slam behind him as he hurried to the car, jumped in, wheeled into reverse. The vehicle came to a sudden stop, Julius slid the body into the backseat, and dropped in beside it. Seth coasted out the driveway and accelerated down the road.

"Thanks. You got the job, Kid. What's Ruth doing here? She oughtn't be anywhere near this place."

"Do you think you're the only one who can be fearless?" She turned to look into the backseat. A look of horror crossed her face. "What have you been doing? Who is the unfortunate woman you have there? The blood dried on your face makes you look only a tad bit better than she does."

"We need to stop and pick up Michael." Seth slowed down for Lewis's driveway.

"Probably Mrs. MacDonald too," Ruth said.

"Why?" Seth's brow furrowed, and he shot her a puzzled sideways glance.

"Who's tending your friend there, Julius?"

"We can't fit two more people in this econocar." Seth scowled.

Julius leaned forward and spoke across the back seat. "I think Michael should drive from here. He knows the back roads. We'll need to get to Frankie and Johnny's, like our earlier plan. Then Ruth can drive Melody on to the hospital. We're cutting it close. Ruth, I need your cap." Julius, with a tender touch, felt the top of his head. "With this cap on do I have blood in any obvious place?"

"You look pretty rough, but I'll run in, borrow a shirt from Lewis, a warm washcloth, grab Michael and Mrs. MacDonald, and be right back." As it came to a stop, Ruth jumped out of the car and rushed into the house.

Like bees swarming out of a hive a few minutes later people descended from the house. Michael slid into the driver's seat, Ruth in the middle, and Seth on the outside, with Mrs. MacDonald on the other side of Melody.

"What happened to the young woman?" Mrs. MacDonald said sliding into the back seat.

"Shh," Julius said as something in his pocket began to ding. They coasted to a stop at the end of the driveway as Julius answered, "Hey," His companions could hear a whisper on the other end. "Okay, we're on it," Julius said before dropping the device in his pocket. "Destination Frankie and Johnny's, Michael."

They pulled out of the drive and began a steady acceleration. "Hang on everybody." Michael spoke as the scenery blurred by.

"There were a couple of guys, the ones responsible for this young lady's condition. They have quite a head start on us." Julius filled in the details. "I don't know how we can even hope to beat them, but they haven't shown yet. Someone at the club is antsy waiting for them to bring something."

Michael pulled around and parked by the back emergency exit at Frankie and Johnny's. "How's this for an out of the way spot?"

"Good. All of us fellows get out. Ruth, get her to the emergency room. Her name's Melody, but I don't know anything else. Ma'am," he spoke to Mrs. MacDonald, "You keep a hold on Miss Melody, and we'll see you later." He slammed his door and turned to the two young men as the car pulled onto the street.

"Michael, go with him." Julius tucked his clean shirt in while he talked. "You are watching for two yahoos. One is tall and thin, the other is shorter, and he's about medium weight. Seth, you look for our contact. She needs to let me in this door. When you see two fellows that fit the description—they'll likely go right through to the back when they come in. I want you to start a diversion." Julius melted into the shadows close to the exit as Seth and Michael strolled to the front door. After a short wait, Julius slipped inside the back door.

Thirty minutes elapsed before two men that fit the given description rushed inside.

Men's voices rose, loud and angry. Women screamed, and people of every sort pushed and shoved to get out the front door. The emergency door erupted as an agitated man backed out dragging a blonde woman, followed by a familiar figure.

"Get back! Get back! Don't come any closer!" The man held a knife in the air.

"Let her go. You're just making it worse," Julius said.

Michael materialized at the exit door, grabbed the knife hand and put a choke hold on the man. Michael pulled an object from his pocket. "Gun wins over knife. Drop it."

The knife clattered to the ground. The man let go of the woman and began a tussle with Michael. Breathless, and shaking, the woman leaned against the side of the building.

Julius grabbed the man, drew his gun and held him. "Thanks. I'll take it from here." Several police cars arrived, and a policeman pointed a weapon at them. "Undercover." Julius held up his badge. "Where's Chief Mallory?"

"Right here." Mallory came out of the crowd from the front. "I'll vouch for him, officer,

Mallory said as he cuffed the crook. "Read this guy his rights, and get him to a squad car." He turned the man over to the policeman.

"We need time...no outside contact, no phones until we get the last of this tied up," Julius said.

"You've got it," Mallory said.

"I don't know what you're doing here," Angie said to Michael and swung her long blond hair out of her face. "but I'm sure glad to see you." She turned to Julius. "Thanks, Cowboy."

"You gotta be careful. There are some mean hombres out here," Julius said.

"Take care..." Angie smiled at Julius, "and thanks." She winked at Michael.

Michael smiled. "Hey, whatever works."

Mallory waited while Angie disappeared into another squad car. "Yeah, our second team is ready. That was fast thinking. Those fellows won't know they're suspects. They'll just think they're at the station to press charges. I'll catch up with you in a bit. There's a car waiting for you."

"Thanks, Chief. I need to retrieve the other part of our threesome." Julius wove through the mess outside the restaurant.

"Wow!" Michael, following Julius, stepped around two people, a gum machine, and an empty newspaper holder. "Look at all the mess. And look at..."

"It's his fault." Seth pointed at Julius.

"Hey, don't blame me." Julius put up his hands. "I told you to start a distraction. I didn't say find the biggest person in the place and punch him in the nose."

"I didn't punch him in the nose." Seth dusted himself off. "I tripped. I've always been graceful like that. The guy in front of me took exception to being pushed. The good lookin' chick he embraced was unhappy. Her escort now." He shook his head. "Hmm—he was more than unhappy." He frowned and shrugged.

"Kid, you have a way all your own." Julius shook his head. "Let's get going. There's still work to do. I hope we got these loose ends tied up. I don't want someone waiting for us when we get to the end of this trail. Chief has a car for us."

Chapter—39—

The house sat dark and forbidding in the bright moonlight washed landscape. "Shine that flashlight in here." Julius found the recording equipment and radios stowed under the tarp in his trunk, threw them in a pack, and slung it over his shoulder.

"You look like Santa Claus and a pack," Seth snorted as they came out of the breezeway.

"Yep, these are presents alright. You should stay at Lewis's, Ruth," Julius said.

"No, I'm coming. Then we can get on with our life—you can get on with yours."

"Yeah. Time to fold up and get out." Julius frowned.

"That's not it at all."

"My mistake." Julius' feelings were a jumble. *This is it. It's make or break time. After tonight I can walk away from here—if I survive.* "Ruth, I'm sorry. Seth and I have a job to do. I think you should stay at Lewis's and leave this to us. And after tonight you should be free, as you said, to get back to your life." *The moonlight made her eyes large and pathetic. She looked too much like Miranda. What if he made a mistake? It would be like losing Miranda twice. The first time almost killed him, the second time surely would.*

"Mom and I discovered Meecham's little business out here. She used to walk late at night when she couldn't sleep. Then the Mac-Donald family moved here and Michael and I began investigating, and continued on this. We deserve to be in on the wrap up." Ruth said.

Seth sighed. "Man, let's just get this job done."

They crossed the pasture and veered off into the grove of trees.

"Michael is supposed to be here any minute. Anything more I should know about these drops, Ruth?" Julius whispered as he concentrated on running antennae and setting up a recording machine.

"Meecham parks around here, but never in the same spot," she whispered. "The night mom and I saw him, he was stationed at the other end of the dirt road." She indicated the direction.

Julius passed out two-way radios. "Do not use these."

"Well—" Seth said.

Julius held up a hand, "Let me explain to Ruth. Seth will go that way, and I'll go this way. If we don't find him, we hit this button. Seth, you hit yours once. That will be your signal. Mine is twice. Ruth, here's your radio. I want you to stay here and wait for Michael."

"What do you want us to do when Michael gets here?"

"Monitor this machine. I want you two to sit tight until we get back. Seth, if you do happen upon Snidely just hit the button, lay low and keep quiet."

JULIUS AND SETH DISAPPEARED in their own direction while Ruth found a natural seat and perched on a fallen tree limb. *Patience has never been my strongest virtue. Waiting is the hardest part of this.* Picking up a catalpa leaf with a gentle movement she fanned herself. Memories stirred in her heart as she studied the grove across the road. She and Reuben had played dragons, knights, and damsels in distress amongst those trees. *How foolish and innocent. Good always triumphed in that world. What's keeping Michael? He should have been here by now.* She heard Julius signal all clear. Julius had said to stay here, but surely she could slip over into the grove and wait there since Julius hadn't found their quarry.

JULIUS FROWNED IN EXASPERATION as he returned to base; Seth had signaled all clear as well. "To get this close," he muttered. "I'm sure we intercepted those stooges in time, I don't know what happened." The anger began to rise. He never failed. *Careful* he calmed himself as he came back to the base. *There are two times when folks get careless; when they get angry and when they get—*

"Where's Ruth?" Michael's voice demanded from the cover of the trees.

"She's not here?" Julius turned.

"No, she's not," Michael said.

"I left her here to wait for you." Julius heard Michael's movement.

"Where're you going?" Julius grasped Michael's arm.

"Meecham's out there," Michael growled, shaking off Julius's grip.

"No, wait!" Julius grasped his arm again. "I heard a single key but—" Suddenly the recorder came to life.

"Is that you, O'Brien?" The voice was unmistakably Phil Meecham's that came over the recorder.

"Oh! Phil Meecham! What are you doing skulking out here at this hour? It's a little late to be checking the quality of your hay isn't it?" Ruth answered.

"I wouldn't have thought you'd have the nerve to be out by yourself." Phil Meecham again, his words held a type of bitterness. "Where's your pal?" He sounded a bit closer.

"You'll just have to guess, won't you?"

"So, you're out here all by yourself? This occasion only happens in my dreams. Ruth, I"

"Not alone. I'm a child of God..." Her stomach churned. Could she see a glint in his eyes, or was it just the moonlight?

"A lot of good it did your mother." Meecham frowned.

"I can't comprehend a person who would kill someone. What did you use?" she asked. "Then watch as they die. Sadistic isn't it?" Ruth shuddered. *Calm, you must remain calm.* Remain calm? His very nearness made her feel nauseous. The smell of his cologne made her stomach roll. She stepped back to reposition herself.

"I didn't. I couldn't hurt your mom..." He shook his head. "Why are we talking about this? Ruth, listen, I—In my dreams, the subject is much different."

She could see the gold flecks in his hazel eyes. *Too close. Too close.* "Why did you kill her?" Ruth took a small step backward.

"I didn't I told you. I need you, Ruth. In my dreams I see your eyes, your face, you haunt me waking and sleeping."

"Why did you kill her?"

"It's like the report said. I came in the back door. I knocked and heard what sounded like a struggle, so I came in. Dad and Grandpa said I had to get rid of you two, but I put it off..."

"Your Dad and Grandpa?" Her eyes were wide with horror.

"Dad has made the business what it is. I was supposed to prove that I was man enough to do the things that were necessary." He reached out to caress her face. "Then I met your mom. I was at the Molly-Mart picking up a pack of cigarettes, when this big voice from a little person behind me said, 'you know those things'll kill you don't you?' And she took it from there to studying the Bible."

Ruth gasped. "Studying the Bible? Then who killed my mom? The report said..."

"I saw him—. He heard me come in the back door. I caught a glimpse as he ran out the front. Dad thought I did it, so he had Biles do a cover-up. But, Ruth, I have to tell you—Don't back away from me, Ruth," he said. "I didn't tell Dad about your mom and you that night. I didn't start that rumor about you and me. I would of given anything if it'd been true. I just wanted you." The recording continued. "There were always people. I could never get a chance," his speech rambled. "I've waited..." He choked on the words.

The airplane droned in the distance. He cursed, and she prayed.

Julius seized him by the shirt, swung him around. The next time Meecham woke up he was in a squad car— but not his own.

"IT ISN'T THAT I PANICKED or anything." Ruth's hands trembled as Julius handed her a cup of tea as they sat in Laura's living room. "Things were more than tense." She closed her eyes and took a deep breath of the steam.

"When I got back to base you weren't there. In Michael's frame of mind, he wasn't the one to go looking. We have the conversation on tape."

"But he didn't say anything." Her hands shook almost spilling her tea.

"Not true," Julius said.

"He said he didn't kill my mom. That can't be true. He said he saw..."

"He reinforced his previous statement. And with his testimony, we know who it was, and why can't it be true?" Julius looked at her with a one-eyed frown.

"Everyone knows he..." Ruth stared at Julius.

"Ruth, we can all be in error. Only God is all-knowing. Philip Meecham has a lot going against him. People judge him by his family reputation and his own actions. Not at all a good situation, but I've seen him put aside all of that and do his job well."

"I'm so sorry. He said they were studying the Bible. That sounds like Mom. But it couldn't be... The report said Meecham didn't think it was—that would mean..." She began to weep into her handkerchief.

"Oh, Ruth," Michael said with a groan as he slid out of his chair and knelt beside her. "Ruth, you're exhausted. You've had too many bad days." He scooped her up. "You need a good night's sleep." He carried her up the stairs as she continued weeping into her handkerchief. He knelt as she sat on the edge of the bed. "Let me help you with your boots. You'll sleep better without them." He pulled them off and set them by the dresser. "Good night and sleep now." He covered her with a blanket. "Mom is on her way."

"No." Her eyes flew open, and Ruth grasped his shirt sleeve, "No, Michael, don't wake your mom. She's had enough—"

"It'll be all right." He brushed her hair away from her face. "Go to sleep." He watched until her eyes closed.

JULIUS AND SETH SAT at the kitchen table grasping their coffee cups. Julius raised an eyebrow as music floated down the stairs. "Go on up to my room. It won't make any difference now." Julius rubbed his hand over his face. "I'll wait here."

Chapter—40—

Saturday, June 27th: Julius and Michael washed their hands at the laundry room sink then filed into the kitchen.

"After breakfast, we need to go into the police station. I'll call Donna to come over so mom can sleep." Michael thumbed to his selected passage for their Bible reading.

"Yes—" Ruth plunked platters of ham and eggs on the sunporch table as they entered the kitchen. "Mrs. M had breakfast started when I came down this morning. Her doctor's visits are very tiring for her in the first place, and last night . . . at her age she doesn't need the trauma. I sent her back to bed."

Michael cleared his throat and took a sip of coffee. "What do you need to be ready to go, Ruth?"

She pushed her hair back out of her drawn, pale face. "I'll just clean up the kitchen a bit, and a quick shower," she said and sat down.

"Psalms 30:4-5," Michael said before reading, "Sing praise unto Jehovah, O ye saints of his, And give thanks to his holy memorial name. For his anger is but for a moment; His favor is for a lifetime: Weeping may tarry for the night, But joy cometh in the morning," he finished.

"How long until you'll be ready?" Julius slid a couple of eggs, a couple slices of ham, and two pieces of Texas toast on his plate and began to eat with gusto.

"After I finish this breakfast? About forty-five minutes," Michael said. "I need to hit the shower. You still look pretty rough."

"I feel pretty rough too. I don't need any more days like yesterday." Julius finished his egg, made a sandwich out of his ham and toast. Ruth picked up his plate and stacked it with Michael's.

JULIUS GLANCED AT THE clock when he entered the kitchen. "Ten minutes to spare."

Ruth smiled wanly. "I'm ready and waiting too." She looked up as Michael entered. "Did you call Donna?"

"Yes, she'll be here shortly," he said. "She may have to leave a little before we return, but Mom's eyesight has improved, and— Oh, must be the Lone Ranger," Michael said as footsteps thumped down the stairs.

"He was almost ready when I was upstairs," Julius said.

"I hear Donna's car in the drive, so let's go," Michael said.

"THAT WAS AN ORDEAL, but your part's done," Julius said a couple hours later as they pulled out of the police station parking lot. "You must've done something, Ruth. Those things don't just come on by themselves."

"Regardless, I'm just going to praise God," Ruth said.

"When they arrested Tim he broke down and just babbled," Julius said. "He said it was an accident. Something about headaches, and the wrong bottle, and some club and passing a test to get in. He said when he heard someone coming in the backdoor he panicked and ran out the front."

"That just breaks my heart. I really never would have thought in a million years." Ruth dabbed at the tears sliding down her cheeks.

"Something didn't add up and Meecham's story stayed the same. When I investigated the scene the evidence pointed at a third suspect." Julius looked back at Ruth. "I hated what I found, but it was what I found . . . It's after lunch—anyone want some fries and shakes?" Julius turned into a local drive-through. After placing the order he drove to the pick-up window. He pulled over and handed out the food.

"Life under the sun seems to go on." Michael frowned. "They have the best fries in the state. Thanks, Julius." Michael ate quietly, finished his food, sighed, and leaned back. Resting his head on the back cushion, he covered his face with his hat.

Julius chuckled looking in the mirror at his passenger. The back of an economy car is no place for someone over three feet tall. Michael was twice that plus a few inches. He didn't look comfortable, but the gentle swaying of the car traveling rhythmically along the pavement appeared to hypnotize him.

"I'm well fed. Now all I need is to catch a few hours' sleep before supper." Ruth broke the mesmerizing silence. "Thank you for the fries and shake—and for all you've done, Julius. We've been praying about this matter for a long, long time. We try to fix everything ourselves, and when we can't then, we take it to God. We should take it to Him first."

"What about your mother?" Seth asked.

"Excuse me?" She raised her eyebrows.

"Shouldn't God have done something to save her?"

"The important thing isn't that we will die, or how we will die, the crucial thing is our spiritual condition when we die. Mom obeyed the Lord Jesus. Evil didn't destroy her faith." Ruth frowned and examined her hands as they lay in her lap. "I miss my mother, but we can't turn back time."

"There are no magic wands in life." Julius looked sideways at Seth. "You shouldn't allow Satan to sidetrack your mission." Julius glanced in the mirror at Ruth. "The question goes, 'if God is so powerful, why do bad things happen'? We live in an uncertain world. One that Eve and Adam chose—sometimes bad things happen."

"True. There are no guarantees, and our spiritual condition trumps everything else," Seth said.

Julius drove up the driveway and parked. "Ya'll going to be around for a while?" He looked back at Michael then Ruth.

Michael sat up and straightened his hat. "I'll be here for, about half an hour."

"What about you, Ruth?" Julius asked.

"We'll be working on supper."

"Good, give us a few minutes, and we'll join you," Julius said over his shoulder as he and Seth walked to the stairs.

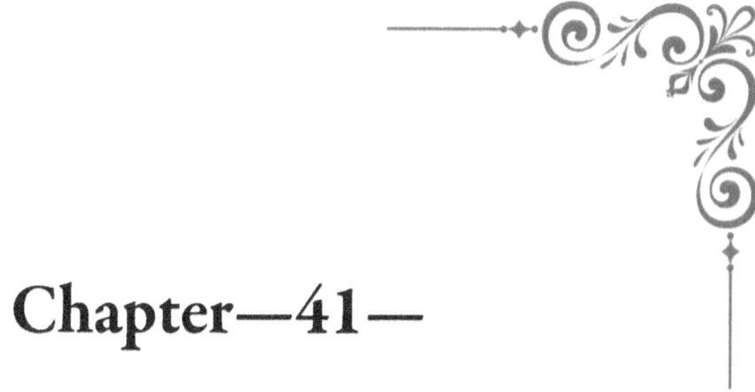

Chapter—41—

Julius and Seth paused looking through the trellis spilling over with climbing roses in full bloom to where Mrs. MacDonald meandered along the garden path in animated conversation. Julius opened the gate and walked down the pea gravel path. At the sound of the gate and footsteps, she looked up.

"Oh, thank God!" She dropped the hoe and opened her arms.

"What's going on here?" Michael said as he and Ruth joined the group.

"Michael, look who's come home!" she grabbed Michael and Ruth and squeezed them also.

"At last—" Michael stopped and stared at the tall too thin young man, clean shaven and just a few years older than himself. "Look at you. That black eye is quite colorful against the strawberry blond hair and blue eyes."

"Michael, let's go and get some refreshments," Ruth said.

"And you sit in the shade, Mom." Julius could, at last, say the word he had waited three weeks to use.

The afternoon breeze sent patches of sunlight glimmering through the leaves of the tree that peaceful lazy afternoon. Ruth and Michael brought the tray of tea and cookies out and joined the conversation.

"From Laura—all the way to Michael there is a strong family likeness. That's why Seth fit right in. Even before his shave and haircut, there was that strong family resemblance." Ruth shook her head,

"But Julius—I would never in a hundred years put you with Seth, or any of the others. Not until yesterday?"

"You've heard the term *disguise*? And what happened yesterday?" Julius asked.

"Siblings are hard to explain, but not hard to recognize." Ruth smiled at the brothers.

"When Joshua came down the path and spoke to me three weeks ago," Mrs. MacDonald said. "He took my hand and that first moment I knew it was him, but he introduced himself as 'Julius'. I was confused. As a little boy, he liked to try on different costumes and imitate others. Such a child. He got himself and others into trouble at times with his, uh—" she paused and raised her eyebrows at her son. "talent."

Ruth smiled at Mrs. MacDonald and changed the subject. "Your doctor's appointment went well?"

"I have thought for the last few weeks that my eyesight is improving. The doctor didn't want to give me false hope before, but the checkup yesterday went well. And it has improved enough to physically recognize objects close at hand—and in the daylight. It's slow coming, but I'm sixty-four."

"What are your plans now?" Michael turned to Julius.

Julius raised his eyebrows. "There are a few loose ends to tie up as Julius C. Armstrong. I need to pick up Seth's few belongings. He can't go back to the bed and breakfast now that he's cleaned up. I'll tell Olan and Rheba he's gone on to better things."

"Your flight leaves early Monday morning?" Mrs. MacDonald frowned at Julius.

"Julius C. Armstrong has to leave. I can only come back as myself if he leaves first."

"Finish your errand, son, at Rheba and Olan's. You two will stay in the gardener's quarters. Laura would insist on it."

JULIUS DROVE TO THE Smith's Bed and Breakfast and perused the outside for a few minutes before he walked to the front door and knocked

"I just came by to pick up Matthew's belongings. Since I've finished here, he went on to other things," Julius said.

"Come in, come in." Rheba held the door. "Have a cup of coffee and a fresh blueberry muffin? Your friend left too early. It's all the gossip today."

"What's that?" Julius joined Olan and Rheba.

"They arrested David and Philip Meecham. The police raided Frankie and Johnny's in Hermon last night."

"Last night?"

"Well, early this morning. I'm surprised you haven't heard already," Rheba said.

"I've had business to take care of. Most of the morning I've spent out of town."

"It happened just west of where you are staying. Lots of rumors." She lowered her voice, "There's talk about everything from drugs and murder, to—" she shook her head.

"I don't think that's the picture of small towns my publisher wants." He smiled. "I'm shipping things out. Thanks for the coffee and muffins. I'll go get those belongings. Mr. Hastings sends you his compliments; he enjoyed his stay. You have a good day, ma'am."

The screen door banged shut behind Julius as he strolled across the wooden porch and down the front steps. At the apartment he, folded Seth's few possessions into a duffel bag, checked the room one more time before he sauntered to his car. What a relief, Mrs. Smith couldn't see what his disguise hid. The bumps and scrapes on his face, his hat covered the patch on his head, and the other scratches and bruises covered by his long-sleeved shirt. Julius scooted the bag onto the front passenger seat and dropped into the driver's side. He felt drained after the few hours of sleep. *Almost done*, he sighed.

He drove leisurely through the quiet town where nothing ever happened. All the shops had closed down for the evening including Mom and Pop's Café. The young punks still sat on the street corner smoking cigarettes. As he drove up the hill, a new family played in the park. Julius waved to be friendly, and they returned the gesture. He drove up the street to where it turned into gravel, and then turned west and drove on home.

He parked in the garage as notes of a familiar hymn floated on the air. Michael, his mother, and Ruth sang:

"Shadows and sunshine all thru the story, Teardrops and pleasure day after day; But when we reach the kingdom of glory, Trials of earth will vanish away."

He came through the breezeway, into the laundry room and began to wash his hands at the sink. They finished the chorus as he dried his hands. *Yes, after the shadows, there will be sunshine; All will be well in a little while. He had survived one last time. I can fly out Monday, a free man.*

"THIS TIME OF THE YEAR when the weather gets stifling it is nice to keep meals simple. Donna and I prepared bacon, lettuce, and tomato sandwich fixen's, and soup before she left for home—while you folks were out gallivanting." Mrs. MacDonald passed the soup tureen.

Julius closed his eyes memorizing the moments. The windows on the sun porch allowed the slight breeze to tease the Austrian blinds. They framed the stunning orange and deep azure sunset that painted the western sky.

"What a surprise this will be for Lewis," Ruth said. She placed her napkin on her plate and pushed back from the table.

"Better to surprise him tonight than in the morning at church. We need to get scooting, though," Mrs. MacDonald said.

"WHAT'S THE NEWS YOU have to share?" Donna said as she came out the back door on to the deck. "Julius didn't come?"

"Yes, where's Julius?" Lewis asked as Mrs. MacDonald, Michael, and Ruth joined them.

"That's our news," Michael said.

"You know, Jo…" They heard Seth's quiet voice as the brothers approached.

Lewis's face blushed, his eyes looked as big as a full moon, and his mouth hung open.

"Close your mouth you're not a cod. And at your age." Mrs. MacDonald clucked at him.

Lewis closed his mouth and swallowed. "So the twins are back?"

"Twins?" Ruth blinked in surprise.

"They're so close in age, and as youngsters they were inseparable. People always asked if they were twins." Mrs. MacDonald smiled.

Lewis ran his fingers through his hair and took a long look at Julius and Seth as they came up on the deck. "They don't look like twins today. Julius C. Armstrong—No wonder you seemed familiar. I'll never forget the time you impersonated the school principal. Had him right down to the toenails…"

"Maybe not that far, but he sure got in trouble when he called school out for the day." Mrs. MacDonald rolled her eyes.

"You need help with the cake and plates?" Ruth asked. She and Donna disappeared inside for a few minutes returning to the deck with cake and plates.

"We thought it would be better to bring Seth over tonight rather than spring him at worship tomorrow," Mrs. MacDonald said. "Here, Ruth, let me pass those around." She helped hand out the plates of cake.

"I'll still be Julius tomorrow, and leave here as Julius Monday."

"And what're your plans, Seth?" Lewis pushed a cake crumb around on his plate.

"I need to go back to Forrest City. I need to try to make amends with my wife. I've tried calling her but no answer." Seth swallowed and looked off in the distance a moment. "Maybe Dad and I—"

"How long you been married? I don't know anyone who won't be glad to see Dad." Lewis sat back in his chair and exhaled.

"Me especially. Almost nine years," Seth said.

"We need to be getting home." Mrs. MacDonald finished her tea.

"Let's bow then before you leave." Lewis waited for silence. "Lord we thank thee for the blessings we've enjoyed. The answer to our many prayers. The return of family, the end of persecution, the blessing as Mom's eyesight continues to improve. For all of these things and Dad's safe arrival, we pray. In the name of Jesus."

"Thank you, son, for all you do." Mrs. MacDonald gave Lewis a hug.

"Good night, see you tomorrow," chorused on the air as everyone piled into the Suburban and rolled down the driveway.

Mrs. MacDonald smiled and turned to Julius. "I'll be glad to call you Joshua again. Your family is well?"

"Don't get used to Joshua yet," Julius said. "and when I'm undercover I'm not in contact with my family. God willing, you'll get to meet them as soon as we can work it out."

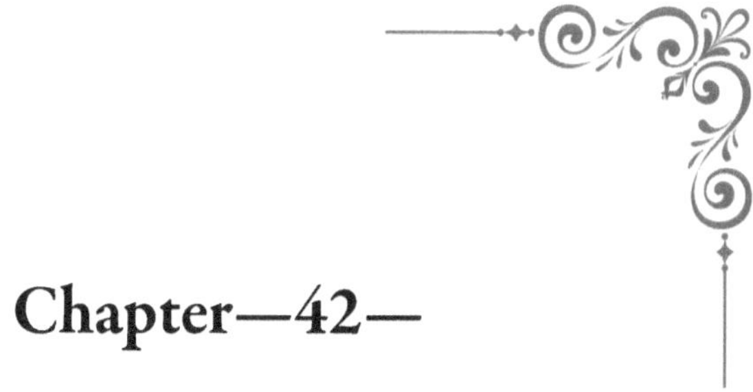

Chapter—42—

Julius rolled over squinting at the sunshine filtering in through the drapes on the east window. He slid out of his side of the bed and smirked. Seth clung to his side of the bed, hanging half on and half off the edge. Old habits die hard. As children, they shared rooms and often had three to a bed.

Many scenes from his last fourteen years filtered across Julius' mind. *How odd to finish the last job in a place I've never been to before. Yet among my family that I haven't been a part of for fourteen years. Oh, God, I don't understand how your hand has led us.* He rubbed his hands through his hair. *How did I walk back into the lives of these people as natural as if I'd just stepped away for a few days?*

He sighed. No disguise would fool Dad and Laura, and only because they are gone, and mother is blind did this whole thing come off at all. He closed his eyes remembering the scripture. *"And it shall come to pass that, before they call, I will answer; and while they are yet speaking, I will hear."*

"Holy, holy, holy, Lord God on high—" Michael and Ruth came through the orchard.

Heaven and earth do seem to be full of God this morning. Julius's heart swelled with thankfulness. "Seth." He prodded his sleeping brother. "Awake thou that sleepest, and arise from the dead."

Seth rolled over. "I've been a whole lot closer than this." Seth sat on the edge of the bed rubbing his hands through his much shorter hair. He grabbed his blue jeans on the way to the bathroom and reappeared a few minutes later, tucking his shirt in.

"You're harder to get moving than you were fourteen years ago," Julius finished combing his hair.

"You were bigger then and meaner than a cat eatin' hot sauce."

"Not me. I've always been mild mannered...Come on, Kid. Let's go down and have coffee and whatever."

"Mild-mannered? Yeah, even the Sage brothers wouldn't tangle with you. But age has improved my technique." Seth laughed as they entered the kitchen.

"You two are a sight for poor eyes," Mrs. MacDonald said.

"Biscuits, bacon, strawberry jam, and coffee." Ruth pointed to the items on the table.

"Strawberry jam? Yes!" Seth's eyes lit up.

"Oh, no," groaned Mrs. MacDonald.

"We aren't five years old anymore, Mom." Seth rolled his eyes and shook his head.

"What were you saying about improved technique?" She wagged a finger at him.

"You can't win with that woman." Julius frowned at Seth.

"Can't win with any woman let alone that one." Seth sighed.

"They just want to change the subject." Mrs. MacDonald laughed. "One time I caught six-year-old Joshua and five-year-old Seth, each with a pint of strawberry jam and a spoon. Jam smeared on their faces, hands, shirts, jam everywhere. Some of the jam had even made it into their mouths."

Ruth laughed and picked up her plate and carried it to the dishwasher. "Bible study's at nine thirty, and worship at ten thirty."

Mrs. MacDonald carried her coffee cup and followed Ruth. "I'm about ready. Lunch is in order, and..." the conversation left with them as the two women started up the stairs.

Michael put his plate on the counter by the sink. "I'll see ya in a little." He followed to the stairs.

"Remember how annoying he used to be?" Seth asked.

"Michael?"

"Yeah."

"Yes, I do, but what a cute baby." Julius smiled.

"We were all cute babies." Seth frowned.

"We were all annoying five-year-olds too," Joshua said.

"Some things really don't change do they?"

"Not really. The jam's all gone. Let's go get ready for church, kid-do." Julius dropped the spoon into the empty jar.

JULIUS THOUGHT ON THE closing message as Brother Wilson wrapped up his morning's lesson. "Our society thinks that cleanliness and Godliness are synonymous. If we wash our bodies enough and spray them with enough good smelling stuff on the outside we are clean," Brother Wilson said. "Holding a form of Godliness—we can hold a form of Godliness outwardly, but until we set ourselves apart, that's all it is. It's just a form of Godliness."

AS THE SANCTUARY FILLED with the words of the familiar song, "Without Him, I would be nothing," Julius watched Seth slide his songbook back in the rack and walk to the front. When the song ended, Seth sat down in prayer.

The congregation waited as the preacher and Seth whispered together. After a pause, Seth stood and turned to the group. "Outside of my family, you folks here don't know me. I wondered whether to wait until Dad arrived back this evening. This is something that he should hear also. But—I know my dad would say, clear it up right away. So, in short, I've had problems in my life as a Christian. I got to a place where I wanted a lazy man's salvation. One that didn't require anything. Like the song we just sang, without Him, I would be nothing. And it's true. Without Him, I have been nothing. I'm here to confess that's not the way I was raised. I have brought shame and reproach upon my Lord and Savior as well as the church He purchased with His blood. And shame upon my family whom I love very much. I want to put that all behind me, to live the way Jesus wants me to. I ask for your prayers to this end."

Lewis jumped up and began the song, "Wonderful, wonderful, Jesus is to me. Councilor, Prince of Peace, Mighty God is He. Saving me, keeping me, from my sin and shame. Wonderful is my Redeemer, Praise His name!" One by one the congregation hugged the returned prodigal.

Mrs. Rudd gave Seth a hearty embrace. Turning to Mrs. Mac-Donald, she said, "Amanda, I wasn't aware that you had another son."

"Sometimes when a person is on a journey, things get lost along the way." Mrs. MacDonald gave Seth a tearful hug.

"WHAT TIME DO YOU PICK up Dad?" Julius leaned back in his chair as the after-service potluck wound down.

"Three o'clock," Lewis replied.

"I won't make it to the airport. Won't be back 'til later—after evening services." Julius frowned.

"You have to do what you have to do," Lewis said.

"You're right. Some things can't be helped." Julius shrugged.

MR. MACDONALD'S PLANE was twenty minutes late. The group waited, each one straining their eyes to be the first to see him stride down the hallway.

Mac had been Mrs. MacDonald's hero since she was five years old. That hadn't changed in the last fifty-nine years. His service papers recorded him as six-foot and one-inch tall, one hundred ninety pounds, and that hadn't changed in nearly forty-five years either. His red-gold hair became a sandy white crown more each year, but his sapphire blue eyes were still as brilliant as ever. His 'natural force' had slowed. However, to look at the man, you knew distinctly that if God called him to lead the people to the Promised Land, he would set out at once.

Mac walked toward the waiting group and greeted them with hugs and laughter. The sandy-haired man did not glance in the direction of his wayward son who lingered almost out of sight in the shadow leaning against a pillar. Mac's children when small had a theory that their father had all-knowing eyes. They could not hide from him. Seth could not hide from his father any more now than he could as a child. As Mac walked toward him Seth held out his hand.

"Son…" the father shook his head, his face wore a look of unbelief. "We have waited, prayed, and longed for this day. A handshake is not sufficient." His father enveloped him in a bone crushing hug.

"Oh, man," Seth gasped. "I think every bone in my body is broken. Between you and Junior, there."

Mrs. MacDonald smiled. People passing by in the terminal would have thought that someone had just returned from a long journey. They were correct, but it wasn't the passenger from the plane.

AFTER EVENING SERVICES, Joe completed the announcements. "We are thankful Brother MacDonald—Mac—has arrived home. It's been a twenty-four hour day of traveling for him. Julius Armstrong left. This morning was his last visit here. We're glad to have the Marsh family back from their trip."

After the final prayer, Mr. MacDonald greeted Mrs. Marsh. "Gretchen, is this your husband?" He shook hands with the tall, thin man beside her. "Haven't we met before?"

"I had a dead battery, and..."Mr. Marsh began.

"That's right. One morning early, I went out to check on some horses." Recognition lit Mac's eyes.

Mr. Marsh cleared his throat. "Well, yeah, but we weren't properly introduced, now were we? My friends call me William T."

Mr. MacDonald smiled, and his eyes twinkled at the memory of a tall, strung out fellow sleeping in his Dodge Charger. "I can do that, William. My friends call me Mac. Glad to be properly introduced now," he said with a wink. "I feel like Rip Van Winkle. I've slept for a hundred years, and missed out on several happenings."

"Yeah," Billy looked up at his dad, then at Mac. "Officer Meecham was arrested yesterday and taken to jail."

"Billy." Gretchen's eyes widened, and she gasped. "Hush, child." She turned him around and hustled him away.

"Well, what do you know?" Mr. MacDonald stepped back in surprise.

"I know these small towns and how rumors fly." Mr. Marsh looked at the ceiling and around the room. "I'd better get Gretchen home. She still gets pretty tired. Good to meet ya', Mac." He held out his hand before leaving.

"Good to meet you too." He returned the handshake.

MAC SLID DOWN ON THE sofa in Laura's living room and pushed back into the lush embrace of its voluminous cushions. "I've been crammed into too many small spaces the last twenty-four hours. Sure feels good to stretch my tired old legs. There seems to be quite a bit of news since I've been gone." Mac's brow furrowed.

"Just wait." Mrs. MacDonald ran her fingers through his hair, and over his face.

"Amanda, you are still the most beautiful woman God ever created." Mac stroked her hair and kissed the top of her head.

She sighed and leaned into his embrace. "When you are gone it is as if my whole life stops."

"Separations are difficult." He gave her a gentle squeeze. "What's the doctor's report?"

"Improving. We have another appointment next week." She smiled. "Mac, there's a surprise. Remember the announcement about Mr. Armstrong?"

"I can't put a face to that name for some reason." He frowned.

"Right after you left on your trip. I was minding my own business. Outside. After lunch. I enjoy spending time among herbs and flowers."

Mac smiled as his wife waved her fingers in the air. "Yes, Amanda, I know you like being outside."

"As I looked for my dignity," she said. "A voice spoke to me, and a man helped me up. He introduced himself as Julius C. Armstrong. He thought he had found Olan and Rheba's bed and breakfast. Ruth's description threw me. The only things he had in common with Joshua were his age and his height. We put him in the gardener's room above the garage."

"Amanda." Mac sighed, reading the script, he filled in the details. "Will you ever stop following your heart?"

"Probably not." Her face sobered and she looked at her hands in her lap.

"So, Joshua has come home also?" Mac questioned.

"Well. He's—" she whispered, "an undercover agent. Tomorrow his flight leaves mid-morning. Sometime after that, he and his family are supposed to come back."

"We need to rearrange this furniture, Amanda. Why someone could walk in through the foyer, and we wouldn't even know it, would we—Joshua?" Mr. MacDonald spoke over his shoulder.

"Julius, sir. I'm still on assignment."

"Is that correct?"

"Yes, sir."

Mr. MacDonald rose and walked toward his son. "God's mercies are never-ending. First Seth, now you."

"It's time to come home, sir. I just want to come home."

"WHEN SETH WENT FORWARD this morning it felt like a knife in my heart." Julius swirled the ice cubes in his glass of tea as they sat at the counter in the kitchen. "In spite of Seth's careless attitude he really cares very deeply. I saw him where I should be. These last weeks I walked a thin wire."

They turned at the clatter as Seth walked in the back door. "Hey, hey! You finally made it in?" Julius said.

"We didn't hear you drive in. Where's Michael, and Ruth?" asked Mrs. MacDonald.

"Right here. I drove the silver bullet." Michael followed Seth in the door.

"Trying to impress your brother? Pride goeth before a fall." Mr. MacDonald shook his head.

"Everyone puts that verse and my car in the same breath." Michael snorted.

"Maybe you'll be able to drive it now that Phil won't be harassing you," Ruth said.

Seth sighed. "Glad this job is almost done."

"This job is done. I've found my Chicago targets, and we're in the process of finishing a cold case—this afternoon I turned in my report, found my family. Tomorrow I'm out of here and finished."

Ruth stared at him.

"It's not going to finish the way everyone thought, but the middle of next week. It's coming. We've had some close calls on this case, but even Melody is going to pull through." Julius looked subdued.

"Melody? It's been a long day for me. That story will have to wait till tomorrow." Mr. MacDonald stood. "Ah-Manda, are you comin' with me, or are you gonna stay here?" He stretched to limber up.

"I told you I'd follow you wherever you go. Good night, all," she said.

Julius, Seth, Michael, and Ruth listened as their footsteps receded up the stairs.

"Fourteen years?" Julius sighed. "Once I started on the lonely path, I kept on going. No reason, just stupidity."

"These last years struck me hard too." Seth looked at the shredded paper napkin on the counter in front of him.

"The last fourteen years have been rough," Michael said.

"Like that scripture, 'Can a man take fire in his bosom, And his clothes not be burned? Or can one walk upon hot coals, And his feet not be scorched?' Sin does that. It hurts everybody." Seth started shredding another napkin.

"When I first showed up no one mentioned Dad. I was afraid to ask," Julius said.

"I just pray you three know how truly blessed you are." Ruth sat so quietly they had forgotten her. "Well, good night." With a swift movement, she rose and fled to the stairs.

"Well, good night, I've had a long day too." Michael put his glass in the dish washer and with a wave headed up to bed.

"THERE ARE THINGS I wish I could change." Seth stared at his glass.

"You can't change the past, only the present, and maybe the future. Regret doesn't get you anywhere, Seth."

"Guess I'll talk to Dad in the morning. Funny how much he's learned."

"Yeah," Julius said, "I used to try to sneak up to my room, or at times, out of my room. That man has eyes, and ears in the back of his head. Tonight I walked into the room as they were talking. I decided to leave. You know their private time and all. Anyway, Joshua, he says, and there's nothing but to face the music. I used to hate that. Yes, sir. No, sir. How do you do, sir? But tonight—" Julius took a deep breath. His emotions struggled across his features. "I've endured much worse in the last fourteen years, from people who were much less deserving, much less honorable, and definitely much less loving. What really shames me is with what Ruth's been through, and she's still a beautiful person."

"There's a storm brewing, bro. When's your flight out?" Seth jumped up to shut windows.

"I need to be at the airport by nine a.m. Not sure when I can make it back."

"Have a good trip and go with God, brother."

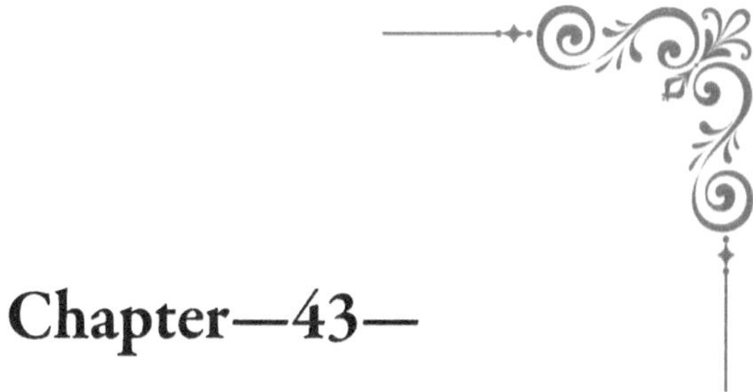

Chapter—43—

There was a slight coolness in the air the next morning as Julius stepped up the curb and walked to the café door. He stood a moment and became immersed in the sights and sounds. He wanted to memorize the mingled smells and savor the laughter and conversation that flowed around him.

"Julius," A voice called from across the room.

He nodded and waved at several people as he sauntered back to his usual booth.

"Say," someone called out to Charlie Anderson. "Was that you and Pat checking out that car Friday night?"

"You mean Stu Bingly's Plymouth?" Charlie leaned forward and looked down the counter at another customer.

"Was that Bingly's car? You wouldn't think he'd have the nerve to come back into the county after the last warning you gave him."

"Some folks learn hard." Charlie took a sip of his coffee. "We were helping him with his tires—"

"Tires? Thought you'd a been doing something besides helping him the way you were talking the last time you caught him making mischief—"

"Yeah, him and that Earl Jacobs they had four flat tires, and lost their shoes by the time Pat and I finished helping them. Hey, there," Charlie greeted Jack and Pat as they joined the crowd. "Good to see you two out and about again. Becky—" he called over the noise of the crowd. "ya got a special cup a coffee for my partner here?"

"Certainly, Mister Anderson," Becky said as the O'Briens sat down at the counter next to Charlie.

Julius chuckled, no wonder he had been able to beat Stu and Earl to Frankie and Johnny's the other night. Charlie and Pat, what a pair. Charlie, the clever talker, and storyteller. And Pat? Well, Pat was just Pat. Kind of quiet, but he knew the value of words, what and when to speak. And folks knew to listen when he spoke.

"Becky tells us you're leavin' this mornin' to go back east," Charlie said as he and Pat slid into the booth across from Julius.

"Yes, sir. I have more work to do, but not here," Julius said. "You know I've grown rather fond of this place. Maybe I'll come back some day."

"You do that," Pat said. "We'll have the welcome mat out and the coffee pot on."

"I must admit to being a mite puzzled." Julius's eyes narrowed, and he looked cockeyed at the two old men.

"Why's that?" Charlie asked.

"I'm surprised they let you two old goats get together anymore." Julius gazed over the top of his coffee cup at the two old farmers.

Charlie harrumphed over his coffee cup, giving Pat a sly sideways look. Pat rubbed a finger over the bridge of his nose and spoke slowly. "There's more'n one way to catch a fish, ya know."

Charlie hooted, and they both wore sheepish grins.

"Take care, boy." They each stuck out a hand, and after they shook hands, they sauntered to the counter.

"No way, buster." Pop held up his hands as Julius tried to pay his tab. "This one's on the house." Then he held out a hand. "Take care, my friend."

"I don't want a handshake, boy." Mom dabbed at her eyes. "This is what 'moms' do," she said with a hug.

Becky blew her nose and tried to laugh. "See ya later, Mr. Caesar."

This is like leaving home all over. Julius all but ran to his car.

"Hey." Jack caught up with him. "Say, if you ever need someone to cover your back—" He held out a hand.

"Take care of that daughter of yours. She's more than special." Julius shook his hand then folded into the driver's seat.

THE CAR ROLLED OVER the brick street, his mind still in turmoil. Flight out at 9:45—why did I think I could make it back by this evening? *If I hit Chicago and turn around immediately, I won't make it back. Not this evening.* The thoughts kept chasing around. How would his wife take the idea of moving to a small town? And his daughter? How would she like the move?

Hermon wasn't far from Beetle River, they could find most of what they needed there. The lovely houses slid by on the outskirts of Hermon. Then there were some mediocre houses. Soon the downtown businesses, a few turns, and Julius saw the sign for the airport. He kept right and zipped into the parking space for his rental car. He grabbed his few items and headed into the office.

"Julius C. Armstrong?" The clerk picked up the keys Julius slid across the counter. He glanced up at Julius with a questioning look.

"That's right," Julius said. "You're not the guy that's usually here?"

"No, he's on vacation." He gave Julius a tight-lipped smile.

What was it about this man? A non-descript average looking bloke, average height, lightweight, light brown hair, tawny eyes—some bell in Julius' computer-like mind was dinging. He'd seen this person before. "Well, you have a good day, now, ya hear?" He had a flight to catch in twenty minutes. A few steps across to the door, he quick-stepped out and to the side of the brick veneer building. He was half a step from the safety of a pillar, when he heard it, felt it rip through his side. He dropped and rolled, aimed and fired. The man shot once more, his bullet catching Julius in the arm. Julius's first bullet dropped the man. It was the tawny eyes like a tiger on the prowl.

Survive, just one more—his face lay on the cold cement, he heard sirens wailing as darkness pulled him down.

He barely heard Chief Mallory shouting, "Get that gurney over here! Now! Hurry!"

Author Bio

Donevy is a primitive artist who has for over forty years worked with raw materials in many different mediums. Not only an artist with paint, canvas, clay, and etc., she is wife, mother, teacher, Bible class teacher, and a writer. She has homeschooled seven children; writes a blog: deborawephraim.blogspot.com; is a member of HAWCN and ACFW. She is committed to continuing to learn and help others learn.

~When you only have words~

Endorsements

This is an amazing suspense/mystery. And, oh, what an ending! The language of the narration is beautiful. Heart-stopping suspense, on the edge of my seat, so tense. Lovely simple expressions of faith, Scriptures at meals and songs of praise. Also, the grace of Jesus and the grace of a family. I am blind, and I appreciate how you portray Mrs. MacDonald as capable. Characters were beautifully done. Delightful, well-developed. I felt myself hurting for their sadness, longing for good to work out for them.

Kathy McKinsey- (Author of Millie's Christmas, etc.) https://www.kathymckinsey.com

I believe your book is one of a kind. I had no trouble visualizing most scenes, especially if houses, furnishings, table settings, or food had anything to do with them. I kept getting hungry from food descriptions.

Marlin Marx (Author of "Between a Road and a Hard Place: One Clueless Wanderer's Story").

Don't miss out!

Visit the website below and you can sign up to receive emails whenever Donevy Westphal publishes a new book. There's no charge and no obligation.

https://books2read.com/r/B-A-TENK-BATFB

BOOKS 2 READ

Connecting independent readers to independent writers.

9 781734 925609